THE ROAD SOMETIMES TAKEN

BAKER OAKS
BOOK 3

AMBAR CORDOVA

First edition 2024 – Cordova Chronicles LLC

Book Cover by Kim•KBG Design with illustrations from Mayhare @mayharte

Copy, Line, and Developmental Edits by Kendra with Spice Me Up Editing

Proofreading by Kendra with Spice Me Up Editing

Formatting by Ambar Cordova with images from 3Crows

CONTENTS

Author's Note   vii
Playlist   ix
Dedication   xiii

Prologue   1

1. Truth Or Dare   7
Contrato, Maluma

2. The Smug Mastodont   21
Long Live (Taylor's Version), Taylor Swift

3. About to Explode   29
Scared to Start, Michael Marcargi

4. Dirty Shirley   41
Rockland, Gracie Abrams

5. Loss Of My Life   49
loml, Taylor Swift

6. I'm Not A Mermaid   59
Mess, Noah Kahan

7. Just Because You Can, Doesn't Mean You Should   71
Work Song, Hozier

8. Jumping Deer   79
Miles On It, Marshmello Ft. Kane Brown

9. Flora & Fauna   87
Blowin' Smoke, Teddy Swims

10. My Toesies Need Some Dirt   95
Stargazing, Myles Smith

11. I Dare You   105
Happy, Craig Lucas

12. The Wilds   115
Young, Wild & Free, Snoop Dogg and Wiz Khalifa & The Roads, Jonah Kagen

13. Crawling Bear   123
Drive, Halsey

14. Boondocking   127
Like Real People Do, Hozier

15. The Big Spoon   137
So High School, Taylor Swift

16. Best Kind of Buzz   145
I Like Me Better, Lauv

17. Runway Strut   151
Style (Taylor's Version), Taylor Swift

18. Shattered   159
Spin You Around, Morgan Wallen

19. Pick Truth   165
Temporary Insanity, Alexz Johnson & Say It, Griffin Peterson

20. Pain or Pleasure   173
Llorar, Jesse & Joy Ft. Mario Domm & Sola, Luis Fonsi

21. Like a Million Bucks   181
reckless driving, Lizzy McAlpine Ft. Ben Kessler

22. You Can Be Rain   187
Let Em Go, Matt Hansen

23. Wear The Hat   197
One Of Them Girls, Lee Brice

24. A Little Taste   205
Cold War, Cautious Clay

25. Bitable Size   213
I'm Gonna Be (500 Miles), Sleeping at Last & Earned It, The Weekend

26. Ready to Eat   225
Me Rehuso, Danny Ocean

27. Nashville Without Us   233
Invisible String, Taylor Swift

28. Chase It   239
A Different Way, Lauv

29. Freaking Adorable   255
Everywhere, Everything, Noah Kahan Ft. Gracie Abrams

30. The Best Seat In The House   265
Wildest Dreams (Taylor's Version), Taylor Swift

31. Pretending   277
Pretending, Glee Cast

32. I'm Going to Kill Him   285
Latch (Acoustic), Sam Smith & Peace, Taylor Swift

33. Gold & Glitter   295
*Flowers, Lauren Spencer Smith & Lose You to Love Me,
Selena Gomez*

34. You Promised   305
Love Me Til' You Leave Me, gavn!

35. Welcome Back   313
Before You Go, Lewis Capaldi

36. The Contract   329
*Millionaire, Chris Stapleton & I guess I'm in Love, Clinton
Kane*

Epilogue   339

What's Next?   347
Join The Babe Tribe!   351
Acknowledgments   355
About the Author   359

standalone but you will see dear characters from The Truth Never Spoken and The Trail Often Crossed.

This book also includes a playlist and the closed-door option. You are welcome to skip until the following chapter when this symbol (⊟) shows up if you'd like to skip the spice. I highly suggest you don't skip it, because each event in the story will lead to the development of who the characters are in the end. However, it is your choice. The playlist is meant to be enjoyed per chapter, but it can totally be read without it.

Now for the reader's precaution themes. There might be spoilers in them so if you want to skip this next part of the author's note, you can. There will be profanity, on page descriptions of explicit sex, death of children (off-page), mental health struggles, a psychological and verbally abusive relationship (not the main character), workaholism (on page), and gaslighting (not the main character).

Thank you again for giving this book a chance.

143,

Ambar.

PLAYLIST

There are no rules on how to listen to this playlist, but to enhance the experience, each chapter has a song title that matches the overall feel of that chapter. Feel free to listen to them after you read the chapter (or during if your brain will let you do that) Playlists are available on Spotify with Lyrics, Spotify Instrumental & Apple Music

Scan for playlists

Spotify

Spotify Instrumental

Itunes

The Smallest Man Who Ever Lived by Taylor Swift

1. Contrato by Maluma
2. Long Live (Taylor's version) by Taylor Swift
3. Scared To Start by Michael Marcagi
4. Rockland by Gracie Abrams
5. loml by Taylor Swift
6. Mess by Noah Kahan
7. Work Song by Hozier
8. Miles On It by Marshmello & Kane Brown
9. Blowin' Smoke by Teddy Swims
10. Stargazing by Myles Smith
11. Happy by Craig Lucas
12. Young, Wild, and Free (Ft. Bruno Mars) by Snoop Dogg & Whiz Khalifa and The Roads by Jonah Kagen
13. Drive by Halsey

14. Like Real People Do by Hozier

15. So High School by Taylor Swift

16. I Like Me Better by Lauv

17. Style (Taylor's Version) by Taylor Swift

18. Spin You Around By Morgan Wallen

19. Temporary Insanity by Alexz Johnson & Say It by Griffin Peterson

20. Llorar (ft. Mario Domm) by Jesse & Joy & Sola by Luis Fonsi

21. reckless driving by Lizzy McAlpine

22. Let Em Go by Matt Hansen

23. One of Them Girls by Lee Brice

24. Cold War by Cautious Clay

25. I'm Gonna Be (500 Miles) by Sleeping At Last & Earned It by The Weekend

26. Me Rehuso by Danny Ocean

27. Invisible String by Taylor Swift

28. A Different Way (ft. Lauv) by Dj Snake

29. Everywhere, Everything by Noah Kahan and Gracie Abrams

30. Wildest Dreams (Taylor's Version) by Taylor Swift

31. Pretending by Glee Cast

32. Latch (Acoustic) by Sam Smith & Peace by Taylor Swift

33. Flowers by Lauren Spencer Smith & Lose You To Love Me by Selena Gomez

34. Love Me 'til You Leave Me by gavn!

35. Before You Go by Lewis Capaldi

36. Millionaire by Chris Stapleton

37. I Guess I'm In Love by Clinton Kane

38. I Love You by Alex & Sierra

DEDICATION

To those who never put themselves first. Who believe others carry their worth in their words and actions. You're enough just the way you are and it's not selfish to tell everyone who doesn't think so to, respectfully, fuck off.

... and to my mom because even though you're always the sun on everyone's cloudy day, you always taught me it's okay to be both sunshine and rain.

PROLOGUE
THE SMALLEST MAN WHO EVER LIVED, TAYLOR SWIFT

September

CARA

"HEY BABE," I answer the phone but the deafening silence on the other end makes my skin break out in goosebumps.

"Cole?" I ask, setting my coffee mug on top of the counter.

"We need to talk," he says, his voice barely a whisper and removed from feelings and tenderness. I've come to expect this call by now. The call that says we need to take some time apart or that I'm not paying enough attention to him while I'm away, but I thought we were done doing this. We talked all summer about our future and how close we were to settling down and hopefully moving in together. *Talk to your boss and we'll go from there,* he said just a month ago—yet here we are again.

"I know we said we were going to push this further, Cara, but I think we just need to end it."

"What do you mean we need to end this, Cole?" I ask him,

annoyed and hurt. Every year he asks for a break. Some *time off* for him to explore without strings attached. Distance and time and blah blah blah. But this time he used the word *end.* You can't just eliminate, erase, and finalize eleven years of love, trust, and friendship. Something that took years to build—and now he can just say he's done?

"Exactly that, Cara. I'm ready to settle down and start a family. I'm done with the back and forth," he says, yawning. Fucking yawning. Like he's bored out of his mind having this conversation that is ripping out my heart and serving on a platter—with a knife through it. I get that I live far away, and the long distance is hard on everyone, but I've lost count of how many times I've told him I'm willing to move back to Baker. I pace in place, trying to make sense of this whole situation before I lose my temper. The last thing I need is for Cole to see how much this is affecting me. How much it *always* affects me.

"Okay, well, I can settle down. We've talked about this. I can move back to Baker Oaks, or you can move here. We can have a family. Together." I choke on the sob I've been holding. I didn't want him to hear me cry but goddamn it, how can I not? I thought I was beyond begging, but apparently, I'm not.

"No," Cole snaps.

I wish I could see his face right now. It's so hard to read his emotions and meaning without seeing him. Is he tensing up? Are his eyes roaming the room? Is he with someone else? Does he mean this for real? My heart is going to come out of my chest, beating so loudly that everything I'm hearing is muffled by the loud palpitations.

I hit the FaceTime button at the same moment he says, "You don't understand, I'm done." He, of course, won't accept it. *Coward.* I'm stuck here, with my phone in my hand, with Cole's voice on speaker as he delivers the death blow to the hope I've been holding on to. One that most people saw coming, but me. So fucking naive.

"No, Cole. You're right. I don't understand," I reply, hoping that what I think is going on is actually not. He can't be ending a decade-long relationship. For what? For marriage? Marriage with who? I'm down to get married. It's all I've wanted from him, for longer than I care to admit to everyone but myself.

"I'm done with us, Cara." How can someone be done with a decade of stories? A decade of shared memories and a decade of growing up together?

"If marriage is what you want, Cole, I can marry you. That's not a big deal. God knows we're old—" But I stop talking when I'm interrupted with the words that no one wants to ever hear. The words are not only hurtful but cruel.

"I don't want to marry *you*, Cara. God! Why can't you understand that? I was trying to let you down gently and let you go, but you can't read between the lines, and I'm done. It was fun while it lasted, but darlin', you are good for a short time—not for the long run."

"Cole—" my voice a broken plea "—don't do this." I hate that I'm begging. I hate that he's hurting me so much I can hardly breathe. I hate that I love him so damn much.

"It's done. I never meant to hurt you, but I think it's for the best that we do this now and we stop fighting the inevitable. Have a good life, Cara."

The line goes silent, and my heart skips a beat. I scream loudly to the void of my apartment and start pacing back and forth, trying to stop this spiral. *I deserve better than this. I deserve better than this. I deserve better than this, I repeat over and over as if saying it out loud will stop the pain. What do I do now?* I can't just sit here in this misery and anger. *When you can't do anything about it, get busy, Cara,* my mom used to say so I do just that.

My mind plays his words on a loop while I deep clean the whole apartment. *I don't want to marry you.* I scrub the bathroom for the second time on my hands and knees, cleaning until the squeaks from the Scrub Daddy invade Cole's voice in my head. *I think it's for the best*—while my tears mix with the water in the toilet bowl after scrubbing it three times until all I see are sparkles. *I'm done with us*—while I bleach the shower curtain, carefully so as not to touch the freaking toxins because the last thing I need is to also get sick from the damn fumes. Because at the end of the day, all those words mean the same: *you're not enough, Cara, and you were never enough.*

"I'm home!" Allie shouts, walking into the condo after shutting the door loudly and scaring the bejesus out of me.

"In here!" I call from the bathroom, opening the sink's faucet and splashing cold water on my face to try and hide my state. Today is Allie's last day with me before her six-month assignment in Florida. I'm going to miss her, but I'm more worried about her. She's been freaking out over going back to Florida and possibly running into her ex, Jake, who she hasn't seen in ten years, but I know for a fact there's no way she'll see him.

Jake lives in Baker Oaks, my hometown, and although Allie wants nothing to do with the place, I visit every summer so I can see my parents. This is how I know that Jake barely leaves Baker at all and, knowing Allie, she won't step foot close to Baker *at all.* I told her we needed one last hoorah tonight before she leaves. I wasn't counting on being totally heartbroken and on the verge of a spiral, but here I am. I must put on a strong front for her and show her a good time. Help ease some of those nerves, regardless of what's going on with me. I can wallow in my feelings tomorrow after she's gone. Her life is so damn boring; maybe she'll get some popcorn and eat it while I tell her how my whole life feels like a movie. Not a rom-com; more like a drama-rom.

"Hey, hey, hey, what's wrong?" Allie asks as soon as she sees me. *There goes my trying to hide it from her.*

"Nah, nothing major. Same old, same old. Cole and I are on a break, *again*. This time may be forever, though. He said, and I quote, *I don't want to marry you.*"

Allie flinches at the honesty of my words but then her face turns from concern to anger. "Cara, that man deserves none of your tears," she says, bringing her hand to my face. "When are you going to kick him to the curb and give yourself a chance at something real?"

"Well, he already did that for me, didn't he? And who knows—maybe it's for the best?" I try to keep it light and change the subject immediately. "I still can't believe you're leaving me again. I feel like I just got you here."

"Cara, let's talk about this. I'm worried about you."

"Don't, Allie. Really. I'm fine; everything is fine. Let's talk about *you*, Miss Traveling-Again-Away-From-Me. I hate it here."

"I know, I know. I'm requesting an area near here next so we can do this again. I love you," she insists and pulls me in for a hug.

"Yeah, yeah, I love you too, bitch. Now let's go get ready. The night is young, and we have places to be, things to drink, and..." I look at her and wiggle my eyebrows, encouraging her to finish my infamous phrase that she hates.

"And people to do."

"Yeeeeees, queen! Let's go!"

The night goes by in a flash. We dance and drink until oblivion. Allie is annoyed at me for keeping her out later than expected while I was trying to find something to make me feel like the ray of sunshine everyone thinks I am. The drinks, the dances, the people—none of it makes me feel anything. All I keep repeating in my head is *If I wasn't enough for the boy I gave everything to, am I even worth it?* And as the hours go by, and man after man tries to touch me while dancing or sends me drinks with the expectation to take me home with them, the more I remember that maybe all that I will ever be good for is a fun time.

1

TRUTH OR DARE

CONTRATO, MALUMA

April

MANNY

"DO you have any plans for the holiday weekend, Mr. Z?" Kate, my assistant—at least, the assistant of this past month—asks with a sensual tone as she wraps a lock of her hair around her finger. I don't know how many times I told Gus to stop hiring girls that are more worried about fucking one of us, *or both,* instead of people who are here for the job. Kate is at least competent, but the flirty looks and innuendos need to stop. I might be known for never having a serious girlfriend and bringing different dates to every event, but I draw the line at work. My heart is not built for the complications a lawsuit might bring and I don't want to have to spend a week in the hospital with high blood pressure. I don't have time for that.

"I'm having dinner with my family tonight and will be flying to the New York office right after," I answer. I try to not be an asshole, but also not a flirt—which seem to be my two personalities. The man behind the suit is not who I am with *my* people; but lately, that's all I've been: Manuel Zabana, co-CEO of Zabana Enterprises. No time for fun or games. This is the first time in a while that I have taken time off. Even if it's just a day.

Gus and I own Zabana Enterprises. We both created the space from scratch and it was our hard work that made it what it is today: a Fortune 200 wealth management company. In the past couple of years, Gus has taken a step back and works more regular hours. Meaning someone had to pick up the slack, which happened to be me. Yes, the company can pretty much run itself; but if nobody's supervising, how do we make sure it stays that way? How do we make sure all our hard work doesn't go down the drain or that the best interest of our clients stays front and center?

"Do you need a plus one?" she asks, walking toward me. Her steps are determined and her hips sway like a woman on a mission. This has been happening more and more now that Forbes added me and Gus as part of their 'Top Ten Empire Bachelors Under Thirty.' It didn't help that the following week, we were in the tabloids for being the most likely not to settle down. People were placing bets on who could make Augusto and Manuel Zabana settle. Jokes on them, I'm already married. My whole life is committed to the two things I love: my job and my family. So the only reason I leave work on a Friday is them, my family.

"I don't. Thanks for offering though," I say, getting up from my brown leather chair and pushing it in under the desk. My office in Jacksonville has a nice view of the St. Johns River. I made sure to position my desk across from the tall windows so when I leave every day, I get the view as I walk toward the exit and get back into the confinement of my car. Even if I don't get a breath of fresh air, at least this way I can see nature. Sort of.

"Goodbye, Kate. Felices Pascuas[1] and see you next week." I close the door to my office, leaving her inside, and get out of this place. Hopefully I make it to Allie's house before she kills me over being late to her dinner.

"¡LLEGÓ EL QUE FALTABA![2]" I shout as I open the door to Allie and Jake's house. The wooden door has a sign that says, *Welcome, come on in,* so I follow that instruction and push the door wide open, stepping in and walking to the living room. I'm so fucking happy my sister finally got over her bullshit and told this guy how she really feels. I don't know what the hell happened between them all those years ago, but clearly it was a mistake because I've never seen her happier than she is right now.

She decided to host Easter at their house and our whole family is coming, except my dad. None of us are close to him but his relationship with Allie is the worst out of all of us. He acts like an asshole half the time, so I don't blame her. I'm pretty sure the only reason Mom is still with him is because he treats her like a queen. But he only loves her like that; everyone else's affection is measured by how successful we are and what we can bring to the table. I guess when Allie decided to become a teacher, knowing she wasn't going to make the type of money he does, their feud started.

---

1. Felices Pascuas: Happy Easter
2. It's a colloquial phrase that means the one who was missing has arrived

Allie planned this weekend and made me swear I was going to give her three days of my time. We closed the office for the first time in years and here we are. At the beck and call of our sister, celebrating her joy.

"Manuel, you're late," Allie snaps, kissing my cheek and giving me a hug before adding, "I'm glad you came, though. Gus is here already; come on."

I take the time to look around and I see my mom sitting with Cara's mom, sipping on wine and talking about who knows what. Gus is sitting on the couch with a glass of tonic water with lime that I can recognize from a mile away. He stopped drinking a while ago and hasn't gone back. Allie disappears into the kitchen and as I follow her, the bounciest girl with sage green eyes walks out and smiles big at me. *Cara*: my sister's best friend who I was sure I would see since the two are inseparable.

"Long time no see, big guy!" Cara exclaims as she wraps her arms around me in a warm hug. Her excitement is infectious—it always has been, and I can't help but feel comfort at the familiar gesture. It's strange how my body always seems to react this way when she's near— a gentle reminder of our shared history and friendship. A history that I've always wanted to be more but considering she's my sister's best friend, it never has.

I pull back slightly, playfully ruffling her hair. Cara is a little taller than average height, standing around five-foot-six or seven; but at six-foot-two, I still tower over her. Despite the height difference, there's something about her presence that makes her feel like she's standing eye-to-eye with me.

"Oh, well hello, Carita, always a pleasure to see me, I'm sure."

She scoffs and walks past me. "I see that you're as insufferable as ever." She plops on the couch next to Gus, putting her feet on his lap and clinking her glass to his with a soft *salud*. That's what I need after a long and tedious day: a drink.

I step into the kitchen, where the air is thick with the rich aroma of simmering spices and fresh herbs. The room is bathed in the warm golden light of hanging pendant lamps, their soft glow highlighting the dark-colored floor and the worn wooden cabinets.

Jake is busy at the stove, stirring a pot with a wooden spoon, and the sound of sizzling and occasional bursts of fragrant steam rise from the pan. The smell of something that could only be described as homey wafts through the room, mixing with the faint hint of aged oak and the sweet undertone of vanilla in the air. Allie always has vanilla something in the air. And even with the food overpowering it, you can still get small hints of the scent.

"What's up, bro? Good to see you." I step closer while I greet him and shake his hand before pulling him into a side hug. The warmth of the kitchen and Jake's friendly smile make it feel like a perfect welcoming home.

"There's beer and peach wine in the fridge, and red wine on top of the counter over there," he replies, pointing to the end of the counter where a bottle of Cabernet sits with a couple of glasses. I opt for beer because I don't feel like passing out on Allie's couch and that's exactly what will happen if I start drinking red wine right now.

I join the rest of the party in the living room. Everyone's casually sitting, talking to each other about nothing and everything at the same time. The doorbell rings and we all look, knowing quite well that not many people would ring the bell when our family is hosting. We're more of a 'welcome everyone in at any given moment' family.

Four people walk in. Two I know but forgot their names from back in high school and two I've never seen before. A huge dude covered in tattoos and an *I-might-kill-you* stare holds the door open for everyone else. Before anyone can introduce them, the tiny, tatted pixie blonde says, "What's up, everyone? I'm Roe, this is Saint, and this is Natalie and Nick." Cara all but hops off her seat and runs to tackle both girls.

Natalie and Nick. I remember Natalie from school. Pretty redhead who was always glued to Nick's hip, the team's linebacker. She's still gorgeous but something in her eyes makes her seem... I don't know, tired, maybe? I offer my hand to both of them and to Saint. I wish I could say the same for Roe, but she disappears into the kitchen with Cara in tow.

"How come they don't get any shit about being late?" I ask Allie. She scoffs as she passes me with utensils in her hand and shakes her head, ignoring my comment and carrying on setting the table.

"Do you need help?" Mom asks.

"No, dinner's ready and everyone's here. Let's eat," Allie answers her, tapping her fingers gently on top of the wooden table.

The rustic dark brown table is set with chairs for all of us, with a variety of dishes in the middle. This looks like a good combination of Southern and Dominican food. There's arepitas, locrio de chuleta, collard greens, and creamed corn. The table is huge, and it takes up most of the space in the large dining room. Everyone sits after Allie and Jake hover behind the chairs they're sitting in and before I know it, there's only one chair left, directly across from Cara.

Cara and my sister have been friends all their lives. Our moms are best friends and even though we moved to a different town when we were kids, they've always been inseparable. Cara has a little sister too, Nellie, but we don't hang out with her much since she's like eight years younger. She might be with her dad, since neither are here.

You'd think that growing up with Cara always being around, I wouldn't be plagued by the thoughts racing through my mind right now. But I've always found myself wondering about the possibilities with her. There's something almost magical about her—her incredible figure and the way she moves with such confidence, so unapologetically herself. I remember when her hair was light brown, but she's been rocking blonde silky waves since high school. Regardless of the change, she remains absolutely stunning. Her mossy green eyes, flecked with glimmers of gold, seem to connect with me every time and I find myself lost in them more than I should. No matter where she is in the room, my eyes always gravitate toward her. It's both a blessing and a curse.

"Do I have something on my teeth?" she asks, snapping me out of it.

"What? No, no I was just looking at your face proportions." I wink at her and she rolls her eyes. I love getting a rise out of her. She's always keeping everyone else on their toes so when I get to do the same to her, it always feels good.

"So, Gus, what are you doing the rest of the weekend? God knows that Manny will be working the whole time he's not in this house. Have you ever considered telling your brother that he can chill a little?" Allie asks, ignoring the fact I'm sitting right here as she throws jabs my way.

"Going to Savannah to spend the week the minute this weekend is over," he replies with a mischievous look on his face, and to that Allie sticks her tongue out at him.

"Oh, my sister will be in Savannah too, celebrating her twenty-first birthday," Cara adds and I'm shocked, to say the least. I still remember little Nellie running around terrorizing all of us but suddenly she's old enough to drink. Where has the time gone?

"Maybe she has a friend she'd like me to meet. You know I've gotta let some of this energy out," Gus teases, pretending like he's fucking under the table.

"Por Dios, Augusto. ¿Cuándo vas a madurar, muchacho?[3]" Mom asks while Allie smacks him on the shoulder. I don't think he'll ever grow up, but people can say the same about me. Yes, I spend a lot of time at work, and I don't play around with my business; but when I go out to dinner or bars, I act like a twenty-one-year-old. And sometimes even worse. It's the best way to get out—what was it that Gus called it? *Energy*.

"Cara," my mom says, changing the topic of this conversation. "Your mom was telling me you're moving back. That makes me so happy, sweetie."

"Yeah, I just need to sort out the details," she replies, her voice trailing off into a thoughtful murmur. Cara stares at the table, her fingers fidgeting with the edge of the table. "Even if it means selling her." Her gaze remains distant, a hint of sadness flickering in her eyes.

"Even if I have to fly to get you, Cara, you're both coming," Allie insists, and Cara brings her hand to her lip, blowing her a kiss.

"Who is *she*?" I ask, confused by the conversation. "Do you have a puppy or something?"

Cara smirks and shoves a piece of biscuit into her mouth. She doesn't answer my question and just continues eating her food.

I look at Allie, trying to get answers, and she explains, "It's her van. She won't drive it on the highway, especially not towing a trailer full of her stuff, but she also doesn't want to sell it."

"Because it's my baby," Cara whines. "I refuse to leave her behind, but I also don't want to drive it for endless hours by myself. So I have to figure something out."

"What about that boyfriend of yours you always keep around?" I ask, thinking of the same guy she's been with since

---

3. When will you grow up?

high school. Every time I see her, he's there, staring at every man who comes near them as competition. But every girl that passes gets ogled like they're dessert, no matter that the most beautiful girl in the world is by his side.

As soon as the words leave my mouth, the room falls into an uneasy silence. Heads turn, but everyone avoids my gaze. The only person who doesn't look away is Cara, and she's staring at me with wide eyes as if she's just seen a ghost.

"What?" I add, breaking the heavy silence.

Natalie, of all people, is the first to speak up. "Let's just change the topic, okay?" she suggests, her tone firm but tinged with discomfort.

"It was just a question," I say, raising my hands in a gesture of surrender. Yet, despite my better judgment, I press on. "But really, Cara, if the van's important to you, shouldn't he be helping out?"

"Enough," Mom interjects, her voice sharp and uncharacteristically stern. "Stop pushing it, Manuel. I raised you better than this. Show some manners and eat your dinner."

Everyone quickly turns their attention to their plates, resuming their meals with a quiet intensity. The conversation is buried, but Cara's sudden shift in demeanor makes it clear that the topic hasn't been forgotten.

AFTER DINNER, we're all outside by the fireplace, talking. The sky is illuminated by bright stars, a typical view in Baker that never gets old. Baker is far enough from the city that you feel close to the stars—not that I've ever stopped to look at them more than just a glance. The fire casts a glow around my friends'

faces and I wish I could say I stopped to appreciate them all, but my eyes are always glued to my sister's best friend. *Fuck.*

I try to keep my mind off Cara and catch up with my mom. She's hands down my favorite person in the world and sometimes I just want to sit by her, lay my head on her lap, and let her talk to me like a little boy. I don't, of course, but that's what I want.

The tattooed blonde walks out with a tray of shots and sets them on a table, calling us all to come closer to a circle.

"This is our cue," my mom says, grabbing Cara's mom by the arm and standing up.

"Adios, Ma. Hablamos pronto[4]," I call.

"Si, mi amor. Love you guys, good to see you." They both go around the yard and leave through the garden gate. This is a beautiful property and every detail I notice makes me appreciate it even more.

"Alright, party animals, it's time for truth or dare," Cara shouts with a grin, handing out shots to everyone. "I know you forgot how to have fun without having your dick six inches deep into your fuck of the week, but this is what we're doing," she adds, catching my annoyed glance.

"More like nine," I shoot back with a playful wink.

"Seriously, you two need to cut it out," Allie interjects, exasperation clear in her voice. "Can we just be civilized for one night? For me?" We both nod in agreement. "Cara, let's keep this light. We're not twenty-one anymore."

Cara sticks her tongue out at Allie but then turns her attention back to me with a mischievous glint in her eye. "Since you were being such a pain, Manny, you can kick things off."

I meet her gaze with a smirk. "Right back at you. Cara, truth or dare?"

---

4. Goodbye, mom. Talk to you soon.

"Truth it is, hotshot. Let's keep it easy for your vanilla sister over here," Cara says with a mischievous smile, settling herself playfully on Allie's lap and planting a kiss on her cheek.

"Who says there's anything vanilla about Allie?" Jake teases with a smirk, and everyone laughs except Gus and me.

"Gross," I add while Allie blows a kiss my way.

The girls all do a kind of oohs and aahs and Cara wraps her arms around Allie in a tight hug before sauntering over to the spot directly across from me. "Don't worry, Jake, I won't be stealing your girl tonight. But when I move this summer, I'll definitely need to squeeze in some more quality time with my girl, okay?"

"Sure," Jake adds, smiling and sipping on his beer.

As soon as Cara says that I remember nobody really gave me details on why her boyfriend won't drive her back or why everyone was being weird about it. She picked truth, and because I have zero self-preservation skills, I use my question to ask, "Cara, why can't you ask what's-his-face to drive you back?"

"Coño Manuel, por Dios[5]," Allie snaps.

"Cara, you want me to punch him in the face for you?" Roe —*was that her name?*—asks, acting like she is about to stand up, but her guy pulls her back.

"It's fine," Cara insists. She puts her forearms on her thighs and stares at me head on. "Manny, since you clearly forgot your manners or when to drop the topic, I'll answer your question. But you better watch it because I'm coming for you next." She downs the wine she was drinking as if it were the shot on her right hand and fire blazes in her eyes, darkening the color to a deep forest green. *Ay coño[6].*

"We're not together anymore," she continues. As I start to

---

5. Shit, Manuel. For the love of God.
6. Oh shit.

respond, she raises her index finger and adds, "Before you say you've heard this before, let me make it clear: it's over. He's engaged to someone else now. We don't discuss it. We've moved on, so please drop it."

I take a deep breath. "I'm really sorry," I admit, my voice tinged with regret because this one I clearly fucked up. "I didn't know."

"You're not. You wanted to know and now you know. Now, drink. I answered, so you lose," she sasses.

"That's not how this game goes," I protest.

"It's the way we play," Natalie says.

I shrug, grabbing the shot in front of me. I chug it, letting it burn my throat —my dignity with it. If I didn't feel like an ass before, I sure do now.

"Who's next?"

We play for rounds and rounds. I lost count after the fifth and to be honest I'm too tired to even attempt to count anymore. Everyone takes a turn asking a question or setting up a dare. I've had to call out from work Monday, call my mom to sing to her, answer how many women I have been with and because I don't fuck and tell, I choose the shot. This is supposedly the last round, and I can't wait to be done with it so I can go to bed. I've had enough to drink to not drive back to the city. JJ, the company's driver in Jax, will come get me. I already messaged him and he'll be here in ten.

"Manny, truth or dare," Allie says, with her know-it-all face and I immediately know I'm fucked either way.

I decide to at least go down with flair, so I answer, "Dare."

"I dare you to take time off and fly to Cara's in June to help her move back home."

Cara spits her drink at the same time that Roe shouts, "Oh shit!" Cara continues to cough, her eyes wide with surprise.

Saint and Jake laugh. Nick and Natalie shake their heads,

and Gus smacks my shoulder before saying, "You did this to yourself, bro."

I could just drink the shot, walk out of here, and it won't be a big deal. I could shake this off and pretend like I don't want to play games. But sometimes, surprising everyone by doing the unexpected is the way to go.

"When's your last day at your current place, Cara?" I ask, keeping my tone steady but curious.

Cara looks at me with a mix of irritation and resignation. "Don't listen to her, Manny. Just take the damn shot," she snaps, her eyes narrowing.

I raise an eyebrow and remain unmoved. "When, Cara?" I ask again, my voice flat.

Natalie, leaning casually against Nick, chimes in with a hint of mischief. "June fifth," she says, her eyes sparkling as if she's loving this more than a telenovela.

Cara's frustration is palpable as she whirls toward Natalie. "Whose side are you on, Nat?" she snaps.

Natalie, unfazed and smiling, replies, "Yours, sweetie. It's a win-win. Just take it."

"The hell I will. Manny has zero time for anything, let alone to drive me back home. It's dumb. Take the shot, Manny," Cara bites.

"He won't have to worry about work," Gus offers, and I look at him, throwing mental daggers at his forehead.

"You know what? Maybe he's too chicken to actually do it. But what do I know—I just met the guy," Roe adds, and the group of drunks just burst out laughing. Everyone but Cara. Cara is sitting there with her arms crossed over her chest and as red as a tomato.

"Cara?" I say, raising my eyebrows at her.

"Take the shot, Manuel."

There's a moment of silence, at least between us. The rest of the group is shouting and hollering. Some are screaming "Shot!" and some are saying do it. I can't think straight but all I know is I'm not a quitter and I'm a man of my word. I give a small, knowing smile and stand, placing my still-full shot glass on the table.

"See you in June, Carita," I murmur, my voice carrying a note of finality. "Buenas noches[7], everyone. Until next time."

____

7. Good night

2

THE SMUG MASTODONT

LONG LIVE (TAYLOR'S VERSION), TAYLOR SWIFT

May 31st - Now

CARA

"I'M GOING to miss you too, sweetie girl," I tell Azalea, the little girl I've worked with longer than any other student. "I'm sure you'll have the best summer ever."

Teaching Special Student Education, or SPED as we call it, doesn't give me a traditional classroom with students. Every county and district do it differently; where I work, I have my own room, but my students are more long term instead of saying goodbyes after one school year. Azalea, for example, has been on my caseload since she was four, and now she's about to start fourth grade. I would have had her for two more years, but moving to Baker Oaks means I won't be coming back to my current school. It's also too far for me to visit frequently, so this week has been bittersweet, to say the least.

It's not like I'll stop teaching in general, but my heart is drowning in sorrow from leaving all my small people behind. I know they'll move on and they'll have another teacher who will love, teach, and support them—but it doesn't change the fact that I'm heartbroken. This is the first school I taught at after graduating college. The first group of students I've grown with. The littles have helped shape me into who I am today, regardless of how crazy they drive me sometimes.

Azalea gives me a huge hug before running across the cold SPED classroom to her mom who's waiting for her by the door. Her mom waves at me before walking away, leaving me with Luke. Luke has been my bestie boy for the past year. He joined our school after getting kicked out of another elementary school due to fighting. He had no social-emotional skills and couldn't identify his zones of regulation. He would go from zero to a hundred in a heartbeat without even being able to identify his trigger or how to regulate his body. We worked hard, and now everyone else sees the sweet boy I know he is. He carries his little ring of emotion cards to cue him into what some of the feelings are. Right now, he's holding it in his hands with the worry card facing him.

I slide onto the ground next to him and ruffle his hair. He might be a big second grader now, but he will forever be my little Luke.

"Hey, bud, are you okay?" I ask, softening my tone so he can see that I'm here if he needs to talk. It's so important for kids to know that we care about them and that we have big feelings, like they do, while also modeling for them how we can be strong. Show them with our actions what we convey with our words.

"Who's going to believe in me, Ms. Thompson?" *Be still my heart, this chicken nugget.*

"Oh, pumpkin! Tons of people believe in you. Your mommy,

daddy, everyone at our school. I will always believe in you even if I'm far away. But you know what, Lukey?"

"What?" he asks, looking up at me with glassy eyes. It's taking everything in me not to tear up right along with him.

"Do you know the most important person who should believe in you, buddy?"

"Who?" he asks, his little lip trembling.

I hold his hands in mine, dropping the cards on the floor and touching his nose before saying, "You, sweetie. You have to believe in yourself. You have all of us in your corner. Always. But you must believe with all your heart you can do hard things."

I offer him my pinkie and he wraps it with his. Tentatively at first but as soon as he hooks it with mine, it's a confident squeeze. We both repeat at the same time the phrase we say every morning before starting school.

"I am strong. I am bright. I am brave and I can do hard things."

He drops my finger and wraps his arms around me, hugging me tight and making me consider every choice I've made about not coming back next year. Maybe he *does* need me here. Who will take care of them when I'm gone?

I hear a throat clearing and looking up, I see Luke's mom standing by the door, wearing a soft smile and warm eyes. I smile and wave at her and when she nods at me, I know she understands.

"Come on, sweets. It's time to go home. I'll give your mommy my phone number, okay? Maybe we can chat sometime," I tell Luke, squeezing him tighter before I get up.

"Okay," he whispers, standing up and grabbing his backpack. He runs toward his mom and hugs her tight.

The dim fairy lights cast a soft glow in the room, mingling

with the lemon scent that usually brings comfort. But today, instead of feeling warm and reassuring, it feels like a bittersweet goodbye.

"I know, baby, I know," his mom says before looking at me and smiling softly. "Thank you, Ms. Thompson, for everything you've done. Luke grew so much this school year. We're happy you're following the path you need to take but we're definitely sad to see you go. You're a gem and any school would be lucky to have you."

Well, shucks. This will bring the tears out for sure. I take a deep breath, bracing for the hurt. Just as I feel them about to fall, I catch a glimpse of someone standing behind her and have to blink twice to make sure I'm not imagining it. Luke's mom looks over and smiles when she turns back to me, probably curious about who's there. To my surprise, it's none other than Manuel Zabana standing there, looking like a damn snack with his fancy suit and tie, and a bouquet of flowers in his hands.

"I'll let you go, Ms. Thompson. Have a great summer, and please send us your phone number through the parent app. We'd love to stay in touch," she says.

"Bye, guys," I add, still in shock at what I'm seeing. I'm torn between feeling annoyed and being utterly surprised, not quite sure which emotion should take the lead.

"Manny, what are you doing here?" I snap at him, trying my hardest not to look at the beautiful flowers in his hands. I don't usually like flowers as gifts. I think they look better planted or carefree in a field somewhere, and the prices in some arrangements could buy me things that will last longer. But these flowers., These right here are a mix of all my favorite flowers—gerberas, Calla lilies, and hydrangeas. All in beautiful bright colors form a bouquet that has my full attention.

"Congrats on finishing another school year, Ms. Thompson," Manny says with a warm smile, handing me the bouquet of colorful flowers. He leans casually against the door frame, his presence filling the space with his relaxed confidence.

"Thanks?" I reply, my voice trailing off as I try to process the unexpected gesture.

"Don't look so surprised, Carita," he chuckles, clearly amused by my reaction.

"Manny, this is my place of work—" I start, but he cuts me off with a grin.

"Not anymore," he interrupts, his eyes twinkling with mischief. "Not after today."

"If you would let me finish talking," I snap. "If this wasn't my place of work, I would have said a couple of grown-up words. But I guess *what are you doing here* will have to do."

"I told you I'd see you in June, but then Allie informed me today was your last day, so I came a day early. I didn't want you to think I was going to break my dare."

What in the actual fuck? He can't be for real. It was just a game. "What are you talking about?" I ask, pretending I don't remember the dare he agreed to months ago. If it wasn't for the perfect flowers in my arms, my body language would be very different from what it is now.

"Allie's dare? I'm supposed to drive you back to Baker Oaks," he quips and I'm sure my face looks as astonished as I feel right now. *I'm going to kill her.*

I turn around to grab my bag and the last box of supplies I need to pack. I wish I could carry everything, but the damn flowers—no, I didn't mean to say "damn," beautiful flowers, I'm sorry—just won't fit. I'm on the verge of throwing a tantrum like one of my students when Manny steps in and takes the box and my bag from me.

"You can just hold the flowers, Cara," he insists with a reassuring smile. "Come on, let's go."

"'*Let's*' is one too many people, Manny. *I'm* going. You can go back to corporate America where you usually live." I try to take the box and bag from him, but I can't. He holds both above him. I look up at him and his giant self, and I know he is too tall for me to try anything. Add the extra height of his arms, and it's worse.

I stomp my foot and roll my eyes at him. "Agh, 'kay. Let's go."

He follows behind me as I walk past some rooms and wave to the teachers who are finishing up their day. I go past Beth, our school's mom. She's really our school's secretary but I don't know how any of us would survive without her.

"I'll be back tomorrow to do my end-of-the-year checklist and return my keys, okay?" I ask and she walks around her desk, wrapping me in a hug.

"I'll see you tomorrow, sweetie. I'm soaking up all the hugs I can get today," she replies, her voice warm and affectionate. "Are you going to the end-of-the-year dinner tonight too?" She looks at me with those earnest eyes that make it impossible to refuse her.

I hadn't planned on going because I'm running on empty and would prefer to indulge in s'mores pie while binge-watching One Tree Hill. But now, with this mastodon standing here looking insufferably smug, my plans might change.

"I'll be there, Ms. Beth," I reply, trying to sound more enthusiastic than I feel.

"Well, hello there," she coos, turning her attention to Manny. Her gaze softens as she takes in his smile.

Manny places the box gently on the floor and extends his hand toward her with a confident smile. "Manny Zabana, nice to meet you."

"I'm Bethany, but you can call me Beth." She shakes his hand, but her eyes are on me, smiling mischievously.

Great. Just great.

Now everyone will be asking me about this guy.

"Ms. Beth, this is Manny, my best friend's brother. He was just leaving," I explain, pulling Manny by his arm and trying to walk out of this place.

"I'll see you tonight!" I shout before stepping through the double doors and out into the hot day.

3

ABOUT TO EXPLODE

SCARED TO START, MICHAEL MARCARGI

Manny

CARA IS WALKING with purpose toward what I assume is her car, her movements sharp and determined. As she walks, she mutters to herself in a low, indecipherable tone, her golden locks swaying with each step. She throws her hands up in frustration, then turns to me, her face flushed a deep red like a cherry tomato.

"Woah, woah, why do you look like you're about to explode?" I ask, taken aback by her intense expression.

"Maybe because I am! What the hell are you doing here, Manny?" she snaps, her irritation palpable.

"I already told you, little firecracker. I'm here to drive you back to Florida," I reply, trying to keep my tone light.

"I thought you were joking. I didn't even know you drove anymore, Mr. Fancy Pants with a driver," she sasses.

"I do drive, and I never back down on a dare. Allie dared me, I took it, and now I'm here to fulfill it. Tomorrow is the first day of June, so I'm here to take you back," I say with a grin, flashing my best charm. It doesn't seem to sway her, as she scoffs and heads toward a vehicle that looks straight out of a Barbie movie.

She opens the door of the pink van-microbus-looking thing, probably from the sixties. It has flowers decorating the side doors and the inside looks like it came out of a vintage movie. The seats are beige and very well taken care of. There are pink and flower details everywhere and a disco ball hanging from the rearview mirror.

She places the bouquet inside and looks at the box and bag I'm holding, opening her arms in a silent request.

"Excuse me," I say, reaching behind her to place the items in her pink-galore van.

"Cara, you do know you're not a real-life Barbie, right?" I joke but it falls flat.

"What I drive is none of your business. This," she says, tapping the van's door, "is my baby. Liking pink doesn't make me a Barbie."

"This is the baby you couldn't leave behind?" I ask, puzzled.

"Is it that you didn't ask your sister what I needed help with or the color throwing you off?" she counters.

"No, it's because what thirty-year-old drives a pink vehicle?" I ask before realizing I've stepped on a landmine. She slams the door, gives me a sharp smack on the shoulder, and climbs into the driver's seat. The van comes to life, and I scramble to open the passenger door and hop in before she drives off.

"Real-life Barbie," Cara mocks in a cartoonish voice, backing out of the parking lot and driving away from her school.

"You didn't have to come. I didn't ask you to." She puts one finger up and says, "First, I was going to drive myself back, thank you very much. Second—" She lowers her hand to signal the right turn she started making without signaling. I buckle my seatbelt with a loud snap and sign the cross on my forehead and chest.

"You're so dramatic. It was just a tiny turn," Cara snaps. "As I was saying. Second, stop acting like you're above pink. Pink is just a color. The best one if you ask me, but it doesn't make this beautiful thing any less."

I smile and say, "Sure, sure, sure. Just make sure we make it in one piece. By the way, where are we headed?"

"I'm going to my house. I need to finish packing, I have a dinner party tonight, and I'm still working tomorrow. Now, if you'll excuse me, I have to call your sister to give her a piece of my mind." She pulls out her phone, sets it on a sparkly holder on the dashboard, and tells Siri to call "The Bestie" on speaker.

"Cara," I try to say but she just looks my way and narrows her eyes.

"Cara?" Allie asks, answering the phone.

"Allison Marie Zabana, you have things to explain," Cara snaps, looking over her shoulder before merging lanes, again without her signal being on. *Por el amor a Jesus, nos va a matar.*[1]

"What did I do now?" Allie shouts.

Cara looks at me sideways. When I don't say anything and she rolls her eyes, I take it as a sign and say in a clipped tone, "Hi Allielicious!" Allie used to be obsessed with Fergalicious by Fergie for a long time, so Gus and I started calling her Allielicious as a joke and it just stuck.

"Happy to hear he made it."

"What the fuck do you mean 'he made it?' Allie, you didn't tell me he was coming. I hate surprises, you know that, and I told you I was going to drive myself back."

"Cara, in no good conscience I was going to let you take a

---

1. For the love of Christ, she's going to kill us.

road trip for weeks by yourself, in your van that hasn't left the city in who knows how long." *Weeks? Did she just say weeks?*

"Mmm... unless Cara's moving around the world and back, there's no way it's going to take her two weeks to make it back to Baker Oaks. What are you talking about?" I ask my sister, hijacking their conversation.

Cara pulls up into a neighborhood, parking the van in an empty spot in front of a beige townhouse with a yellow and lemon wreath on the door. When she parks, she grabs the phone from the holder and hits the FaceTime button. After a beat, Allie's face shows up on the screen with a triumphant smile on her face.

"You didn't tell him?!" Cara asks. "So, you didn't tell *me* that you actually got *your brother* to join me on a road trip that I told *you* I was going to take by myself? But you also didn't tell *him* it was more than just driving me back to Baker Oaks?"

She smiles and says, "Sounds about right. I have to go though. Good luck!"

The call drops and Cara drops her head on the steering wheel with an audible "Agh!"

"Hello, tierra a Cara[2]," I call, lifting a strand of the softest hair—silky smooth between my fingers. A jolt of electricity courses through me from the tip of my finger, and it's obvious I need to get laid if touching this girl's hair makes me feel more than I have felt in months.

Yeah, the media talks about me having a flavor of the day but I haven't had a girl in a bed in months. I say *a bed* because I've never brought anyone to my own place. Or places, if you count my condos in every city where we have a corporate office. Maybe I'm bored or maybe I'm old. Either way, I'm tired of the same shit, so driving for almost seventeen hours seemed like a

---

2.   earth to Cara

good idea. Freshen up my mind, widen my horizons, and put me in a new scene. But two weeks? I can't take that much time off.

Cara gets out. I want to follow her but I remember the bag, box, and flowers so I open the back door and gather her stuff. She stops by her front door and mumbles something under her breath.

"Sorry, Carita, I don't have supersonic ears."

"I said," she pauses for theatrics, "I need my keys from my bag."

I hand her the bag, and after she opens the door, we walk in. Stepping into this home feels the way I imagine Malibu Barbie's house would. The first thing I notice is the smell of lemon and vanilla. Like a scone at a bakery. The house is decorated with pink, lilacs, greens, and yellows. Patterns and solids. Flowers and lines. It feels soft in here but almost not real. Cara leaves her shoes by the door, walks to the pastel pink fridge, grabs a Poppi Cola, and throws herself in a pink recliner. There are boxes strewn across different areas of the house with what I assume is the stuff she's moving, but there's still enough space to walk around and sit.

"Drinks are in the fridge, Manny. Make yourself at home while I try to figure out what just happened."

I set her stuff down and sit across from her. I may not be a huge dude, but I certainly feel taller than my six-foot-two in this matchbox-sized home. My eyes keep wandering the room and when they land on Cara, she's looking at me with her eyebrows raised.

"Got anything to say about the house? It doesn't pass your minimalist and expensive as shit vibes?"

I smirk at this because she's not wrong. I do like minimalism, but not for the reasons most people think. It's just easier to work from home in a place that doesn't feel homey. It makes Mom sad that I think like that but it's the truth. One day, I'll devote my life to something else—or someone else—and maybe they can make my house a home. In the meantime, black, gray, and beige with abstract decoration works.

"I'm surprised but it also suits you," I say. "Cara, I know this took you by surprise, but can we please talk about your plans? I don't have a lot of time before I have to make a decision about what I'm doing."

"Manny, just go home or go to work or wherever you need to be. I'm a big girl and I can handle it. And by the way, I'm not thirty yet, you ass—that's still two years away," she adds, and I'd forgotten I even mentioned age earlier. Maybe that's what hit a nerve and now she's in a sour mood. Half the time I forget I'm twenty-six, so I really didn't mean for it to be a big deal.

"Talk to me." I loosen my tie and pull it over my head, setting it on the cold table beside me. I unfasten the top buttons of my shirt deliberately, feeling the fabric shift against my chest. As I slide my jacket off, I catch her gaze as her eyes flicker to me. I roll my sleeves up, exposing my forearms, then slip off my shoes, the soft thud echoing in the quiet space. Placing my arms on my lap I add, "What were your plans? And how come just two months ago, you didn't want to drive?"

Her eyes scan me before she lets out a huff and answers, "I hate driving. I hate people on the road acting stupid, and I hate all the variables. Do you know how many people die in car accidents every day? Too many, Manny, too many. So, I didn't want to drive."

She stops momentarily, then puts her head back and closes her eyes. My attention should be on what she's telling me, but my eyes wander to her pouty pink lips and to her long lashes. Then to the tiny piece of skin between her dainty blouse and her slacks. I've always been attracted to Cara. She's gorgeous and her personality adds to the appeal. However, she's older than me, has always been with the jackass, *and* she's my sister's best friend so it has never been a possibility. Just a crush. A want. A what if.

"Are you even listening to me?" Her voice is coated with a mix of frustration and hurt. I can feel the weight of her words hanging in the air.

I know better than to offer anything less than a simple, earnest affirmation, so I nod and murmur a quick, "Yes."

"Anyway," Cara continues, her tone shifting, "that's why Allie was supposed to drive me back. But then I decided to be a grown-up and take the road trip I've always dreamed of. Allie and Jake are all starry-eyed and caught up in their honeymoon phase, and honestly, I don't want to be around that. Nor do I want to be the one to have them spend two weeks apart after not being together for so long. That would be really bad juju, and God knows I could use all the good vibes I can get right now."

"What trip?" I ask, unable to keep the curiosity out of my voice.

"Manuel," she sighs with a hint of exasperation, "you ask too many questions for someone who's usually glued to his phone."

"Yeah, that's what happens when you run an empire, Cara," I reply, a trace of defensiveness creeping into my voice. "But it doesn't mean I'm not capable of holding a decent conversation that is not about business."

"Isn't that what you do for a living? Smooth-talk people into doing whatever you want them to do? Well, it won't work on me, Manny."

"Actually, not at all. I help people make financial decisions that make sense for them. But also, I don't need to butter you up, Cara," I counter, my tone softening. "I'm just trying to be a friend."

She lets out a frustrated sigh, her eyes narrow. "Fine. What is it?"

"What is what?" I ask. She's always going a mile per hour.

Always laughing, running, dancing, and her jumping. Her actions and words blend together into one big explosion of joy. Right now, all that energy is about to explode, and I don't think joy is what will come of it.

"What is it that you're truly doing here, Manny? Are you really here to just drive or are you here to meet a quota? Is there a reporter out there, seeing you with the charity case of the month? Or are you getting ready for the newest article—" She jumps up and stands on top of the couch, puts her hands under her chin like a microphone and says, "We're here outside the residence of a sweet school teacher, where Manuel Zabana is currently donating his precious time and money to help her to stop spiraling."

Cara continues rambling, performing for me and I just want to laugh. I don't think this will do either of us any favors, so instead, I get up and clap. I clap like I'm her audience and she just put on a show. This catches her off guard and she finally stops talking. I grab her hand and pull her off the couch. She jumps down with a yelp, right into my arms.

"Settle," I whisper gently against her forehead. I learned early on that telling someone to calm down doesn't help, especially after growing up with an anxious sister and trying to help her through difficult times. I found that "settle" can work sometimes, and when it doesn't, I have a list of other phrases ready to go. Not that I use them often, but it's reassuring to know they're there.

She tenses at my touch, but I don't let go, wrapping my arms around her even tighter. I can try to be the ground she needs right now or at least I can try.

"Cara, breathe." I even my own breaths, hoping that she'll match them and when she does, her breathing slows as her shoulders sag. "That's it, breathe for me."

"I need to go outside," she insists, stepping away from my

hold and heading back to her front door. I follow her outside and around her house. There's a narrow stepping-stone path leading to a wooded area near the water. She leaves her sandals behind and walks barefoot over the stones; her steps deliberate as she heads toward the trees. She plants her heels firmly into the ground, takes a deep breath in and then lies down on the grass.

I'm not doing that in my Tom Ford pants, but I can stand by her and try to figure out what's actually happening. She might be losing it, but right now, laying on the grass with her eyes closed and her lips slightly parted—she looks more beautiful than ever. And fuck me because I need to focus, but Cara's proving that to be harder and harder the more time I spend with her, and this is not even day one.

"I've always wanted to go on this epic road trip. But there's always something to do and somewhere to be," she says. "I want to be able to explore and hike; swim in random places, go to a country bar in a town nobody knows me and... let go. I want to sing karaoke and thrift shop to go to an event." Cara lets out a breath and turns around to face me. "I want to travel and see the world. I want to live outside of the two cities I've called home my whole life and this summer I can finally do it. My parents agreed that I don't need to work at the diner and with me moving back, I have time before I have to be back at work in August. I have six weeks to do whatever I want—well, three really, if you count when I need to be in Atlanta for my friend Alex's wedding, but yeah."

"What's stopping you, then?" I ask, staring at her lying on the grass with her eyes closed and her hands digging into the dirt.

"I hate driving," she admits, blowing out a breath and her eyes fluttering open to look at me.

"But you like exploring more, no?"

"Well, duh. But the more I think about it, the more I don't want to do this alone," she replies and closes her lips tight before her watch lets out an alarm.

"Shit, shit, shit, I have to go!" Her voice is frantic as she leaps up from the grass, her movements hurried. She starts to walk past me, but I quickly grab her hand. A jolt of electricity zips through my fingers, and I can tell she feels it too—her eyes snap back onto mine, wide with surprise.

"Breathe, Cara," I say, my voice calm but firm. "You're moving a mile a minute. Where do you need to go?"

"I have that stupid end-of-the-year dinner," she says, her words tumbling out in a rush. "They're throwing a goodbye party, and I'm already late if I want to shower and pick up a gift for my boss."

"How about this?" I reply, trying to keep my tone calm and hoping it rubs off on her. "You go take a shower, and I'll handle the gift. What do you want to get him?"

"Of course you would think my boss is a man, Mr. CEO. My principal is a woman, and she loves wine, so I was going to get her some fancy bottle of wine."

"I can handle the wine. Just go shower, and I'll figure it out."

"Alright, but the keys to my van are inside," she says.

"I'm not driving that," I reply. "I've got this, Carita. Just go."

Cara heads into her house, leaving me outside. I pull out my phone and dial Lucia, my assistant for the past month.

"Mr. Zabana, how can I assist you?"

"Change of plans, Lucia. I need you to send a car to my location right away," I say into the phone, my tone clipped with urgency.

After ending the call, I stand there for a moment, the evening air brushing against my skin. I glance around, and I feel the weight of the situation settle in. I'm left waiting, my mind already racing. The streetlights flicker on, casting long shadows on the pavement as I wait for the car to arrive and think about how the hell I found myself in this situation and what am I going to do about it.

4

DIRTY SHIRLEY

ROCKLAND, GRACIE ABRAMS

Cara

"GO SHOWER, *Cara*. Let me handle it, *Cara*. Go do your thing, *Carita*," I grumble to myself while I scrub furiously. Fucking Manuel Zabana had to be here and throw everything off. I'm going to kill Allie, too. What kind of friend doesn't give her best friend a heads up about sending her obnoxiously hot brother to go *rescue* her? What in the actual fuckety fuck?!

What about me trying to be independent and shit? What about me trying to find myself after being locked in a two-life spiral? My life is split evenly between school and summer breaks in Baker. Now that both of my worlds have crumbled, I can freely do whatever I want. Not that I couldn't before; but when Allie decided to leave Baker Oaks, cut out everything from that town aside from me and our friendship, it was hard juggling the secrets and the lies. But I would do that for her twice over in a heartbeat. Now, if she had told me what kept her and Jake separate all those years, I would've put some sense into that brain of hers. I know why she did it but now, at twenty-eight, I don't think it needed to happen. Not my call though, so I kept being the supportive friend she needed.

Every summer, I set up my townhouse for rent and travel back to Baker to help my parents out at Ronnie's. Ronnie's was Grandpa's legacy, and he left it to my dad; one day, it will be mine, too. Even though my passion is not running the eclectic homey diner, I still love doing it. I love serving others and getting to know them better. I can tell when Sue is having a rough day because she drinks her coffee black, or when Roe's on a creative streak because she orders food she doesn't normally eat and sits and doodles. I've seen people meet there and then go on to have relationships, and I've heard more town gossip at Ronnie's than anywhere else.

I do love working there but I don't love anything more than teaching. I've known I wanted to be a teacher since I could remember and there's nothing that makes me want to leave this profession I love. Not the hard days, not the sad days, not the long days. I love it. So when my best friend moved back to Baker and got a job teaching at the elementary school—the same one I attended as a kid—I called Mr. Ryan and begged for a SPED position. Their previous teacher quit so it was meant to be. *Luck*, he said. *Serendipitous*, I replied. There's very little in life left to luck and a whole lot that is just meant to be. *Fate. Magic.*

This meant I could jump right back to my favorite place, with my favorite people, and do what I love most. All perfect, except, my stupid ex lives there and now he's engaged to Jake's ex. They were supposed to move out of Baker, but who knows when that will happen.

So I wanted to do something for myself and take the road trip I've always wanted to take. I asked Cole to go with me multiple times, but he could never take the time off to do it. If it wasn't something he wanted to do, there was never enough time in his eyes. He did suggest I take the trip with Allie, but she was always working crazy hours and only did day or weekend trips with me. I didn't feel like going with anyone else, so it just didn't happen.

"Shit," I groan to the empty room as cold water hits my skin. After getting out of the shower, drying my body and dressing in my favorite green dress with a daisy pattern, I blow out my hair and add some blush so I don't look dead. I open the fridge, the cool air brushing against my skin, and reach for the pitcher of sweet tea. I tilt it, pouring the tea into my iced coffee cup, the clink of ice echoing as it fills. With a satisfied nod, I sling my purse over my shoulder, the familiar weight comforting against me. Almost two hours later I'm ready, so I take a deep breath, push the front door open, and step outside, the summer air warming my face immediately.

"Whoa, where are you going so fast?" Manny asks as I almost run smack into him. He's standing there with a gift bag the size of a wine bottle in one hand and three other shopping bags in the other. He's wearing a different shirt than before—this one dark and fitted as if it were tailor-made for him. Of course it fits perfectly; Manny always looks like every piece of clothing was designed just for him.

I'm not sure when I first noticed how attractive he was—maybe around his seventeenth or eighteenth birthday—but now, seeing him as a fully grown man, he's undeniably stunning. His navy button-down shirt, slightly unbuttoned at the collar, and his dark jeans highlight his well-defined figure. The little bracelet he always wears adds a subtle touch of sophistication. He looks and smells expensive, with an effortlessly polished vibe. Meanwhile, I'm a crumbling mess.

He clears his throat, bringing me back to reality and I remember briefly how he said he would go get a gift for my boss.

"How did you get changed so fast? Is that wine for my boss?" I ask.

"Hotel room, yes, and these are for your other staff friends. I know you said your boss, but I assume you have an assistant principal and the way you were talking to... what was her name?"

"Beth," I whisper.

"Yeah, Beth. It seemed like she is important so I got her something, too."

He's always been this thoughtful—even though the media makes him seem like a superficial asshole. He's such a good brother and friend to Allie and in part, he has been to me too, as much as I want to kill him sometimes with his antics.

"Mm, thanks? I have to go. Are you coming or...?" I ask.

"I thought you'd never ask. Our car is waiting," he says, pointing at a dark SUV idling behind him. He opens the door for me and steps aside letting me in first, and then stepping in closing the door behind him.

"Where to, Mr. Zabana?" the driver asks.

"Where are we going, Cara?"

"Uh, to Limoncello," I reply and the driver nods, puts the directions on the screen and we begin our twelve-minute drive to the restaurant. The SUV smells new so I know it's not his, but I'm still shocked from the whole outfit, gifts in hands, and vehicle waiting for us to say anything.

"Talk to me about this party. Are we staying for long? Are these people fun? Do I need liquor to deal with your coworkers, or are they cool and I can drink wine?" he asks.

"Who invited you to stay with me?" I ask, raising my eyebrow and turning my body so I can face him.

"I'm coming along; no need for an invitation," Manny quips with a lighthearted voice. "I want to hear more about this road trip and everything else you've got on your to-do list for moving back. My siblings conspired against me, so I'm off work duty until Sunday."

"You're taking four days off? I didn't think you could stay away from work for even half a day," I reply, a hint of disbelief in my voice, bringing my hands to my chest and dropping my mouth open.

"No, I'm just not required to show up anywhere. I'll be working from my hotel room tonight and tomorrow. But since I'm already here and don't know anyone in the city, I figured some fresh air and a bit of distraction would do me good."

Manny's casual demeanor contrasts with the stress that's been weighing on me, and it's infuriating yet oddly comforting to have him around. As we drive through the city, I watch the neon lights blur past. The roads are bustling with life, the occasional honk of a horn slicing through the hum of the city.

We arrive at Limoncello, the sports bar that stands out from the surrounding buildings with its vibrant colors. The exterior is painted a warm, sunny yellow, with large arched windows framed by lush green plants. Soft, glowing lights are strung across the entrance and they cast a cheerful, welcoming glow. A vintage wooden sign with elegant lettering hangs above the door, swaying gently in the evening breeze.

We step out of the SUV and walk in; all the while, Manny's hand doesn't leave my back. It lingers there as he leads me where we're going. It's such a simple touch but one my body has craved for years. I've been so starved of physical touch that this little contact has my skin on fire. I've slept with plenty of people and had my shared fun but the subtle lingering touches, the protective touches—those don't happen anymore and apparently I've missed them. The wind carries his scent of pine and something citrusy and maybe even mint, but all of it overpowers everything else going on. He either wears the best cologne there is or I have to get laid, stat.

"Ms. Thompson!" Derek, one of the science teachers, shouts when he sees me. Everyone waves and smiles at us as we walk up to the area reserved for our school. This has become a tradition now: between the end of the school year and before our post-planning days, we have dinner at Limoncello on a Thursday. They have karaoke and the VIP area is right near the stage so we have free entertainment all night.

I wave my hellos and walk to the bar so I can order and start drowning my emotions in alcohol. I wish I could name them all, but somewhere between ending the school year and Manny being here, makes the move and the start of a new era feel all too real and I hate change.

"Hi angel, what's your best local IPA?" Manny asks the bartender and with a giant smile she gives him a list. He orders one that I've never heard of and turns to me. "What about you, Carita, what's your poison today?"

"Can I have a Dirty Shirley?"

"Sure thing, coming right up," she says and Manny smiles at me.

"What?" I snap.

"I didn't take you for a grenadine girl," he answers, smiling bigger.

"Well considering that I have the taste of a five-year-old, Dirty Shirleys are where it's at. Plus, Natalie spoiled me with her delicious wine and now everything I taste is too adult-ish for me. Speaking of my little kid taste, can you order chicken tenders too? I'm starving."

The girl comes back with our drinks, takes the chicken tender order along with some potstickers for Manny, and passes him a napkin with her phone number and a wink. I roll my eyes at him after he puts it in his pocket.

"What? Can't blame me, I just smiled at her," he chuckles.

I get up with a groan and join my coworkers in the area reserved for us. There are maybe thirty people present, not many for the size of our school but all of my favorites are here and that's what matters.

"Cara, come sit here," Beth calls and I join her and the rest of the front office crew.

"Who's this handsome man, Cara?" Colleen, Beth's right hand, asks. But before I can introduce him, Manny takes charge of the conversation.

"Hi, I'm Manuel but you can call me Manny." He grabs her hand and kisses the top of it while winking at her.

"Where were you hiding this gentleman?" Colleen swoons, and all I do is smile and nod before I pull Manny by the arm and make him sit with me, on the opposite side of the table.

We talk for a while about my plans and the new school. They tell me how much they'll miss me and how the school won't be the same without me. I give the gifts that Manny bought and when my boss opens the wine, I see it's a freaking expensive wine. She's appreciative, of course, but I just want to kill Manny because what in the actual fuck? The room is dark and it's crowded, making the air feel thicker as the time goes by. Between the singers choosing different music from upbeat tempos to slow songs and Manny keeping my Dirty Shirleys refilled, I'm feeling great but don't want to overdo it. I'm about to call it a night when the person on the mic calls my name to go sing.

"This must be a mistake because I didn't write my name down," I say to really no one but also to everyone around me.

"You said you wanted to sing karaoke this summer so I wrote your name down," Manny explains, and if looks could kill I'm sure he would be dead.

"What do you mean you wrote my name down, Manny? I'm not singing in front of all these people," I snap but I don't have time to say anything else because the whole area claps and shouts for me to stand up. *Gotta love working with teachers.*

"Okay, okay, I'm coming." I stand, pulling my dress down and shooting daggers at this guy because I will kill him. I will.

I walk up to the DJ stand and ask for a minute so I can pick a song. He starts a song and promises the audience he'll be back with more karaoke in no time. I look at the book and although I could pick so many of the upbeat and cheery songs, there's one in particular that calls my name. Seeing it in the choices made my heart skip a beat because it's so new, I didn't think they would have the instrumental version for it.

"Can I sing this?' I ask and when I do, his face brightens.

"You can but this one is a little different—if you're up for a challenge." His smile could light up the whole room. His eyes shine with something that looks like hope.

I can't let him down now so I say, "I'm always up for a challenge."

5

LOSS OF MY LIFE
LOML, TAYLOR SWIFT

Manny

SHE MIGHT CUT off my balls. When I think of her face, I'm sure of it. I didn't think signing her up would be a bad thing though. I thought she just needed a little push to start her whole summer list of things she wants to do.

> Me: on a scale from 1 to 10 how fucked am I if I signed Cara up for something she didn't know about?

> Allielicious: It depends on what the something was?

> Me: Karaoke at a bar with half her school faculty?

> Alliellicious: 💀 💀 💀

> Allielicious: Buena suerte

Fuck.

The song stops and Cara walks to the mic in the center of the stage. She's pulling a stool with her and at the same time, the DJ steps out from behind the booth and walks toward the back corner of the stage where a dark piano sits. I can't tell if it's black or brown, but whatever color it actually is makes a good contrast with the yellow and blue framing the whole stage. She sits on the stool, adjusting the height of the mic and before she speaks or sings, she looks at me with a murderous glare and moves her lips in what looks like *you own me.* I'm guessing *you owe me* is more like it.

The DJ starts playing the piano behind her. A soft melody that I can't place and then Cara says, "Good evening, Limoncello." Her voice is cheerful as she smiles big at the audience—a complete contrast to how I know she feels, but she's a master of her craft and she hides her true feelings well.

"I've never done this here before, but my friend Manny thought it was a good idea as a farewell to this city that has given me so much in the past years. Mike over there," she says, pointing at the guy on the piano and he smiles and nods at her. She flips her hair over her shoulder and smiles back at the crowd before continuing, "He said that this would be a good opportunity for him to play one of his favorite new Taylor Swift songs. So make sure you give it up for him as he performs with me tonight."

I'm not surprised at how effortlessly she has the crowd's attention, laughing at her subtle jokes and smiling with her. Cara is like the sun and we're just all in her orbit.

"So without further ado, let's begin."

The audience claps before the melody on the piano changes and as soon as it does, a hush falls over the crowd. Cara closes her eyes, lets out a gentle breath and starts singing. Her voice starts soft, her eyes still closed and her hair cascading in soft waves around her shoulders. She's not only singing—she's telling a story. A story about a couple who are dancing around each other for years. A story about memories and patiently waiting and taking further steps into a relationship.

She opens her eyes as the melody changes into what feels like the chorus of the song. Her eyes sparkle looking around at the crowd, which is completely enamored by her tone and her voice. Then she says something about the love of her life and stops singing, letting the piano take over to the next part of the song.

You can only hear the melody dancing in the space. It's like the whole bar is completely frozen in place, captivated by her sweet voice. Suspended in time while she continues telling this story. The same way I have been completely lost in Cara for as long as I can remember.

As the song keeps going, the tempo picks up and her voice changes to a deeper tone. A sadder tone. She's singing about goodbye masked as love and she's delivering a message with both her voice and her eyes. Her voice is haunted now and she's casting a spell over all of us.

Even the bartenders, who were previously cheerful and focused, have now paused, listening to the sound of her voice as it reverberates through the space. Then as Cara delivers the last line of the song, changing love for loss, her eyes close one more time and the melody fades. The bar remains hushed for a beat longer, as if nobody wants to let go of the enchantment. Then the spell breaks, and the room erupts into cheers and a loud applause. Everyone stands up and when she finally opens her eyes, her whole demeanor changes. Before the song, she was like a ray of sunshine, full of warmth and color. Now, she resembles a wilting flower, withering away as the melody ends.

Cara offers a shy smile, one that doesn't reach her eyes. To others, they might think it's her real one, but I know her better than that. I can see the quiet sadness that lingers just beneath the surface, hidden behind a mask she's learned to wear. Her eyes don't wrinkle at the corners the way they do when her joy is real, when it spills out effortlessly and fills the whole room. They don't sparkle with that familiar warmth, that unguarded light that makes her who she is. Instead, there's something distant, almost hollow, in their depths. The smile, too, is a half-hearted thing—just a shadow of the one she used to give, the one I became too accustomed to growing up and the one I tried my best to pull out of her. This is compliance, the kind she has perfected over time, the smile she offers when she's trying to follow some unwritten rule to pretend she's okay when I can see how far from it she really is. And I ache, wishing she didn't have to hide herself but also wondering if I had anything to do to with it.

She brings the DJ to the front and gives a curtsy, pushing him forward so people can clap for him too. She leaves the stage, walking past the crowd as they clap for her and when she passes by them, she keeps her head held high and smiles at them. She slides into the seat next to me, puts the straw between her full lips and downs her whole drink.

"Cara, my goodness, I didn't know you could sing like that," Beth admires, her voice full of awe, a warm smile spreading across her face. But I can't tear my eyes away from Cara—how she stands there, the soft glow of the stage lights catching in her hair even from afar, the way her hands hover nervously by her sides like she's unsure if she's allowed to be proud of herself, proud of this moment.

"I sing for the kids all the time," she responds, her voice soft and almost apologetic, as though she's justifying something she doesn't want to be seen for. "It's the adults that I don't like." Cara blows Beth a quick, lighthearted kiss, trying to brush off the compliment like it's nothing. But I can see it; that little break in her composure, the way her lips quiver before they settle back into something almost forced.

"That was amazing," I gush before I can stop myself, the words tumbling out with more weight than I intended.

"I'm ready to go," Cara announces suddenly, her tone shifting again. It's like the performance is over, the curtain falling, and she's already retreating into herself. She reaches for her purse, the subtle click of the clasp snapping shut louder even in the busy restaurant. She pulls out cash and starts to count it out mechanically, as if paying for drinks is all that matters right now.

"Put it on my card, please, and close the tab," I tell the bartender, my words coming out more abruptly than I mean them to. There's a sharp edge in my voice, like I'm angry.

"You really don't have to pay for my drinks, Manny," Cara protests, her voice tight and almost clipped, as she watches the bartender swipe my card. There's a trace of frustration in her tone, but underneath it is something more—a quiet, brittle thing, like she's angry at herself more than anything else.

"I'm sorry," she whispers, just loud enough for me to hear, but I don't think she's even talking to me anymore. I think she's talking to herself.

"I know I don't have to," I reply. "But I want to, Cara."

"Thanks," she murmurs, her tone softening as she heads toward the door. The tension in her shoulders seems to ease slightly as she walks away. The glow from the bar's neon sign reflects off her silhouette, casting a warm amber hue on the polished wooden floor beneath her. She exits into the night, the door swinging open and then closing with a soft, resigned thud behind her.

"Cara, wait." I walk behind her. Once outside, she turns her body to me, and that is when I see it. She has rosy cheeks and tears behind her eyes.

"Why did you do that?" she asks, smacking me on the shoulder with her bag.

"Woah, woah, why are you sad? That was an incredible performance."

"I didn't say I wanted to sing karaoke in front of everyone, Manuel. That was so embarrassing."

"Embarrassing?" I repeat. *What the fuck?* "Were we both not in the same place? Because that was so damn good you left us all speechless. Not an ounce of what you did out there was embarrassing. That was the best damn performance of the night. Hell, I don't think I've ever heard anything better."

"Don't try to win me over now. That was shitty! You didn't even ask!" Cara shouts and at this point, we're making a scene out here. I know she wants to go so I message the driver. I told him to stay on standby and in just a couple minutes he pulls up to the curb.

"Come on, let me get you home."

I open the door for her and step right in behind her. She sits on the opposite end of the SUV and looks out the window, giving me the cold shoulder.

"Cara, talk to me," I plead, reaching over to hold her hand. "I'm sorry I did that. If I had known it was going to upset you, I would've never."

She lets out a breath and says, "It's okay. I just hate surprises and today has been a day full of them. I'm ready to go home and go to sleep."

Ouch, she hates surprises and today I'm responsible for three of them.

"Okay, I get that. Sorry for pushing you to do something you weren't ready for," I tell her. Her body immediately shows me that was the right move. Her shoulders relax, her eyebrows are not frowning anymore and she lets out a big breath, melting into the seat.

"All of you Zabanas are good at saying sorry huh?"

I don't think so, I want to say, because I don't usually apologize for anything. Apologizing is taking the blame for something and I'm usually right. But with Cara, it has always been easy. Easy to talk to her, to spend time with her, even when I was being the annoying best friend's little brother.

"What do you mean?" I ask and she places her legs on top of my lap.

"All of you are always saying sorry, even if it's not your fault. Especially your sister. You meant well, Manny. I was just surprised. And honestly, the whole move has me a little jittery," Cara adds, grabbing her hair and twisting it in a messy bun behind her neck.

"What's stressing you out about the move?" I add as my phone vibrates on my lap, showing a business client's number and I dismiss it. I cringe at the act. I don't remember the last time I skipped a call but it can wait. Right now I need to figure out what's going on with her.

Cara's eyes trace the movement of my hand to my lap, sees me silencing the call and then her eyes shoot right to mine.

"You can answer that. I can cover my ears and say *lalala* until you're done if you don't want me to listen to your important business call," she jokes, adding quotation marks to the business call part.

"It is a business call, Cara, and it can wait."

"At this time? That's probably a booty call," she adds, sticking her tongue out and shaking her head.

"I don't get those, sunshine. I don't give my phone numbers to the women I fuck and I don't date, so here we are. If someone's calling me on this number, it's business related, trust me." And I mean it. In the beginning, I used to have my phone number listed but I stopped after I had a couple of stalkers—women *and men*— calling me at all times of the day to ask to come to my place.

Now, I have two numbers: one for family and friends, and one for business. It leaks every so often but I've had a good streak.

The phone rings again and I decline the call.

"Then still, answer it," she says.

"No, I'm talking to you. You were saying?" I add, turning my phone off. *That's new.*

"Honestly?" Cara pauses, her voice trembling slightly before she continues, "I just want to do this one thing for myself. I want to explore, travel, and see all the places I've always dreamed of. I don't want to do it alone, but I'm done begging people for their time. I'm tired of never being at the top of anyone's priority list. I'm done pleading for people to want to be with me."

Her words hang in the air, heavy with a mix of frustration and resignation. Cara turns to look out the window, her gaze distant as if searching for answers in the dark sky. As she shifts herself further away from me, I feel the immediate loss of her warmth, a sudden coldness replacing the comforting heat that had been there. The absence is palpable, a stark reminder of the emotional distance between us. The SUV feels emptier now, the silence more pronounced, and I can sense the weight of her words settling heavily in the space between us.

"Then do it," I insist.

"It's not that easy, Manny. I want to believe that I'm this independent can-do-it-all woman, and I'm sure I can, but I don't want to. I don't want to go on this road trip by myself. I think I like people too much. I like being around people too much."

We pull up to her house and she tries to open the door but I hold her hand. That movement freezes time. A simple touch and everything changes. I can feel it in the air. I can feel it in the way she slowly turns her face toward me and when her emerald eyes get hooked on mine. I'm about to do something that I've never done before—I think I might take her up on this crazy trip. I might actually stop working and help her make this dream come true.

"Wait, let me," I insist as I open my door, stepping out and offering my hand to help her get out of the SUV. She takes it and steps out, giving me a soft smile.

We walk in silence to her door. The wind blows softly bouncing through the leaves in the trees around us and Cara's hair flowing with it. The soft light from the streetlamps reflects on her face and her eyes shine when I look at them. I'm doing this. I can't look at her like this, so full of dreams but so sad at not making them.

"Let's do it," I announce. I want to sound confident, like I know what I'm doing, but I think for the first time in my life I sound unsure. Hesitant.

"Do what?" Cara asks.

"I'll take you on the road trip. We'll go and do whatever you want. Just make the list and I'll take us there."

Cara rolls her eyes. "Yeah, like you would leave your precious work for that long to do this for me. It's okay, Manny. It was a dare, not a contract," she adds.

But it's not just the dare. There's no easy way to say no to Cara and there's no easy way to let her down. Seeing a glimpse of sadness on this girl who is usually such a light to everyone around her, it's hard enough. She said she's not been a priority to people, I'm about to make her mine.

"I'm not backing out on the dare," I say, because what else can I? How do I say that I don't want to see her sad without making her feel like I pity her. "We're going."

"Manuel," she starts.

"Cara, we're going. I'll stop by tomorrow and we can finalize plans, okay?"

"You're impossible," she groans, grabbing the keys from her purse and opening her door.

"To say no to?" I tease, smiling and she smiles back.

"Bye, asshole, I'll see you tomorrow." She steps into her house and turns around. "Are you sure? Don't get me all excited for nothing." This vulnerability that she's showing me. This uncertainty is not like the confident Cara I've known for years and I'm thankful for it. I'm glad to see the friendship that I thought we've had through the years is there. The honesty in her words and in this moment is more than I thought would happen and I'm grateful for it, even if she doesn't believe me.

"I'm a man of my word, Carita. See you tomorrow." I wink at her and she flushes.

I wait for her to close her door and then walk to the SUV that's waiting for me. And I think about how the fuck I'm going to make this work.

6

———————————

I'M NOT A MERMAID

MESS, NOAH KAHAN

Cara

SO MANY PEOPLE are pretty criers. They have soft tears landing on their cheeks. Their eyes glow and get lighter and they look more kissed by the rain than anything else. I'm sure that's what it feels like to be God's—or whatever entity's above—favorite. I, on the other hand, am not. I look more like a blowfish. My eyes get puffy and red. My usually light green eyes get as dark as emeralds and my skin gets blotchy. Definitely not kissed by the rain; more like you threw me in a pond while fully clothed and with regular mascara on. That's exactly what I look like now after leaving my school for the last time. I'm a complete mess.

Saying goodbye to my friends from the past near-decade was not easy. It wasn't pretty. It was so hard, in fact, that I almost considered throwing all my plans away and staying. Saying goodbye to the kids yesterday was rough, but saying goodbye to those who have become family was definitely not what the doctor ordered.

I make it home and get out of the van, but when I walk up to my house, I see Manuel standing by my door, looking fresh while I look like an absolute wreck. He has the whole 'mysterious rich boy' vibe that he always carries; but this time, with nice dark jeans and a dark collared shirt, he looks like the boy next door. Nice, approachable and hotter than sin. *Jesus, I need to get laid. Can't be lusting over this man.* His back is against the wall and he's holding a coffee in one hand and a bag from Lost Larson—my favorite bakery.

"Manny," I greet him, reaching up to kiss his cheek. The Zabanas are Dominican and it's part of their culture to kiss on the cheek when you say hello and goodbye. I have been a part of their family for so long that it is somewhat expected. I don't mind it, and usually I just throw myself at Allie when I see her and I can ignore her brothers, but after hanging out with Manny last night and him actually trying to make my life a little easier, I sure as hell should show him some manners. Except the minute our cheeks touch, I feel the familiar zing on my body I've been getting lately when we touch, and I still don't know how to deal with that.

"Hola, Carita," he replies, smiling and handing me the coffee. "Coffee and croissants for my lady."

"And from my favorite bakery. Are you trying to score brownie points? To what do I owe this pleasure?" I ask while I open the door and we walk in. There are some boxes in the living room but there's still enough space to sit and walk around.

"We need to plan the road trip, so I figured we could make that happen now. I have my assistant on call waiting to hear from us so she can finalize plans," he explains, sitting in a recliner that looks too small for him.

"I'm not having one of your cutie assistants plan my dream trip for me. I can handle it." *Who does he think he is? Coming in here and telling me what we're doing.* I still sip on the fucking delicious coffee he brought me, though.

"First off, she's not cute. Second, that's fine. Then what are we doing?" Before I can answer him, I open the bakery bag and see a croissant, take a piece off, shove it in my mouth and set the bag on the table.

"Well I need to finish packing, I need to rent a trailer for my boxes and then I need to make an itinerary for the trip. Also, how long do you have? How long can we take? Those are the things I need to know so I can plan what we're doing and when we're going," I add. It's so kind of him to want to go on this trip with me but I also hate to bother him or take him away from his fancy job. I'm twirling my hair with my hand and my knee is shaking, waiting for him to say something.

"I can hear you thinking, Cara," Manny says.

"Well, say something then," I groan.

"I told you we're going. And I also told you I am a man of my word. So how long do you want me? A weekend? A week? Three weeks? You say it and you got me," he insists, reaching forward and grabbing my hand, pulling it away from my hair.

"I mean, could you come back? I still have to finish packing and make the itinerary and do shit and I can't do all that today. I don't want to pull you from work for that long and maybe I'll be ready by Monday?" Holy run-on sentence. *Breathe, Cara, breathe.*

"Cara, breathe for me," he adds as if he can hear my inner thoughts and sense the turmoil.

"Okay," I whisper and Manny lays his hands back on his knees, sitting back and relaxing in the recliner again.

"Okay, so what's on this checklist of yours? Because I'm sure you have it hiding in one of the girlie notebooks in your purse," he teases and I want to roll my eyes but I grab my bag and pull out my pink planner instead. I let out a nervous squeal because showing someone your plans is never easy, especially when you're trying to share the plans with them. I open it to the page that has my 'Move Back to Baker' checklist and hand it to him.

1- Packing:
Living Room
Kitchen
Bedroom
Bonus room
2 - Bags for road trip
3 - Itinerary
4 - Leave Key with Colleen
5 - U-Haul
6 -Book hotels
7- Get supplies
8 - Snacks?

Manny mulls over the list. "Okay, this is not that bad. Are you planning on road-tripping with a U-Haul?

"No, silly. I'm pulling a trailer with the van!" I exclaim, taking my notebook from him and putting it on top of the flower side table.

"You're planning on road-tripping, *and* pulling a trailer, with that Powerpuff Girl bus?" Manny questions me with a surprised tone that mirrors his expression. I'm so annoyed at this whole conversation that I'm about to throw all the plans out the window.

"Yes, I'm taking my girl with me back to Baker. I've told you this how many times now?"

"Okay, okay, but I thought you meant you would load everything up and send it back with movers and then just drive your bus, Cara. Can that even sustain a long trip like that, pulling a trailer full of stuff? And boy. Buses are boys," he corrects.

"Are you giving me a gender lecture right now, Manuel? If I want my bus to be a girl, it'll be a girl, and yes, it can. It's in great condition, I take it to the shop every other month."

"Vans are girls, and I guess you do call it a van even though it's a bus," he quips and I give him a death stare. "Okay, okay, just in Spanish I guess," he groans, raising his hands and then pinching his nose. "But like have you thought about how much easier it would be to road-trip without pulling a trailer?"

"Manny, I'm on a teacher's salary here. Do you know how expensive it would be to ship all my crap?

He lets out a breath, looking me in the eyes and considering his next words. Then he says, "In a perfect world, if everything from your list was ready tomorrow, could you leave tomorrow?"

"Yes, but that's impossible," I say.

"Leave the impossibilities to me, sunshine. Can you do that or not?"

"Yes, I guess." God, he's insufferable.

"If I could have someone here to pack your stuff, would that be okay with you?" *Pack my stuff? What stuff?*

"What stuff?" I ask sipping on my coffee, I close my eyes and moan because this shit is so good, I need to inject it into my veins.

"Your stuff. What was on your list? Ah yes, living room, bedroom, etcetera, etcetera."

"Who's gonna pack my shit, Manuel? Not all of us grew up with hot daddies and nannies," I add and he physically shrinks. Mr. Zabana is actually a total asshole and he might be good looking for his age, but I don't play around with older men. I'm too much of a child to embrace *adulthood* this early. I know I'm almost thirty and I should *grow up* or whatever, but we haven't reached that point and I'm not rushing it. The rise I get out of

Allie and her brothers about me calling their dad hot though? Worth it.

"Stop calling my dad hot, please. I have contacts; is that okay with you?" he asks. He's being so docile and respectful, I wonder what happened to the Manny who is usually goofing around and not taking anything seriously but his job.

I nod gently and he smiles at that.

"Okay, let's go." Manny stands up and walks toward the door.

"Let's go where? I'm tired, I look like shit and I want to take a nap."

"You could never look like shit," he scoffs with his megawatt smile. Then he adds, "We're going to get some checks on that checklist of yours. I know how much you like to cross things off." He winks and I grab my bag, following him out and into the van.

"Wanna drive?" I ask as I wiggle my eyebrows, thinking that he will say no. Manny surprises me when he opens his palm and lets me throw the keys at him.

"Might as well get used to driving this explosion of girliness."

"Oh do tell, why do you need to get used to it?" I ask, walking around the passenger side and hopping in the front seat.

He gets in the van and adjusts the seat while he swears in Spanish. His sleeves bunch up at his forearms, drawing my attention to them and I get caught staring because when my eyes meet his, he shows me the cockiest grin and says, "Well, I'm driving this thing on this bucket list trip, aren't I?"

Manny pulls out of the parking lot and heads into town.

FOUR HOURS later and I'm exhausted, but... hyped? Ready to fall asleep, but giddy? I can feel my body bouncing in the seat both figuratively and literally. Manny drove me around town until I got everything I needed. We bought our weight's worth of snacks and drinks, grabbed scrapbooking supplies, and some other things we needed for the trip. Well, I needed, I guess. Manny, forever the gentleman, drove around without complaints. He carried my bags as I shopped, and overall was great company. His phone never stopped ringing but other than answering a few messages and a call here and there, he didn't remove his attention from the task at hand.

We decided to grab takeout for dinner and head back to my place. He ordered sushi—or his assistant ordered sushi, I guess—and we're pulling up when I see a U-Haul parked right outside my place.

"Manny?" I ask but he stays quiet and just parks the van. He silently walks around to open my door and offers me his hand like I need help to get out, but I take it anyway. I grab some of the bags of stuff we bought, but he takes them from me and carries them inside with the takeout bag, too.

As we walk to my place, I see movers shoving things into the U-Haul and after stepping in, I confirm my suspicions. My whole house is packed and ready to go. Not the furniture, though. I'm leaving it fully furnished and renting it to the girl who did her internship in a kindergarten class at school. She's very 'rainbows and butterflies' so she didn't even bat an eyelash at my quirky house.

The U-Haul is almost full and upon further inspection, I notice they're bringing out the boxes from my room, which were already packed. Thank God for that, because I would have fainted at the thought of strangers going through my drawers.

A leggy brunette walks out in high heels and a tight fancy skirt. She seems as tall as the ceiling. I'm usually not surprised by tall women, as I'm five-foot-seven myself, but this woman is more than tall. She demands space with every step she takes. She demands all eyes on her. So fucking confident. And that makes me pull my shoulders back more and stand taller myself.

She walks past me and straight to Manny. She gives him a big smile that he doesn't return and says, "All set here, Mr. Zabana. Things will be delivered to your sister's address and we'll keep you posted."

"Thank you, Lucia. Have a great night. I won't need you again here. Can you send a car for me in about an hour? We need to have dinner first." Manny's voice is commanding and *holy moly* does that made him hotter. His business-like tone, his serious demeanor, and the respect that he used to give her instructions, while not treating her like she's any less. His mom is a great lady so I'm sure that's where he gets his good manners from but *fuck me* because that was both hot and sweet.

Lucia walks out of the house and closes the door behind her. The house is empty now. No boxes anywhere. No people roaming around; just me, Manny, and the food. He sets the table and I join him, sitting down and opening the first container to see if it's my sushi roll. I grab the chopsticks and the yum-yum sauce and start eating.

"That's not really a sushi roll. That's more like breaded rice with chicken inside smothered in sauce."

"And who are you, the sushi police? Let me eat my Highway Seventeen roll in peace, please." Deep-fried deliciousness with cream cheese, avocado, and chicken inside. The perfect combo.

"Sushi without fish shouldn't even be called sushi," he argues.

"I don't like seafood, fish, or anything that breathes underwater, Manny. Why would I trust it? I'm not a mermaid. If it breathes underwater, I'm not eating it. Let me live happily with my chicken sushi, please."

"Whatever you say, Carita, whatever you say." Manny shakes his head before laughing loudly.

This might be my favorite thing about all of the Zabanas: how easy it is to talk and laugh with them. How easy it is to just be with them. Allie and I have been friends for forever so her brothers were always part of the package. Manny's twin brother, Augusto—Gus for short— is funny as shit too, but we really don't talk as much.

Manny was the one that I could always talk to, either because he was always nagging at me or because he was always asking me how I was. As we grew older, Manny became more than Allie's little brother—he became my friend too. He became someone to talk to every now and then when I needed a pick me up, because I knew I could count on Manny to make me laugh. He became someone that I wanted to share things with because he always replied quickly, no matter what it was, and this led to us talking frequently. He became a good friend.

However, since adulthood, it's been harder to spend time with him, or any of them actually. Jobs all over the country, relationships, responsibilities, and whatever else gets in the way. Whoever said that growing up was a fraud was right. This shit's for the birds.

"So Cara, you bought a whole stationery set... what are you doing with all that?"

"Funny you should ask," I say, getting up to grab the bag of things on the table and pull out the new journal. It came with tabbies to match the colors on the cover and I have never been happier. I'm surprised Manny saw me pick out these things since he was on his phone during this part of the shopping spree.

"See here?" I ask, opening to the first page to show him the bullet points in my journal. "This is a bullet journal. You can use it for many things, but I got it to document the road trip and to write the itinerary. I'll be working on that tonight. I want loose plans, if that's okay with you. I want to be able to seize the day and enjoy it—does that make any sense?"

I hate that I turn into this jittery mess when I'm trying to ask for something. I used to be able to ask for what I wanted head on. But in all the years that I was with that ass-who-shall-not-be-named, he made it seem like I was being annoying. *You ask for too much, Cara. Just chill.* I can hear his words echoing in my brain. My therapist says that I need to let go of the girl I tried to be when I was with him and embrace who I am now. Who I always knew I was deep down. Go back to the things that make me happy without daring to think of who might like it or not. I'm trying but it's not always easy. Journaling is just one of the many things.

"Whatever you want to do works for me. I'm yours for the trip and I'm down for whatever," Manny answers and I raise my eyebrows at him. "I mean, I will draw the line at some crazy shit that I'm sure you'll try to pull off, but I'm game. You said three weeks, you got three weeks."

"I said it was going to take me two weeks to do this road trip, not three," I add and he looks at me and smiles. His soft smile. Not the 'I want to seal a deal' smile. This is his 'I'm comfortable with you' smile. The one that reaches his eyes and makes them gleam. The one where his eyebrows are soft and relaxed. The one that could make any girl jealous he's not flashing it at them. And he's showing it to me.

"But you also said you have to be in Atlanta in three weeks for your friend's wedding, right? So why would you cut your trip short to go back out, unless you want to? I figured we could add some more stops to that one-in-a-lifetime dream trip of yours, I can drop you off at this wedding, and after we can drive straight to Baker. Does that work for you?"

"Is this what makes you a great businessman? Your attention to detail?" *Did I just say that aloud? Fuck my whole life.*

"What? Are you surprised I remembered you have that wedding? It's not hard, Cara," he says it nonchalantly. Other than my friends—my close friends, the friends who will never get rid of me friends—I don't think anybody pays attention to what I say. My parents do, but I won't bother them with trivial things. The people at work, we just talk about work. And all the boys I've dated, including Cole, seemed to be more interested in my pretty mouth than the words coming out of it. So no, not easy at all.

My expression must say it all because he shrugs and continues, "You like to talk, you need to be around more people who like to listen. Hell, you should be around people who pay attention to what *you* have to say."

The air grows thick as Manny's dark eyes find mine. I want to squirm and look away—that's what I do most of the time—but not now, not in this moment. Right now, I want to be the cause for that intense stare, even if it's just for *this* moment. There's a table and over two decades of family friendship between us, but right now I wish there was nothing. I wish he was looking at me like this because he wanted me. I wish he was looking at me like that because he meant those words in ways more than just being kind to his sister's best friend. His phone rings, snapping us both from this moment.

Manny looks at this phone, clears his throat and says, "I'm sorry, I have to take this." He gets up and walks out the back door onto the porch and I plop my head on the table. Except the plate full of sushi smothered in sauce is there and now my face is covered in both.

I get up and walk to the sink to wash my face. This day needs to be over. I'm ready for a warm bath and music to take the edge off because I can't go on a road trip with this man without bustin' one out.

"What happened to your food?" Manny says as I dry my face and I wave my hand to brush off his comment. I grab the plate and toss the rest of it in the trash.

"Hey, I gotta run. But would you be ready tomorrow? Can I come in the morning?" he asks.

"Yeah, I can be ready, but why don't I just pick you up? You're the one doing me a favor."

Manny smiles and nods, walking over to kiss my cheek before saying goodbye. He leaves and I go to my room to do all the things I wanted to do, but in reverse order. Maybe after coming undone with the help of my little pink friend, I'll be able to act normal around Manny again.

7

JUST BECAUSE YOU CAN, DOESN'T MEAN YOU SHOULD
WORK SONG, HOZIER

Manny

SAVED BY THE RING. That's what I'm calling what just happened. Cara is stunning, funny, kind, and loyal. Growing up around her gave me an appreciation for true friendship like nothing else. Not that I would consider her a close friend, but she's best friends with Allie and we got friendly by default. I've always known how gorgeous she is and when I was sixteen, she was the only girl I could see. It was so bad, Gus joked all the time that I had a thing for older women. Cara is not even two years older than us so he can chill, but yeah.

Through the years that crush never went away. But rather than being mature and doing something about it, I decided to bother her and do anything to get a rise out of her instead. Her cheeks get all flushed when she's annoyed and I love nothing more. However, whatever that moment was in there, and whatever has been happening every time I touch her recently, has got to stop. I can't be going on a road trip with my sister's best friend and constantly wondering—what she would look like screaming my name, what she would look like with my dick buried inside her pussy. Constantly wondering if she tastes as good as she smells. Questioning if her blushing throughout today was because of her annoyance or because she felt the same spark.

Part of me thinks it is the latter; that Cara felt the connection we've always shared and that I wish it was more. I do know for a fact the physical attraction I've always had is rising again and my dick thinks the same, considering that it's hard against my jeans. I could go out and bring a girl home to take this edge off but I don't think it would work. Right now, all I can think of are green eyes and soft blonde waves falling on pretty curves. Waves of hair that would look damn good over the charcoal sheets covering my hotel bed. And against the wall in my bathroom. And bent over my desk. *Que maldito desastre.*[1]

I drop my wallet on the desk in the hotel room and walk into the bathroom, undressing as I go, leaving the clothes on the floor. I'll get to work planning out my week after I handle the dick issue.

I turn the water on in the shower, making it as hot as possible because if I'm about to jerk off at the thought of my sister's friend, I might as well suffer a little too. There are so many things wrong about it, but damn it, it doesn't feel like it right now. Right now all I want to do is get some relief and hopefully get it out of my system.

The bathroom is steamy. Small droplets of water fall slowly on the tile walls. The mirror's completely fogged, hiding the reflection. Like it also knows how fucked up this situation is. I step into the fogged glass shower under the scalding hot water, my skin tightens under the spray. It's too hot, but not as hot as my thoughts right now. I lean back on the wall, letting the water

---

1. *Que maldito desastre:* What a fucking disaster

fall on my body as I grab my hard aching dick. It's been fighting with me all day, and the time has finally come.

My hand grabs the tip and I slowly slide it back, gripping it with slight force down to the base. I repeat the movement until I can feel pre-cum on my fingertips. I increase the tempo and close my eyes, but all I can see is Cara's smile. All I can hear is her voice. All I can think about is how she would feel. It doesn't take long after that for me to explode. I let out a guttural grunt and ask myself how I'm going to get out of this mess. As I shower, I hope that this will be enough and that I can go back to not thinking about bending Cara over the nearest surface every time she walks by me.

I'M SITTING on the hotel bed with my computer on my lap when my phone lights up with a FaceTime call from Gus. We talk most days; sometimes it's about work and sometimes it's about life. I guess when you've shared everything with someone from the womb, it makes it hard to live completely independent lives. Add that to the fact that we own this company together and there's always something we need to talk about. His face lights up on the other side of the phone and I nod to him.

"Keloke[2] manin,[3]" Gus says on his side of the line. He's wearing a suit and his hair looks put together, so that means he's either coming back from somewhere or is about to leave to go out.

---

2. Keloke: Commonly used in the Dominican as a what's up or hello
3. Manin: slang for brother or bro

"Aqui tu sabe, leyendo correos y viendo como voy a dividir el tiempo en este viaje con Cara.[4]"

"You don't have to worry about work, manin. This shit, this empire we built? It runs on its own. You have to let it, Manny, or it's gonna eat you alive, man," he says.

"Lucia and everyone else who called me today disagree, Gusti. I don't want to let people down—they expect me to do things," I retort, rubbing my face and shaking my head.

"When was the last time you went on vacation? Let me answer that for you. Years. You took a weekend away a few months ago, and then you took a week off three years ago when you had the flu. That's it. You've earned this vacation, so take it."

"Esa mierda se va echar a perder sin mi, Gusti,[5]" I say, now more annoyed than anything.

"If our company collapses because you take three weeks off, then we did something wrong. Go to sleep and enjoy the time away. Learn something from Cara; she lives carefree enough for two people. You could use some of that in your own life."

"Adios. Hey, call Allie and check on her, okay?" I ask.

"Okay, don't call Lucia to check on the company. Bye."

He hangs up and I set my phone and my laptop on the nightstand. Tomorrow's another day to finish reading those emails. Right now, I need to get as much sleep as possible to be ready for whatever craziness Cara has planned.

---

4. Here just reading emails and trying to figure out how I'm supposed to split this time with work and Cara.

5. That shit's gonna go bad without me

I MAKE it to Cara's place before she has a chance to pick me up. I know she's an early riser—she always has been. When we were kids, I would always find her playing by herself in the living room of whatever vacation home we were in, or hiding in the kitchen snacking on something before everyone else was awake—so I know she's up. I knock on her door and before I'm done with my third knock, Cara opens the door with a big swing and the first thing I notice is the huge smile on her face.

Her hair bounces with her, not at all being held down by the bandana with orange dots that she has on top of her loose waves, as she moves up and down clapping and making a squeaky scream. She has a slew of bracelets on her arm in orange, pink and teal and one of those old-style shirts with a washed-out bus that looks just like hers.

After she's done with the most adorable jumps, Cara throws herself at me, wrapping her arms around my neck. "Thank you, thank you, thank you! I don't think I've even said that once in the past two days. But this morning I finally realized that you're making my dream trip come true and I'm so grateful. Gracias Manuel, gracias, gracias, gracias!"

I hold her close to me and I really don't want to let her go because she feels incredible against me, and she smells like sweet summer days. Her hair is so soft against my cheek and neck and I'm not sure if it's her shampoo or what, but she smells like a lemon blueberry scone.

"Alright, alright," I say as she steps back into her house. I drag my suitcase with me—I had Lucia pack it for me since I didn't come prepared for three weeks of travel—and set my weekender bag on top of it. She has a suitcase and a couple of bags by the couch too, all pastel colors of course.

"I'm just doing one last sweep and then we can go. I do need to take the key to Colleen before we head out."

"You got it, Carita," I reply and lean against the wall. I

check my phone, and I don't have any emails or phone calls from work, which is weird. I send a quick text to Lucia before putting my phone in the pocket of my jeans.

> Me: All good over there? Send me an update when you can.

It's early, I know that, but emails are usually flooding my phone by 6:00am every day. I'm not waiting for her to reply; I said I was going to try and relax so I will. This is why I'm here wearing slacks, a T-shirt, and a baseball cap on a Saturday in June. Relaxed Manuel activated.

She tries to grab her bags, but I look at her and order, "Don't, I'll be back to get those. You, my darlin', worry about yourself."

"I can take my own bags, Manny."

"Just because you can doesn't mean you should, sunshine. Just come on, let's get this into that vibrant bus of yours."

"Fine," Cara huffs before walking toward her bus. She slides the door open for me, allowing me to set our suitcases in.

"Well thank you, my lady," I say, adding a bow and winking at her.

She rolls her eyes and says, "You're so annoying, let's go."

Cara waits for me to get the rest of the bags, locking the door of the house behind me. I think she's following me out but when I turn around, I find her with her forehead against the door, eyes closed. The breeze is blowing gently, taking her hair with it, and making the moment seem serene. Holy. I feel bad even witnessing it, especially when she brings her hand up to the door, her palm flat against it as she whispers, "Thanks for the memories."

She turns around with her eyes still closed and lets out a soft sigh before snapping her eyes open and finding my gaze on her. "Have you never said thank you to a place that saw you grow?

Because this—" she points at her place "—was more than a place to live," she heaves, and that's when I realize she thinks I might be judging her.

"I've never been in the same place for more than a couple of years. That was just beautiful," I admit, and Cara softens, lowering her shoulders and relaxing her brows. "The only thing that has seen me grow, grows with me," I wink at her, trying to lighten the mood. She scoffs and walks toward the bus.

I get in the driver seat, putting the keys in the ignition and cranking the motor up after I shut the door next to me. I'm still not over the realization that this is what I'm going to be driving around for the next three weeks. Cara's fidgeting in her seat, clearly uncomfortable about something and I can bet money is because we're about to go on this trip and she's not the one controlling it all. Yes, she has the itinerary—but I'm the one behind the wheel and this, after all, is her baby.

I place my hand over her bouncy leg and ask softly, "So where are we going first?" I want her to let her know even though I'm driving, it's her call. She's the one in control.

"After Colleen's? Matthiessen State Park," she replies, and I add the coordinates to my phone.

"We're only two hours away from there; are you sure this is the first stop you want to make?" I ask, pulling out of the parking lot. She has her journal from last night open in her lap, with a list of things to do on each stop carefully drafted across the pages.

"Yep, this is one of my favorite places and I want to start our trip there. Now, Manny," Cara adds, pulling her phone from her bag and connecting it to the stereo. "Any particular song you'd like to add to the playlist?" She smiles at me and wiggles her eyebrows, and I do the only thing that I can in this moment —laugh. I have to laugh so I don't keep thinking about this adorable woman sitting next to me; how we're about to spend three weeks together, without anyone else, and I'm not sure if I'll make it without trying to kiss her or touch her. *Yo nada más que me jodí*[6].

---

6. Yo nada más que me jodí: I'm so fucked.

JUMPING DEER

MILES ON IT, MARSHMELLO FT. KANE BROWN

Cara

For the past hour we've been on the way to the park to see the waterfalls, riding in comfortable quiet. Taylor Swift dominates the playlist with a sprinkle of other pop songs and some Wisin & Yandel that I know Manny likes. I'm not fluent in Spanish but I know some words here and there and understand even more than that. My family spent many summers with the Zabanas growing up and I picked up on a phrase of two.

Their music was constantly played by Manny and Gus, so I was hoping he'd like the addition. And I was right. Every time one of their songs comes up, Manny sings like he's in center stage. He shouts and pretends his fist is a microphone. He dances to the beat—as much as he can, anyway— and smiles the entire time. Pride rises in my chest as I realize I still know him well enough to choose music to put him in a better mood. Pink van and Cara one, Manny and his *I won't drive the Power Puff bus* zero.

"Oh, look! Jumping deer!" I shout, mimicking the yellow sign with my hands near my chest and pretending I'm jumping, and Manny twitches, gripping the steering wheel harder.

"Jesucristo, Cara! What the heck was that?" he cries, his knuckles white and eyebrows furrowed.

"Oh!" I cackle. "Sorry. I guess I should've warned you. I love the highway signs, and that one back there was a jumping deer. It's fun to shout their names as I see them."

"You mean the deer crossing sign?" He turns right and pulls up to the park's entrance. "And by fun, do you mean producing early onset heart attack symptoms?"

I roll my eyes. "So dramatic. What's the fun in *deer crossing* when you can have a jumping deer? Plus, have you ever really looked at them? They look like they're jumping, not crossing." I smile at him, before grabbing my journal and making a check-mark next to our first stop.

"WHERE IS THIS TRAIL TAKING US?" Manny asks, walking beside me. This park is near Starved Rock, which is really pretty, especially in the fall, but it gets crowded quickly. This is like its little sister—with less people and more room to roam. There's no camping or lodging allowed here, but for a quick stop it's perfect.

We walk alongside each other, navigating through the dry trail surrounded by oaks and cedars. There are some blooms along the way and so far, we haven't seen one single person. It's quiet and peaceful and we're taking it all in. The coneflowers and the milkweed are everywhere, adding color to the trail and making me feel at home. *This,* this is where flowers belong. Out in the wild, blooming beautifully around us. Not in some vase inside someone's home, dying slowly.

We had a full argument about what Manny was wearing to hike. He was so frustrated, going on and on about how not all of us were planning on strenuous terrain. When he told me he was wearing slacks and I laughed about it, he snapped with a *"What the hell am I supposed to wear, Cara?"* After I explained that he would need more of a workout outfit, regardless of what it looked like, he listened to me and looked in his bag for something more comfortable. He's wearing joggers and Nikes instead. which are not the best option with this terrain, but better than before with the dress pants and Ferragamos. Add *Buy Manny hiking boots* to the mental to do list.

Tiny birds flutter their wings around us and make low tapping noises in the trees as we walk by. We can hear the water falling, alerting us that we're almost to the waterfall—the main reason I wanted to come here. Manny may travel the world for work, but sitting at the bottom of a waterfall is not on brand for him. Sometimes you need to disconnect to be able to be yourself again. *This* might give him that. It might give *me* that.

Walking around the bush-lined trail, we hear the splashing water intensify, and then we see it. The waterfall is spectacular; as Manny's standing, taking it all in with his hands on his hips, I grab my phone and snap a picture. Putting my phone away, I get the picnic blanket out of the backpack and lay it on the ground. We have the perfect view of Giant's Bathtub Falls and as its name says, it looks just like a tub. I sit, grabbing a couple of juice boxes from the bag, and wait for Manny to notice.

I wait to say anything because I've never seen him so in tune with what's going on around him. His shoulders are not as tense as they usually are, and he hasn't checked his phone once.

That's also a first. He's been walking and watching. Taking it all in. His dark green shirt is tight against his arms, and it stretches across his back showing off his muscles. For someone who works as much as he does, his body is book-boyfriend-worthy. All chiseled, like a sculpture. He knows it too because every chance he gets, he flexes his arms or lifts his shirt to tap his abs. He's so damn confident, and sometimes, I just want some of that for myself.

He finally turns around and when he sees me, he smiles at me a moment before speaking. "Cara, this place is beautiful." He sits next to me, putting his backpack down and taking the juice from me. He raises his eyebrows at the Capri Sun, and I have no other choice but to smile back.

"The taste of a five-year-old, remember?" I say, popping a grape into my mouth. I brought a snack tray in my cooler backpack, and it was the best decision. Because even though it's not really lunch time yet for regular grown-ups, I'm still on an internal school schedule and our lunch tends to be early, so I'm starving.

"I didn't know you liked hiking this much," Manny admits, grabbing some vegetables and holding them in a napkin.

"Do you want the long story or the short?" I ask, hoping he says short because I don't know if I truly want to go into full detail...but also secretly hoping he does say long because he's a great listener.

"Long, always." He smirks and I throw a grape at him.

"Grow up, Manny."

"You're the one eating a ham and cheese Lunchable with a Capri Sun, and you want *me* to grow up?" he adds, shaking his head. He lays down on the blanket and puts his arm behind his head. His arm flexes just right to show how well the shirt hugs it —making me almost drool. *The story, Cara, the story.*

I clear my throat and explain, "When Allie and I moved to

California, most of the people our age wanted to party all the time, but your dear sis was mourning after losing Jake. She wouldn't talk to anyone. So, at first, I did try to go to parties and do what everyone else was doing, but it just wasn't all that fun when I was constantly worrying about her. I started reading on ways to cope with loss, because even though he was alive, she did lose him. One of the things I found was that being in nature helps." I stop talking and eat some crackers and cheese, closing my eyes and letting it all in. The memories, the hardships, the moment we're in now and everything in between.

"She of course didn't want to go anywhere, and bugs scare her half the time so I would take her on little outings to spend time outside. She was okay with it and eventually she started enjoying going out with friends—dinners and small gatherings. Those are my jam too. So of course I was happy, but I realized that I missed being outside more than I thought. I was reading a book about the benefits of nature on mental health and found that for some people medicine and exercise makes them happy; for me it's this."

I wave my arms around, gesturing to the world around us, and lay down next to him. He tilts his head toward me and smiles. I return it and add, "With dirt under my toes and the sun above my head, I'll be as happy as I can be for the rest of my life. It recharges me. A few years ago, I found a yearly challenge where people try to spend at least one thousand hours outside in a year and I've been trying to hit that goal ever since."

"Like a sunflower," he says. His eyes sparkle as he searches mine. Dark and haunting, calling me to him.

"Wh—what?"

"You're like a sunflower; you need your feet on the ground and your face toward the sun." Manny brings his hand to my eyebrows, smoothing them. I hadn't noticed I was frowning, but he did, and judging by his expression he doesn't like it. "No need for that frown on your pretty face. I was just echoing what you said."

I hadn't noticed how close we are. Now I'm acutely aware of his feet near mine, barely touching but still there. His eyes—oak brown just like the trees behind him—are focused just on me. And his scent, spicy but almost sweet, engulfs me completely. I drop my gaze to his lips but lift it back up to his eyes and when I find nothing but kindness in them, I snap out of it. *He's Allie's brother, Cara. He's your friend and he's just being kind.*

I clear my throat and lay on my back. Closing my eyes and letting the sun warm my face hoping to blame the blush I'm surely sporting on the sun and not to the fact that I'm attracted to Manuel Zabana way more than I knew and definitely more than I should be.

"CARA, CARA." A distant voice says, and at the same time, soft hands touch my shoulder. I open my eyes and see Manny's face right in front of mine. Looking around, looking as dumbfounded as I feel, I notice we're in the same picnic spot, but now there are some people standing near the water, and the sun has gone down a little. Not enough for it to be sunset, but definitely enough to let me know that I fell asleep.

I look back at Manny and smile before saying, "Well, good morning to you, too."

He chuckles and gives me his hand, pulling me up to sit. "I wish I could tell you it was still morning but that would be a lie. We both fell asleep, Cara. Out here, in the wilderness."

Wilderness. I chuckle at that. "What better place to take a nap than surrounded by all this beauty?" I tease, bringing my knees up to my chest and laying my head on top of them.

"You do that often, sunshine? Fall asleep surrounded by nature?"

"Often enough that I'm not worried about it anymore, Manny. There's something about the sound of the water falling and the birds chirping. The soft breeze that carries the trees and flowers' scent. Nature below me and nature above me—that's where I want to spend my days."

He looks at me with wonder. I know it comes as a shock to him, especially growing up in the fast paced family he did, but I just don't want that for myself. I want slow days under the sun. Coffee early in the morning outside while the world sleeps and nature awakens. I want to count stars and catch fireflies.

"Did you add that into your bucket list?" he asks and I look at him confused. *Did I say that out loud?*

Manny smirks. "Counting stars and catching fireflies, did you add that to your list?" *I did, I did say it out loud.*

"Ha, no, I do those things often. And in Baker, it'll be even easier. Why?" I ask him.

He takes a deep breath and touches his forehead. Bringing his hand through his hair and back in front of him. "Can I add things to this road trip bucket list? Because I've never done any of those."

I bring my legs down and into a butterfly pose, perk my chest up and say, "You've never counted stars, Manuel Zabana? Not even when you were trying to woo girls into dating you in high school?" I wiggle my eyebrows at him and he smirks. Before he speaks, I know the snarky remark is coming. I can feel it.

"When you're trying to build an empire, there's no time for stargazing. And I didn't have to woo anyone with stars, Carita. I *am* the star." He looks up when he says that, throwing his fist in the air like he won something.

I roll my eyes at that and laughing softly, I say, "Alright, hotshot, let's clean this mess up."

We pack up our stuff in silence and start hiking back toward the van. I can't believe he's never stopped for one second to look for stars or to catch bugs. To appreciate what's around him. Now, I'm adding to my list to make sure Manny writes his own too. I just need to get him to let me.

I had it in my plans to head toward Ohio today so we can explore for a few days but there's a cool place nearby that I would love to take him. Perfect place for stargazing and getting lost with nature. I pull out my phone, and call to see if there's availability, and when they tell me they have one spot left I take it.

"Where to next?" Manny asks as we put our bags in the back of the van.

"Camp Aramoni, please." I climb onto the front seat and we head out in that direction.

9

___

FLORA & FAUNA
BLOWIN' SMOKE, TEDDY SWIMS

Manny

WE PULL up to a property with lush trees all around and some sort of bungalows in the distance. Cara slides her sunglasses onto her head and gives me her big smile. She claps her hands and starts kicking her feet in the front seat. I've never seen an adult so excited about anything before; but every time I see Cara surrounded by something she's passionate about, this is exactly how she acts. *Every time.*

There's a big wooden sign that says Camp Aramoni followed by a gate. Cara gives me the gate code, and we follow the gravel path toward the main house which looks like a barn. The place is surrounded by nature; from tall, slender trees forming natural archways, to wildflowers and ferns marking paths. There are ruins near the entrance showing what once was here, and on the far end, you can see little houses on something resembling stilts. Once I park and open the door, I can hear nothing but the encompassing sounds of nature. There are no vehicles or people chatting but nature *is* speaking. I can hear water from a stream or river and I feel immediately calm. Like the symphony of the forest is connecting with my senses and telling them to relax.

Cara stands by the door, with her hands on her hips and a cross body bag around her chest. She looks up at the sky and smiles at me. "Come on, hotshot, let's see what they've got for us."

I'm in between confused and amazed but I follow her inside anyway. Stepping in here is like opening a book. The space screams rustic but with a touch of modern. It's not luxury, obviously, but it has high ceilings adorned with strings of soft twinkling lights. Warm sunlight filters through the large windows, casting a glow over the wooden floor and the furniture. The walls are full of trinkets and artifacts that I'm guessing have stories to tell and a fireplace I'm sure keeps everyone warm in the cold months. There's a small shop to the right as well, with clothes, sunscreen, snacks and bug spray.

We walk up to the registration desk and are welcomed by a tall guy wearing casual summer clothing and a friendly smile. "Welcome to Camp Aramoni, how can I help you?" he greets.

"Hi! I'm so happy to be back. I called and someone said that you have room for one more reservation?" Cara asks.

"Sure, let me look it up real quick." Julian—that's what his name tag says—types on the computer for a minute before returning his attention to us.

"We do have Flora and Fauna left. We had a last minute cancellation so it's open today. It's the last tent in our lineup, does that sound good?" he asks and Cara nods, grabbing her bag presumably to get her wallet out. I beat her to it and put my credit card on top of the counter.

"Manny, I got this," she snaps.

"No, I do. Here, Julian, put it on my card, will you?" I also hand him my ID. He emails us the packet with information—since this is a green spot and they don't waste paper to print unnecessary things—and he proceeds to let us know that our ride to the tent will arrive in five minutes.

As we're walking out to grab our bags, Cara turns to me and says, "You know, I can pay for things too. You didn't let me pay yesterday at the store or gas station, or anything for that matter. I'm a big girl, I can handle it."

"I know you can, but again, it doesn't mean you should. Think of this as a bonus for teaching the children. My treat," I insist. The truth is, my sister was a teacher for a long time. I know how underpaid they are. It's not fair that I can make in a month—hell, sometimes in a week—what they make in a whole year. And on top of that, judging by the one interaction I saw from Cara and that little boy, it looks like she's a good one. Allie always mentions how Cara was meant to teach, that it comes naturally to her. The least I can do is help ease some of her financial worries with this trip.

"Well, fine, but don't do this with everything, okay?" she retorts, using her teacher voice on me. Borderline bossy but still sweet. Like the sound of a stream crashing over smooth rocks, it shows its presence but it doesn't break the surface.

"Or what, sunshine?" I tease, and as soon as it leaves my lips I want to take it back because it came out flirty as fuck. Not uncommon for me, but I don't want to push it.

"Try me and find out," she snaps and I smirk at the same time she smiles and bites her lower lip. We're suspended in this moment, with this air of electricity. Like a storm's brewing between us.

The truck that is taking us to our tent shows up, snapping us out of our moment—whatever that was—allowing us to walk away without talking about it.

The drive is serene. The driver tells us a few things about the camp and when dinner and breakfast will be. He tells us that our tent is the last one but as we pass the others, I realize *tent* is a loose description. They are like small rustic houses in the middle of the wilderness. Made from a canvas-like material, each boasts a small porch and seating areas right next to them on the grass. There are all sorts of people staying here. We see some children playing with their parents and couples cozying up together. Some guests are lounging in hammocks, some are reading on porches, and some of the yards are empty. Each site blends seamlessly with the natural landscape and I'm intrigued to know what they look like on the inside.

Once we reach our spot, I notice there's one glamping tent—it looks more like a house but made of canvas instead of whatever material houses are made—and bushes that hide what I assume is the nearby river because the water sounds a lot closer than it did at the main house.

We walk up to our tent and the driver waves goodbye as soon as he drops our bags on the porch. There's a little sign that reads *Flora & Fauna* by the door. It's a small cozy room with two armchairs and a bed. *One bed.* I didn't even think about asking about the space and they probably assumed we were a couple so they also didn't say anything else.

"Oh," Cara exhales, blushing, drawing the same conclusion.

"Don't worry, I'll sleep on the floor," I insist, putting our bags on the bed and smiling at her.

Her brow is furrowed and she shakes her head. "No, Manny, you don't have to do that. It's not a big deal," she says.

"It's not, I'll take the floor, it's only one night. What do you want to do here? Wanna go explore with me?" I ask and flash her a big gentle smile. I can almost hear her mind ticking so I'm trying to get her out of this space. The overthinking and overanalyzing that she finds herself in more often than not. She's been doing this since we were young, or at least I remember Allie saying that. It's hard to notice because in front of everyone else, Cara oozes confidence. She's always smiling, flirting with everyone, and being the life of the party. But behind the smiles and the over the top dance moves, my sister could tell that she often overthinks everything. She's never let me see the version of herself she hides before, or maybe I've never stopped to look for it. I usually get to see the sassy and friends-with-everyone Cara.

"'Kay," she says, "let me freshen up." She opens her bag, grabs a smaller bag from it and heads into the bathroom. I open the mini fridge and see there are a couple waters. I grab one and pull out the drinks from the backpack cooler we were carrying earlier and add them to the minifridge.

"Ready?" she asks, walking toward me with a soft smile. *There she is.* Soft smiles and excited eyes. My favorite version of Cara.

"For you? Always," I wink at her and we walk out heading toward the river. Or we try to but as soon as we walk out of the tent, my phone rings. It hasn't rung all day and when I look at the screen it is Mr. Virgil—one of my oldest clients—and he never calls unless it's important.

"I have to take this; go ahead and I'll catch up with you," I insist and she nods at me.

I sit in one of the cold chairs outside and answer the call.

"This is Manuel."

"Manuel, I thought we were more than *in business together*," Mr. Virgil says, his voice clipped and dense. *Coñazo, ¿que diablos pasó?*[1].

---

1. *Shit, What the fuck happened?*

"Of course we are, Virgil. We're friends, no? What's going on?"

"Well my assistant just told me that you won't be in our meeting next week. I don't feel like dealing with anyone else but you! So what? Now that your business is bigger you're only focusing on larger accounts?"

Que jodia baina[2]. "No, no. I'm taking some time off, and it just happened to be during this meeting. But Augusto agreed to take over or I can Zoom in."

"Just because you two look the same doesn't mean that he's the one overseeing my account," he adds. I can hear the frustration in his voice.

"Virgil, we both own the company. But I understand your frustration. Do you want to reschedule or do the meeting online? I have no trouble joining from my vacation."

"Must be nice to take a week-long vacation. Send the invite and I'll be in touch, Manuel. I only do business with you, got it?"

Got it. "And I appreciate your business. I'll have Lucia send you a new calendar invite and I'll make sure you have my full attention."

He hangs up the phone and I cuss loudly. There's a couple on a porch in the tent nearby and I can see their heads turning to see what's happening. I guess that's the downfall of being out here in the middle of nowhere—there's no noise to drown when shit goes south.

I sit and breathe for a minute and drag my hand through my hair before calling Lucia.

"Mr. Zabana, I thought you were on vacation?" she asks.

"Lucia, why didn't you tell me that Virgil was upset? He called me fuming. I'm sure someone in the office knew of this

---

2. What an actual shit

prior to him calling me. So how am I the last to know?" I bark. I try to control my tone so I don't sound like an asshole. If there's one thing that I take pride in, it is being a servant leader—walking the walk instead of just talking the talk. I learned about servant leadership in college and I connected with the concept immediately. I don't scream at my employees, and the ones that have not tried to sleep with me have stayed with the company since we opened. I try to stay calm, cool, and collected because the last thing I need is for people to see me as another *millionaire* with anger issues.

"I'm sorry Mr. Zabana. Your brother said that under no circumstances was I to contact you. So I sent his assistant an email about the meeting, but I guess Mr. Virgil didn't want to wait. It won't happen again."

"I told you I was going to work on this trip, so don't listen to my brother. Send me important messages and anything that needs to be handled ASAP. Okay?"

"Will do. I apologize, again," she adds. "Anything else I can do?"

"No, Lucia, that's all. Go ahead and send him an email with a new calendar invite for a Zoom meeting. Add me to it and make it as early as he'll allow so I can try and get it done before we get on the road from wherever we are at the time. Talk to you soon." I hang up the phone and immediately text Gus because what the hell.

Me: Augusto, stay out of my business.

Gusti: Disfruta tus vacaciones, Manuel. Dejate de estar contestando el teléfono

3

---

3. Enjoy your vacation, Manuel. Stop answering the phone.

Me: ¿Y los clientes que se van a buscar otra compañía que? ¿A la mierda esos?

4

Gusti: If people can't understand that you took your first vacation in years, they don't need to stay with our company. That's not the people we want around.

Me: You let me handle my shit.

Gusti:

I put my phone in my pocket and get up from the chair. My mood is sour now. Nobody is listening to me and the whole damn company is putting me in a time out. But I can pretend everything is fine and dandy in front of Cara. I refuse to ruin her trip over that.

---

4.   How about the clients? Should those just leave us for another company and we can send them to fuck themselves?

10

MY TOESIES NEED SOME DIRT
STARGAZING, MYLES SMITH

Cara

MANNY'S CALL seems to have stressed him out so I didn't want to push when he sent me on my way to the river. The path between the tent and the river is beautiful. Trees, bushes and flowers framing the slight descent to a trail. The tree's canopies cast shadows on the ground making the area cooler. The scent of damp leaves and flowers is subtle and welcoming. Like I'm Alice walking through the forest on the way to Wonderland.

I'm sitting on the riverbank with my bullet journal, jotting down the adventures from today. I take a quick picture of the journal with the river in the background and post to my Instagram stories with a little text that says 'adventuring.' I post on social media often. Some people say I post too much but I like to share my life with people even if we don't talk every day. I've gotten a lot of followers from adults who want to prioritize time outside, too, so this will be perfect for them. After that, I go back to the journal to add doodles to the page and check the itinerary for tomorrow. I hear footsteps behind me and when I look, I see Manny jogging slowly toward me.

"Carita!" he shouts, plopping his body next to me. *Carita*—the damn nickname he gave me ages ago. I don't hate it but it makes me feel like a little sister as opposed to a woman—a woman he might be interested in.

"Hi, welcome back!" I add and smile at him.

"Whatcha doin'?"

"Doodling in my journal. How was your serious call, Mr. Business Man?" I add, changing my voice to mock him when I call him a businessman.

"It was as fine as a business call could be," he adds and his playful tone before now sounds serious.

"Hey, it's okay if you have to work, Manny. You're already doing so much and going above and beyond. Really, if you need to, go ahead. I'm sure this is the longest you've been away from work in a while, right? That's what Allie is always complaining about," I urge, setting my hand on top of his thigh. I used to be like that too.

He takes a deep breath before answering, "I'm not going to lie. I usually don't take time off but maybe it's needed now. I will have to work some but not too much. Palabra de honor[1]." He kisses two fingers and lifts them up like swearing or taking an oath.

"Goofball," I tease and we both laugh.

He grabs three rocks from the ground and skips them one at a time on the river. After the last one, he pauses with his knees up and his eyes locked on the water. The river's gentle flow of clear water creates the best background music anyone could ask for and I take a minute to appreciate how lucky I am that I get to

---

1. Scout's honor

spend so much time in nature today. "You know, if you truly mean it, it could be so good for you," I murmur after a moment.

"What could?" Manny asks, not stopping skipping the rocks over the otherwise calm river. Growing up, I don't think he ever sat still for more than a few minutes. There were days in some of the vacations where I would find him sitting by the water, just like this, looking at it, skipping rocks, or even just dipping his toes in. Where did that boy go? When did he grow up into a man who forgot life's meaning and to slow down to appreciate the idle time? When did he stop noticing the pockets of time in between life's chaos?

"Taking a pause. Taking time off. Enjoying being outside. Dipping your toes in the water. Feeling the breeze on your face. Thinking about nothing but everything at once. Letting the day tell you what to do and where to go without worrying about people thousands of miles away from you who wouldn't care at all if tomorrow you never called again. A job is always replaceable, even when you're the boss," I urge, locking my eyes on his and swallowing hard before adding, "but your life, your health, and your mental space can't be. Take care of it."

I reach over to squeeze his hand and after a second he nods silently, before going back to skip his stones.

"Are you ready to head back and wash up for dinner?" he asks and I nod. Manny gets up, offering me his hands to help me get up from the ground. When I place mine in his, a spark rushes through my fingers but before I can think twice about it, he pulls hard, lifting me in a quick swoop and dropping my hand as soon as I'm standing. I immediately observe how cold my hands feel without Manny touching them. We walk up the trail through the mix of evergreens and tall trees with their leaves whispering softly in the breeze.

DINNER WAS AMAZING. The barn had a candlelit dinner set up family-style. Beautiful picnic tables were lined up outside with live music and wine. I danced as much as my feet let me and drank until Manny told me that if I wanted to walk back to the tent, I should stop. I should've listened sooner, because we're on the way back to the tent and I want nothing to do with walking.

"Wait, let me take my shoes off," I cry, pulling the long strap wrapping my calf and untying my sandals. I hate shoes. I hate wearing them and half the time they're just a pretty accessory. These sandals are cute and comfortable but after wearing them for hours, I'm done.

"What if something bites your toes?" Manny asks and I laugh because I think he's joking when I should know he's being as serious as a heart attack.

"Whatever it is could bite me with my shoes on, too. Look," I boast, wiggling my toes in my sandals to show him how close they are to the ground.

"Oh, I know, Cara. I wasn't able to pull my eyes away from those pretty dancing feet all night."

I know without looking at myself in a mirror that I'm blushing. Manny is such a flirt, always has been, but being on the other side of his sweet little comments always makes my heart do a somersault. In high school, he often made comments like that in front of me but rarely toward me. Maybe it's because I dated Cole for so long they were never geared at me. But when Manny *would* flirt with me I got that same feeling I'm getting right now: giddy, excitement, and fun. Nothing has ever happened between us, of course, and nothing ever will. But sometimes I wonder if he can back up all that talk. I wonder if he's a shameless flirt or if he truly means it.

"Then why didn't you dance with me, hotshot?" I ask while I unwrap the straps of my other gladiator sandal. I opted for a flowy sundress today with these sandals which wrap up all the way to my knee. My dress is really short, so shorts underneath were a must. I was very glad for my choice when I stood up to dance and my dress whirled up with my first twirl. I'm sure my thick legs were all on display.

"I only dance Merengue, Salsa, and Reggaeton. And none of the dancing tonight was any of those. Also, if you wanted me to dance with you, you could've asked."

"I always want to dance. Take that as an open invitation."

"Oh, yeah?"

"Yup, for the future."

He pauses to look at my sandals now in my hands and shakes his head. "Are you really going to walk barefoot in the dark?"

"Sure will!" I shout.

Manny lowers himself in front of me in some sort of squat, making him look like a horse as he offers, "Come on up, sunshine. Hop on."

"Manny, please. Why? I can just walk," I whine because what in the actual world does he expect—for me to just hop on his back?

"Come on, I don't want something to eat your pretty toes," he urges.

"No, thank you." Giggles escape me as I shake my head and smile at him.

"Do I need to dare you to do it, Carita?"

I put my hands on my hips and square my shoulders as I groan, "If you dare me, Manny, you have to play too."

"I'm already here because of a dare. I'm not afraid to play. I dare you to hop on my back, Cara."

Oh for fuck's sake. I hop on his back, and he slides his big hands under my butt. With a quick boost, he pulls me higher on his back and then he sprints toward our tent.

"Manny!" I shout. "What are you doing? AH!" I scream but it's more of a loud laugh than anything.

"I didn't go for a run this morning so this will do," he shouts over the silence of the forest. We're *so* going to get kicked out of this place if we're not quiet, but I can't help but laugh non-stop until we make it back to the tent.

Manny puts me down, my feet touching the damp grass right outside our fairy-light-illuminated tent, and he lets out a loud laugh before putting his hands on his knees. *That laugh.* That wasn't his usual one. His careful and polished laugh. This one came from deep in his tummy. It rumbles through space and bounces deep into my core. I freaking love that laugh, I decide.

"Manny, shh! It's past ten, it's quiet time around the tents," I press, bringing my hand to his mouth because he won't stop.

He scoops his hands around me and picks me up, cradling me against his chest and walking us toward the black chairs next to our tent. I take my hand off his mouth and stare at it instead. I clear my throat and look away right before he sits me in one of the chairs. Manny walks to the other, sitting and resting his head on the top of the chair and laughing again, this time softer.

"Wow!" He lets out a loud breath and closes his eyes. "I haven't done that in so long."

"You're in the habit of running around with a girl on your back through the grass, Manny?"

"Hahaha, no. I haven't laughed like that in a while," he shares, opening his eyes and keeping them locked on the sky. *Why not?* I think. Because with a laugh like that, I would laugh all the time.

I do the same and lay my head back, looking up at the sky and seeing how clearly I can see the stars. These crisp nights, when the sky transforms into this starry canvas of twinkling lights, give me a sense of awe greater than most things. It's the perfect reminder that we're a tiny part of this entire galaxy. It makes my problems and issues seem so insignificant in the grand scheme of things. It's such a good feeling when all I've thought about for years is about how much of an inconvenience I was. But how can you be anything but precious when you're part of this magical world?

"You should do it more often. It suits you," I add, smiling at no one but the glittering tapestry of shining stars above. The serene silence around us echoes with the burbles of the river in the background and the crickets and other critters serenading us makes this moment perfect as it is.

"Yeah," he muses softly, letting out a deep breath. "There's never enough time."

"There's never enough time for what?" I ask, my voice breaking as I try to contain my emotions so he doesn't see how sad it makes me that, at less than thirty years old, Manny has stopped living.

"For stopping to notice the calm. To notice the beauty. To notice it all."

"But there should be, Manny. We never know when our days will be over, or when our time will pass. We will never know when our last moment will be so why don't you try to make the best of them? You've given your work your all. Don't you think it's time for you to give yourself all of you too?"

His gaze is still locked on the sky but a silent tear slips from the corner of his eye, glistening in the dark night.

"I know it's hard to put yourself first but maybe you just need a reminder," I continue, pulling a bracelet from my arm. "Here."

Manny tilts his head to face me and when his eyes meet mine, I lift my hand to him. I reach out to grab his hand and turn it palm up, placing the pink stretchy bracelet on his palm.

"These always remind me to take a breath and slow down. To count the stars, to smell the flowers, to dance to good music, and to sing my favorite songs. They remind me to leave work on time and to put my phone away after a while. Now you can remember, too."

His eyes glisten with emotion as he slides the bracelet onto his wrist. As much as I'm glad he accepted the band, I hope he doesn't ask why I started wearing them. It's not that I don't want to share, but I fear this moment is already so heavy and I'm not sure I'm ready to unpack it all.

He stares at his wrist before looking back up at me, "Thank you, Carita." *Carita.* The nickname again but this time it feels nothing childish. It feels like a code word to let me know he hears me. To let me know he sees me.

"Twelve," he shares before laying his head back on the chair and looking up at the sky.

"Twelve what? Stars?" I ask, slightly confused.

"It's like you were kissed by them," he adds and now I'm even more confused.

"Manuel, you're going to have to use more words than that or explain a little better."

Manny chuckles softly. "Your freckles, Carita. You have the same amount of freckles as stars in the sky." He looks so at peace as he says that, so calm, like he didn't just say the nicest thing anyone had ever said to me or like he didn't just speak pure poetry.

I bring my hand to gently touch the bridge of my nose. My freckles are barely noticeable, and for him to have counted them is more than I can handle or acknowledge right now.

I wait for the spell to break, but it doesn't. Manny just keeps looking up at the sky. He looks so restful that I grab my phone from the small pocket in my dress and snap a picture of him. *It's absolutely perfect.* The moonlight illuminates his olive brown features. His dark soft curls and his dark shirt are in contrast with the soft lights behind him and his smile—his beautiful smile—shines as bright as all the lights around him.

"Counting stars, Manny?" I ask, tucking my phone back in the pocket.

He brings his eyes to me this time, smiles, and replies, "Yeah, now there are thirteen that I can see." His intense stare doesn't leave my eyes and even though I'm fully clothed, I feel naked under his sight. As if somehow, he can see all of me. Like he can see through me.

"Maybe you should make your own summer bucket list," I tell him, my voice shaking and my throat dry.

"Maybe I should," he agrees. He clears his throat and stands up, giving me his hand to help me get up but when he sees my feet again, he shakes his head. "Do you want me to carry you in?"

"Nope, let my toesies get some dirt, please." He smiles at me and nods and we walk down the path and up the wooden steps.

Manny opens the door for me. The air is cool inside in the dimly lit room and a shiver runs down my spine, making my whole body aware of how chilly it is here. There's no way I'll be able to sleep in the pjs I brought so I go through my bag and grab a pair of leggings and a sweatshirt. Even if it's summer, I always bring a sweatshirt with me for comfort and to keep me warm and toasty, like a marshmallow.

"I'm going to get dressed for bed," I tell Manny, walking into the bathroom and clicking the door shut behind me.

11

―――――――

I DARE YOU

HAPPY, CRAIG LUCAS

Manny

CARA DISAPPEARS into the bathroom and I take this time to cool off. She's been driving me insane all night. No, not insane. Fucking *wild*.

Her dress showed off her body perfectly; not all of it, just enough to keep my imagination going. The top of her dress was tight around her small perky breasts and her waist then flared out. It's short too, showing her perfect long legs. And those sandals. They wrapped around her feet and calves and had me wanting to wrap myself around her body. To top it off, as she danced her dress would lift, showing off her tight shorts underneath. She asked me why I didn't dance with her and the truth of the matter is that every time she got up to dance, my dick got hard at the sight of her—so carefree and so beautiful and so perfect. The crush I've hidden on Cara all my damn life is definitely surfacing now and I'm at a loss at what to do with it.

I grab a water bottle from the fridge and down it in one gulp, before changing from my dinner attire to some sweatpants and a fitted white shirt to sleep. I grab the extra blanket from under the table and a pillow, making a bed on the ground.

I'm laying the blanket down when Cara comes out of the bathroom, her hair pulled to the side over her shoulder, wearing leggings with knee-high socks over them and a sweatshirt that could fit me. It lands mid-thigh on her and I don't know how she can look so stunning in whatever she wears.

She puts the clothes she has in her hands on top of the night table and looks at me with a frown.

"What?" I ask.

"You're not sleeping on the floor, Manny. This bed is huge, come on."

I'm not sharing the bed with her. That's a bad idea on all counts, especially because I'm worried about what will happen once her warm body is next to mine. I would never cross that line between us. But what will happen to me—I will probably die of pent-up *energy*.

"Nah, I'm good, Carita. I'll be fine, right here." I smirk, tapping the floor with both hands before laying down and crossing my legs at my ankles. "See? Perfect. Good night."

She stays quiet for a minute but then she comes closer, squatting down so her face is near mine. Her lemon scent entraps my body, making my skin break out in goosebumps like it is physically touching me.

I look up into her eyes—they look dark now in the dim light from the lamps—and she says the last three words I expected: "I dare you."

"Come again?" I ask, coughing, grabbing the water bottle on the table and taking another sip.

"I said—" she pauses for emphasis, sitting on the edge of the bed "—I dare you to sleep with me. Sleep on the bed with me, not *sleep sleep* with me. You get the gist."

"No," I insist.

"Such a shame, I thought you said you were a man of your word or something." Cara doesn't say anything else, she simply crawls to the top of the bed and pulls the blanket over her legs before laying down.

"Good night, Manny. I can't wait to tell everyone how you avoided a dare."

Por el amor a jesucristo[1]. "Fine, I'll take it," I groan, standing abruptly and dragging my feet to the bed. I bring one of the pillows with me and set it between us, hoping that the pillow will be enough of a barrier to keep us apart.

"Nighty night, Manuel," she whispers, turning her body away from me, pulling the chain on the lamp and leaving me alone with my thoughts. I count the time that passes. Seconds turning into minutes and minutes turning hours trying to fall asleep, which seems impossible with her soft waves spread across the pillow and her lemon scent enwrapping all of my senses. Whoever said that scent was one sense didn't meet Cara. The way she smells starts with that one sense and it takes all of them. It sparks a memory. It sparks a feeling. The way she smells feels like basking in the sun. It smells like a day full of your favorite things, happy and sweet. It tastes like the sweetest drink. And with her laying right next to me, soft breaths coming out and eyes peacefully shut, I don't think I'll ever be able to smell a lemon and not think of her—not see her.

I WAKE up alone in bed. I check my phone and it's 5:10am. I'm surprised I slept past five. I don't set an alarm because I

---

1. For the love of Christ.

never sleep in. My body has a way of reminding me that there are things to do and I can't accomplish them by sleeping. I usually check my emails and then go to the gym or for a run before heading to the office. *But why is Cara up?* Maybe she's on her teacher schedule and her body wakes her up, too. I look around the dark room and don't see her anywhere. Her side of the bed is made, the pillow barrier still in place, and the room is eerily quiet.

I get up and the floor creaks, like it's announcing I'm up but there's nobody here to hear it. I get my shoes and softly open the door to the tent. What I find on the other side is not what I was expecting. Sitting on the steps, wrapped in a blanket with her head low, is Cara. She's moving her hand through her hair, caressing it gently as it falls down her back and her loose waves—dancing in the wind. I have to pinch myself to remember we *are* on this trip together because this scene is too close to what I've dreamed of for years. When I step closer, the floor creaks louder and she turns around. When her eyes look up at me, that's when I can tell. *She's crying.*

Her eyes and cheeks are red. Not like she's cold but more like she's been sitting out here crying for a while. Crying alone with only a blanket and surrounded by nature—the only thing she allows herself to find comfort in. Except I'm here and if she's hurt, she could've told me.

"Hey," I whisper, hurrying to her side and sinking into the floor beside her. She glances down, her hair falling to shield her face, and I catch a glimpse of her trembling shoulders. With a quick motion, she closes the journal resting in her lap, the soft thud echoing in the quiet air. She wipes at her cheeks with trembling fingers, her breath hitching slightly as she fights more tears stopping them from falling.

"What are you doing out here, Manny? I'm such a mess,"

Cara grumbles, turning away from me so I can't see her, but tough shit because I'm not accepting that.

"Hey," I say again, this time softer, grabbing her chin with my fingers and tilting her face toward me. It's still not sunrise but the sky is brightening. I can see it in the colors of blue merging softly with the light caught between night and day. The twinkling lights illuminate her face, highlighting the freckles across her cheeks, beautiful even with the crimson color behind them. "Cara, what's the matter?"

"Nothing, nothing, just ignore me. I'm a mess," she adds, sniffling and trying to take her face from my fingers.

I bring my other hand to hold hers, and squeeze gently before saying, "Clearly something, Carita. What's going on?" I look into her often light green eyes but right now they have darker speckles of green and gold, making them seem like a precious stone. Like little emerald saucers.

"You don't have to hide from me." I drop her face and let her do what she needs, if that's moving her face away from me then so be it but I don't drop her gaze. I want her to know she can find a friend in me. She can find listening ears and someone who won't judge her for whatever is bothering her.

"It's a long story," she says.

"It's a long day," I add, pointing at the sky transforming into soft hues of coral and lavender as it mixes in with the inky blue. "We have all day, no plans, so if you'd like someone to listen, I'm here. What's going on?"

She takes a deep breath, looks down at our hands intertwined together, and lets out a breath. "I was journaling," she begins. I want to ask questions but before I can she adds, "Not like the bullet one, this is more like a diary if you will. I share my thoughts and sometimes feelings. I had a weird dream and I woke up sad so I walked out here and it just all started to come out."

"You wanna talk about it?" I ask as I continue to rub small circles on her hand. Her skin is so soft under my fingers. Like petals of the rarest flower. She is a garden. A field of colorful flowers so beautiful and precious you don't even want to pick them—worried you'll uproot them.

"Like you want to listen to a girl ramble? No, thank you. I don't want your sympathy," she snaps.

"Cara, I always want to hear you talk. I always want to listen to whatever it is you have to say. So if you want to talk about it, I'm all ears. If you don't, I understand that too. I just want to be here for you, whatever that is at this moment."

Cara pulls her hand away from mine, placing it in between her thighs and closing her eyes. She stands up, the beige fluffy blanket still wrapped around her shoulders, with her high socks she wore to bed last night now with hiking boots too. She offers her hand to me and sets her journal on the railing, when I look up at her she smiles softly before saying, "Let's go watch the sunrise and I'll tell you. I need a little walk first."

We walk in silence down the path toward the river with the sky dancing with colors. Gold ribbons on what little we can see of the horizon. The deep blues are almost gone, drowned by the soft warm colors announcing a new day. If there's one reason to wake up early, it's this. We stand by the river and although the air is crisp, it's comfortable. Perfect summer morning temperature. Cara's eyes are set on the water and her cheeks, which were deep red before, have lightened like the sky.

She lays the blanket down and sits, patting the spot next to her and I take it. She rests her head on my shoulder and starts talking. "I had a dream that Cole called me to tell me about his wedding and to invite me but he said I'll only get the invitation without a plus one because he knew I was going to die alone."

I'm going to kill that asshole. My body tenses at her words. I'm trying my hardest not to react like I have no manners and not to say exactly that but the words slip out of me before I can stop them. "I'm going to kill him, Cara."

"Ha," she says, letting out something between a laugh and sigh. "It was a dream, Manny. He didn't actually say that."

"Dreams don't come out of nowhere, sunshine. They come from that beautiful brain of yours—" I tap her forehead gently "—overanalyzing a situation or from deep in your heart when you're trying to process an emotion." I take her hand in mine, bringing it to her chest and letting her feel her heartbeat. I bet if I could hear it out loud it would be as loud as banjos rumbling through the early morning hush. "Is it him getting married that's bothering you?" I ask.

"Honestly? Probably," she answers, lifting her head from my shoulder and laying back on the ground, letting the first sunlight of the day kiss her cheeks. "Have you heard this story?"

"Other than he's marrying that girl we don't like, no." I say we because this chick hurt my sister pretty badly so we all took the stand that we don't like her. Then she went and got engaged to Cara's ex who is part of their friend group. The whole thing sounds like a damn high school drama, not like the real lives of adults.

"Well, he broke up with me last August for the last time. And I say *the last time* because we've been on and off for years. But he basically said that I wasn't wife material and he was ready to settle down. A few months later, they announced their engagement. I didn't hear it from either of them, I heard it from Allie who called to check on me. Allie who also suffered under the pettiness of Tasha—the ex, if you didn't know. The worst part? I don't even wish them ill. I just want him to be happy even if it's not with me. I just wish I knew how to be happy and how to not feel like a fucking failure," Cara explains as silent tears roll down her face.

"Cara," I whisper, my voice thick, the words hanging in the

air like a prayer, as I reach up to wipe away the tears that have begun to blur her vision. She doesn't pull away, but her eyes don't meet mine either—she just stares at the space between us, lost in a place that feels like it's miles away from where I stand. Her pain is palpable, sinking deep into my chest, and I'm desperate to hold it all for her, to take it away. But I can't. I can't do a thing to fix what's been broken inside of her for so long.

"You're not a failure, and you look pretty happy to me," I press, my voice soft but firm, trying to push past the walls she's built around herself. "You have so much to be happy about." But even as I say it, I know it's not enough.

Her lips twitch in that way they do when she's trying to hold it together. But she doesn't smile. Not really.

"There's a lot that can be hidden behind pretty smiles, Manny," she adds, her voice quiet but steady, as though she's already rehearsed this lie a thousand times. And in that moment, I feel it—the break. I can almost hear her heart cracking, like glass shattering in slow motion. Or maybe it's just the sound of it all finally breaking—that fragile shell she's been living inside for so long.

My breath catches in my throat as I watch her, helpless. She's always been the one to hold it all together for everyone else, the one who shoulders the weight of the world with a smile, even when her own shoulders were buckling beneath it. She's the fixer, the glue. The one who reminds everyone else how much they're worth. But there's no one to remind *her*. Not anymore.

"You don't have to hide your hurt, Cara," I remind her, the words barely more than a whisper; like I'm pleading with her to let me in, to stop pushing me away. "You have Allie, and I'm sure Roe and your other friends are there for you." But I know deep down it's not the same. It's never the same.

She shakes her head slowly, her eyes distant, like she's

already gone somewhere I can't follow. "That's not my role in our relationship. I'm the fixer, the one who reminds everyone how much they're worth. I don't get to cry over a relationship that they all saw was a hoax."

Her words hit me like a punch to the stomach. I see it then—the way she's been carrying all of their burdens, all of their broken pieces, while she's crumbled beneath the weight of her own. She's convinced herself she's not allowed to break, not allowed to feel the way I know she does—because if she does, who will hold it all together? Who will remind everyone else how valuable they are, when she's forgotten her own worth in the process?

My chest tightens, and I take a step closer, my voice barely a murmur. "Who reminds *you* of your worth, Carita?" It comes out raw, the emotion I've been holding back breaking free in that single, fragile question. My heart aches for her—aches for the woman I know she is, the one who's buried beneath all the layers she's built to protect herself from feeling too much, from being too much.

I wish, more than anything, that I could pick her up and wrap her in my arms, hold her like she's always held everyone else. I wish I could somehow make her see how incredible she is, how worthy of love and care she truly is, even if she can't see it for herself. How any man would be beyond lucky to call her his. But I don't think she believes it. Not even for a second.

"That's a good question," Cara says quietly, her voice strained like the words are stuck in her throat. She falls silent then, and I can feel the weight of her sorrow settling over us both. Her held words turn into heavy breaths, each one carrying the weight of a thousand unspoken things—things she's afraid to say, things she doesn't know how to say. The wind picks up around us, carrying her pain away in gusts, as if it might be able to take it somewhere else, somewhere far from here.

But it doesn't. It never does. It lingers. It stays. And so do I, standing in the quiet, wishing there was more I could do. Wishing I could be the one to remind her how much she means —how much she has always meant to me, even when she couldn't see it for herself.

Her arms break in goosebumps and I lay next to her, extending my arm. "Come here." She scoots over, laying her head on my arm.

"Thanks," she offers.

"For what?"

"For being a good listener." Then she's closing her eyes again and her eyelashes kiss the top of her cheeks with a sigh.

"Always, Carita, always," I promise, letting the sun warm us up a little more but not breaking this moment. I don't know when we'll be this close again. This vulnerable, this comfortable with each other, so I decide to appreciate it while it lasts. I know I'm fucked because all I keep thinking about is how good she feels in my arms and how I want to make sure she feels cherished and safe forever. She's leaving an imprint in my heart just like this bracelet she gave me is leaving a mark.

12

THE WILDS

YOUNG, WILD & FREE, SNOOP DOGG AND WIZ KHALIFA & THE ROADS, JONAH KAGEN

Cara

We've spent the last three days traveling to the next spot on our bucket list. Stopping in different places and checking more things off our list along the way. We went to a fair and ate our weight in popcorn, cotton candy, and funnel cakes —or at least I did, because Mr. Fitness Manny over there didn't eat much. The Ferris wheel was broken so we're going to try to find another fair so we can cross that off my list.

Manny wanted to see puppies, so we went to an adoption event and got our fill of puppy kisses and pets. I was so surprised when he added *that* to his list, but apparently he's always wanted a dog. Unfortunately, he can't commit to one until he travels less for work which he said he's ready to start thinking about. Manny has been such a champ. He hasn't complained once and even when I caught him working, he just smiles at me and goes back to it.

He hasn't asked about Cole or the crying session from the

other day, but he tells me every night before he goes to sleep that he's there if I need him. We haven't had to share a bed again since that night, which has been good for my sleep. I was restless just from his subtle woodsy and spicy scent—which, by the way, I still haven't been able to figure out exactly what it is.

Now we're almost to our next stop—Ohio. Did we need to go to Ohio? No, but I want to see The Wilds. The Wilds is a conservation center for animals with a ton of acreage. So think zoo, but nicer to the animals. I've been dying to see this place and now that I get to, I'm beyond excited. The GPS says we're fifteen minutes away and I can feel the excitement in my bones.

My phone buzzes in my lap and I turn it around to see it's Allie in our group chat.

The Bestie: How's the trip going? You owe me a FaceTime call too, btw.

I haven't talked to any of them since the first day at Aramoni. Not that they haven't texted, but more like I want to be blissfully unaware of anything that's happening in real life. This trip has been a dream, and I'd rather not wake up from it. Other than posting on Instagram every now and then, I've been blissfully ignorant, and I like it.

The Badass: Nobody Facetimes me.

Me: Roe, you hate talking on the phone.

Me: The trip is one in a million, tbh. I never want it to end.

The Bestie: Manny behaving?

Me: He's being a gentleman. Your mom raised him right

The Bestie: He's a good one for sure

> The Badass: Why is he single then?

> The Bestie: Oh, he's not.

He's not single? What? I look up from our conversation and smack Manny on the arm.

"Jesus, Cara, what?!" he shouts, looking at me in between attending to the road and surely wondering what that was for.

"You have a girlfriend?" I ask. I don't even know why I'm mad. It's not like there's anything going on between us other than my hungry wandering eyes because I'm a horny mess. Yes, he has been kind, and talking to him is kind of nice, but he's my best friend's brother, right?

"Where the hell did that come from?" he asks. "I do not. I don't date, Cara."

I look at him, confused, but before I can elaborate another text message comes from Allie.

> The Bestie: He's married to his job. But whenever he gets the chance to put that aside and give his heart some attention, the girl he finds will be lucky. He's one of a kind.

> The Bestie: Well two of a kind. Gus is pretty good too.

> The Badass: Sounds like your parents raised all three of you right, huh?

> Me: Allie's mom is the best. We love her.

> Me: OMG! We're almost to The Wilds. I'll send pics later.

"Hellooo?! Cara, where did you get the idea that I have a girlfriend?" Manny asks, turning left onto the road that will lead us to our destination.

"Something Allie said—that you weren't single. I was just

worried, I don't know, that I was overstepping, maybe?" I ask in full-blown run-on sentence mode.

"Overstepping with what? Spending time with me? Because other than sharing the bed that one night, nothing has happened. We're friends, right?" he asks, looking at me for a split second and then waiting for my response.

We sure are. "Yup, we are. A girlfriend wouldn't want you sharing a bed with another girl though, regardless if you're friends or not," I add.

"And I wouldn't have done that if I *did* have one, but I don't, so move on." He looks back to the road and when I do the same, I see The Wilds.

"Aaaaah!!!" I scream, clapping my hands and pulling my phone out to record. The road winds through undulating hills, giving glimpses of expansive meadows and green areas that go beyond what I can see. I lower the window and I can smell the scent of the earth and greenery. I hear birds in the distance, making an ever-changing soundtrack. Even with the noise of the bus, I can hear the sounds of nature. I can feel it too. I stick my head out the window, closing my eyes and feeling it all.

We drive through the rustic wooden gate near the entrance, following the paved road that leads to a gravel path for the visitor center. I unbuckle my seat belt and get ready to leap out of my seat the minute Manny pulls up to a parking spot. As soon as the van comes to a stop, I'm leaping out of it and on the move.

"LOOK AT THE GIRAFFES!" I shout, as we wait on the

safari tram, not so patiently, for them to come near. "Do you know what a group of giraffes is called?" I ask Manny.

"No, but I'm sure I'm about to find out. Since you've taught me about all the other animals we've seen today," Manny replies.

"A journey or a tower. So that's a pretty big tower of giraffes," I add, giggling like the dork I am. I had a student a few years ago who was obsessed with the group names of animals. He learned a new one every week and all he wanted to do was to quiz me to see if I could remember them. Now it's my jam, too.

The tour guide announces that the giraffes will start sticking their heads in the tram's windows for us to feed them. I grab the leaves he passed around earlier and get up like a flash of lightning, knocking a bag onto the ground.

"Oh, no! I'm so sorry," I exclaim, picking the bag up and smiling at the woman who has been a trooper dealing with my excitement all afternoon. She smiles back but then her face turns into complete horror at the same time that I feel something pulling my hair.

"Don't move," Manny commands, moving his leaves into the air as he helps me up.

"What was that?!" I ask, shaking my body like that could remove whatever just happened.

"Oh nothing; just a little giraffe trying to eat your hair because you're so close to those leaves," he says, pointing to my leaves. They're on top of the seat and apparently, my hair was too close to them.

I laugh loudly and Manny flashes me a big smile.

"Come on, Cara, you'll miss your *tower* if you don't feed them now."

"Eeek!" I squeal, grabbing the rest of the leaves and feeding the smallest giraffe. I grab my phone and pose to snap a picture of this moment to post later in my stories.

"I'm out of leaves," I hear a little voice whine. I turn to find Lila, the only little girl in our group, who I was geeking over animals with earlier. She has the saddest frown I've seen in a while. I hear her mom telling her they're also out of leaves and it breaks my heart to see her so sad. I grab the leaves I have left and walk toward her, trying to avoid the hungry giraffes.

"Here, I'm all done feeding them, you can have mine," I offer and immediately her face lights up.

"Thank you so much," she says.

"You didn't have to do that. You already entertained her enough at the beginning of the safari," her mom adds.

"It's not a big deal, really. She can have them," I insist and walk back to my seat.

"That was very kind, Cara," Manny says with an emotion in his eyes I can't pinpoint. Like he wasn't expecting me to do something like that.

"Are you surprised I'm nice to children, Manuel?" I ask.

"No, not even one bit," he quips, smiling softly at me and maybe I misread that situation because he looks at me with what seems like pride. "Do you want my leaves, Carita?"

"Nope, you can feed the giraffes. Look how cute they are," I add, pointing at the one currently trying to reach Manny's leaves.

"Here," he says, handing me what he has left. "You looked so happy feeding them, just do it. I'm good here."

I grab the leaves, jump off the seat and feed the softest giraffe ever. She sticks her long dark tongue out, and in one quick lick, she takes them all from me. We're only five days into this trip and I feel like it's Christmas. I still can't believe it's actually happening. Every time I talked to Cole about doing this with me it was excuses after excuses. *Just go to a regular zoo,*

Cara. Aren't you too old for safaris? That's too long to be on the road. Don't you have better things to do, Cara? It was never yes with Cole. 'Because I want to' was never a good enough reason. And it's so damn refreshing to actually get what I want without having to beg. Sometimes without even having to ask because Manny's taking the time to watch, and to notice.

We leave the giraffes and finish the safari before heading back to the visitor's center. We laugh and smile at every experience from birds to rhinos and everything in between. We're stepping out of the tram and Manny offers me his hand to help me down.

"You guys are so cute. I hope you have many years to come together. You should put a ring on it," one of the ladies from the tour says, walking past us and leaving me speechless.

"I should put a ring on it, huh?" Manny asks, smiling and wiggling his eyebrows, taking away the awkwardness of the moment.

"Oh, be quiet. Let's go, we have places to be," I say, pushing him slightly with my hand and turning on my heels to head back to the van. I don't want to talk about the jitters I got when he said that. It's probably just me crushing over the fact that he's making my dreams come true with this trip.

We're leaving tomorrow for our next stop so I want us to take advantage of our day in this area. The Wilds was everything I wanted and more and I wouldn't be here if Manny hadn't come on this trip. At least, not this summer.

"Hey," I say softly, stepping into the van after he opened the door for me.

"Yeah?"

"Thanks. This was a dream," I add.

"Siempre, lindura, siempre.[1]"

---

1. Always, Cuteness, always.

Manny walks around and settles into the driver's seat with ease. I'm sure he can feel the leather warm against his skin just as I did a second ago. As he turns the ignition, a low rumble fills the air, mingling with the faint scent of wildflowers and gasoline.

"Can I take you somewhere?" he asks, a hint of warmth in his voice, his eyes sparkling with a blend of mischief and happiness. He points the AC vents toward himself, feeling the cool breeze that brushes against his face, a momentary escape from how hot today was. His fingers move slowly over the buttons on the dash as he hits play and waits for me to answer.

"Ooh, you have more of your own stops planned now?" I ask, taking my shoes off and rolling the window down to put my feet on the sill.

"Something like that," he teases, winking at me before putting directions in his phone and leading us out of the parking lot.

13

CRAWLING BEAR

DRIVE, HALSEY

Cara

Leaving behind the expansive fields, the winding roads take us into a small downtown area. It's quaint and beautiful, giving the "everybody knows everybody" feel. Manny parks in front of a small cafe and after telling me to wait in the bus for him, he comes back out with a couple of bags. He doesn't say anything though, he just smiles and gets the bus rolling back on the road.

"Crawling bear!" I shout after we pass more wooded hills and greenery slowly turning into smaller hills with creeks in between.

"Where?!" Manny screams, slamming on the brakes and looking panicked.

"Oh, just the sign—" I point at the side of the road to the bear crossing sign we just passed "—a little bear crawling."

"Cara, you scared the shit out of me. I thought there was an actual bear crawling?" Manny laughs and continues driving, the silence broken with the sign. "Why crawling, though? That looks just like a bear walking."

"There are different types of bear signs. When I see a bear walking, I'll shout it out," I say and smile big, laying my head back and watching the road.

The sun is starting to lower and the whole atmosphere has a warm glow. Holding my hand out the window, I feel the gentle breeze under the warm sun, which reminds me of toasted crois-sants and hugs. Cozy, calm. Exactly what I want to feel. We pass an area that looks like an industrial museum and he parks right next to a giant machine-looking thingy.

"Come on, let's go," Manny says, grabbing the two bags from the cafe and his backpack before stepping out of the van.

I follow him toward the structure with a sign that reads "Big Muskie Bucket." I think I remember reading about it but I didn't mention it before, so I'm not sure why we're here.

"Care to explain?" I ask.

"Come on, Carita. Be spontaneous with me," he adds, putting the bags down and pulling a picnic blanket from his backpack. He lays out the blanket on the grassy area near the exhibit.

"What's this?" I ask.

"A little picnic, just sit and enjoy the moment," Manny insists and I don't know who this guy is right now—backward hat and so carefree, taking the day by the reins and enjoying it as it goes—but I'm thankful it's me who gets to experience him.

"Picnic lunch? We already checked it off the list."

"But we didn't really eat. We fell asleep so we need a redo, and I read online about this area and it sounded cool," he says.

"Did *you* search online or did you have—what's her name again? Ah yes, Lucia—look it up for you?" I ask, trying to get the bag of food but he pulls it away from me.

"Matter of fact, Lucia did find suggestions, but I picked the cafe where these came from, happy? Now be nice or I won't show you what's in here," Manny teases, shaking the bag in his hand.

"Gimme, gimme, pretty please," I plead, clapping my hands and sitting on my knees.

He unzips the bag and pulls out neatly wrapped sandwiches, golden scones, and two bottles of water. The smell of fresh bread mingles with a hint of citrus from the scones and I can bet my left kidney those are lemon. He hands me a bottle, cool and refreshing in my palm, and grins. "You pick first," he insists, his eyes sparkling. "I like all of these, so I'll happily take whatever you leave behind."

"Eeek, thank you!" I shout, grabbing the chicken salad sandwich and the lemon scone with tiny purple dots. *Lemon blueberry, my favorite.* I take a bite of the sandwich and kick my feet because this is fucking delicious. Salty but perfectly balanced with a hint of sweetness. Definitely not what I was expecting. I open the top portion and see that there's mozzarella cheese and some balsamic glaze too.

"What in the fancy chicken salad is this?" I ask and Manny laughs.

"It's a Caprese Chicken Salad. It looked good, so I grabbed it. I'm glad you like it." He goes to take a bite of his sandwich but before he can his phone rings. He lowers his gaze to it and, shaking his head, he gets up and says, "I have to answer this, I'm sorry. Excuse me." He walks away, while answering the call, and I feel the emptiness as soon as he's gone.

In these past five days, I've gotten used to his company. He's easy to be around. Easy to talk to. More than easy, he's interesting to talk to. His views on the world and life are so different from most people I hang out with. Actually, it's different from his sister's, too. It's like he's a free soul trapped in the body of a business guy or whatever it is that he does. Even more than that, he's interested in what I have to say. And it makes me realize I didn't see how little attention Cole ever paid to me. True attention.

The guys I've dated over the years paid some attention; not like Manny, but definitely enough to seem interested. I don't know if it's because I was keeping Cole in the back of my mind, but I was never in the present moment with them either. It's not that I'm dating Manny or anything like that, but by being around him, I find myself not thinking about much other than the next stop on our list.

I've never felt more like myself or less judged than I do when I'm around Manny. It's refreshing but also kind of scary because I don't want to get too close to him. Not when I know he will go back to his corporate world. I don't want to grieve whatever friendship is forming on top of Cole and the move.

I pull out my phone from my shorts and snap pictures of the picnic and the view, before opening my social media and posting a photo dump of the day so far. Pictures of feeding the giraffes, smiling with rhinos behind me, of my feet hanging from the window, and the picnic right now. I add a picture of Manny in the distance, his joggers and T-shirt making him look like any regular guy. But once you see his posture against the tree, with his backward hat and the phone on his ear, you can tell that there's more to him. Every part of his body is hard under his clothes, muscles galore. And his damn jaw is even tighter now that he seems to be arguing on his call. He looks both mysterious and like the guy next door. It's mesmerizing. I caption it *Ohio's been wild*, post it, and continue with my food, wondering what he's talking about that has him all worked up. Actually, I'm wondering *who* he's talking to.

14

BOONDOCKING

LIKE REAL PEOPLE DO, HOZIER

Manny

"I UNDERSTAND you're upset but I told you we're handling this," I argue, not actually knowing if anyone is handling anything. The contrast of the peace and quiet around me with the loud voices on Virgil's side of the line is astounding. I can hear the sharp tone of everyone around him and the grunt of his words could make the earth shake. But I'm not going to turn into an ass like him. I've got to control the situation.

"What are you handling? Are you still on vacation? Are you back in New York?" he asks, like I need to be physically somewhere to do my job.

"The market conditions have been extreme lately. You wanted to take an aggressive approach and not preserve cash flow. Sometimes it backfires and sometimes it works. It looks like it's backfiring, but we're watching the market to make sure we do what's best for you. The setbacks are hard to predict but we are working on it," I add. It's like talking to a little kid who's not getting his way. This is the worst part about this business—when people don't understand that they won't always win.

A loud clap of thunder echoes through the trees, and when I look up, the sky is rapidly turning ten shades of gray. The weather in this area is so volatile, way more than I expected.

"Extreme conditions or not, this is a disaster and not a solid investment. And now I'm looking at significant losses." Virgil's anger is clear, echoing through the phone line. I could go on and on about how we diversify and employ risk management strategies and how the market has affected even the most stable investments, but that won't help.

"Virgil, we're actively working on a revised strategy to mitigate these losses. Would you like me to call you in forty-eight hours with some options?"

His voice is a mix of skepticism and exhaustion as he replies, "I need concrete steps and a timeline for recovery. If things don't improve, I'll have to reconsider my options." This man has been with me since we opened the company. He's just trying to act all tough.

I look up and see Cara picking everything up because the sky just went from gray to almost black and the rain could start any moment. "We will provide you with a comprehensive plan and timeline by the end of the week. Your trust is important to us, and we're doing everything we can to restore it," I say, and he hangs up. *Maldito hijo del que lo parió*[1].

I rush to help Cara with everything. "Here, here, I'm sorry—let me help you." I grab the bag from her hands and run with her to the van. The rain starts to fall, cold and wet on my cheeks as we run. I usually hate rain. People don't know how to drive, making it impossible to get anywhere in a decent amount of time. My sister had a weird crash last year on a rainy day and

---

1.   *Son of a bitch or motherfucker*

that doesn't help either. It also reminds me of how sad life can be. As if the planet gets it too and it gives us rain so we can remember her tears. After I open the back door and we put everything in, I turn to hear giggles from Cara. She's run back out to the middle of the grassy area and is spinning in circles, letting the rain fall on her.

I lean against the van, my gaze fixed on this ray of sunshine personified as she twirls and laughs, sticking her tongue out and letting the rain soak her. There's thunder rumbling in the distance but nothing seems to be phasing Cara in this moment. Her laughter rings out like the sweetest melody mixed with the rhythm of the now-heavy rain. The flowy dress she's wearing is clinging to her body, showing off her soft curves and her hard nipples peeking through the light fabric. But my eyes focus on something else . I focus on the bright smile she wears as she dances and moves in the rain. There's nobody here but us, the dark sky, and the rain but she makes it seem like the world is her stage and we all just exist to watch her. Like the rain is falling just so she can dance in it. As if the sky is darker so she can shine even brighter. She's the sun, we're in her orbit, and the entire planet knows it.

"Manny! Come dance with me!" she calls out, her voice bright and cheery despite the downpour.

"It's pouring, Cara!" I shout, my heart racing both with the anticipation at what she might do and with the sight of her carefree self enjoying this moment instead of hiding from it. The rain keeps getting more intense and her laughter gets louder.

"Don't be a chicken, Manny! Come on," she yells, stopping her twirls and facing me. When she sees me shaking my head, her face lights up and she starts running toward me. I'm still mostly dry considering I'm standing under the giant tree we parked under. But that doesn't stop her from throwing herself at me. Cara wraps me up in her arms with her soaking wet body and not a care in the world.

I tense under her cold wet touch as she continues, "It's just rain, Manny. Just a little rain. When was the last time you danced in the rain?" She pulls me by my hands but without moving me. *Never*, I want to say, but I don't because is that really what she needs to hear? I almost say no and run inside the van to hide from it all but then I notice the bracelet and remember her words. *These always remind me to take a breath and slow down.* The pink bracelet wrapped around my wrist makes me stop and wonder: do I *want* to hide from this moment or have I been wired to think that? Have I been wired to think that rain is bad and that dancing under it is childish and annoying?

"It'll be fun, I promise!" she calls over the rain, her eyes sparkling with joy and invitation. It's impossible saying no to her so I push myself off the van and run with her.

The rain intensifies and now that we're in the middle of the clearing, Cara stands in front of me and smiles. She opens up her arms, letting her head fall backward and closes her eyes.

"Have you ever felt this free, Manny?" She grabs my hands and twirls under my arm, dancing with me as I stand still. The cold water splashes on and around us, creating a pattern that's music to her ears judging by the way her body moves.

"No, Cara, I haven't," I confess and she stands still for the first time in the past ten minutes, looking me in the eyes and letting out a deep breath. She adjusts her dress and I try my best not to look down, knowing how little her dress covers now that's see-through.

"Then dance with me," she whispers, moving a piece of hair away from her face.

I grab her hand and pull her toward me, close enough to touch. I bring my hands to her lower back and her palms land on my chest, resting carefully there, like there's no turmoil happening under her touch.

My heart is pounding in my chest so hard I'm afraid it will come out. Cara looks up, her green eyes gazing into mine, and her lips part slightly as we sway with the percussion of the rain on the ground. I lower my gaze to her lips as she licks the rain off of them, like she knows I'm dying to kiss her and to find out what the rain tastes like on her skin. My eyes linger there, wondering if her lips are as soft as her hands or if they're as warm as her heart. I wonder for a second, then two, then three.

The energy in the air is electric and I wonder if it's from the storm or whatever is pulling me to her. We keep swaying under the water, falling into movement with each other matching the rhythm of the rain. I lift my hand, tracing up her back and her arm slowly. Goosebumps form on her skin from my touch. I reach for her hand and intertwine her fingers with mine. We don't say anything, but our gazes never falter.

Cara lifts to her tiptoes and lifts her face closer to mine. A small movement but enough for me to notice it. Enough for me to wonder what she's doing. She tilts her face and now her lips are close to mine. I may not understand what's happening between us on this trip, but I know what *this* is. *Lust.*

She's feeling all the energy around us, and the rain touching every inch of her skin is causing sensations that her brain is always craving. Her brain is seeking more. Hence why she's trying to kiss me. And if it was anybody else, I would take the opportunity and taste her lips. And *that* would lead to me tasting her skin and every inch of her body. Eager to learn what makes her scream, bit by bit. But this is not just a random hook-up or a girl I won't ever see again. This is Allie's best friend and as much as I would like to, I can't.

I turn my face, dropping my hands from holding her body

and feeling the emptiness under my fingers immediately. I grab her shoulders instead and whisper, "Cara, we can't."

I see the panic on her face but I don't get time to say anything before she exclaims, "Oh my God! I'm so sorry, Manny, please ignore me." Cara slips out from my hold and leaves me wet and cold as she runs toward the bus. She climbs in the back and shuts the door, closing the privacy curtains and leaving me out here. I'm sure she's changing so I don't want to interrupt her but I also don't want to just leave her like that.

"Cara!" I shout as I pound on the door, hoping she's not completely overthinking things in there but knowing damn well she is.

A few minutes pass before Cara opens the door. She's wearing an oversized shirt now and her hair is wrapped in a towel. "Come in, come in, quick!" she shouts.

I step in, trying not to soak the floor or her cute decorations. There's not enough space for both of us to change clothes without crowding each other but the storm is picking up and I'm thankful she let me in.

"Cara," I say, my voice low and deep.

"Manny, don't worry about it. I got carried away. Just get dressed." She climbs into the front seat and turns around, giving me privacy.

After I change into dry joggers and a different shirt, I sit on the bench behind the front seat and ask, "Cara, can we talk, please?" The rain intensifies outside and the loud taps on the roof of the van makes it sound even louder. Like Mother Nature is screaming and she wants us all to listen. Lightning flashes, illuminating the dark sky followed by a loud rumble of thunder in the distance.

"Manny," she whispers, closing her eyes and shaking her head. "Please, just let it go, okay? I said I got carried away. You said you loved to hear me talk but that you would respect me if I didn't want to. I don't want to. So, let's just go wherever we're going next."

I hear the regret in her voice and I just want to hug her and tell her that it's okay and the reason why I couldn't kiss her. But she's asking me to drop it and I will respect that. I can pretend like nothing was happening between us—try to forget I wanted to kiss her too.

"HOW FAR DO you want to drive today?"

Cara is currently wrapped in a blanket on the front seat, scrolling on her phone. The rain has not let up so I'm driving slower to try to keep us safe. Far too many people die every year on highways in car accidents and I like to avoid them as much as possible.

"Wherever, really. I just need food and some place to sleep," she answers. Her voice is shallow, like she's trying to stop herself from saying something she doesn't want to. I need to get her out of her head and I might know just the thing. We've been sitting in silence for the past hour and a half so when I keep driving she doesn't question me.

I pull over to park when I find the spot I'm looking for. It looks like a lot of nothing in the rain but I'm hoping by the morning it's clear and we can watch the sunrise. I also hope she's not going to yell at me for what I'm about to do.

"Where are we?" Cara asks as I park the van under the canopy of trees.

"We're staying the night here. There's a bed and we have food, the two things you asked for," I say nonchalantly, rolling the windows down slightly and turning the van off.

Cara rolls her eyes. "There's one tiny bed in the back, Manny, you won't even fit there."

"I will, I promise. Don't you have something on that check-list of yours called boondocking?" I ask with a smile, and when her eyes open wide and her brows furrow, I know I got her. *Busted.*

"Yeah but I didn't take you for the kind of person who would do that so I didn't mention it . How do you even know?" she asks.

"What boondocking is? I Googled it..." I laugh and she does too, finally breaking up some of the tension.

"No, silly. How do you know I had boondocking on my list?"

Because I've memorized it, I want to say, but instead I answer, "I read it by accident the other day. Let's just get ready." I let her through to the back and as she goes past me, I notice she's not wearing anything under her shirt. *Fuck me.*

The entire backseat area is as whimsical and cozy as her home. A mix of vibrant and pastel pink and purple flowers everywhere and cushions and throws lie on top of the fold-out bed in the far back. She shuffles some things around, pulls the sofa out, turns it into a bed, and then climbs on it. Book in hand, she pulls the soft pink blanket over her bare legs and lays her head on a couple of pillows and goes straight to reading. Her book has a couple holding pinkies on the cover in what looks like a campground and it's the most adorable thing I've ever seen.

"How fitting," I muse.

"What is?" she asks with a puzzled look, lowering her book so she looks at me.

"You reading a camping book while we stopped in the middle of nowhere for the night," I tease.

"Ha, not camping at all. Actually, the female main character hates the outdoors but she's trying her best."

"Interesting. Are you liking it?" I ask, looking closer at the cover. Over the purple hues of the sky, there's the title *A Lodge Affair by Rachel LaBerge* right above a campfire and a couple of chairs. The cover is pretty and it matches Cara perfectly. What is it that she says? Her *aesthetic*, it matches her aesthetic.

"Are you mocking me, Manny?" she deadpans.

"I could never," I gasp, my hand over my heart. "Remember I grew up with my mom, her library and Allie devouring books. I don't love reading but I think it's so cool that people can get lost in books."

"Well, I love this one," she adds, lifting the book again and going back to reading.

I take the opportunity to climb over the seats, cursing everyone who built this tiny fucking thing that they call a bus before making it to the back. What I should've done is ask her more about what she's reading. What I should've done is even take the book away from her hands and set it on the table just so I can have her attention solely on me. Maybe even give her that kiss she tried to steal earlier and kiss her so deeply she'd want to get a new bracelet just so she can remember it, over and over again. That's what I should do but just because I *can* do those things, doesn't mean I should. So instead, I pull my laptop out of my bag and get to work instead.

15

THE BIG SPOON
SO HIGH SCHOOL, TAYLOR SWIFT

Cara

I READ a couple of chapters and put my book down because I want to savor the end and right now my mind is spiraling thinking about the fact that I tried to kiss Manny. I want to slap myself. *What the hell was I thinking?* I wasn't, that's what it was. I got carried away by his warm skin and the way his eyes flared when he saw my body through my soaked dress. I got completely carried away by how his scent blended with the rain —my favorite smell in the world—and how he seemed to swallow hard every time I laughed. I hate that he has this effect on me. Making me lose all my bearings. And now we're sleeping in this tiny van and I'm about to lose my shit with him so close and over the fact that I'm lusting over Allie's little brother.

He's sitting across from me, his feet crossed in front of him and his laptop on his lap as he types quickly. He looks serious and annoyed, and the only time I've seen this side of him is when he's working. I feel sad. Nobody should get this tense and upset about a job they've invested so much of their life into.

Nobody should be this upset about what's supposed to be their dream. His hard work should bring him joy or at the very least fulfillment.

"Manny, why don't you take a break from your job I still don't fully understand?" I ask, jokingly and setting my book to the side and patting the empty spot on the bed. "Bring me a sandwich too, pretty please." The rain has slowed down outside but it's still enough that there's a gentle patter dancing on the roof. It's soothing, and watching it fall outside the dark windows is an awe-inspiring display. I love the rain and I love its sound. I could stay here forever and live happily ever after.

"Sure," he sighs, closing his laptop and grabbing the leftover food from earlier and setting it on the bed. He sits on the opposite end and looks out the window. His expression softens immediately. "Do you want to understand?"

"It depends—do you love your job, Manny?" I ask, reaching for the sandwich and chips he's handing me from the brown paper bag.

He takes a slow sip of his water before answering, "I'm good at it."

"That's not what I asked," I say, my curiosity piqued and patiently waiting to see if he'll dodge my question.

He pauses, looking thoughtful. "I don't think anyone really loves their job, Cara. It's something we do, and we make the best of it. I get a rush when I see a client's portfolio grow, and there's something deeply satisfying about helping people reach their financial goals. But as for loving the job itself? I'm not so sure about that."

I shake my head in protest. "I do. I do love my job. There are things about it that I hate—like how severely underpaid we are or how some policies don't have the best interest of the child, or how some parents struggle to get their kids the support they need because of misinformation. But I love it so much. I couldn't imagine doing anything else. It sure as hell doesn't make me a grumpy pants every time I think about it," I add, popping a chip in my mouth and waiting for his reply.

Manny closes his eyes and shakes his head. "Grumpy pants?"

"You're all fun and games all the time but the minute 'Manny-the-Business-Owner' is activated, you turn into a grump. It's not on brand for you," I scold.

"It's not the job itself," Manny groans, frustration clear in his voice. "It's this one client who's been a real pain in my ass. He's giving me hell over his portfolio, especially since I'm on vacation. But I just checked it again, and everything's looking great. Now he's insisting on a face-to-face meeting, but honestly, there's no need for that."

"So just tell him to fuck off," I suggest.

"I wish I could," Manny replies, shaking his head. "But he's a major client. I've got to handle this carefully."

"Don't you have a bunch of those? A bunch of big clients? Nobody who disturbs your peace deserves your attention and heart," I insist and as soon as the words come out, I realize how much of a hypocrite I am. How messed up I am in the head that I can see it clearly in someone else's life, but when it was my life that was absolute hell, I never saw it happening.

In the moment, I never saw how bad Cole was to me. How shitty he behaved half the time. As long as I was enthralled by him and I didn't want anything for myself, he was fine. But the minute I spoke about something I wanted to do or a career I wanted to pursue, I was being selfish or he didn't want to be with me anymore. I can pretend in front of everyone to be this happy-go-lucky ray of sunshine, but the truth is that with Cole, I always felt like I wasn't enough. Like I needed to try harder. I needed to look prettier and grow up faster. I always felt that even at my very best, he still saw the worst in me. But of course I didn't see that until he proposed to someone else and I drove myself sad over it. Beyond sad, I thought I was worthless. In a hole of despair. Over what? A shell of a man whom I loved?

"Yeah, you're right but it's also a business. A business I own with Gus and I can't let him down either. I'll figure this one out, don't worry your pretty little mind," he says. Taking his shoes off and climbing on the bed—the tiny bed.

I throw my trash onto the ground and make a mental note to pick it up tomorrow. When I look over, I laugh hysterically at the sight. Manny's legs are dangling off the bed, and half of his upper body is resting on the side of the van's wall. This vintage microbus was in a junkyard when I found it. I really *really* wanted it and I asked around at school about mechanics until Colleen told me she knew someone who could work on it, and he turned it into a dream. It's fucking iconic and it gives cozy nostalgic Barbie vibes. The bed can fold up into a sofa, and I've always dreamed of using it to sleep under the stars in the middle of nowhere. But I never imagined it would end up being used by a gigantic man I'm not *sleeping* with.

I fit just fine and if I'm being honest, Cole would've too. At five-foot-nine, Cole isn't that much taller than me, and considering that I'm a cuddler, there wouldn't be a need for space. But Manny? He's tall and broad and taking up so much space it's borderline comical. He's laying back with one arm tucked under his head but half of his body is clearly not going to fit and it can't be comfortable at all.

"Manny, Jesus, just come here," I plead, wriggling back on the tiny fold-out mattress. The bed is adorned with a faded orange cover and surrounded by my favorite things I've collected, and it seems even smaller with each passing moment. The walls, lined with colorful bead curtains and painted flowers, feel like they're closing in as I try to make space.

"I'm good, really. Just go to sleep," Manny says, his voice

muffled as he tries to make himself comfortable on the narrow bench that converts into a bed.

"Don't be stubborn, please," I insist, my voice tinged with desperation.

He turns to face me, his expression a mix of frustration and concern. "Even if I scoot over, there's just not enough room. Please, just drop it."

I take a deep breath, feeling the tension and the emotional distance between us. Then, before doubt can creep in, I blurt out, "I have an idea."

I roll over, turning my face away from him and going into fetal position—child's pose if we were in yoga class—and lift my arm, waiting for him to give me his.

"What are you doing?" Manny asks.

"Give me your arm, be a big spoon and we'll fit."

"No," he says sharply. Thunder rumbles in the distance again. I don't have the patience to deal with this, I just want to go to sleep. I know he's probably wary after that almost kiss we just experience but I hope this is the olive branch we need for him to see I can be respectful.

"Manuel Zabana, please don't make me argue with you right now. Come on."

"Cara, no," he snaps.

"I will throw a giant fit, Manny. And trust me, I know how to nag until I get my way. I'm a daddy's girl after all. Come on, just give me your arm."

So fucking stubborn. He doesn't move so I turn again, grabbing his arm and trying my best to pull him over my body. He lets me, because there's no way I'd be able to move him without his help, and when I do, I put my body in the same position as before. "See? You just need to do the same and we'll fit."

He huffs but eventually bends his body to mold against mine. And though I knew we would fit on the bed, I just didn't realize how perfectly we would fit *together*. My head is right on his chest, letting me hear his steady heartbeat. His chin rests over my head and even though I can't see if he's comfortable or not, I can feel his body relaxing against mine so I'll take it that he is. His usually hard muscles don't feel as hard when he lets me put his hand around my belly or when his knees fit perfectly behind me. And to top it off he's wearing the bracelet I gave him, making a perfect contrast with his skin and adding even more to how perfect this moment is. *Perfect* is the only word I can think about and I don't know how to feel about it. I close my eyes repeating that word over and over in my head before drifting to sleep.

I OPEN my eyes with light streaming through the window and something hard against my back. I try to move but there's also something heavy over me. I let out a big yawn and then everything about yesterday comes rushing back. The Wilds, the picnic, the rain, and *oh my God,* I tried to kiss Manny and then told him to spoon me. *What in the actual fuck, Cara?!* I suck in my belly and try to slide off the bed when Manny's body tenses and he turns away from me suddenly. *Great.*

"Good morning, sugarplum!" I say, hoping to ignore the fact that his giant boner practically woke me up this morning.

"Good morning to you too, sunshine!" he whispers, voice groggy with sleep and ignoring the problem between his legs. *Phew, okay, we're both ignoring it then.*

I get up from the bed and search my bag for a pair of shorts because I went to bed without wearing any and then asked him to cuddle me. Good thing I don't inspire anything in him other than friendship because that would've turned out pretty steamy otherwise. I clearly need to let out some tension if I'm going to make it the rest of this trip without asking him to fuck me. *Would he even say yes?* Probably not. I'm not his type and he already told me no to a kiss, he definitely won't say yes to more. It'll be fine, everything will be fine. We'll go to a bar and I'll get drunk and into someone's pants as soon as possible.

"I'm going to go watch the rest of the sunrise." I grab my blanket, my phone, and a pair of sandals before stepping outside. I walk toward the water, and there's a giant lake that I couldn't see last night with the rain and how dark it was. But in the morning light it's breathtaking. The soft orange light of dawn stretches across it, bathing everything in a beautiful golden hue. I wrap the blanket around me and stand in awe of the sight. Little birds chirp in the distance and the gentle rays of sunshine warm the water's surface.

I hear some twigs snap and leaves rustle behind me, followed by the intoxicating blend of earthy-spicy scent of Manny. I look to the side and find him standing there, his hair disheveled and his shirt wrinkly but he looks like a walking advertisement. I smile at him and turn back around to watch the rest of the sunrise.

"Beautiful, isn't it?" I ask.

"Stunning," he replies, his voice just above a whisper. When I look over he's not looking at the sun rising, or at the water's changing reflection as the sun gets higher in the sky.

He's looking at me.

I can feel my cheeks warming, surely shifting to a darker color and my breath catches but I won't think more into this—I *will* let it go. I smile at him, tucking a piece of my hair behind my ear, and turning around to finish watching the sun and its slow but steady ascent.

"Where to next?" I ask.

"You're the one with the lists," Manny replies as he bumps my hip with his, settling my heart and stopping me from spiraling.

"You have a list of your own, hotshot. Where to next?"

"Are you ready for some whiskey?" he asks.

I snap my head back, mimicking his habit, and smile at him before saying, "Lead the way!"

16

BEST KIND OF BUZZ
I LIKE ME BETTER, LAUV

Cara

"You two are so damn funny," exclaims Kacey, the short and sweet woman who has been hanging out with us in the last leg of this bourbon tour. She and her husband, Keith, are on their honeymoon from Florida and we connected with them when I started talking about how I'm from Florida, too. They've been nice to talk to and of course, Manny has taken the lead in the conversation, and we're all enamored with him. It's a little past noon now and we've been drinking, talking, and snacking on this tour and they've been with us every step of the way.

It took us two days to make it to Louisville. We left the lake while the weather was perfect, so we explored and hiked instead of driving through. By the time we made it out of Ohio and into Kentucky, it was nighttime and we booked two hotel rooms so we could shower and sleep in real beds. We explored Lexington and rode horses, and I never would've imagined that a giant man on a horse would be graceful until I saw Manny riding. He was effortlessly flowing through the trails like he wasn't over six feet tall. Me on the other hand? I have a few bruises to help me tell a better story.

"Birth defect," Manny jokes and they laugh again. I just roll my eyes and sip on my I-lost-count-what-number bourbon that is actively helping my mood. I have the best kind of buzz. I'm happy and elated and I haven't thought about anything but the right here and right now in the past few hours.

"How long have you guys been together?" asks Kacey. "Keith and I have talked so much about us and we didn't even ask about y'all. It must be forever because you two are so comfortable together! I hope that's us one day," she says.

But before I can correct her, Manny speaks again. "We've been together forever. Our parents are friends, so we grew up together, and one thing led to another, and here we are," he explains, pulling me to him and tucking me under his arm. *What?!*

"Congrats, man. I'm sure it's so nice to grow up with your soulmate," Keith admires and I try to hide my panic by finishing my drink and grabbing Manny's from his hand.

"It's the best feeling, right bebé?" he asks, kissing my temple. I can feel his soft lips against my skin and his smile broadens as he tightens his hold on me. *What is going on?*

"Alright, everyone. This is the last stop, so you can come back with us on the bus or stay here. It's up to you. Remember, there's the derby-themed party tonight at Harbor's Bar," the tour guide shouts over the crowd, creating a massive wave of people leaving their seats at once.

"What's a derby-themed party?" Manny asks.

"It's just more drinking, food trucks at a bar by the water, face bets on past races, and people dress up like they're attending the Kentucky Derby. I saw the flier in the last distillery we went to," I explain.

"We're heading back to the bus. Are y'all coming?" Keith asks, standing from his stool and helping Kacey slide off hers. We shake our heads no and they wave goodbye. They smile at each other and after a gentle peck on the lips, he places his hand on her back and guides her out.

As soon as they're out of sight, I smack Manny on the shoulder. "Manny, what the hell?! We've been together forever?"

"If people are going to assume we're a couple, Cara, might as well go with it. A lot easier to pretend than to explain the whole road trip. Also, how fun would that be? We can just make up stories and pretend. You want to be a fashion designer mom of two? Be it. You want to be a popstar? Be it."

"Who are you and what did you do to Manny?" I ask.

"What? Do you think you're the only one who can play games? With all your weird animal sign shouts and your truth or dares? I can be fun too," he boasts. Placing some cash on the bar, Manny stands and offers his hand to help me off the stool.

"You're fun, as long as you forget about work," I tease, sticking my tongue out at him and holding on tightly to his arm. I'm 100% buzzed and the quick movement has my head spinning and tongue tingling.

"This is me forgetting about work. Welcome to Mannyland. I have an idea. Do you trust me?" he asks. When I smile and nod, he pulls me until we're outside and he's checking for an Uber.

"What if we go to this derby thing and pretend we're not who we are? I don't want to be Manuel Zabana today. I want to be Manny, Cara's carefree husband, and have a blast," he suggests.

We only wait a few minutes in the busy street before a dark sedan pulls up by us. Manny opens the door for me to step inside and after he slides in next to me, he just looks at me with a devilish grin.

I shake my head. "Manny, people are not going to believe you're my husband."

"Oh, but they will. You can't resist my charm and truthfully, neither can they," he adds, tucking his phone away after he sent a couple of texts. He's such a multitasker, I can't even believe it sometimes, everything he does at once. Make plans about tonight, call an Uber, answer texts or emails while making sure I don't fall to my ass after drinking my body weight in alcohol— it's astounding.

"Where are we even going?"

"To buy derby-appropriate clothes and hats," Manny teases, pulling his phone back out and showing me the stores he has pulled up on his browser. Some off-the-wall boutiques that I'm sure will cost more than my mortgage for one dress.

"Manny, those are going to be so expensive. It makes no sense to spend a lot of money on something we're going to use once." I'm a little concerned about this small outburst of spontaneity.

"I'll pay for it, it's fine," he replies.

"No, no, no, no, no! Are you crazy? It's going to be hundreds of dollars for something we're going to wear once."

"Says who? I'll wear a fancy hat again." Manny smiles and slides his fingers across his forehead as if he were swiping a hat on his head.

"To go where?" I snap back, lifting my eyebrows at him and crossing my legs.

"Fancy places, Cara." *Oh my god.* I roll my eyes at his reply.

"I have a feeling the fancy places you go to are more like black tie and expensive wine than mint juleps and hats. Not that the derby is only about the hats, but you get what I mean." My hands rest over my lap, and the chuckle he lets out makes my body come to life. This whole interaction has me annoyed; but more than anything, I'm extremely aware of how freaking attracted to him I am if a simple chuckle has basically altered my brain chemistry.

"I do get what you mean, but really, we can just go and get what we need. Have you ever considered not arguing with people about everything, Cara? Go with it for once," he drawls, grabbing my hand and smiling at me. *Why is he so freaking cute? Like a damn adorable brand-new puppy.*

"What is it that you say all the time? Just because you can doesn't mean you should? Let's not be wasteful, okay? I have an idea," I hint, grabbing his phone and changing the address of where we're going. We have one hour, two max, to make this work and I'm determined we will.

17

RUNWAY STRUT

STYLE (TAYLOR'S VERSION), TAYLOR SWIFT

Manny

"HERE, HERE, HERE," Cara shouts, pointing at the big white and blue sign above the old-fashioned entrance door.

"What is this?" I ask, confused as to why we're pulling over in front of a charming but very vintage thrift store.

We get out of the car and walk toward the timeworn building showcasing slightly faded paint with large windows. Blue shopping carts swarm the entrance, but before I can ask her again what we're doing here, she gets out cash from her purse and hands it to me.

Raising my eyebrows at her, I try to open my mouth to say something, but she brings her index finger to my lips and says, "Shh! Listen. You have ten minutes and twenty-five dollars to find me an outfit for this party. I will do the same for you. Meet me by the changing rooms in ten. Got it?" She winks at me and runs through the doors and into the store.

I walk around the thrift store, holding a couple of dresses

and skirts in my hands, completely annoyed at the fact that I don't understand this game. And if I'm being honest, I've been annoyed all day at the fact that I want to undress her. I want to be exploring every inch of her body and not finding more ways to cover it. In the end it doesn't matter either way, because she's off limits and I know that. It doesn't hurt to dream though.

"Time's up!" I hear Cara shout from across the store and the clerk by the dark register chuckles at that. I shake my head and walk toward her, clothes in hand and a smile on my face because it is impossible to look at how happy she is right now and not match it.

"Lemme see, lemme see." She has the biggest smile on her face and her hands together in front of her chest like she is two seconds away from a cheer clap.

"Three outfits and a hat to match," I say proudly, holding up the garments in my hands.

"Ah! Good job!! Those look like me!" Cara shouts.

Handing her the clothes and pointing at the cart next to her, I ask, "What about you?"

"You're going to have to wait and see. Go try it on and come out to model for us."

"Who's us?" I ask, lifting my eyebrows and looking around. That's when I notice the two employees sitting by the dressing room doors. "Well hello, ladies," I croon, giving them each my hand to shake.

"You're such a flirt. Let's go," Cara taunts, pulling me by the arm and dragging to the dressing room. The rooms are side by side, divided by a thin wall and even though I can't see her, I can hear her ruffling around with her clothes.

"Cara, you okay over there?" I ask as I change into the first pair of dress pants and white collared shirt. This is already a no. It smells like Abuela's closet, and I look like I'm going to prep school.

"Hush and get dressed," she shouts from her side and I snicker because this is ridiculous—but who am I to say no to her?

I hear the door to the changing room open so I get out of the small stall and stand across from her showing off my outfit. Cara tries to contain her laughter but instead she nods to one of the women sitting down. A Taylor Swift song plays —hard *not* to know it's a Taylor song after Allie listens to her non-stop— and she struts down toward them, swaying her hips and walking to the beat. She's wearing white pants that don't reach her ankles with a pink top and a fluffy hat. I added that hat as a joke, but of course, Cara can pull it off. She spins around, walking in my direction, and when she reaches me, she grabs my hand and pulls me, leading me toward the space she just walked by.

"What?" I ask, wondering what the deal is.

"Model for us, hotshot, let's see your runway strut," she urges, clapping her hands to the beat of the song.

These girls want a show? Then it's show time!

I start walking down the made-up runway, exaggerating my steps as if I were a model putting on a show. When I make it to the racks of clothes, I turn around and smile. I walk back and repeat the same. Walk, pose, smile, repeat. With a loud round of applause, I make it back to the dressing room area and Cara's laughing now. So damn hard. So cute, too.

I get right next to her, bringing my hands around her back and pulling her to me. If pretending she's mine is what I'm doing today, then I'm playing along every chance that I can. "Do I get a ten?" I ask, whispering into the shell of her ear and causing her to shiver and tense under my touch.

"I don't know, why don't you ask the judges?" she manages to ask and I swear she's trying hard as hell not to be affected by me. Why am I playing with fire when I know I can't let it burn?

I let her go, turning around to see the ladies and ask, "So is that a ten?"

The shortest of the two ladies smirks and coos, "Honey, you get a twenty," making everyone laugh. Good thing this store is empty or this would be bad for business. The employees are sitting down, staring at two complete strangers making fools of themselves trying on clothes and having a fashion show.

We go back to our changing rooms, and although more laughter fills the air as we get ready to head out again, I hear a sharp, frustrated curse from Cara's dressing room, followed by a loud thud that echoes against the walls.

I frown, my heart skipping a beat. "Cara, are you okay?" I call out, straining to catch any hint of her tone over the noise.

"Yup! Perfect!" she replies too quickly, her voice a pitch higher than usual, tinged with something that doesn't quite match her words.

I get out of my own dressing room and step closer to her door, the faint sound of her shuffling and a muffled sigh reaching my ears, layered beneath the chatter from the store. It's a struggle, the kind that seems to reverberate in the air—her breath hitching as she tries to keep it together while she mumbles something under her breath.

"Are you sure? It sounds a little... chaotic in there," I say, trying to keep my voice light, but concern lingers just beneath the surface.

"Just a minor wardrobe malfunction!" she calls back, though I can hear the strain in her words, the way they crack like thin ice.

I take a deep breath. "Do you need help? I can come in." Do I want to go in there? Do I want to be close to Cara in this enclosed space? Yes. Should I? Probably not. If self-preservation was a gift, I have none.

"Nope. Absolutely not. Definitely not!" she shoots back, but I can hear her moving around again, the rustle of fabric and the scrape of something heavy hitting the floor.

"Cara," I press, leaning against the doorframe, my voice softer. "Just open up, alright? I'm right here."

There's a pause, the silence thick with unspoken words. I can almost hear her weighing her options, the tension hanging heavy in the air. Finally, she exhales slowly. "Fine! Just give me a second!" She opens the door and lets me see what's going on.

I try my hardest not to laugh, but Cara seems to be stuck in one of the dresses I grabbed for her. This particular one seems to be fitted, which means she's currently wearing a piece of fabric that is practically painted on her body except for the top part. *That* is tilted sideways halfway through her chest. She's covering her breast with one hand while the other is twisted, trying to grab the zipper.

My unreleased laughter dies on my throat because Cara's perfect body is in full display in front of me and her cheeks are rosy from the exertion of trying to get the dress on or off. I swallow hard, my eyes roaming her whole body until her words snap me out of it.

"Well don't just stand there, take this dress off!" she cries, turning around and showing the culprit. The zipper is stuck halfway through her back. It got hooked on some fabric, making it impossible to move.

"Alright, alright," I reply and when I get close to her, I bring my hands to her shoulders. Leaning down, I add, "Don't move."

Cara tenses under my touch and at the sound of my husky voice; I both love and hate how affected and responsive she is to me. The way her body reacts to my change in tone, to my subtle touches, and to my cologne. I've noticed it even when she tries to hide it. Whoever said forced proximity brings out feelings that are not usually there was right. Not for me, of course since I've been gone for this girl for over a decade but surely for her.

I bring one hand to hold the top of the dress while the other one yanks the zipper down in one quick and hard pull. Her breath hitches at the same time the zipper makes it to her tailbone, right above her perfect round ass.

Now that the dress is open, her whole smooth back is on display, showing a trail of tiny almost imperceptible freckles that lead to her neck. I get the sudden urge to trace them, and before I can stop myself, I do. I trace them softly with my knuckles and her velvety skin prickles under my touch. The air is thick around us and Cara's skin is so perfect all I want to do is run my hands all over her. My tongue all over her. I bring my gaze up to the mirror in front of us and I catch Cara's eyes on mine.

It's getting harder every day to ignore the way I feel about her. Hell, the way I've always felt. And maybe, just maybe, I should act on this—maybe get it out of my system. But I don't know how I could taste her, touch her, once and not want more. I don't drop my gaze and neither does she, her cheeks warm by the seconds the same way that my hands itch with the need to touch her. It's not a want anymore but a need.

"Everything okay over there?!" someone shouts from outside, breaking the spell we were both in.

"Yes. Just a moment," I call loudly before lowering my voice and telling Cara, "You're unstuck." My breath blows gently on her back and I can see her tense immediately backing up.

"Thanks," she murmurs as her eyes finally leave mine and she pulls the dress up to cover both her breasts.

"I'll get out of your hair," I add, stepping out of her dressing room and back to the front to wait for her and do our next runway strut.

We repeat the same process a couple more rounds until we're both happy with what we got. We leave the store wearing our derby clothes, leaving the clothes we brought in behind. We promise to come get them tomorrow but the ladies are more excited about our fun date than anything else. They said that romance isn't dead if a young couple of newlyweds could have this much fun. And damn what I wouldn't give for that statement to be true.

"Are you ready for this party?" Cara asks, looking out the taxicab window before turning to me and returning my smile. I'm not the only one. Everyone who meets her ends up smiling too. Her energy helps everyone be in a better mood.

"I am. Did you figure out who you want to be?"

"No, who do you want to be? I can adapt," she offers.

"No; thank you for entertaining me with this whole outfit experience but now, you pick, and I will adapt," I insist, and I can see her physically shrink. Seeing her shoulders sag or her brows frown when she has to make any decisions is bizarre, especially for this girl, who oozes enough self-confidence to affect others. I can't put my finger on why it bothers her, but I will figure it out. Maybe that's what should go on my bucket list for this trip—lift Cara up the same way she does for others.

"Manny, I don't know! You're the one who wants to play this game. You pick," she pleads.

I don't have time to say anything before the taxi pulls over in front of a venue filled with people and music so loud that we can hear it even from inside the car. I don't know why she wants to pretend something different—I can pretend to be hers forever.

"Thank you, sir," I say, handing him cash to pay and tip. "No need for change." I open my door, stepping out of the car and extending Cara my hand to help her step out of the car. When she does, I lower my head and whisper in her ear, "If I'm picking, then you'll be Mrs. Zabana tonight, just like the rest of the day. Would you be okay with that? With me calling you my wife tonight?"

Cara catches a breath at that, her body tensing under my touch. I look at her and see her swallow hard before she whispers, "Sure thing, Mr. Zabana." Her voice comes out shaky and she clears her throat before saying, "Now let's go party like newlyweds."

18

SHATTERED

SPIN YOU AROUND, MORGAN WALLEN

Cara

THE MUSIC IS loud and although I was expecting a lot of people, nothing could have prepared me for this. The middle of the room is crowded with people dancing shoulder to shoulder on the dance floor. Everyone is dressed in fancy clothes with perky hats and holding drinks while they dance to some upbeat song I don't recognize. Around them are high top tables, decorated with pastel tablecloths and three-tiered centerpieces holding bite-sized tea party cakes.

Manny's hand drops to my lower back as he guides me through the garden toward the bar. The bar is near the river and with the sunset's warm hues behind it. It's picture perfect. I grab my phone from the clutch Manny picked to match my outfit and snap a quick pic before placing it back in the purse.

Manny, the forever gentleman. Manny, the *"Would you be okay with me calling you my wife tonight?"* guy. Manny, the stupid hot little brother of my best friend, has my head spinning with his damn gestures, damn manners, and his damn games.

After the tipsy galore at the bourbon trail, I needed time to sober back up so I know it's not the alcohol. I know there's more to it but I'm going to need a drink soon if I'll make it out tonight without trying to do something about my feelings, *again*.

"What can I get you guys?" the bartender asks.

"My wife first," Manny says, setting his forearm on the table and turning his body to face me. It should be illegal to look as good as he does and to have perfectly curled hair in this weather. And calling me *his wife* on top of that? A crime. When he suggested this whole 'let's pretend we're married rouse,' I didn't think he meant it but he has spent the rest of the day acting like I'm his wife. I'm not going to lie, I don't hate hearing those words come out of his mouth but playing pretend could be dangerous in this situation. I can get carried away and start believing it.

"You know what I'm going to order," I coo to Manny, tracing his shirt with my finger. "A Dirty Shirley, please," I tell the bartender and Manny puts in his order too—Vodka tonic with lime.

"I never want to assume what you're in the mood for, wife." If I had a drink I would've choked on this because the innuendo behind his words is palpable and I'm literally just a girl.

"Such a gentleman, husband," I sass, smiling at him and letting my eyes roam the space before looking back at him.

"I try," Manny adds, winking at me.

We get our drinks and walk past the tables and to the dance floor. I wasn't sure if he was going to dance after the last time I danced the night away he said he only dances to Latin music. But judging by the smile on his face and the way he's swaying effortlessly to the music, I guess he's in the mood now.

He walks ahead of me, keeping his hand behind him to hold mine, guiding me through the crowd and making the way to a small opening in the middle. Passing people too enthralled with the music and lost in their own moves to notice us, he turns, spinning me around to face him while smiling at me.

"Ready to dance, sunshine?" Manny asks, moving to the beat of "Lunch" by Billie Eilish.

"Always," I reply, taking a sip of my drink and moving my hips side to side. This dress he picked flows effortlessly as I move, swirling with me, making me feel like a dancing queen.

The people around us move nearer, and Manny closes the space between us, caging me in but not touching my body. I don't blame him, though. Last time I was in his arms, I tried to kiss him and he was very clear that kissing me was not in his plans—and that's fine by me. I like his company enough and maybe kissing him would make it all weird. I don't want weird, I want easy. I want to be a priority. None of that can happen with Manny, because we all know his job will always come first and I need to get over it. If it wasn't for the amount of time we've spent together in my van, I don't think that would've even happened. I like him—a lot. He's funny and sweet but that doesn't mean that I like him like *that*. It's just a little lust because of how good he smells, because of how good his hands feel around my back, and how much I need to bust one out.

The music fades and "Spin You Around" by Morgan Wallen hits, changing from an upbeat tempo to a slower melody. He takes one more sip of his drink, before stretching his arm to set his short glass on a high top table.

"We can sit this one out," I say because I don't want him to feel pressured to slow dance with me tonight. I already dragged him to thrift store shopping and to this party. He, being the good sport he is, has not complained once but I don't want to push it.

"Do *you* want to sit?" Manny asks at the same time he grabs my hand and pulls me flush against his chest.

"Maybe?" I whisper, bringing one hand to his shoulder and keeping my left hand down, holding my barely-touched drink.

Lowering his face and brushing my ear with his soft lips, Manny says, "Your body is saying otherwise, Carita. Listen to it and dance with me. Besides, couples usually slow dance when the opportunity arises and that's what we are tonight, right?"

"I'm not sure which couple you're thinking of, or maybe just in the movies, because I had to beg for the few slow dances I got," I add.

"You're too pretty to beg, sunshine. You deserved to be spun around on the dance floor, especially to a slow song."

Our bodies are so close there's not an inch of space left between us. My head is on his chest as his hips are squared with mine. His spicy, earthy scent wraps me up, sending goosebumps all over my arms and back. When his head rests on mine, I turn my head to look up, and find his eyes are pure fire now locked on my own. And maybe what I find in his eyes is just lust, or comfort, or familiarity—but regardless, I could drown in them forever.

As we sway to the music, my body tenses against him. I'm overpowered by the slight alcohol buzz, the slow song, and his overall presence. His hand gently presses on my back before he says, "Loosen up, sunshine. People are not going to believe you're my wife if you don't relax for me."

"But I'm not really your wife, Manny," I whisper. I was hoping my voice would sound steady, but it comes out breathy instead.

I do know how to pretend. I've been pretending for years. Pretending I'm happy when I'm not. Pretending my heart is not in shambles from a long-term relationship that didn't work out. Pretending I'm strong when I'm not. Pretending all the damn time. But when I look into Manny's eyes and I see his want, or at least I think I do, I don't have to pretend I like slow dancing with my husband in the middle of a crowded room. I don't have to pretend I like him *a lot*. Because I do and the only person I'm pretending for right now is me.

He swallows; I can see his Adam's apple bobbing at the same time his hand traces slowly over my shoulder and down my back, finally resting firmly right above my ass. Manny repeats the feathery touch over my hand, past my elbow, up my arm and down my back. If he couldn't tell before how much he's affecting me, I bet he can now. There's no hiding the small bumps on my skin caused by his touch. My breath catches when he presses his fingers into my back and suddenly, I can't breathe. I need air. I blink quickly, trying to calm my heart before it skyrockets out of my body.

And when he gently whispers, "Cara," mere inches away from my face, I lose all my bearings and accidentally drop my drink, the glass breaking into a thousand pieces onto the floor—shattering the moment and my damn dignity with it.

"Holy shit, I'm so sorry," I apologize frantically, lowering my body and starting to pick up the pieces.

"Cara, stop," Manny whispers, his shoulder brushing gently against mine and his hand covering mine.

"I'm such a klutz. I'm so sorry."

"Don't pick up the glass. You'll get cut. Just stop. Let's get some help," he instructs as the people keep dancing around us like nothing happened. His touch elicits an electric charge in my body and although I'm still freaking out, his calmness is seeping into me.

"I got it," someone standing behind us says. A bartender appears holding a broom and a dustpan, ready to clean up the mess I made. My toes are wet from the splatter and I need to compose myself.

"I'm going to run to the potty." I leave without uttering another word, walking fast through the building toward the restroom. *Potty. Like I'm still at work and I'm five years old.*

19

———

PICK TRUTH

TEMPORARY INSANITY, ALEXZ JOHNSON & SAY IT, GRIFFIN PETERSON

Cara

THE BATHROOM IS QUIET, not a soul sharing the space with me. Perfect opportunity for me to have my freak out in peace. I turn the faucet on, dipping my hands under the cold water and splashing some on my face. Good thing I didn't wear makeup today or this whole situation would be even worse. *Breathe, Cara, breathe.* Is this the time when I message Allie and tell her that I almost kissed her brother... twice? Is this the time when I tell Manny to take me home instead of continuing this trip and ruining my life?

As I'm washing my hands, I notice the bracelets framing my arm. Damn it if they don't remind me to stop being a chicken shit and to tell him how I feel, but how does one even go about telling someone *Hey I think I have a crush on you* as if I was a horny high schooler? I know I promised to seize the day every time I look at them but this is uncharted territory and I don't know if I can.

I turn the water off and grab a paper towel to pat my face

dry. Refreshed and hoping I can control my words and my body, I leave the bathroom. And just outside the door, I find Manny leaning against the wall, in the ridiculous outfit that somehow makes him look like a movie star. But instead of his usual smile, he's frowning.

"What's wrong?" I ask, bringing my hand to his face on instinct. I try to pull away quickly when I realize what I'm doing, but he's faster and holds me in a gentle grip.

"Do you want to get out of here?" Manny's voice hangs in the air, laced with a tone I can't quite grasp. It's a tone I've never heard before—raw and unnamable. Usually, I'm pretty good at reading people, but this feels like a foreign language I can't decode. They say humans are complicated, hard to please, but I've always believed it's about paying attention to the little things: a subtle shift in posture, a shallow breath before a lie, the flicker of a gaze that reveals too much. Yet here I am, lost. I can't tell if he's angry, sad, or something in between. Maybe I'm losing my touch—just like I lost sight of the truth with Cole. I never saw the end coming, never realized he didn't love me as fiercely as I loved him.

"We just got here," I reply, my fingers still entwined with his, but the warmth is beginning to feel like a chain pulling me down. Not to the ground, but into a spiral because I'm three seconds away from spilling everything I'm feeling and I don't know if that's safe.

"You're uncomfortable, though," Manny observes, his eyes searching mine, desperate for clarity. "If you think this was a mistake, we can leave. It's okay, really."

"Why do you think I'm uncomfortable? Just because I dropped that glass?" I shoot back, the defensiveness creeping into my voice. I'm not just a clumsy fool; I'm an emotional mess of highs, lows, and confusion, and I can't shake the feeling that everything is spiraling out of my control.

"No, not because you dropped it, but because of how you reacted to dropping it. Let's go to the hotel or let's go sit, yeah?" he asks, wrapping my arm with his and guiding us both out of the hall.

"I don't want to go," I whisper so quietly I think he may have missed it. But he nods, letting me know he did, per usual showing me how easy it is for him to listen to me. To respect me.

We walk back outside to the boisterous crowd, but instead of joining them like before, he leads us to a set of tables in the garden near the water. The view is spectacular. Many people say they prefer things like glaciers or mountains, and they don't appreciate the natural wonders in front of them every day. For the people here, this may just be a river, but for those who have never seen a river, this is a miracle.

Manny pulls the seat out, letting me sit down before he takes the one across from me, sitting down and propping his feet up on a bar under the white metal table between us.

We sit there in silence before it's so uncomfortable I have to break it. I used to be able to sit with myself and be fine in the silence, just being in the moment. But sometimes my thoughts are my worst enemy and I'd rather fill my thoughts with joy instead. Fiddling with my bracelets, I remind myself that even if joy is not real, it's better than the alternative and sometimes you have to fake it 'til you make it, right?

"Are you excited about Nashville tomorrow?" I ask.

"Are you going to change the topic and not tell me what happened back there?" Manny retorts, nodding and pointing his chin toward the dancing area.

Because suddenly you make me nervous. Because I can't think straight when you're around. Because I shouldn't want you but I do. Desperately.

"It just slipped," I say shyly, my cheeks burning.

"Why are you hiding from me?" His frown deepens, and for

a moment, his gaze flickers away from mine, landing instead on the pretty waitress gliding toward us. She's wearing a tiny black dress that clings in all the right places, her long dark hair cascading down her body.

"Can I get you guys anything?" she asks, her smile bright, as if the world revolves around her.

"I'll take a water," I reply, trying to keep my voice steady but it wavers like my heart, which feels like it's teetering on the edge of something painful.

"Same," Manny agrees, but there's a subtle shift in his tone, a hint of annoyance I can't quite place.

"Coming right up!" she chirps, and as she puts her hand on Manny's shoulder, a flash of irrational fire ignites in my chest. What the hell?! Why does this bother me so much?

"Cara," Manny starts, leaning forward, his forearms resting on his lap, as if he's bracing for something.

"What?!" I snap, the tension in the air crackling like electricity, the fear of losing him—losing this moment—making me crazy.

"No, no, don't snap at me, sunshine. I need you to talk to me. What happened back there?"

I wanted you to kiss me. The thought is at the tip of my tongue. I fidget with the skirt of my dress and look down at my lap, trying to avoid this conversation and his stare. I feel soft hands under my chin, slightly tilting up until my eyes are on him and he has nearly closed the space between us.

"Truth or dare, Cara," he asks, serious and certain. He might be asking me to play this game but his face says the opposite. It feels like a challenge; more profound than the silly game I like to play. Isn't that what we've been doing though? Using this game as our arsenal? Playing dirty under the disguise of a dare to get the other person to do what we feel is right. His eyes lock onto mine, piercing and intense, as if he's searching for something buried deep within me.

"I don't want to play this game now. Just drop it," I add.

"You've never been one to back down from a truth or dare, right, Carita?"

My eyes roam back and forth, switching between his eyes nervously, waiting for a tell to clue me in on what's actually going on here. *Give me a sign, Manny.*

Maybe it's the universe conspiring against me or maybe it's telepathy but Manny says, "Pick truth, Cara. I want you to tell me the truth."

Shivers run down my spine and I close my eyes. My eyelashes gently brushing my cheeks and letting out a deep breath, I reply, "Truth." I hope I won't regret this but I'm so tired of hiding.

I open my eyes and find Manny's eyes on mine, looking at me with unwavering focus as he asks again, "Why did you freak out back there?"

I look at my lap, while my heart races in my chest. I'm sure he can see my hesitation and although the temperature around us is dropping, I can feel my skin flushing and heating me from the inside out. I've never backed out of a challenge so, despite my uncertainty, I say, "I thought you were going to kiss me."

"Cara, look at me," Manny commands with a firm but sweet tone. Bringing his fingers under my chin, he lifts it up so my eyes are right on him.

I do and find him frowning. He swallows hard. I can see him straining to keep his hands in his lap. "The thought of kissing me was so bad that you dropped a glass and were ready to run for the hills?"

"Well considering you rejected me the other day? Yeah. The thought of wanting you to kiss me and realizing you don't find me attractive enough for even a pity kiss in that moment I thought we were sharing, definitely had me spiraling."

I get up from the chair, following the deep shades of twilight above the river, and walk as fast as I can away from Manny. The quiet murmur of the water barely breaks through the loud music left behind. But the further I get from the party, the more I hear the rest of the world around me. Loud cars passing by on the road and over the bridge, horns in the distance, and crickets in the garden. Before I can fully distance myself from the moment, Manny reaches out and grabs my hand in his gentle but firm grip.

"Cara, stop, please," he whispers, pulling me toward him. I turn to face him and he adds, "Why on earth do you think I don't find you attractive?"

"Well, I'm not your typical conquest," I snap, my voice trembling with a mix of frustration and raw vulnerability. "You know, brunette, skinny, and leggy. So maybe I've been misreading things, and I freaked out, okay? Happy now?" My eyes burn with the intensity of my emotions, feeling like they might spill over any second.

I turn away sharply, needing to put more physical space between us, as if that might help me regain some semblance of control.

"Just... let me keep whatever dignity I have left," I beg, my voice softening but still strained. "Give me a minute, and we can leave in a few."

The air between us is thick with tension, almost suffocating. My plea hangs in the silence, and the weight of what I just said seems to linger in the space around us. Even with my back to him, I can feel it. I can feel the unspoken understanding of what's been said. *I just told him I want him and he didn't say anything back.*

"No," he finally says, and considering how I feel my whole

body warms up even more, I'm sure he can tell. Manny slides his palm into mine, his fingers gently cupping my own and then he's pulling me toward him. He grabs my hand and brings it softly to his mouth, kissing it gently before placing it over his chest, right above his heart. I can feel his heart beat fast, matching my own. The hand that previously held my hand slowly goes up my arm, over my shoulder and holds my neck.

The warmth of his hand contrasts with the cool evening air, and there's a brief, electric pause before he says, "I don't know why you would think you're not everyone's type, Cara. And I didn't kiss you the other day, yes. But not because I don't find you attractive, totally the opposite actually. I think you're the most beautiful girl I've ever seen. It was because I don't think I can kiss you once and ever stop kissing you, Carita mia."

My breath hitches with that revelation as his soft breath tickles my lips. Before I can say anything, he tightens the hold he has on me and leans in to touch his lips to mine. His kiss is gentle, as soft as the way he whispered my name while we danced. Each movement is careful and tender as if he's savoring the delicate connection between us. He takes his time kissing and caressing my lips, allowing every bit of emotion between us to build up.

He starts changing the dance between our lips from slow affection like a ballad to a faster, deeper, rhythm like a tango. Both of us explore each other's lips. The kiss shifts, growing in intensity as his hands find their way to my face, holding me in place as if I was a precious thing he didn't want to lose. The rhythm quickens, now more urgent, and the sweetness of the beginning gives way to a consuming heat, pulling a moan from my lips and that's when I remember what's happening. *I'm kissing, Manny.*

I pull back, snapping my eyes to his, and cover my mouth with my hand leaving a gasp hanging in the silence between us that was just filled with the rhythm of the dance we just had with our lips.

"Cara, stay with me. Don't get lost in that pretty little head of yours," Manny adds, taking a step forward and smiling gently at me. "And before you can ask me, this was not a pity kiss. There was never a reason for me to give you a pity kiss. I've been dying to kiss you since I can remember."

"Please, don't lie now," I scoff after dropping my hands.

"I'm not," he says softly, his hands guiding my face to his and tenderly stroking my cheek. The warmth of his touch is at odds with the absolute chaos inside me, and his eyes, filled with genuine concern, only intensify my confusion.

"Don't do this, Cara. Talk to me," he urges.

"I just want to go back to the hotel, Manny," I reply, my voice strained as I struggle to keep my emotions in check. The last thing I want right now is to figure out what just happened between us. He told me not to get lost in my head, but that ship has long since sailed, leaving me adrift in a sea of conflicted feelings.

He takes my hand, his grip firm but comforting, and I can feel the weight of Manny's gaze as he searches for some sign of where I stand. I know he's looking for a hint about how I feel after that kiss. The truth is, I can't admit that it was the best kiss I've ever had—one that left me breathless and wanting more. I can't tell him that every part of me is screaming to keep kissing him, even though I know I need to stop. My heart and mind are in a tug-of-war, and I'm caught in the middle, desperately trying to cling to whatever sense of control I have left. And to try to make sense of what the hell just happened.

20

PAIN OR PLEASURE

LLORAR, JESSE & JOY FT. MARIO DOMM & SOLA, LUIS FONSI

Manny

IF SOMEONE HAD TOLD me two weeks ago that I would be sitting in the back of an Uber, on the way to a hotel room in Kentucky with Cara Thompson sitting next to me, looking all flushed and jittery after I just kissed her senseless, I would have said they were lying. Kissing Cara has always been a pipe dream. Cara—the girl who always irradiates joy. The girl who everyone wants in their corner. The girl that would make any man feel like the luckiest guy in the world. The girl who taught me how to tie my shoes at six and how to jump off a tire swing at ten. The girl who has been driving me mad for years, and I thought never saw me as more than her friend's brother. And somehow, she kissed me back today, even after thinking I would only kiss her if I was taking pity on her.

Cara sits quietly, her fingers drumming against her knee as she keeps her gaze fixed on the blurred view. Each passing streetlight accentuates her expression and I can see the turmoil behind it. She fidgets with the hem of her jacket, lost in that beautiful brain of hers.

As the car pulls up to the hotel, I open the door and help her step out, letting her walk in front of me. Stepping into the polished wood and comforting leather scent of the lobby, I guide us toward the elevators still in silence. The elevator ride is smooth but feels endless, with the biggest elephant in the room between us. Cara's unease increases as we get closer and closer to our floor. We walk the worn carpets until we make it to our side-by-side rooms.

"This is me," she whispers, pulling her hotel key from her purse.

"I know, I'm right there," I add, pointing to my door.

Cara looks down, passing the hotel key between her fingers and avoiding my stare. I bring my hand to her chin, tilting it up so she can look at me but she doesn't. Her face is toward me but her eyes are everywhere but on me.

"Cara, bebé, don't hide from me," I sooth, getting her to look at me with the prettiest green eyes.

"I'm not hiding, I'm just... can we just forget that happened?" she asks. *Forget? She wants to forget?*

I let out a sound, a mix between a scoff and a laugh. When her eyebrows frown I say, "I'm pretty sure it will be impossible for me to forget that kiss, sunshine."

I drop her chin, fighting the urge to touch her as she lets out a sigh. "I don't have the brain capacity to deal with this right now, okay? Let's just forget it for the moment. Grab that memory, put it in your pocket, lock it, and throw away the key," she says, bringing her index finger and thumb together and twisting them in the air as if turning a key.

I take a step toward her, and she takes a step back, and we repeat the movement until her back is against the door. I bring my arm up, placing my hand next to her face, caging her in with my body and dropping my face to her forehead.

"You can try and pretend it didn't happen, Carita, but I know you know better. That kiss?" I say, smacking my lips together, my voice going deep. "That kiss was not one you easily forget. It was a kiss you crave, knowing one could never be enough. I'll let you live in denial for tonight. Tomorrow though? I want to talk," I add, before kissing her on her forehead, grabbing her hotel key from her hand and sliding her door open after the beep.

"Go ahead and try to erase that kiss from your mind, sunshine. I dare you to try. I'll be here waiting for you to tell me when you can't."

She steps backward into her room, eyes wide and breathing slowing as she closes the door without saying a word.

This is the main reason I didn't want to kiss her. Not that I haven't thought about it a million times. Even joked around with my friend that I was going to marry her someday, but the truth is that she's always been out of reach. First because I was the annoying little brother, then there was the jackass ex-boyfriend, and now, well—I've been trying to avoid this exact spiral. In what world does she think she can walk around being the complete ray of sunshine she is without people falling heads over heels for her? In what realm does she think that one can look at her beautiful rosy lips and not want to kiss them?

I walk back to my room, taking the coldest shower known to man, before lying in bed. Tomorrow will be another day. We'll talk about whatever that was and we will figure it out. I'm not expecting her to just say she wants anything serious with me—nobody really does. They're just in it for the money and maybe the way I look and since that's not Cara's vibe, I'm sure the kiss was more of a lapse in judgment. One thing's for sure, I need to make sure she understands that nothing about that kiss was pity.

Not one ounce was unwanted. I wanted it. I wanted her. I've wanted her for so long and I'm not sure how I'll let her know.

> Allielicious: What did you do?

I READ Allie's text that came through at 7:00am. I wait, expecting more info, but no others appeared. Allie usually texts in a series of explosive messages, one rapid fire after the other. This one. Came alone. No follow up, no explanation, no details.

> Me: More details would be fantastic, sis.

> Allielicious: Cara's spiraling. What did you do?

> Me: Rude of you to assume I did anything.

> Me: Have you actually talked to Cara or are you just assuming?

> Allielicious: She sent an SOS text but has not replied. Not like her. Whatever you did, fix it.

> Me: I didn't do anything!

> Allielicious: Then go check on her

> Allielicious: and tell her to call me

I go to put the phone down but as soon as Allie's texts stop, a phone call comes through. *Gusti.* I hit the green button, answering the video call and bringing my arm behind my head to rest. As I'm holding the phone I play with Cara's bracelet, just thinking about all these little moments we've lived together the past few days and how happy they've made me. Happier than I've been in years.

"Keloke, manin[1]," Gus says but I can't see him, hidden between the shadows behind the darkness in the room he's in.

"Are you done playing house yet?" he asks, a smirk dancing across his face, his tone light and playful. But what he doesn't understand is that there was nothing pretend about it for me. I wish I was playing house with her. Damn, I'm ready to buy the damn neighborhood if that would get her to stay with me forever.

"No, Gus. I'm not playing house. That's not what I'm doing here. I'm on a trip with Cara, and I'll be home in less than two weeks. I'll be back to real life."

His eyebrows raised skeptically. "Are you liking it, though?"

"Actually, I am." I pause, reflecting on how long it's been since I truly enjoyed my time away from everything. I try to remember the last moment I could be present, doing anything other than work. It dawns on me that it might have been back in high school. Even then, it was hard to focus on what I wanted because there was always something else demanding my attention—homework, extra classes, advanced Spanish in the afternoons, and even trying to keep up with my friends. Many kids hate school but for me, school was a refuge. It was the one place where my only responsibility was to finish my assignments and be done with them. High school allowed me to pursue something for myself, and while I did have to maintain good grades, it felt good to concentrate on something I genuinely wanted to do.

The bar was high at home. And having Allie as a sister didn't make it any easier. She could finish her homework on the ride home and have the rest of her evening free, while I had to study for hours to keep up. I worked hard for my grades, which

---

1. It's a colloquial way of saying Hi brother in the Dominican Republic

taught me a lot about self-discipline and perseverance. However, it also made schoolwork feel like a chore, like something else on my to do list to please my parents. At school though? I thrived.

"You enjoy spending time there?" I want to answer his question honestly, but just then, a flash of movement catches my eye behind him. He frowns, noticing something on his phone, and immediately mutters, "Shit."

"Have some company?" I tease. It's unusual for him to have people over, especially this early in the morning but he also seems to be somewhere else, not at his main home. He rarely has girls sleepover; he's more of a casual dater, like me I suppose.

"Yeah, let me call you back, okay? Good luck with the outdoors and... whatever." He hangs up the phone abruptly, leaving me alone with my thoughts.

The day is bright ahead of me. I change into workout clothes, leave the hotel room, and hit the gym. I haven't exercised since the trip began, which isn't a big deal with how much hiking and walking we've done. I still feel restless and the best way to clear my head is sweating. Especially since I can't stop thinking about Cara and how I'm going to resist kissing her again—when I can't stop remembering how her lips felt against mine and how she fit perfectly in my arms.

THE RUN WAS EXACTLY what I needed. There's nothing like listening to my favorite music while getting my heart rate up. I told Cara I'd check with her around ten, since she mentioned wanting to sleep in. I want to respect her space, but my mind is unraveling wondering what is going on in her head. I know she's probably spiraling about our kiss and I do need to bring it up at some point so Allie doesn't kill me. She might be losing it, but I'm still trying to wrap my head around the fact that she kissed me. She wanted to kiss *me*.

I'm giddy at the possibility of this becoming more—or at least, of her letting me in her heart a little bit more. After having that conversation with both Allie and Gus, I actually realize how much I'm enjoying this trip and how I think about work less and less every day. That's never been possible before and I kind of like it—a lot. There are so many memories of good times but very little are actually in adulthood, most of them are from when I was young and coincidentally, Cara is in most of them too.

I can't shake the memory of the first time Cara showed me her heart. I was five and she was seven, and we were running around inside the house during one of our family vacations. Our families stayed in touch over the years, often vacationing together, whether at busy amusement parks or quiet beach houses. My favorite memories were the times we spent at the lake, playing games, and enjoying family time. There was this one beach house I vividly remember because it was the first time I felt seen and I was just a little boy. Our moms set up an ice cream bar at the kitchen table and yelled for us to come inside.

Cara had been swimming for what felt like hours, and so was I, but at five years old, who could keep track of time? I bumped into her when she ran inside the house, and fell to the ground, trying my hardest not to cry. My parents had always told me to be tough, not to cry—to be a rock so I kept repeating those words over and over in my head.

Cara, however, looked at me like I was a fragile little thing. She looked so apologetic, and said, "Oh no! I'm so sorry. Are you okay?" She gave me a big hug and when I sniffled, she told me, "It's okay to cry if I hurt you or scared you. It's okay, Manny."

Her angelic voice and the sincerity of her concern left an imprint on my heart.

We were just kids, and it was an accident, but that moment marked the beginning of something special. That entire interaction helped me understand that it was okay to have big feelings and to express them if needed. I could tell even then that I was drawn to her glow, and I always knew that my life would be intertwined with hers in some way. Even if it was from afar as I watched her glow. Except now I'm not sure she was actually as happy as she let on.

I walk up the stairs, bypassing the elevator entirely, still needing the physical effort to ground myself. Making my way up, I mentally prepared to check on her—wondering if she needs anything, if she's eaten today, and to check on our schedule for the rest of the day.

My skin is slick with sweat, and I wipe my forehead as I approach Cara's door. Just as I raise my hand to knock, I hesitate. I hear faint sounds from inside. At first I think she's hurt but then I hear it—a soft, unmistakable moan. My heart races, and I can't help but feel like that sound is rooted deep within my soul. It's not a sound of pain but one of pleasure, and I know it's wrong to stand out here, listening to whatever is unfolding behind that door.

Yet, a primal part of me wonders—is she touching herself, lost in thoughts of me? Is she thinking about what could've happened last night? Is she thinking about our kiss? The idea sends a jolt through me, and my entire body reacts to those sweet sounds cementing the fact that we're both so in tune with her, my dick and I of course. I stand frozen in place, caught between wanting to respect her privacy and the overwhelming urge to know what is happening inside. But before I can hear more, I make myself walk away and into my room to take another cold shower and leave her alone in her private moment.

21

LIKE A MILLION BUCKS

RECKLESS DRIVING, LIZZY MCALPINE FT. BEN KESSLER

Cara

YESTERDAY IS A DAMN BLUR. From the bourbon tasting and people giving Manny and me compliments about our relationship, to the party, the closeness between us, and the kiss. The perfect kiss. I'm a good kisser, or I thought I was, but *that* kiss is making me question if I've ever even been kissed right my whole life. I never knew a kiss could not only touch your lips but reach your soul. Set your senses to overdrive and give you sensations only described in movies. Just one kiss and I'll never be the same again. Where's the new bracelet for that? The one that will help me remind me of that feeling.

My mind has been in overdrive since last night, reading between the lines and overthinking all the scenarios. All the what-ifs dancing in my mind and my body—well, my damn body. The slightest touch from Manny and my skin is on fire. He looks at me with his stupid smile and his backward hat, and I get goosebumps. And his damn cologne or soap or whatever it is that makes him smell spicy, woodsy and manly has me sizzling.

Add the kiss to the equation and my body doesn't know what to do.

We're supposed to get ready to go to Nashville. My number one stop on this trip. I can't wait to dance my heart out and to listen to live music for days on end. We rented a B&B because we wanted to take our time. I've been so excited to finally get there, but instead of rushing out the door to leave, I'm here sitting on my hotel bed, wrapped in a towel, hot and bothered. My body is begging for relief and I might just give in. I think I have to if I want any chance at enjoying my day without jumping on Manny the minute I see him.

I search my bag for the beige pouch I keep at the bottom. A little pouch that holds a girl's best friend. This one, particularly, is my favorite. It's small and pink but damn powerful. I got it because it's supposed to be amazing for couples but when I brought it up with Cole, he got all defensive and asked me if his dick wasn't enough—so I hid it. I'm also not going to bring a toy out with random hookups or with guys after a date or two, so I mostly use it by myself and I fucking love it. It has a small part that sits on my clit while I reach the perfect spot. I get goosebumps just by thinking about how good I'm about to feel.

I lay back on the bed, unwrapping the towel and touching my pebbled nipples. I close my eyes and get lost in the feel of my cold hands against them. The contrast of the warmth of my breasts against the chill of my fingers sends shivers down my spine. I touch one softly, drawing circles against my skin with one hand and lowering my other until I reach the spot that has been dying for attention. I rest my feet on the edge of the bed, dropping my knees. My fingers trace between my folds; sliding through them, I touch my needy clit which is ready to be teased. I circle it a few times while I pinch my nipple and moan, filling the room with the most indecent sounds. Sounds of pleasure and satisfaction; what better sounds are there? I can feel my arousal building, so I grab the vibrator, turn it on and slide it in gently, adjusting until it hits the right spot.

"Jesus," I whisper to no one, but this feels so good, I can't keep in words or sounds. I bite my lip, at the same time that I squeeze around the toy. I squeeze as I rock my pelvis in circles as I let the pressure and the vibrations touch my most sensitive parts and reach all my pleasure points. I continue to motion, chasing the high. I know it won't take long because I've been on the edge for far too long.

After licking my lips and letting out a guttural moan, I explode around the toy, squeezing it tightly with my inner muscles and turning my face on the bed, screaming a loud and borderline obscene *yes*. I let myself come down from the high, shaking my head at the fact that I just made myself come so fucking hard thinking about Manny's face between my legs. *I'm in so much trouble.*

I CLEAN UP, put some makeup on, and play country music so I can get in the groove. I start swaying as I sing with Kelsea Ballerini, putting on jean shorts and a loose spaghetti-strap shirt. I decide to go braless because it's too damn hot for anything else and grab my tennis shoes. Space buns pin up the front of my hair with the rest in messy waves down my back and when I look at myself in the mirror, I feel like a million bucks. I'm hot and I just orgasmed, nothing can sour my mood today. I just have to avoid talking about the kiss and everything will be fine.

I walk toward the door and when I pull it open, Manny's standing there, coffee in hand with troubled eyes. He has dark jeans on and a button-down olive green shirt that makes his features pop. His skin practically glows in contrast with the color of the shirt and his soft curls are unruly as if he passed his hand through them.

"Well, hello, Manny. Personal space?" I ask, trying to go past him but he keeps staring at me, so hard I look down to make sure I did actually put clothes on and I'm not out here embarrassing myself. "Mmmm, hello?"

He swallows, his Adam's apple bobbing down and he hands me the coffee. "Here, cafecito para ti[1]."

"Well thank you, kind sir. Did you get your milk in yours?" Manny has a perfect ratio to the way he likes to take his coffee. A shit ton of the darkest roast you can find and slowly poured cold milk into it. It's so bizarre the way he takes it, so I'm always wondering if when he goes to order coffee, he explains exactly how he likes it.

"Nah, but a latte is the closest thing, you know?" he replies, grabbing my suitcase and walking toward the elevator.

"I can carry my own suitcase," I insist, trying to reclaim a bit of independence and my bearings. I underestimated how much he would affect me after last night and what I just did in my room at the thought of him.

"Do I need to say it again?" Manny's tone is firm yet playful, leaving the rest of the statement hanging like an unfinished thought. I don't mind his chivalry—there's something comforting about being around someone who genuinely cares about my well-being. But I also feel the weight of my thoughts— the fine line between allowing him to be a gentleman and fearing that I might never find someone who truly wants to be this way with me. Finding someone who will let me make the calls on how I want to spend my time and what I want to be doing together instead of what *he* wants to do all the time.

---

1.   a little coffee for you

Someone who knows I *can* do hard things but who still wants to make my life easier, even if just by bringing me afternoon coffee or dragging my suitcase down to the bus.

I'd been with plenty of men over the years, especially during those breaks between Cole. I'd focused so much on having fun and enjoying life that dating had taken a backseat. Casual encounters filled the gaps, but they never lasted. I sabotaged myself, always searching for something serious while convincing myself I was okay with something fleeting. It was a cycle that had gone on for a decade, with both of us drifting in and out of each other's lives like the tide, never quite finding solid ground. But I want solid ground; I just thought Cole was going to give it to me someday.

Allie and Roe often remind me that I'm too good for him. I made excuses for his behavior in my mind, convincing myself I didn't deserve better or that *he* was the best I would ever get. Maybe I'm not mature enough or I'm too volatile. But deep down, I know there are others out there searching for someone like me, someone to settle down with. Yet, here I am, feeling like just one of the "bros," destined to remain alone forever.

As the elevator doors slide open, I take a deep breath, determined to shake off the heavy thoughts and enjoy the rest of this trip. I just have to remind myself that I am worth more than the cycles I keep repeating and that *my* someone is out there. Even if I haven't found him yet. I don't want to waste more moments without turning them into memories. In the meantime, I'll keep pretending nothing happened with Manny and maybe the feeling that that person might be him will go away.

22

YOU CAN BE RAIN

LET EM GO, MATT HANSEN

Manny

WE'RE STUCK IN TRAFFIC. We've been stuck in traffic for the past two hours. We ate everything we had and now we're counting the minutes until we get to Nashville. Cara took a nap at some point but now she's restless in the passenger seat. She's moving, reading, singing, dancing, and

everything in between. She has gotten calls from what feels like all of Baker Oaks. Some on FaceTime, some voice messages, and some calls. She talked to Allie, Roe, and Natalie for what felt like an eternity and they just kept going back and forth calling each other names for not being in Nashville together. It was both amusing and disturbing. As soon as she hung up the phone with them, Cara's easy smile turned sour as she whispered to me how much she wished they were here with her.

I, on the other hand, turned off my phone. Not having signal on my phone for a day back in Kentucky and completely forgetting about work while I spent time with her on the Bourbon Trail had me itching for more time disconnected from everything. I texted Gus to let him know, and I'm hoping for the best. He said, 'fucking finally' and that was it. If Zabana Enterprises is truly well-run, then it can survive a few days without me checking in. Or at least I hope so.

The view entering Tennessee shifted seamlessly from flat land to now a tapestry of green hills and forested areas, giving way to the urban sprawl as we approach the city. The closer we get to Nashville, the more buildings and traffic we encounter. Other than GPS indicating we're close, the cityscape with the skylines and tall buildings emerge on the horizon. Cara gets another call, and after the loud ringtone, she answers with a perky hello.

"My girl," the deep voice on the phone says and Cara's whole face lights up. ¿Quién coño le dice *my* girl?[1] Tightening my hands on the steering wheel, I wait for her to continue the conversation because the irrational side of my brain is going full Neanderthal with uncalled jealousy right now.

"Alex! Very soon you won't be able to call me *your girl* anymore, big guy," she replies, still smiling at the phone.

"You'll always be my girl, Carabear. Livie's fine with that, right baby?"

"One hundred percent! I don't want that title. Calling me Liv, and soon enough calling me your wife, is enough for me. Cara earned her title dealing with all of you stupid asses," a girl says in between laughs.

"How's the wedding coming along? Next week you guys

---

1. Who the hell calls her his girl?

will say forever. I'm pumped for you both," Cara says softly. You can hear the pride in her voice as she shares those words.

I continue driving, pretending I'm not overly aware of their conversation. Instead I take notice of the contrast between the natural beauty of the countryside and the city as we make an entrance into the heart of Nashville.

"It's going well, I think. Livie and her parents have done most of it. I was only given a few tasks and that's why I'm calling, actually," this guy Alex says. "Two things—I need to confirm if you'll have a plus one, and...," he pauses, "Cole and Tasha are coming together for the wedding. I know you and everyone knows they're together but I wanted to give you a heads up. We already shifted tables so at least you won't be sitting together. I'm sorry, girl."

"Don't be sorry, Alex. You have nothing to apologize for," Cara insists but her once-cheerful voice now sounds down, almost eerie. I look her way and she forces a smile. It doesn't reach her eyes but she continues talking. "They're both your friends, I would feel weird if you didn't invite them." She's reassuring him but her whole demeanor has changed. Her smile is smaller. Her shoulders sag. Her light is dimmer.

"I'm sorry, this whole situation is so shitty. He was so shitty to you and I'm sorry."

"Again, not your fault. It *is* shitty but there's not much we can do. Your friendship means more to me than being uncomfortable around them."

"I don't know what we did to deserve your friendship but thanks for not making this whole thing harder," he says and her face softens for the first time since he brought up that jerk. "What about the plus one?"

"Just me and my big personality," Cara replies. I watch her eyes, careful not to crash this bus into another car and when she finds mine, I point at her phone and mouth *mute it*, hoping she understands.

Her eyebrows frown but she looks back down and says, "Give me a sec, Alex." She taps her phone and looks at me before asking sharply, "What?!"

"I can go with you to the wedding," I offer, turning left on the road as the GPS tells me to.

"No, I don't need a pity date," she snaps, tilting her phone down so Alex can't see her face. *Pity*, there's that word again. As if I'm not already hot at the thought of her going by herself. Then add the fact that the jerk is going to be there with the new girlfriend, fiancée, or whatever she is; but if I tell her that right now, she'll fuss and say no so I need to play my cards right.

"I'm going to be there either way and this way I don't stay in the room like a loser," I reply, "You'd be doing *me* a favor."

Cara shakes her head. I know she doesn't really want me there, but maybe it's not that she doesn't and more that she thinks she's bothering me. But I know the one thing she can't refuse is when someone asks for help. I hate using her weakness against her but in this case, I will. "I haven't asked for anything on this whole trip, Cara. Please, let me come party with you. Plus, I'll see Jake and we can hang out while you and Allie dance the night away."

We pull up to a quaint house nestled in a tree-lined neighborhood. The front yard is well-maintained with two small flower beds brimming with colorful blooms of wildflowers. The marked parking spot, framed by shrubs and flowers surrounds us now and after shifting the bus to park I ask, "Please, Carita?"

Her features soften as she lets out a sigh and picks her phone back up, tapping the screen and saying, "Sorry about that. Is it too late to add a plus one?"

I throw my fist in the air like I won a trophy and she shakes her head, shooting daggers my way with her eyes.

"Not at all. Does this person have a name?"

"Manuel Zabana. I gotta go, though. See you next week!" Cara shouts and hangs up the phone.

"I better go shine my dancing shoes," I add, laughing and pretending to dance Salsa. Funny Manny is the only thing that's left if I won't bring the kiss up. She clearly regretted it, or at least that's the lie she's telling herself but we both know that's not the case.

"You have dancing shoes?" she asks and I can tell she's nervous or sad or anxious. Maybe a combination of the three but definitely not the upbeat Cara I'm used to. The more we're together on this trip, the more I realize that she may show everyone her funny, sweet, kind, happy side but that's not what fills her mind. She has these moments when I've seen glimpses of her life when she feels other things but she hides them. She hides her true feelings and it breaks my heart. It tears it apart because I know that she's the first to encourage her friends and family to be honest, to feel, to talk about what they're going through, yet she hides it all behind the 'happy' mask.

If there's one thing I want her to get out of this trip, of the week we have left together, is that she should trust her people into showing them what she's feeling. She doesn't have to show herself as flawlessly composed all the time to be who she is.

"That was a joke. A way to get you to relax and stop over-thinking it, okay?" I reach for a strand of her hair that fell out of her bun and twist it around it, tucking it into her hair tie and dropping the back of my fingers to caress her cheek. She closes her eyes, her eyelashes kissing the top of her cheeks, and lets out a breath. I give her time. Time to figure out what she wants to say or if she even wants to say anything at all. I give her time to just be. Be with herself and her feelings. Be in this space, without feeling like she needs to be anywhere else, like she needs to be something else.

"It's okay to let it all out," I whisper, granting her the permission she feels like she needs. She lets a breath out with a slight shake and when she opens her beautiful eyes, I can see they're full of tears.

She blinks rapidly, once, twice, and then the first teardrop falls. She drops her face into her hands and whispers, "God, I'm so sorry."

"Hey, hey, hey," I soothe, squeezing her shoulder gently. "There's nothing for you to be sorry about. Let yourself feel it, whatever it is that you're feeling, Cara."

"I'm sorry... I didn't mean to start crying. I just feel so stupid right now," she mumbles, wiping her eyes with the palm of her hands.

"Cara, bebé, please stop apologizing." Can't she see that I would give every single dollar I have and more to be her soft place to land?

She looks up, her eyes swollen and red, and a soft smile appears on her face. "It's okay, I'll be fine. Let's go inside. It's late and I'm hungry," she says quickly, her voice still trembling.

I shake my head, offering her a reassuring smile and adding, "You don't have to apologize for *feeling*, and you sure as hell don't have to apologize for letting me see this part of you. You don't have to hide from me and if you want to talk I'm here. I really mean that."

"What if I don't want to talk about it?" she asks.

"Then we don't have to. But the offer still stands, I'm here if you do want to and sometimes, letting it out is all you need. When was the last time you shared what you were truly feeling?" I squeeze her hand, gently rubbing the top of her soft hand.

Cara lets out a breath, placing her head back onto the pink seat and closing her eyes. There's no sound other than the soft melody of the background music and Cara's soft sniffles.

"You'll think I'm pathetic," she says softly, still with her eyes closed.

"Never, Cara, never," I remind her as I squeeze her hand one more time.

"I just hate the whole situation, you know? Our friend group is in such a tough place with Tasha and Cole's engagement. Everyone's walking on eggshells around me and Allie. Allie isn't close with most of them, so it might be easier for her, or at least I hope it is. But these are my people, Manny. I grew up with Nick, Alex, Jake, and Cole. Natalie too. Tasha joined our group later, but the rest of us go way back. They're like my siblings as much as they are my friends. And yeah, we all thought I'd end up marrying Cole one day, except Cole himself. But now he's marrying Tasha? Who also used to be with Jake? It's all just too much. The icing on the cake is that all of this is happening now when we're all going to be forced to be together. I knew it was coming, but Alex's call made it all feel so real. I think I got overwhelmed and that's why I started crying, but I'm okay now. I promise."

"Hey, it's okay. You don't have to apologize for feeling this way. I can see how heavy all of this is on you. It's completely normal to be overwhelmed and to cry. It's a lot to process," I reply. "But Cara, you don't have to pretend to be okay with any of it. The situation it's all fucked up. It's okay to be pissed or sad or whatever you want to feel," I add, trying to reassure her with my eyes but my voice is betraying me because my tone is clipped as all I want to do is rip his head off.

Cara looks down at her lap, her voice barely above a whisper. "I just don't want to be a burden. I've already cried over him enough and everyone's already on edge about this. I'm done bringing everyone else around me down."

I shake my head and add, "You're not a burden. And also, I don't think *you* even know the light that you are in everyone's life. You don't bring people down, you lift them up but sometimes, you need to let others do the same for you. We all need rain sometimes."

"What? What do you mean?"

"You're everyone's sunshine, Cara. Pure, happy, warm. But sometimes we all need rain, and you can be that too. Show others that you *are* both." I smile softly again, not dropping her eyes and getting closer to her. In these moments, these little pockets of time, I feel like nothing exists but us. I feel like she's looking at me with more than just friendship but want or adoration. I feel like maybe she could see me as more, even if just for this trip, even if just for this moment.

"Everyone sees rain as a bad thing, me included sometimes, but rain helps things grow. Rain can cleanse. Rain can restart a cycle. What if we didn't have rain? We wouldn't even know we needed the sun. Bask in both, Carita. Be both."

"Like a bracelet moment," she whispers. I let the time pass so hopefully she can sense that I'm giving her the time she needs. I want her to share whatever she feels like sharing and I'm letting the sound be as loud as it can be right now. *Talk to me, Carita. Trust in me.* Then she continues, "I started collecting these because of Ollie, a student who passed away a few years ago. He was pure sunshine, Manny. He cheered everyone on and he collected his hospital bands as bracelets because he said each one reminded him he had another day to live."

My throat is dry at this confession, at her sharing the reality of the bracelets. She told me they reminded her to slow down, but knowing *why* is deeper than I thought. My heart aches at the thought of what the kid went through.

"He used to walk around handing out regular bracelets to everyone when they shared a good moment. He gave me this one," she says, showing me a thin orange bracelet she rarely takes off. "He gave it to me the day he learned how to tie his shoes. Funny how that's such an everyday task and I didn't think anything of it when he asked me to teach him. But to him, that was such a win. He passed away in his sleep a few months after that and to be honest, my life has never been the same. It changed my perspective on how I see things, I just need to remind myself that all moments are worth keeping, even the hard ones."

"We learn from them all," I agree, thinking about all the moments in this trip I've loved and how they'll stay with me forever. Cara, unknowingly, is carrying on with this kid's legacy, helping people like me slow down and appreciate it all.

She drops her gaze, and I take advantage of the moment and press a gentle kiss on her forehead. "We love the sun but we need the rain too. You carry everyone else's highs and lows. You need someone to help you carry yours, but you have to let them see it, Carita."

Slowly, she lifts her eyes to meet mine. The redness still lingers, but there's a softness there now. "Thanks. I guess I'm just hungry, and that's not helping."

I let out a soft laugh, narrowing my eyes playfully. "How about we find something to eat soon? A little food will help for sure."

Her lips curl into a tentative smile. "That sounds good. Dinner and drinks?"

"The perfect plan."

23

WEAR THE HAT

ONE OF THEM GIRLS, LEE BRICE

Manny

"COME ON!" Cara shouts over the pounding music, tugging at my hand as I sit on the wooden barstool. The dim, neon-lit bar in Nashville pulses with energy; the floor is packed with people dancing, their laughter mingling with the loud beats of country tunes. Her voice cuts through the noise, "Come dance with me, please! I love this song!"

Cara's back to her usual self—a whirlwind bubble of energy. She's been on the dance floor for the past hour with me in tow. She hasn't stopped dancing for more than a few seconds to drink water and then goes back to it. Her blonde hair bounces with every movement, reflecting the strobe lights that dance around the room. If excitement was a person, it would be her, moving with a rhythm that seems to flow effortlessly from one song to the next. She knows more songs than anyone I've ever met and has been dancing non-stop. I've tried to keep up, but I'm drained and need a break. I'm not made of endless energy.

"Okay, I'll dance with you again, but right now, I need to

rest. I need to hydrate a bit, too. We'll both be done by the end of the night if we keep this up and someone has to drive us home." Today has been a long day and we keep adding drinks and non-stop moves, making us more tired than you'd think.

Cara pouts, her lips curving into a mischievous grin. "Where's the fun in that? Where's the fun Manny from the other day? The 'won't you pretend to be my wife' Manny?"

Her tone is playful, and I know she's just goofing around, calling me on my bullshit. Probably just high on music as she says she gets when she listens to too many of her favorite songs in a row. Still, there's something about the way those words sound coming from her that I can't quite ignore.

"He's right here, still having fun, but he needs a minute," I say, lowering her cowgirl hat with my index finger and adding, "Let's sit this song out, and I'll dance with you again on the next one, okay? But you can go dance your little heart out if you want."

"Fine," Cara says, adjusting her hat and pulling her hair back onto her shoulders. With a dramatic turn, she stomps away in her pink cowgirl boots, her heels clicking against the wooden floor. When she said she wanted Nashville's country scene, I didn't realize she meant it so literally. She stepped out of the B&B room tonight in sparkly pink country boots, the tiniest white dress I've ever seen, the hem touching right where her ass ends and her legs begin. If she bends forward you can see the edge of her ass cheeks and paired with the lacy bottom and the cleavage on top, the dress leaves little to the imagination. Her pink cowgirl hat and bouncy curls make her look like a real-life cowgirl Barbie. My gaze lingers on her, unable to ignore how incredibly hot she looks. Her energetic movements keep drawing not only my attention but everyone else's too and I'm still shocked she doesn't see that.

I still can't believe she doesn't see that she commands every space she walks into, and she lights up the room with her smile. *Her smile.* By far my favorite part of her, and tonight, she has the biggest smile I've seen on her in days. It's as if her soul is shining through her smile and we can all see that she's irradiating happiness.

I'm not sure if it's the music, the food, the drinks, or the lively crowd around her that's making her smile more tonight. Maybe it's the fact that she's in a place she's been wanting to visit for long. Or maybe it's that she needed to cry and let it all out and now she feels better. Maybe it's a combination of it all. But a little voice inside of me tells me maybe she's hiding behind that pretty smile and that she's just plastering joy for everyone to see while she dies a little inside. Whatever it is, I'm going to figure it out. If it's the first, then I'm damn happy she's finding joy in this trip but if it's the latter, I'm going to do everything in my power to make sure that smile becomes a genuine one. I will make sure every damn moment for the rest of this trip is worth a new bracelet for her.

"Ready for another one?" the bartender asks, pulling me from my thoughts. I didn't even notice her come near me, too captivated by Cara's movements and laughter.

"I'll take another one and two waters," I say. Cara will definitely need some after she's done dancing. My eyes roam back to her and it's like I can hear her laugh even above all the noise.

"You're lucky. Not only is she fucking hot, respectfully, she's the life of the party here. I wouldn't leave her dancing alone for long or someone will try to sweep her off her feet," the bartender comments as she disappears behind the bar before I can respond.

She's not mine, I want to tell her, but I can't quite convince myself to say the words. It's been so hard listening to everyone who thinks we're together, that we've been together for a long time. They tell us how good we look together. I would like nothing more than for that to be reality, but it wouldn't be fair to her. There's nothing I can bring to the table that she doesn't already have.

Yes, I have money but she doesn't care about that, never has. Her family and mine have been friends for a long time. Her parents might not have the money my family does but they have always worked hard to earn what they have. She's not like all of those girls who chase me down so they can climb the social ladder or to get the latest designer bag. I have my business, but Cara was born to be a teacher and she loves it. I don't think she'll ever want to stop teaching. I could say I could give her a sister, but she already has one, and my own sister is like a sister to her, too. I could show her a good time but that's not even true. Cara's the life of the party all on her own. She also deserves time. She deserves to be someone's priority and if I give up time at work, which I clearly would for her, would she even consider me?

I watch as some guy walks over to her, grabs her hand, and twirls her around, spinning her in his arms. As they dance to the beat of the honky-tonk music, her smile is bright so I know she's not uncomfortable, or at least not from what I can see. I grab my drink and take the last sip while I keep watching. They move in perfect sync, following a two-step rhythm she picks up on almost instinctively. Almost as if she knew the dance before he pulled her to him. They dance so closely, and I can't help but notice how her head tilts toward him, as if on the verge of a kiss.

I can feel my ears burning as I grip my whiskey glass tightly, nearly shattering it in my frustration. I remind myself that she's not mine and she's free to do as she pleases. But then, just two days ago, she kissed me. She. Kissed. Me. And then, she didn't talk about it again, killing me inside. The memory lingers, I find it hard to forget. I can't shake it off, especially since she has treated me exactly the same as before, as though nothing ever happened between us. I want to take the damn bracelet off and show it to her, to remind her how she told me to live in the moment. To stop and see the wonder. But what about her? Is she stopping to take it all in? To let herself feel it all? Because if she was, she would let herself get lost in me. At least I hope she will.

I told *her* to let me know when she couldn't get over the kiss but, in the meantime, I'm the one still reeling from it. I'm the one on edge all the damn time from that one kiss. I'm the one who hasn't forgotten and I might be in big trouble. Because her hat falls on the ground and when he goes to pick it up and tries to put it on his head, I immediately get up from the stool and stride toward them, quickly.

Her back tenses as soon as she realizes he's not giving the hat back. Her arms are crossed in front of her and I can't tell if she's saying anything. I make it right in time to hear him say, "Wear the hat, ride the cowboy. Let me put it on, sweetheart, so you can take it from me and we can get out of here."

"I wouldn't put that hat on your head if I were you," I snap. Cara turns immediately to face me with drawn eyebrows.

"Why? I was dancing with her first, jackass. Besides, she's not stopping me, right sweetheart?" he says, with a smirk on his face that I want to erase with my fist.

"You saw an opportunity to get her alone and took it. And don't call her sweetheart," I bite back.

"I'm perfectly capable of handling myself." Cara stomps on her feet and narrows her eyes at me.

"Do you want this ass to put your hat on, Cara?" I ask, ignoring the dude standing next to me, hat still in his hand.

He leans in closer, a mocking glint in his eyes. "My name is Dale, not ass. Why don't you say that to my face though? Ask *me* if I want to put the hat on. This is a bar, not a courtroom, and it seems to me the lady was having a good time and I'm here to have fun, too. Looks like the problem is you, so if you can't handle that, maybe you should back off."

Cara's frustration boils over. I can see it in the way her cheeks flush, her arms fly up to her chest crossing over it and her eyes narrow. Oh, she's pissed. She steps between us, lowering her hands to her hips.

"Enough! I'm not some prize for the two of you to fight over. Just let it go and give me my damn hat." She pulls the hat away from him and storms out of the bar.

"Cara, wait!" I shout, barely keeping pace as we burst out of the wooden double doors and into the humid, bustling street. The air is thick with the scent of street food and exhaust, but Cara's focus is unwavering. Her hips sway with urgency as she turns left into a narrow alley, away from the chaos of the crowded avenue. Horns sound in the background as the music fades from the different bars.

"Cara, por favor, slow down." My voice is a broken plea as I walk as fast as I can behind her, trying to catch them, but she doesn't slow. Her heels echo faintly but sharply on the ground as she seems fuming and more annoyed the further away she walks from me. Finally, she stops, her shoulders heaving with frustration. With a dramatic movement, she puts on her hat and spins around, her eyes blazing with anger.

"What the fuck was that?!" she shouts, her voice bouncing off the alley's walls. Her hands fly to her hips in an exasperated gesture. "You're giving me mixed signals, and I can't keep up with this! One minute you're all sweet and charming, and the next you're treating me like a little sister."

I close the distance between us, my own frustration boiling over. "Cara, it's not like that. I didn't mean to—"

"Not like what?" she interrupts, her voice rising. She's standing so close now that I can feel the heat radiating off her. Her eyes are locked onto mine, and there's a raw intensity in her gaze. "One minute you're kissing me and touching me gently, calling me bebé and shit, and the other you're just winking and smiling at everything that crosses in front of you. But then when someone else tries to get close to me, then you turn all caveman on me. Protective like I am ten and need my big bro to come and set a boundary."

"It's not protecting you like a brother, Cara," I add between clenched teeth.

"Then what, Manny? You clearly don't want me, but God forbid I want someone else."

"You wanted him, Cara?" I ask, getting even closer to her and letting my words hang in the air between us, mingling with the stale scent of the alley. "Because wear the hat—ride the cowboy, right? That's what he said... is that what you want? To go home with him?" Her breath intertwines with mine, and I can see her swallowing hard. Whatever this emotion she's feeling is, anger, frustration, *lust,* is palpable, fueling a sudden, electric tension between us.

Her back is against the wall now and I'm caging her in with my hands right next to her face. "I got all caveman on you like you said not because I think you're a sister to me, Cara." I pound my fist on the wall and bring her hand to my chest. "You feel that? That's my heart about to come out of my chest because I was fucking jealous, not because I thought you needed saving. I've been dying to kiss you again every second of every minute of every hour since our first kiss. I told you I had never kissed you before because I knew that once I had a taste of you, it wouldn't be enough. And I was right. I want more, Cara. I need more."

"Manny," she whispers and I close the space between us, crashing my lips to hers. This kiss is fierce and demanding. This kiss is urgent and filled with all the emotions we've been dancing around. The rough brick feels cool against my hand, a stark contrast to the heat of the kiss but if I bring my hands down to her body, I won't be able to stop myself from touching it all. She arches her back, pressing her breasts against my shirt and all I can think is fuck it all. Fuck all restraints and all inhibitions. If I want her, I need to let her know.

My hand glides down her back and under her ass, lifting her slightly and she wraps her legs around me. I press her hard against the wall, biting her lower lip, and licking it before continuing to kiss her. And *that* I do. I kiss her. I kiss her until time has lost all its meaning and everything else ceases to exist. I kiss her until I can't breathe anymore and the only air I'm breathing is hers. I kiss her until there's not two of us anymore but one tangled mess of each other.

Our breath is ragged as we break apart, our foreheads resting against each other's with the hat forgotten. The alley is silent now, or at least it feels that way, because right now all I can hear is her soft breaths and all I can see is her green eyes looking at me. Everything else fades away.

24

───────

A LITTLE TASTE

COLD WAR, CAUTIOUS CLAY

Cara

"MANNY," I whisper, my voice trembling completely out of breath. His lips are so close that I can still taste the whiskey and spice lingering on them.

His hand frames my face, while the other rests possessively on my hip. I look down and realize my legs are wrapped around his waist, and he's holding me securely because apparently, I climbed him like a tree during our kiss. I was so lost in that perfect moment that I didn't even notice.

"Yes, Carita?" he murmurs, his eyes closed as he gently caresses my cheek.

"Put me down," I manage to say. He complies, easing me back to the ground. I close my eyes and exhale deeply, my hands coming to rest on his chest. As I steady myself, my mind reels with everything that's happened in the past ten minutes—or maybe even the last hour. I keep replaying how I was blissfully lost in the moment with Manny until that other jerk tried to interfere. Now, here I am, caught between confusion and clarity. It's not about that idiot anymore; it's about what's happening between Manny and me. There's something undeniably real here, and I can't keep ignoring it.

"Why did you kiss me?" I ask, my voice trembling despite my best efforts to stay cool, calm and collected. My heart races as I glance up at Manny, unsure of what to expect but hoping to God he wants me as bad as I want him.

"Because I've been dying to kiss you nearly my whole life," Manny replies, his gaze locking onto mine with an intensity that makes my breath catch. "I've told you this before."

"Yeah but did you really mean it?" I press, my stomach fluttering uncontrollably. The weight of his words and the depth of his stare leave me both anxious and hopeful, each second stretching out with a mix of anticipation and longing.

"With every fiber of my body." His gaze darkens, his expression shifting to one of raw, palpable desire. "But if I'm being honest, I want to do more than just kiss you, Cara. Watching that man's hands all over you, hearing him say he was going to have you tonight—it had me seeing red."

My breath catches in my throat, a mix of confusion and excitement swirling inside me. "If you wanted to have me tonight, you know, you could just wear the hat." I try to lighten the mood with a playful tone, though my nerves betray me, making my voice quiver. I smile softly at him as I wait for his reply.

"I want you tonight, tomorrow night, and every damn night since I can remember." Manny's lips curl into a smirk. He lowers his body slowly, his movements fluid and purposeful. He picks up the hat from where I dropped it, and he acts as if he will slide it onto his head but instead, he drops it back to the floor and brushes his fingers against my skin with a charged, lingering touch.

"I don't need a damn hat to show you how much I want you,

and if anything," he adds, bringing his arm in between us and snapping the pink bracelet on his wrist—the bracelet I gave him. "I was claimed by you days ago, whether you realized it or not."

The sweat glistens on both of us, our breath coming in heavy uneven bursts as the night wraps around us. *The bracelet.* He has not taken it off but I didn't think it was because he thought I was claiming him. Was I?

"But if we're doing this, it won't be because I want you to, you need to make that decision, bebé. I want you," he adds, pressing his hard dick against my hip, "in case it wasn't crystal clear. But I need you to want me back. I need you to say yes."

I can't fight this anymore so I wrap my hands around his neck, pull him flushed against me and kiss him again.

Manny kisses my lips like he might not ever kiss me again. Carefree but not careless. He kisses, and bites, and licks, and when I open my mouth to let his tongue in, he hums as his tongue dances with mine. I'm lost in this kiss and this man, I don't even care where we are. I don't even care who might see.

I break the kiss to come up for air, and he kisses my chin, my neck, going down until he licks my collarbone and squeezes my hips, making me moan. His hand immediately comes up to cover my mouth as he whispers in my ear, "You have to be quiet, Carita. I'll make you feel good, I promise but I need you to be quiet." I nod, slowing my breathing and trying not to lose my mind in this moment.

"Can you be a good girl and be quiet for me?" *Holy shit.* I open my mouth and bite his fingers gently, his skin's hot and salty against my tongue, at the same time that I nod again.

"You listen so well, Carita," Manny praises as his hand drops from my mouth and traces along my chest to cup one of my breasts. His mouth is hot against my ear, kissing and pulling at my skin as his fingers find my nipple and squeeze. When my nipple pebbles under his touch, he hums again and groans, "These are fucking perfect."

He squeezes my breast again and when I arch against his touch, he lowers his hands to lift me up, my legs wrapping around him and his mouth having better access to my chest. Manny uses his teeth to bite the fabric of my thin dress out of the way before closing his hot mouth over my nipple.

I let out a soft moan and he shakes his head, reminding me to be quiet. I bite my lip instead because this is too hot, out here in the open where anyone can see.

His mouth stays on my breast but he slowly stands me back up, lowering his mouth and kissing my chest and belly, before coming back up to kiss my lips. He lifts my dress over my exposed nipple, covering up again before bringing his hands down to my thighs. His fingers crawl up my legs and under my dress until they reach my hips and hook into the fabric of my underwear. My skin is on fire and I can feel my clit pulsing with every touch of his hands. With every second that passes and his body is this close to mine.

Manny's eyes are locked on mine as he pulls the panties down my legs, licking his lips showing me a smirk. I part my lips, catching my breath, and when he notices, he smirks again, dropping down to his knees to lower the panties all the way down to my ankles. My chest heaves as I try to control my breathing and not come just from the view of Manuel Zabana kneeling between my legs with my underwear in his hands.

He hooks a hand behind my knee, lifting my leg, and pulling the panties off one foot and then the other. He brings them to his nose and inhales. "Fuck, Carita, I knew you would smell good. I can't wait to see if you taste as good too."

I shiver at his words and as if he can sense how unraveled I am by that action, he smirks, putting my underwear in the back pocket of his jeans, and slides his hands up my thighs. He lifts the bottom of my dress slowly, saying, "You've been driving me wild with this dress all night, and I've been dying to get under it. Spread your legs for me, Carita."

I widen my stance, arching my back against the wall. I pull his hair as his tongue licks between my folds. He licks, once, twice, before humming against my pussy and bringing his hand up to spread the lips wide while he licks me undone.

"Fuck," I whisper and he stops licking me.

Manny's eyes look up at me as he says, "Silencio, Carita or I'll stop."

"You wouldn't dare," I say.

"Oh, I will stop and then you'll have to wait until we get back to the house to let yourself finish. Or you can be a good girl, listen, and I'll continue feasting on this perfect pussy. Which one is it going to be, Cara?"

When I don't say anything, he smiles and adds, "That's my girl. Now keep quiet please; I have a meal in front of me, and I'm starving." He lifts my knee higher, hooking it to his shoulder, allowing him more access to my pussy as he brings his mouth to it and licks right on my clit. *Jesus, I might die today.*

He takes his time, licking, and kissing. He flicks my clit with his tongue, then holds it between his teeth and sucks gently. His hand leaves my leg and comes straight to tease my entrance.

"So fucking wet and perfect," Manny coos before going back to lick my clit. He slides two fingers between my folds and right into my pussy, making me see stars. Every part of me he's touching with his hands or with his mouth is on overdrive and I'm so close it hurts. I'm sure he can feel it because I'm squeezing around his fingers with every pump and with every lick of his tongue.

He continues the pattern until I'm about to combust. I can feel my arousal building. The warm sensation pools in my belly until there's nowhere for it to go. I pull him closer, using the leg that is over his shoulder and when he bites my clit gently, I let go. I explode around his fingers, pulsing against them and letting out a silent cry. I shake, *hard*, until I have nothing left in me, and I become putty in his hands.

He licks my clit one more time, before sliding his fingers out, and standing up. He looks me dead in the eyes, when he brings his fingers up, my arousal all over them. He brings one of them to his mouth and licks it clean.

"Damn, Cara, you taste like heaven. I want to take my time savoring every last drop of your cum." He brings the other finger to his mouth and proceeds to do the same. Licking them both clean, right in front of me, turning me on again.

There's something so hot about everything that just happened that I say, "Bummer... you're going to have to do it again later and let me get a taste. I've never been told I taste like heaven before and you just had it all."

His eyes widen with mischief, bringing his hand to my chin, and kissing me hard. I can taste myself on his lips. Before he tasted like whiskey and spice, but now he tastes a little tangy and sweet. He breaks the kiss and says, "There, a little taste. Now let's go, I'm not done with you tonight. And for what I have in mind, we need some privacy."

He grabs my hand and pulls me toward the road, never letting go. We weave our way through the most alive road I've ever seen—people dancing in sync with the city's heartbeat, strolling without a care in the world, laughing with a joy that's coming from their bones. A kaleidoscope of rhythm, color, and noise. A living tapestry of feel-good and good times. Maybe it's not the happy city, and it's just me, with my pores craving input. Craving emotion, because whatever that was back there with Manny, has just woken parts of me I didn't know existed.

We make it to the van, I reach to open the door but he twirls me around and pins me against the sliding door. His hand smooths up to my neck, his fingers caressing my nape. He holds my head, pulling lightly on my hair, he tilts my chin up as he lowers and takes my lips in his.

He kisses me tenderly, not like the kiss shared in the alley. That was rushed and passionate as if he was going to lose me any second if he didn't claim every single part of my lips. But this one is not feverish. This kiss is soft and sweet like I'm delicate, and he might break me if he kisses me any harder. It's slow, as if we have all the time in the world and he wants to save every single second that his soft lips are on mine.

"Manny," I whisper but he doesn't let go. He kisses me again.

I bite his lower lip gently, and he smiles against my mouth, the kiss breaking but our connection remaining. His nose brushes against mine, sending a shiver of excitement through me. He whispers softly against my lips, "We have time. I've dreamed of the moment you'd let me get lost in you and I want to take my time. Let me commit every kiss, every taste of your lips to memory, Carita. Let me savor this moment."

The sweet, intoxicating scent of his breath mingles with the faint trace of cologne he's wearing. The reality of kissing him, something he says he's dreamed about for years, is even more thrilling than I had ever imagined. Nothing in my wildest dreams could have prepared me for how incredible this feels.

"Let's go back to the house," I suggest, my voice trembling. Manny responds with a tender kiss to my forehead. He carefully opens the front door for me and then slides into the driver's seat. The van hums to life, and as we pull away, he reaches for my hand, holding it tightly for a brief moment before letting it fall back to his side and start heading back.

25

BITABLE SIZE

I'M GONNA BE (500 MILES), SLEEPING AT LAST & EARNED IT, THE WEEKEND

Cara

"I CAN HEAR YOUR THOUGHTS, CARA," he says before glancing at me, his eyes soft with concern. "Stop overthinking it, okay? We can talk about it later, or even now if it will make you feel better."

I can't help but let my thoughts swirl, grappling with the intensity of everything that happened today. "I want to talk about this," I say, my voice shaking.

Manny's eyes flash with a quick, reassuring smile before he focuses back on the road. "Oh, yeah? Let's figure it out then. Talk to me, Carita," he says.

"I need to understand what's happening. You mentioned you've been dying to kiss me for years. If that's true, why didn't you say anything before now?"

"When would have been a good time to say I had a crush on my sister's best friend? When you were twelve and started looking older, but I was just a ten-year-old boy? Or when you were sixteen and all of your inner beauty was bursting out and started changing you into the woman you are today? I was just the annoying little fourteen-year-old brother, right?"

"You were annoying. You were always nagging and taking shit from us and getting us to buy things for you or take you places, even when we didn't live in the same city."

"Yeah, because I was trying to spend as much time with you as possible. I got to see you two or three times a year. I wanted to be around you, but I was a damn kid and that's the only way I knew how."

"But at some point, Manny, you weren't a kid anymore," I add softly, my eyes searching his.

"Yeah, and you were seriously dating the same guy that you'd been with for years. Plus you know just because I think Jessica Alba is hot and kind and cute, doesn't mean I'm gonna ask her out if I ever meet her," he says smirking. When I roll my eyes, he adds, "You know what I mean. I didn't know how to tell you then, and I didn't know how to deal with my feelings. I sure as hell didn't know *when* to tell you as you turned into this smoke-show of a woman. And you were with the stupid ass for years. I know my place, and it was as your friend's brother, not as a guy you could see yourself with."

"I am not Jessica Alba. Her, you've had a crush on forever for what I can remember."

"No, you're right you're more. She's a person I've seen on screen, and I may have had a platonic crush on her all my life, but you, Cara, you I *know*. The person you are doesn't compare to her or anyone. My feelings for you are tangible... You're also hot as hell, don't get me wrong, but I need more than a pretty face." He smirks and winks at me, eliciting another eye roll.

"If the hundreds of gorgeous women you date are also decent humans, then how does the rest of the population have a chance?" I ask as he pulls into the parking spot of our B&B. He looks at me eerily, silently, before stepping out of the van and walking around to my side. *What in the world?*

He opens the door, offering me his hand to help me step out, his eyes searing into mine, he says, "I don't date. Not really. Those women? They're a good time. Fun for a night and that's all I wanted. None of them are you. None of them *look* like you, did you notice that too? I couldn't be with someone who had any resemblance to you because nobody could measure up. I don't like spending a lot of time with many people in general, but with you? With you, I could spend a lifetime."

How is a girl supposed to recover from this? I swallow hard and look at him, leaning on the van, with my arms crossed over my chest. My heart's racing, and the steady beat drums loudly in my chest as time ceases to exist. Manny stands in front of me, giving me his full attention.

"Any other questions? If you're done asking, I'd like to kiss you now," he asks, bringing his hand to my face and with a feather-light touch caresses my cheek.

I always have questions, that's the problem. I could talk for hours and ask a million questions and be a happy girl for the rest of my life. Right now though, the only question in my mind might be the craziest one. "Are you going to kiss me again or should I dare you to do it?"

"You never have to dare me to do something I want to do," he says softly before his mouth crashes back into mine. His mouth is a contradiction to his tone. Where his voice was barely above a whisper, soft and careful, this kiss is anything but. Three kisses we've shared tonight, all of them different, and all of them the best kisses I've ever had. I don't know how I went years without being kissed like this because I truly was missing out. Missing out on tenderness, sweetness, and passion. Hell, I was missing out on lips that command attention, and at the same time respect boundaries, falling into cadence with mine.

He bites my lower lip, his teeth sharp, drawing pain but quickly soothing the spot again with his tongue, building pleasure deep in my core. I pull him closer to me with his shirt, and when his hips press against mine, I can feel how turned on he is. The fact that I elicit that response from his body with just a kiss, has my mind lost in the moment. So lost, I forget we're still in the driveway when I let out a loud moan at the second bite.

He slips his hands down under my ass, lifting me up, and as I wrap my legs around him, he walks us toward the house, never dropping his mouth from my body. Whether it's my lips, my neck, my ear, or my cheek. His mouth is on me, at all times, making me feel like a dessert he can't get enough of.

Blindly we go through the door, and after he kicks it closed, he walks us both to his room. He places me on the bed and steps back. Now that he's not touching or kissing me, now that he's standing in front of me, I notice how hot he looks. He lost the backward hat he was wearing at some point tonight leaving his hair a mess—unruly but perfect. He pulls his shirt off, grabs the back in one quick swoop and tosses it on the ground. My eyes go directly to his chest and his perfect abs. I don't think I've ever noticed how stupidly in shape he is and before I can continue assessing him with my eyes, a deep chuckle brings me back to reality. My eyes snap up to find his, filled with pure heat, looking at me.

"You're a sight for sore eyes, Manny," I say, trying to stay flirty and not sound like a total fangirl.

"Well, thank you," he adds, grabbing my foot and pulling me toward the edge of the bed. He lowers his body until he's face-to-face with me, caging me between his strong arms. "I've been dying to see, touch, and kiss every inch of your body. Now I just need your permission to do it."

Silence spreads between us. My breath catches at his admission and definitely takes me by surprise. I don't think I've ever been with someone who has me spread wide open in front of him, with my panties in his back pocket, and still waits for confirmation that I want this but God do I love it.

"Do you want to undress me yourself or should I, hotshot?" I add, and that's all the permission he needs.

"I've been a patient man, Carita. Not only were you driving me wild all night with that dress, but I've been ready to burst since I heard your sweet moans outside your door this morning."

He what?! My eyes open wide and I'm sure I look twenty shades of red by how hot my face feels all of a sudden. I can hide behind this feeling or I can put my big girl panties on and tell him what I'm really thinking.

"What if I told you I was thinking about you? What if I told you I was coming undone at the thought of your hands on my body?" I say, mustering the courage I didn't know I had and tracing my breasts with my fingers.

I shiver at the same time his gaze darkens when he hears that. Manny smirks before licking his lips and shaking his head in amusement.

"Then I would ask you to let me touch you so I can find out if that's exactly how you'll sound now that I have my hands on you. Allow me to rip this sexy-ass dress off of you."

I nod and Manny brings his hands to the bed before adding, "Let me do it all." He drags his hands over my hips and under my dress, around the back to caress my bare ass, and lifts the dress slowly over my body and off over my head. He throws the dress down, joining his shirt on the floor, and then he stands. His hand covers his mouth as he shakes his head. I see his eyes darkening and his jaw clenching when she sees my bare breasts. I'm team no bra and in this situation, is working in my favor. The corner of his mouth pulls into a soft smile under his hand before he adds, "Damn it, my imagination betrayed me. I knew your body would be deliciously gorgeous, but fuck if every inch of you is not anything but perfection."

His eyes roam my body, his words lingering in my ears, and I can feel the heat rising on my cheeks. He lowers his body over mine, caressing his lips with mine, in a soft kiss. The softness is such a contrast to his heated words. I expected him to kiss me with the same frenzied intensity as before but this kiss is not rushed. It's tender, sweet and patient. Yet not hesitant, he knows what he's doing, he's just slowing everything down—and driving me crazy.

"Manny, just fuck me already!" I plead, letting go of his lips.

He flashes me a smile and bites his lower lip. "Oh, I will fuck you, bebé. All night long, but I will take my time. I've dreamed for years of how many ways I would take you if I ever were to have you and now that I have you, I want to take my time. I will take my time getting to know what you like and dislike. Getting to know what you love. Let your body do the talking, Carita mia. I want to listen."

His mouth lowers, peppering kisses from my jaw to my neck to my ear, nibbling on my earlobe as his hand roams up my body. When he reaches one of my breasts, he groans against my ear and the sound alone has me breaking into goosebumps immediately. He lowers his mouth over one of my small breasts while he cups the other and gently twists my nipple.

"Oh God," I whisper, arching my back when he bites my nipple.

I can feel the smirk against my skin, with his mouth full of my breast. "These are perfect, Cara," Manny says.

"They are small," I add. I love my body but I've been inse-cure about belonging to the itty bitty titty committee since I can remember. The only good that comes out of having small breasts is the no bra situation but most people love big boobs, I wish I had them too. Judging by the way he groaned and smirked against my nipple, Manny seems to be loving them more than I thought possible.

"They're bitable. Perfect size for me to grab, to kiss, to suck. I said you're perfect, take the compliment." He continues kissing down my body, under my breast, to my belly button and on my hip, right above what would be my panty line if this man didn't actually steal them earlier today. His hand moves under my ass and grabs it while he hums against my skin.

"Manny, you already went down on me once, you don't have to do it again, really."

"Cara, I know I told you that I love your voice, and I do. But the only sound I want to hear coming out of your mouth right now is a moan, or my name when you can't fucking hold it in anymore. If I want to taste your perfect pussy again, I will, unless you don't want me to?" he asks, lifting his eyebrow and looking at me. The view of his head between my legs, hands under my ass, and his eyes full of fire on me, is more than I can handle.

"It's not that I don't want you to. It's that I want you to know you don't have to. I haven't even returned the favor." I blush as soon as I say that and he smiles softly at me, making me feel at ease.

"You think tasting you is a favor? You think that having your sweet taste all over my mouth is not the biggest treat I've had in a damn long time? Because if that's what you think, Carita, I'm about to prove you *so* damn wrong. I knew I would want more. I knew I would *need* more after one taste. I *knew* I'd crave you. I can't get enough of you. Now drop your legs and open up for me. Let me see all of you before I taste you again."

I follow his command and spread my legs open more, letting my knees fall until they hit the bed with a soft bounce. He stops to look at me and I feel my cheeks flushing again. I consider closing my legs but his words '*Don't hide from me*' repeat on a loop, giving me the confidence to own this moment. He's standing there frozen in time, his eyes devouring me whole without even laying a finger on me. He makes me feel so beautiful, so desired.

"I wish you could see yourself, Cara. I wish you could see this perfect pussy glistening, so wet and ready for me."

His mouth goes straight to my clit, sucking gently and pulling a moan from me. When I arch my back at the sensation, he uses his hands to lift my ass off the bed giving him better access to all of me. He grabs one of my legs and places it on his shoulder, as he lowers his tongue to my entrance and starts licking, kissing, and sucking. If he continues like this I will come all over his mouth again. Twice in one night. He brings his thumb up to my clit and presses gently while his mouth explores the rest of me.

He slides his tongue in between my lips, making me see stars. "Fuck, Manny, yes." I wish I could say it's quiet, but it isn't. It's loud, and primal, coming from the depths of my core because I'm so close to the edge that I could scream his name over and over until he makes me come again. My hands are gripping the bed but it's not enough so I bring them down and grab his hair, pulling gently at his soft waves while pushing his head down against me to try and get more friction. He looks up and smiles at me, my breathing is heavy as I say, "I'm so close, please make me come."

"You don't have to beg, bebé," he groans, going back to my pussy and pressing hard with his thumb over my clit. When his other hand grabs my ass, strong and possessive, like he can't get enough, it sends me over the edge and I explode on his tongue. I can feel my arousal coating him but that doesn't stop him from moving his tongue and his thumb all over my clit. I feel every shudder, every sensation. I feel it all.

I quickly grab a pillow and smash it over my face, muffling

my loud cries. He slows the strokes, helping me come down from my high, and then removes the pillow from my face.

"What did we say about hiding?" he asks. "I want to see it all. I want to hear it all. Let me see you come undone," he whispers, climbing up my body and kissing me gently. This kiss is sweet and tangy, his lips full of my arousal and that might be the hottest thing I've ever experienced. Now I got to experience it twice, in one freaking day. *What is this life?*

Manny drags his hand over my clit again, making me shiver because of how sensitive it is, he slides two fingers in my wet pussy making me gasp against his lips. He brings them out as he lets go of my lips with his mouth. He brings his fingers up and coats my arousal over my bottom lip as he says, "You wanted a taste, so suck, Cara. Taste how sweet you are."

I bring my tongue out, not dropping his eyes and when I taste the tanginess on them, I suck them in and bite, letting out a moan and tilting my hips to him. I want him to know how ready I am for him, *again.* I want him to know how much I want him but even though I can feel his hardness against me, he still has pants on and we need to do something about it.

"Manny," I whisper against his lips. "You have way too many clothes on."

He smirks, kneeling and unbuckling his belt. "Oh yeah?" He stands and continues to undress himself.

"Yeah," I say, rising on my elbows so I can enjoy the view. His body is perfect—both smooth and strong. He finishes taking his pants off and when his dick springs into view, my mouth waters at the sight and I bite my lips gently. He grabs his wallet out of his pants, fishing for a condom before dropping them back to the floor.

"Let me," I add, grabbing the condom from his hands and trying my best to open the package without dropping it. My hands are shaking, which is a first, but something tells me there are plenty of things about to happen with Manny that will be firsts. Starting with the size of his dick and how it'll fit in my damn vagina.

He grabs his dick and strokes it while maintaining eye contact before asking, "Are you going to keep looking at it or are you going to do something about it?" I laugh and then he adds, "There she is. Get out of your head, bebé. We're in this together and we stop when you want to stop. Okay?"

I nod, but the fact that he thinks I want to stop is mind-boggling because I want anything but. "Come here," I say, sitting up and waiting for him to walk to the edge of the bed. His dick has beads of precum that I use to glide my hands down him when rolling the condom over it. I grab his balls and feel how full they are at the same time he lets out a hiss.

He grabs me by my elbows, lifting me to my feet, grabbing my face, and kissing me. He kisses me deeply, hungrily, and ready for more as he lays me on the bed. He continues to kiss me as he lines up his dick with my entrance. When his hand crawls under my neck to hold me tightly, he enters me in one slow thrust.

"Jesus," I whisper against his lips and he smiles again.

"I didn't know you were so religious," he adds, looking at me and showing me his easy smile. He's at ease, I can feel it in my bones. I can see it in the way he looks at me or the way he smiles. The glimmer in his eyes even with the fire in them. He truly wants this.

"I'm not, I'm just at a loss for words right now," I breathe, smiling against his shoulder as he thrusts deeper into me, slowly, letting me adjust around him.

"My name would do, Carita mia. If you need something to scream, let it be my name." he adds, drops a kiss on my shoulder, pulling another moan out of me as he slides in deeper. He's so big and thick. He feels like damn perfection as I stretch around him. He allows me the time I need until he's so deep all I can do is gasp. He smiles as soon as I do and when my eyes meet his he starts moving again.

Manny's finding a rhythm that will work with both of us with every thrust. His eyes are on mine, full of desire and want. And even when the pace quickens, he's still all in. His eyes, his arms, his body, his full attention in this moment. I bring my hands up to his back and dig my nails into his skin as he drives into me over and over again. I arch my back against him and bring my leg around his ass, digging my heels into him, he lets out a guttural moan and that's all it takes for me to explode around him, again. In no time, he's falling right along with me.

"Cara," he growls as his strokes slow and his body tenses at the same time that I drop my legs, completely spent.

He drops next to me, our breathing heavy and in sync, mixing with our body heat and sweat as we both come down from the high. I turn my face to look at Manny and I find him staring at me, smiling. "What?" I snap, wondering what the heck is so funny that he is even composed enough to smile at me like that.

"You look so fucking pretty right now," he says.

"Oh really? All sweaty with messy hair?" I ask, bringing my hand up to my hair and shaking it up.

"More like sated, unraveled, and in my bed" he adds, bringing his lips to mine for a quick peck and getting up to use the restroom. I assume it's to discard the condom, and I use that opportunity to close my eyes and think about whatever the hell just happened.

26

READY TO EAT

ME REHUSO, DANNY OCEAN

Manny

IT'S SO HOT, is my first thought when I open my eyes to the ray of sunshine on my face. We were too busy last night to close the curtains and the morning sun is heating the room. I can smell Cara's shampoo or whatever it is that she uses that makes her smell like a lemon vanilla scone. I've ordered a lemon scone in each store we go to this whole trip trying to find the exact combination that reminds me of her. They all come close, but none of them are the exact thing. I want to recreate that scent. Bottle it up and bathe in it.

When I look down, I see her soft waves on top of my chest. Her head is tucked under my arm, with her hair covering her face. I gently lift her hair and when I see her peacefully sleeping, I can't help but to smile to myself. Cara's arm rests around my torso, her legs intertwined with mine in what feels like a pretzel, but she is sound asleep. Eyebrows relaxed and lips slightly parted as her even breaths go in and out. *No wonder I'm so hot.* There's so much body heat between her naked body and mine, but I wouldn't change one bit of it. I wouldn't change a second of last night. Maybe I would have changed not kissing her sooner but then again, maybe it was the right time to do it. Now I just have to figure out how to get her to keep kissing me at least for the rest of this trip because now that I know what it could be like, what it could feel like, I don't want to give it up.

I see her bracelets as I trace her arm softly with my fingers and all I can think is about how I want to make more 'moments' with her. I want her to wear them all like bracelets in her arm. I want them branded in her brain to the point when she looks back on this trip it brings her nothing but good memories and maybe, just maybe, she'll keep me around for longer.

I feel her shift softly in my arms, as she scrunches her nose and wraps her arm around me tighter. She has small goosebumps down her back, so I gently move to grab the blanket and pull it over her. I'm not sure how she can be cold right now but she clearly is and I want her to be comfortable. Time moves both slowly and too fast with her in my arms. So slow that I've noticed which eyelashes kiss her cheeks and which ones curve up.

She has three freckles on her right cheek, so light you can barely see them, adding to the other twelve I've noticed before, but they are there, outlining what would be a heart if I traced lines through them. The girl who wears her heart on her sleeve also has little hidden hearts on her body.

And her body, I notice how every curve molds with mine seamlessly. How her thick thighs are like pillows around mine, making me feel like I'm surrounded by a cloud. And when I trace them with my fingertips, I can feel light stretch marks showing me how her body has changed through the years. The body of a woman under my hands. The body of a Goddess. She tastes like heaven and she feels like it too. Time passes too fast because when she moves again she tenses, realizing how she's tangled with me. Now, the sun that was on my face before, is nowhere to be felt.

"Good morning, sunshine," I whisper against her forehead, squeezing her shoulder.

"Hi," she replies, her voice sleepy. Unwrapping her body from mine and leaving me feeling hollow and cold as soon as she does. Her eyes snap to mine and I can see a flash of the one thing I hoped she wasn't feeling: *regret*.

"How did you sleep?" I raise my hand to her hair and tuck it behind her ear. Finding any and every excuse I can to touch her.

"Great, I guess. I don't think I moved even once, and this is the first time in my life I've slept naked without feeling uncomfortable. So, ten out of ten?" she adds, smiling and turning on her back to face the ceiling.

"Talk to me, Cara," I urge, my voice a gentle but firm plea. I can see the tension in her shoulders, the way her hands grab the sheets tights. Her words may not be saying what she's feeling but her body betrays her.

"Do we have to?" She brings a pillow to her face that I immediately remove.

"Are you going to freak out if we don't?" I counter, watching her eyes flicker with uncertainty as she looks at me.

"I feel like I'll spiral regardless, but mostly because I don't want you to think that this has to be like a relationship or whatever," she says and I knew it. I knew she was going to try to complicate things more. What I didn't know was that she was going to say that this is not a relationship.

"We already have a relationship, Cara. We're friends. We're friends who are attracted to each other, and clearly have fucking chemistry too, you can't deny that." I know I'm not relationship material for her. I know that I'm only good for a while even though I would give what I don't have to be just what she needs —to be someone who she may want to spend her life with.

However, that's not who I am and what I'm really good at is making her feel good, and I'm happy to oblige.

"That's not what I meant," she adds, sitting up and pulling the sheets around her, covering her body from me. I can feel the wall she's trying to put up between us, marking her boundaries. "What I mean is, I know that you don't do relationships and maybe we just got carried away—so we can put it behind us."

"Or," I say, earning me a quick snap of her head back to look at me. "Or we can keep having fun for the days we have left on this trip. We can draw all the boundaries you want, but didn't you have fun last night? I sure did."

"Last night was... something," she says, blushing instantly and looking down. I didn't think Cara had a shy bone in her body but on this trip, I've seen more and more that she uses her wittiness and extroverted personality to mask what she truly feels. But by some miracle, she lets me see pieces of her that I haven't seen before and all I want to do is treasure her and show her that it's okay to let others see when she's not okay.

I place my finger under her chin and lift her face up to look me in the eyes. "Last night was what?"

"Perfect." Her eyes flutter open, revealing a sparkle of wonder. "I didn't realize I could feel so much. I didn't realize I could feel so good. You made me feel alive in a way I've never felt before. It was incredible, Manny, truly. But don't get it twisted—I'm not planning on holding on to you like some kind of lifeline."

I chuckle, a playful smirk tugging at my lips. "So, you're not ready to walk down the aisle just yet? Here I was thinking you'd be tossing me aside now that you've had your fill."

A flicker of amusement tugs at her lips before she shakes her head. "You're insufferable."

"And you secretly love it," I tease. "Look, let's not overthink this. We still have time on this trip, and we're both adults. We both liked what happened, so why not just enjoy it?"

"I don't want things to get awkward," she says, her gaze shifting uneasily.

"Then let's keep it from getting awkward," I counter.

She hesitates, her eyes darting between mine as if searching for the right answer. Finally, she speaks, her tone firmer. "Then we need some ground rules."

"A contract?" I suggest, raising an eyebrow.

"Stop mocking me, Manuel," Cara snaps, crossing her arms and blowing a strand of hair out of her face with a frustrated puff. "I'm serious. We need clear boundaries."

"I'm not mocking you, I mean it. I already did something once on this trip you didn't like and I'm never doing that again. I need approval of everything from now on. A verbal contract. I'll go first," I say, putting a pillow over my dick because seeing her this flustered, in the morning light, wrapped in nothing but the bedsheets has me harder than should be necessary. "Kissing allowed."

"Oh my gosh, Manny. I'm serious," she exclaims, her frustration bubbling just beneath the surface.

"Then you make the rules, Cara," I reply, trying to keep my tone light, even as I sense how important this moment is.

"Don't 'Cara' me," she snaps back, her sass cutting through the tension like a knife. It's a familiar dance, one we've done many times before.

"Okay, go ahead. Tell me your rules," I say, softening my voice. There's a hint of a smile playing at the corners of my lips, but I'm fully aware that I'm inviting her to share the boundaries she desperately needs to set.

"We don't tell anyone. The last thing I need is for people to call me a cougar or something." Her tone shows how serious she is about this, leaving me with nothing to do but laugh. She narrows her eyes at me and I shake my head.

"Two years, Cara. You're two years older than me, not ten but sure, done," I add. Not that I kiss and tell but I also don't have many people that I actually talk to. Sadly, I'm only close to my siblings.

"Number two, no sleeping with other people."

"You think if my dick is inside of you, I would be able to have it inside of someone else? Also, there is no one else. Next," I laugh. Does she think I'd be able to think about anyone else for the rest of my life after I know what she feels under my touch?

"It stops when the road trip ends," she adds and even though I knew she would, it still shocks me. It hits me right in the heart.

I want to be done with this conversation as soon as possible. I want to understand her boundaries, but I also don't want to talk about all the things I can't do. I *want* to talk about all the things I can and will do with her, to her, around her.

"What about the things we *can* do? All these cant's are leaving me thinking you don't want to do anything at all.

Cara turns her body to me, the sheets showing every curve of her body under it when she says, "You can touch me all you want." She smiles at me as she traces her body with her hands taunting me.

"Agree, you can touch me too," I say.

"You can kiss me all you want and you can fuck me all you want to." Her cheeks redden when she says that. Somehow that makes her look even sexier. I pull her to me in one quick swoop and she yelps before saying, "Wait, though, I have one more."

I raise one eyebrow hoping it's not something too crazy but nothing could have prepared me for how deep what she says hurt.

"When this is over... you still need to be able to be my

friend, deal?" Cara adds. It stops me for a moment, my whole body tensing. I know I'm not end game for her and I know she deserves better but it still hurts to hear it come from her lips. I know I won't be able to move on from this trip but I'll happily give her the week of her life. The more I think about it though, the more I realize that one isn't going to be that hard because I'll take whatever she'll give me and hell if she upgrades me from best friend's brother to friend, I'll take it. Even if it kills me slowly in the process.

"Are there any rules about what to have for breakfast?" I ask, brushing her hair behind her ear and hoping she doesn't see how she's breaking my heart in the process, even before I can fully give it to her.

"What?! No, you know you can have whatever you want for breakfast because I don't really care about eating this early."

"Then I know exactly what I want," I say, grabbing her leg, draping it over mine, and bringing my other hand to her neck. "I'm ready to eat." And without waiting another second, I crush my lips to hers.

27

NASHVILLE WITHOUT US
INVISIBLE STRING, TAYLOR SWIFT

Cara

"I CAN'T EAT one more thing today, Cara," Manny says, holding his belly and bending over like a toddler who just ate something they don't like.

"We have one more stop and then we can go do whatever you want. Pretty please," I beg, holding his hands. We've been walking around trying different foods in Centennial Park but I really want something sweet now. I feel like I could eat a cow today and I'm not sure why. Maybe because we spent approximately six hours lost in the sheets last night and then two sessions this morning before we left the house. Both a first for me. I have been with plenty of men but most of them were hookups. Cole was my longest relationship and that man never went more than once. He sure as hell didn't do more than he needed to. Definitely didn't spend hours kissing every inch of my body, making me laugh, or taking pride in the way he was making me feel. *That*'s what Manny did. It was as if my pleasure was directly tied to his. Like he enjoyed making me feel good just as much as I enjoyed feeling it. Two days he spent getting to know everything I liked in and outside of that house. I'm sad the Nashville trip is coming to an end soon because it has been my favorite stop of this trip by far.

"I have a stop I want to make, too," he says.

"Oh? Do tell," I reply, shoving the last piece of pretzel into my mouth.

"Let's go to the other side of the park to look at the Parthenon," he says and I jump, clapping my hands. I've been wanting to go there for a while but I didn't think he would've liked going there.

"You want to?" I ask, moving my eyebrows and practically dancing out of happiness.

"Yeah, it's on your list too, right?"

"Yes, but do *you* want to go?" I ask as we walk toward it.

"I do, Cara, but even if I didn't want to, you want to and that's enough for me," Manny adds, holding my hand and looking around as we make it close to the building. The Parthenon is a museum in Nashville but it's also the only full-scale replica of the Parthenon in Athens, which I think is really cool. We're almost there when he drops my hand and stands behind me instead. I try to look back at him but he holds my shoulders, keeping me looking forward.

"What?!" I shout but he just squeezes my shoulders.

We continue to walk until I hear someone near me shout, "I can't believe you thought you could do Nashville without us."

I turn around quickly and this time he lets me, and immediately I see something, or rather someone, that I thought I wasn't going to see for another week. Roe, Allie, and Natalie all stand side by side, smiling ear to ear and looking damn adorable in their dresses and cowgirl boots.

"Eeeek!" I shout, running to them and throwing myself into

Allie's arms. Roe's not a hugger and Natalie is constantly trying to get pregnant so I would hate to squish the new baby if she's pregnant. "What are you guys doing here?" I all but scream at them, not letting go of Allie for one second.

"You're going to smother me to death, Cara," she mumbles with her mouth full of my hair. I let her go, holding her hands and looking at all three of them. My girls. My sisters that life gave me. They are all here and I can barely believe it.

"You said you wished we were here with you so we made it happen, babe," Roe says.

"But, like, how did you know I was going to be here?" I ask and they all look at Manny. *Manny?* I turn around to look at him, and he's looking back at me with a big smile on his face and his hands in his pocket.

"You sounded so sad when you told them you wished they were here, so we made it happen," he shrugs, his voice warm with understanding.

In an instant, I throw myself into his arms, the world around us fading as I bury my face against his chest. The rhythm of his heartbeat is steady and reassuring, grounding me even in the middle of my swirling emotions. "Thank you," I mumble, my words muffled but full of gratitude, feeling the comforting weight of his arms around me. Not even caring about how weird this must look to Allie but this is so sweet, I don't know how else to react to it.

"Well, you're welcome, Carita," Manny replies, his smile brightening his face. He pulls back slightly, his hands lingering on my shoulders as he ruffles my hair playfully, the gesture making me feel both cherished and light-hearted. "Now, I'm going to make myself busy and go work for a few hours. Pick you guys up at 5:00?"

Allie leans in, planting a soft kiss on his cheek. "Thanks for this, manito[1]. See you in a bit." Her voice is laced with warmth, a testament to their bond.

He beams at her, his eyes twinkling with affection, then waves goodbye before heading off in the opposite direction from the museum.

"Stop it right now! I can't believe you guys are here!" I shout, my heart racing with joy as I spin around, unable to contain my excitement.

"We don't have a lot of time if we want to go inside!" Natalie exclaims, her voice tinged with urgency. She tucks a loose strand of her gorgeous auburn hair behind her ear, her eyes sparkling with determination. Grabbing my hand, she pulls us three toward the entrance.

"SO WHAT ARE the plans for the rest of the day," Allie asks. We toured the museum and walked around before messaging Manny to see where he was. We decided to wait for him by the water and we're all currently sitting on the grass, spending some very needed quality time together.

"Plans? You tell me! You three were the ones who showed up here making all of my dreams come true. This trip has been everything I've ever wanted and more, and now this," I add, pointing at the three of them and smiling. "This was just the cherry on top."

"A dream come true, huh?" Roe asks, lifting her shades from her eyes and adding, "I thought you hated Manny. So you're

---

1.   short for hermanito which means little brother

either filled with rage and you're ready to kill him, or you guys fucked, and that's why you're so radiant."

Allie chokes on the apple she's eating and I open my eyes wide at her words. I need to come up with something quick to say so I shout, "I am always radiant, thank you very much. That's why so many people call me sunshine, darling."

"Darling? Are you twelve and in the countryside?" Roe sasses back.

"We live in the countryside," I add, going back to the water I'm holding. Roe's goose backpack is like a grocery store. When we sat here she opened it, getting so many snacks and drinks out.

"We are sitting on the countryside," Natalie says, adding to this useless conversation. That's what I love the most about them, about my bestie girls, the fact that we can talk about everything and nothing all at once. I can see them once a year or every month, every weekend, or not at all and I know that their love and friendship remains.

"Can we also not talk about my brother fucking anyone please and thank you?" Allie adds, tossing a rock in the water. I forgot how much I missed them. I got to see them a few times this year but it's never enough. I don't want this day to end, especially not after having all my girls together for the first time in forever. And not especially with everything our friend group is going through. I know I'm seeing them again next week for the wedding, well not Roe since she's younger than us and didn't go to school with us, but it still not enough.

"So what are we doing?" I ask.

"Dinner, dancing, and seltzers?" Roe asks, taking a bite of a Twizzler she also had in her bag and laying on the grass.

"Sounds like a plan to me," I hear Manny speak from behind us and this is the moment I realize just how much my body is aware of him. Not because of how my skin prickles when I sense him near me or how my heart races when I hear his voice, but because of how comfortable I feel the moment I know he's near. His presence alone puts a smile on my lips, and I've never felt that before. Maybe it's just the rush from the past twenty-four hours or maybe it's us being together for so many days without anyone else around. Maybe it's both. Either way, my whole body just came alive from hearing his voice.

I find both Allie and Natalie's eyes on me as soon as they see him and I try to mask the fact I think I just got caught reacting to his voice and ask, "Are you ready to drive us around and let us get wild and wasted?" I get up from my spot on the grass and smile at Manny quickly, trying not to draw more attention to us.

"Sure, but how about we go get dinner first, I have a place in mind," he adds, offering his hands to his sister and Natalie to help them up.

Roe gets up on her own, never accepting anyone's help as per usual and then walks up to me, whispering only for me to hear, "Can't fool me, Cara. You got rocked by that man and it's written all over your face. I want details."

Astounded, I try not to acknowledge that and walk, falling in place behind Manny, Nat and Allie while ignoring Roe's comment. If Roe can tell, how am I supposed to hide this from Allie too until the day after tomorrow when they head back?

"Are you girls in the mood for some wine?" he asks, as we climb into an SUV waiting for us at the park.

"What happened to the van?" I ask.

"It's back at the place. We don't all fit, it's okay, I've got this," he replies, closing the door and climbing in the front seat. He gives directions to the driver and we start rolling.

28

CHASE IT

A DIFFERENT WAY, LAUV

Cara

AS WE DRIVE up the hill, we see a small cottage with the warm summer sun casting an amber hue over the land next to it. There are rows of grapevines shimmering under the clear sky and that's when I see the sign that reads Arrington Vineyards. Laughter fills the air as Roe finishes telling a story about a tattoo, she just did on a frat boy. We pull up to the entrance, and Manny, forever the gentleman, gets out and opens our door, and helps us out one at a time.

"Just wait until you see the view from the terrace," Manny says, his hands tucked casually into his pockets as soon as he closes the door. We weave our way through the entry room of the wooden building which looks like a mix of a tasting room or a barn. It smells like a mix of grapes and berries and something sweet. As we walk through the entrance it's eerily quiet, as if the place is closed and we're the only people here. When we step out onto the terrace, the scent of fresh grapes mingling with the warm breeze shocks me. Or maybe I'm shocked from seeing Jake standing in the middle of the paved courtyard, a confident smile on his face as he waves at us. At Allie, I should say, since his eyes are only on her.

"What's going on?" Allie asks, her brows furrowed in confusion.

Jake grins wider, his eyes sparkling but before anyone can react, he reaches for Allie's hand, gently pulling her away from us. "Come with me," he says, leading her to the edge of the vineyard, where the vibrant green vines stretch endlessly behind them.

As they reach the perfect spot, Jake turns to face Allie, his expression shifting from playful to serious. The laughter fades into the background, and the world feels like it shrinks down to just the two of them. He drops to one knee, pulling a small velvet box from his pocket. "Allie," he begins, his voice steady and filled with emotion, "I wish I could say that my life has been filled with only joy since I met you but the truth is that's not really life. Life is messy and sometimes painful. It feels like we've been through so much already, not only together and in our time apart," he says and Allie is already a mess of tears. Her curls cover half her face and she tries to tuck some strands behind her ear. Even though it doesn't work, it's keeping her hands busy with the task as the love of her life proposes to her. "I could go on and on about why I think you're the woman for me but I think we both know, and all of our friends know, that the day your eyes met mine, I knew you were it. Even in the ten years we were apart, there was no true happiness without you. I'm done waiting. I'm done giving it time, waiting for something that we both know deep down is what it's supposed to be. I belong with you and you belong with me so, could we make it official? Will you marry me, honey?"

Allie's hands fly to her mouth, eyes wide with disbelief. The moment stretches, the anticipation thick in the air. The rest of us stand frozen, unable to contain our excitement. "Yes! Yes, of course, I will!" she finally breathes, her voice breaking with joy. Jake slides the ring onto her finger, creating a memory that will linger forever. She pulls Jake up from his knees and throws herself into his arms, kissing him deeply. They don't care that we're all here, that we're all cheering and clapping, they get lost in their kiss.

I look around at the semi-empty vineyard, asking myself how the hell this even happened. And what I find is Manny looking at his sister with pride in his eyes. No tears but definitely pride. I walk toward him, leaving Allie and Jake to their moment. "How on earth did you pull this off, Manny?"

"It's a long story but I didn't do it all alone," he answers, pointing at the back area of the vineyard where I see his brother Gus, Santiago, and Nick.

"How in the world?"

"A lot of frequent flier miles, a few text messages, and wanting to see my sister get her happily ever after sooner than later. Really it was all Jake's idea. When Allie messaged me to tell me she wanted to surprise you for the weekend, a few hours later Jake messaged to tell me he wanted to surprise Allie and propose. It was a lot of coordination and keeping things from my two favorite girls."

"Two favorite girls, huh?" I ask him, raising my eyebrows at him and smiling because no matter what he says next, I love the sound of that.

"You two have always been my favorite girls, Cara," he replies as we stand together, eyes on each other, suspended in time, until a voice breaks the spell.

"Cara mi amor[1], how's it going?"

"Gus," I say, turning my body around, kissing his cheek and

---

1. my love

giving him a side hug. It's crazy to me how these two look almost the same but I can tell them apart by miles because of how different they are. When they were kids, they looked even more alike than they look now. With the years Gus' skin has darkened more turning into a terracotta brown when Manny is more of like tawny brown. Gus wears his hair short and Manny wears it longer, with his ringlets free when not carefully styled with gel. Still, their eyes and features are the same. Two drops of water split evenly in half, and even though the reflection is the same, they feel and sound different. Even their essence is different. Their voice, their disposition, and even their likes are different, but now that I've been closer to Manny, now that I've had his body on mine, I can tell that even in the way Gus's arms feel around me, they're different. "Fancy seeing you here."

"Only once in a lifetime your sister gets engaged, I had to be here, Carita."

"Don't call her that," Manny snaps at the same time I flinch at hearing the nickname I've started to associate with lust and comfort in these past couple of weeks. They've both used it in the past and it never bothered me, until now. It has become our thing, Manny and me, and it feels wrong coming from Gus's mouth.

"She's our Carita. Of course I can call her that," Gus says, winking, pulling me to him and hugging me. The eternal flirt but this time, I don't think Manny is too happy about it.

"She's not and I said to not call her that," he snaps. Gus tries to open his mouth but the look Manny gives him is enough to prickle my skin. I'm sure they have their own secret twin language because Gus backs up with his hands up and shakes his head, showing us both he got the message.

"I'll let you two alone so you can figure out whatever the hell it is you have going on."

"Gus—" I try to say but I get interrupted quickly.

"Don't, Cara. Not my business," he adds, looking between us and taking a deep breath. "I have enough business of my own to be minding someone else's. Just be careful, both of you," he says, shaking his head and then adding, "It's not only *your* hearts on the line here."

He looks over where Allie and Jake are taking pictures. I knew this whole thing was messy but damn it if I didn't think how it could affect Allie. Nothing will happen though because this is just a road trip fling and then things will get back to normal. He'll go back to his corporate world and I'll go back home.

"What was that?" I ask Manny after Gust walks away to hug his sister.

His eyebrows furrow and he lets out a breath before saying. "What was it that you called me the other day, caveman? Clearly, I turn into one when it comes to you."

"Are you always this honest?" I ask because what the heck?

"I hate lies. I don't see a purpose to them, especially when half of the shit that goes wrong in the world happens because of lies. Plus, I'm asking *you* all the time not to hide from me. Wouldn't it make me a hypocrite if I did just that?"

I didn't expect that reply but again, Manny keeps surprising me, and the more time I spend with him, the more I talk to him, the more I realize that maybe we're both hiding who we are. I hide from the world, the hurt, and the pain behind the pretty smile and he hides from love behind his job.

"Maybe but it would have been easier to just tell me that you were joking or something," I say, twisting my hair around my finger, trying to appear nonchalant, and not that my heart is currently racing a million miles per hour.

"And miss the opportunity to show you, I'm not willing to share? Nah, not a chance. This contract might be temporary but my promises aren't, Carita. For as long as you're in my arms, I'm not sharing." He winks at me, squeezing my arm gently, and walks away to talk to his sister and his soon to be brother-in-law, leaving me breathless.

"It's not every day that I see you speechless," Natalie whispers next to me.

"Jesus, where did you come from? I was about to go get wine, want some?" I ask knowing she doesn't drink wine but trying to deflect and avoid the conversation I know is about to happen.

"I have water, I'm good," she replies, lifting her plastic cup with iced water at me. She's so beautiful and freaking kind and it makes me happy seeing her enjoy her life a little. Since she had Bella so young, she had to grow up so much faster than we all did. And for some reason beyond me she thinks that going out or traveling without her daughter makes her a bad mom. When in reality, Natalie is the best mom I've ever met, and Bella is lucky to have her.

"I'm sure they have stronger things if you want me to ask," I add.

"I'm good, Cara. Not drinking right now, but thank you." When she says that, her eyes get slightly glossy. She's not an emotional person so I'm sure that whatever it is, must be huge. *And she's not drinking.*

"Nattie, are you pregnant?" I whisper and she replies with a silent tear rolling down her cheek and a soft smile.

"Please don't tell anyone, I haven't even told Nick."

"Of course not," I promise, grabbing her hand and pulling her toward the nearest white metal chairs on the patio. "I'm so happy for you, sweetie girl. Is everything okay?" Natalie and Nick have been trying to get pregnant for the past five to six years, and because of her health issues it has been really hard on her body to get pregnant or stay pregnant. I can't imagine how hard that must be for both of them.

"Yes, I think so, or at least the doctor says so," she replies, taking a deep breath in and looking far away toward the beautiful vineyards. "After everything we've been through, I just don't want to get my hopes up or Nick's. He seriously can't take another heartbreak, but it also feels like I'm cheating this baby of being wanted and loved when I won't even tell the dad."

"Oh sweet, sweet girl, that baby knows how much you want her. Yes, I'm going to assume is a girl so I can continue my girl aunt era," I say, pulling a smile from her and that's exactly what I was aiming for—to help her lighten the load. "You take your time telling people and when you're ready, we'll be here to shower you, baby, and Bella in love. Nick, too, I guess."

"Thanks, Care, you always know how to say the right thing. Don't think I'm going to forget about whatever that was going on back there but I'll give you the same courtesy and let you tell me whenever you're ready. I do have a question though..."

"Oh lordy, Nattie, what?"

"Is this a rebound thing from the whole shitshow with Cole?" she asks and I'm too damn sober for this conversation. What am I supposed to say? *No, I like him?* Or say *yes* and treat it like I told Manny we should treat it, like a casual summer fling?

"I'm not sure, Nat. We're having fun is all I can say for right now." I look up and find Manny's eyes on mine as he sips on a glass of wine from across the vineyard. I feel the warming sensation all over my body every time his eyes are on me and the more I think about it, the more I think they always are.

"Okay, I trust you know what you're doing, just tread lightly, okay?"

"I will! Now, let's go say congratulations to our girl who is finally getting her happy ending."

"Before we do, Cara," she says, holding my arm and stopping me from standing up. "I'm sorry about Natasha. I never saw that coming." *Natasha*, her best friend who now is engaged to my ex. Natasha, who was sleeping with Cole while we were together.

"None of us did. She's shown her true colors twice now; we can just cut ties, or at least I did. Also, Natasha? Since when do you call her by her full name?"

"Since she slept with my other best friend's boyfriend and wrecked my relationship with Jake, I've had it. The drama, the backstabbing—it's exhausting. Sometimes, you have to cut out the people who threaten your peace, even if you care about them."

"I'm sorry, Nat. I know you two were close," I add, squeezing her hand.

"But were we? When you're close, you share the truth. You let someone see all of you. I thought we had that, but maybe I never really knew her at all—not until now. And this version of her, I don't need in my life."

I get up and give her a hug, squeezing her tight, but not too much, afraid to hurt the little miracle growing inside of her when I hear Allie say, "Why are you two hugging?"

I leap out of Natalie's arms and into Allie's knocking her down to the grass and squealing. "Eeeeeeek!!! Congrats, bitch! You're going to be the most beautiful bride!"

"Cara, what the hell?!" Allie shouts, pushing my face away from hers as I try to pepper her whole face with kisses, making them in the air instead.

"I can't wait to go dress shopping—" kiss "—and pick flowers —" kiss "—and pick colors—" kiss "—and watch all of your dreams come true. You deserve it all!"

"You psycho, stop it before you kill me and I miss the chance to think about the wedding." Allie laughs loudly, hugging me tighter and reminding me how much peace she has found this past year.

I drop my head by hers, inhaling one of her wild curls so I roll over to her side while coughing, "Your hair almost killed me, Allison."

"It wouldn't have happened if you didn't tackle me to the ground, Caroline."

"Blasphemy!" I shout while gasping and sitting up, pretending she just shot me in the heart. "Not my name, Allison Marie."

"It sure is, Caroline May. Just because you don't like it, doesn't mean it's not real. Also, you called me Allison first."

"Are you two done?" Jake shouts from where he's standing, holding two champagne flutes and lifting one up when we look his way. We fall into heavy laughter and with the help of Manny and Gus who came to rescue us from my burst of love, we get up. I shake off my dress, pulling down my skirt, making sure I'm not showing anyone my ass and give Allie a proper hug.

"Congratulations, Allie. Nobody deserves this more than you." Her eyes glimmer with genuine joy, showing her smile wide and warm as I try to mirror it. I'm so damn happy for her and Jake.

"Thanks, Cara. Love you. I'm so happy you were able to witness this." I can feel the warmth wrap around me like a cozy blanket, making this moment even more special.

As I step away from her, my heart races, excitement bubbling up inside me thinking about all the things we need to plan for. I know I'll be the best bestie girl to ever exist, bridesmaid or not. I glance at Jake, and my smile softens. I walk over, pulling him into a hug, feeling the steady beat of his heart against mine.

"Don't fuck it up this time, big guy," I say, my voice half teasing, half serious.

"Never again, Cara." His eyes are filled with sincerity and I feel like a little girl on Christmas day. My two best friends finally pushed all their bullshit aside, communicating and getting engaged. We all knew they were end game, it was up to them to realize it too.

"Congrats! You two deserve all the happiness in the world. And the babies, all the babies," I add because I know that Allie has always wanted to be a mom.

"One step at a time," he adds, letting me go and walking to get his girl.

After everyone finishes all their hugs, claps on the back, and blessings to them, we sit at the picnic tables outside and enjoy wine, food, and the beautiful scenery. Manny and Gus reserved the whole place for us so the service has been nothing but top-tier. The food is incredible and so is the conversation. We learn about how the guys planned this in mere days and how they were able to pull it off. We eat, drink, and laugh. We share ideas and good memories . Allie cries a lot, as usual, and Roe rolls her eyes. It's honestly the best night I've had in a while, surrounded by all the people I love so much.

I get up to use the restroom and after spending longer than necessary in the bathroom, trying to compose myself and not jump Manny at every chance I get. Being around Manny and all of them has been hard. I don't want to lie to them but I also can't help my lingering eyes after he talks or the way every time I look at him, he seems to be looking at me first and that makes me feel many different ways—desired, pretty, alive. *Get it together, Cara. One night. Just make it the rest of the night without letting everyone see how much you like him.* I rinse my hands and face and open the door, to find Manny standing right outside of it.

"Jeez, you scared me," I say, but I'm immediately rewarded with Manny's lips on mine followed by him pushing me back-ward, shutting the bathroom door, and locking it behind us. "Manny," I moan between kisses against his lips.

"Yes, Carita?" he asks, pulling back and keeping his eyes on mine. The fire behind his eyes make my knees weak and I just cannot.

"What are you doing, hotshot?" I ask, grabbing his collar but not stepping away from him for more than the few inches between our lips.

"What does it look like I'm doing, bebé? Kissing you like I've been dying to all day, and I finally got you alone."

His words hit me like a spark, setting off something inside me that's been smoldering for hours. I can feel the weight of his gaze, the hunger in it—like he's not just kissing me, but devouring the space between us, wanting *more*. His fingers find the small of my back, pressing me closer to him, the heat of his body against mine sending a jolt of desire through my chest, straight to my core. His lips crash against mine, hungry and insistent, like he's been starved for this kiss and I'm glad I'm not the only one.

There's something powerful about knowing I'm the woman unraveling Manny. "They're going to know we're in here doing this," I say as I turn my face sideways, giving him access to my neck. My pulse races as I try to ground myself. But he's already moving, his lips trailing down the curve of my jaw, nipping and kissing with a delicious slowness that makes me ache for more. He knows how to leave me hanging on the edge, wanting more, but never giving it all at once. His mouth moves lower, his lips brushing against my throat, and I feel it before he even reaches that tender spot—my pulse quickening in anticipation. I don't need to say a word; he knows exactly where to go.

My body reacts to this whole thing, melting into him and arching my back so I can close whatever space there is between us.

"Doing what? Kissing? Or do you want more to happen?" he asks, biting his lip and smoothing his thumb across mine. My eyes flare at that question and I can feel my cheeks burning up too, keeping me from hiding how much that sounds like what I've wanted all day.➡

"Do you want me to fuck you in this bathroom, Cara?" I suck in a breath because judging by the instant tingle between my legs and my stomach doing a somersault, I guess I do want him to fuck me in this bathroom.

"Manny," I whisper.

"That wasn't a yes, Cara. You're not shy, so tell me, bebé, what do you want me to do?" he asks, bringing his hand to my neck and holding my face in place so I can't move it away. So I have to look into his eyes as I try not to fall apart.

"Yes." My voice is barely above a whisper, covered with need and want. Covered in whatever spell Manny has put me under that gets me to say yes to him railing me against a wall and now in a bathroom with all of our friends in the next room.

"Yes, what?" he asks, eyes on me daringly.

"Fuck me in this bathroom," I command with a sultry tone, looking him dead in the eyes. He makes me feel so confident, so desired, so perfect, when he looks at me like this, so the least I can do is hold his gaze too and tell him exactly how I feel.

"I thought you'd never ask," Manny whispers against the shell of my ear, dropping his hands to the back of my legs and lifting them slowly. When he gets to the curve of my ass, he hisses against my neck, licking the sensitive spot right above my collarbone.

"No underwear, sunshine? Were you thinking about me when you got dressed today? Were you thinking about my fingers fucking you in dark places when you decided to wear this perfect dress, those damn cowgirl boots, and no underwear? Or were you thinking about my dick, filling every inch of you somewhere public? Which one was it?"

"Both," I breathe, because that's exactly what I'd thought about this morning. About how much I enjoyed his face between my legs in that alleyway the other night and how ready I was for that, or anything else for that matter, to happen again. Soon. Here. Anywhere, really. He stops kissing me, looking at me with desire in his eyes, making me feel on fire from the inside out.

He drags his fingers up my ass, squeezing hard and pulling me closer to him, letting me feel his hard dick against my belly. "You see what you do to me? Just grabbing this perfect ass and the thought of you walking around all day with nothing underneath this dress has me ready to shoot in my pants. You're driving me wild, bebé."

Manny crashes his lips to mine, stealing my breath and reducing me to ashes. His words, his touch, his smell, all of it is too much and I need more. I part my legs when I feel his knuckles against my pussy, and instantly feel the tip of his fingers slide between my lips, finding my clit and teasing it.

"Oh," I say in a hushed tone, trying not to let the whole vineyard know what we're doing. But I'm losing control because of the way he's making me feel. He touches my clit softly, giving me just enough friction to make me go crazy but not enough to tip me over the edge. I've never been this close to coming in my life with so little but the anticipation of him fucking me in this bathroom and making me come while screaming his name, has me almost seeing stars. Or not screaming because the last thing that I want is for everyone out there to know.

He slides a finger in me, then two, pulsing them slowly, and pressing against the spot that makes me lift one of my legs around his ass, and dig my heel onto him.

"Are you this wet and ready for me?" Manny asks and all I can say is a broken moan. If I don't come soon, I'm going to go insane. "We don't have a lot of time, Carita. Are you going to come for me all over my fingers like the good girl I know you are?" He's pressing me against the door, using the leverage to pump in and out with his fingers. He brings his thumb to my clit, pressing hard at the same time he bites that sensitive spot on my neck, right under my ear. At this rate, I wouldn't be surprised if there's a bruise there. The perfect spot and he knows it.

I clench my pussy against his fingers and when I think this couldn't feel any better, he slides another finger in making me feel so full and stretched out around them.

"Fuck, Manny," I gasp, moving my hips in circles, using the back of my heel as leverage.

"Chase it, Cara, ride my fingers, use them. I want them soaked in you," he says, and when he presses all of his fingers into my body, that's all it takes for me to reach the peak and fall over. "Fuck, so hot, so wet, so perfect," he praises against my ear, watching me come down from my high.

My chest is heaving, as I bring my hands in front of me, opening his belt and trying to get his dick free. He kisses me as I fumble with his belt. His kisses are rushed, passionate, and wild. And with every kiss, he reaches farther than my lips. I'm being kissed like he's a dying man and I'm air. Everything else fades to the background and the only thing that matters is this moment, this one kiss.

I pull his pants down and his hands grip my ass, lifting me and sitting me on top of the sink. I'm at the perfect height, aligned with his body, and when his lips clash against mine again, I wrap my legs around him, guiding him into me. His dick stretches me to the point of both pleasure and pain and sends tingles all over my body. I break the kiss, trying to catch my breath, and tilting my head back letting out a soft moan. He takes advantage of the neck access and peppers wet kisses up and down my neck.

I start to relax around him so I guide his body in tempo with mine, using the heels of my boots against his firm ass. We move in synchrony, letting our bodies feel, and getting lost in the moment. His pace quickens and when I moan again, he brings his thumb to my clit, pressing against it and helping me reach my climax again.

"Yes, Manny, right there," I whimper, shaking in his arms and clenching against him until he lets out a guttural groan, and then I feel him tense. We both come down from the high, our chest heaving out breathing erratic. His sink in my hair, as he pulls back gently, gaining more access to my mouth, kissing me again. This time, tenderly, patient, and kind. Soft kisses, allowing my body to settle.

"We didn't use a condom," he balks and he's right. I didn't even think about it, letting myself get lost in the moment.

"I'm on the pill and I got tested not too long ago..." I let that thought fizzle into the air because I don't want to think about telling him that I got tested after I found out that I was being cheated on for God knows how long.

"I haven't gotten tested this year, but I've never fucked without a condom. I'll get tested first thing in the morning though." He leaves a soft kiss on my lips, before adjusting himself back into his pants. He brings both my legs down and helps me stand.

"Never?" I ask.

"Never," Manny replies. He brushes his hands through my hair, fixing it and helping me feel more put together than the mess I'm sure it is right now. I reach to get some toilet paper to wipe myself when his hand stops me. As he brings me back toward the door with his body, and his hand pins mine to the door, he says against my ear, "Don't wipe it off, Carita. Leave my cum inside of that pretty little pussy of yours. And every time you feel it in you or running down your legs, touch yourself. Touch it, feel it, hell even bring it to your lips and lick it. Let it be a reminder of the fucking goddess you are." As he brings his other hand to my sensitive sex and slides two fingers back into my pussy.

He palms my pussy as he pushes his cum deeper inside of me and this shouldn't be as hot as it is, but goddamn. I could come again if he keeps doing that. He slides his fingers back out, bringing them to my lips. "You said you liked the taste the other day, so lick them clean. Suck them off and taste both of us this time."

Manny's eyes flare as I do as he asks, swirling my tongue around his fingers and tasting the salty but tangy combination on his fingers. This is obscene and sexy and hot all at once, and I fucking love it. I didn't even know I had a kinky side but fuck, I love this.

"God, you're so fucking perfect. Look at you sucking my cum off my fingers. You were made for me," he coos. I open my eyes wide at those words but if he notices he doesn't say anything.

"Let's go before I have to fuck you again." He tucks himself back into his pants, bringing his hands to the sink and washing them clean. He gives me a peck on the lips before opening the bathroom door, looking around and then letting me step out in front of him.

He pulls the back of my dress down and walks closer to me, so he can whisper, "I don't know about you, but I could go for round two. If you want to call this celebration a night. Just say the word and we're gone." Manny gives me a soft kiss on the top of my head and walks to the front of the vineyard while I head to the back where my friends are waiting for me.

29

FREAKING ADORABLE

EVERYWHERE, EVERYTHING, NOAH KAHAN FT. GRACIE ABRAMS

Manny

"THANK YOU FOR EVERYTHING," Allie says, hugging me and stepping back to stand by Jake. After Cara and I's sex escapade in the bathroom, we finished dinner and the bottles of wine we were tasting and now we're all ready to part our ways. They all leave early tomorrow since this was such a quick trip but I'm happy we were able to make it happen. Allie and Jake are staying longer to explore Tennessee before going to Atlanta for their friend's wedding, but the rest of the group is going back to Baker. Except for Gus—who knows where he's going next?

"That's what brothers are for. You guys be safe and see you in a few days."

"You're going to the wedding too?" Jake asks.

"Cara's bringing me as her plus one so yeah, I'll be there," I reply, putting my hands in my pocket and looking down, trying not to show any reaction. My head is racing with thoughts of Cara in a formal dress and also taking it off her after.

"Good, see you then. Thanks again for helping with this."

"No need to thank me, just don't fuck it up. Kay?" I warn and he smiles and nods, walking with Allie to one of the vehicles that came to pick us up. With the amount of wine we've all had, I didn't want to risk anyone driving so I ordered everyone a car to take them back to their hotels. The one for Cara and me is waiting in the back of the driveway, with Cara already inside. She said her feet hurt so after she hugged everyone, she got in the car.

After everyone's safely on their way, I find Cara sound asleep on the backseat. I give the driver directions to where we're going and lift Cara's head onto my lap so she's more comfortable. She wiggles against me so I try to soothe her back to sleep, "Sh, sh, sh," I whisper, brushing her hair off her face and behind her ear.

In between bringing her arm around my lap and a yawn she says, "I really like you, Manuel Zabana, I hope you know that." Her words stop me in my tracks and I start thinking about the possibility of her letting me in—maybe giving me a chance— even if I'm not enough for her. Maybe she'll give me a chance beyond this trip and I will find it in me to prove to her that I'm worth her time. Maybe if she gives me the chance I can work to show her every minute of every day how worthy she is of it all. I want to be one of those damn bracelets, captured in a timeless token into a memory she doesn't want to let go.

"LOOK AT THIS PLACE," Cara says in awe. We woke up early and after breakfast, we left the house to explore Nashville. We took the city tour and have been hopping on and off the bus all day. We're at our final destination for the day and Cara's highlight of the trip, according to everything that she has said. The Grand Ole Opry is stunning and she seems to think so, too. The wooden beams overhead seem to hum with the melody of the artists who have performed here over the years. You may not be able to hear the music but you can feel it the moment you walk inside. The walls are covered with photographs of country music icons, their smiles frozen in time, each telling their own story. It's perfect and watching this place through her eyes has got to be the most magical thing I've ever seen.

We wander further into the venue, the stage surrounded by beautiful light. I can almost imagine the strum of a guitar and the laughter of an audience from years past. I can almost hear the room filled with melodies and singing. Cara glances up at the giant chandelier, its crystals sparkling just like her eyes, like stars in a night sky. Her eyes are alight with joy, taking it all in and when I think she couldn't get more excited, her skin breaks out in goosebumps as she takes the space in. Her hands grip her arms, rubbing them up and down while she says, "This place is beautiful."

I pause next to her, bringing my hand up to her chin, lifting and tilting it so she can look at me. "You are beautiful, Carita." Her cheeks blush as she goes on her tiptoes and kisses my lips with a soft kiss.

"Thanks, now hush, let's go." We pause at a small exhibit showcasing some artifacts—an old cowboy hat, a vintage microphone, and handwritten lyrics. Each piece feels like a whisper from the past, inviting us to share the moment with them. This is why I like museums and exhibitions; it's like history lives through them and there's so much to learn, if not only from the exhibition itself but from all the hidden truths between them.

"Thank you for coming with me on this trip, Manny," she whispers. "I didn't think I needed anyone to make this trip better but you sure have. Thank you."

"Happy to do it, Carita mia," I reply, pulling her under my arm and kissing her head. We walk side by side until we join a small group waiting for our tour guide. "Want to ditch the tour?" I ask and that earns me a big smile and her eyes shine with mischief, as her gaze locks with mine.

I grab her hand and pull her toward the exit, my thumb gently rubbing the back of her hand as we walk fast past people waiting to enter. I grab my phone as we walk down the steps and toward the garden, Cara giggling at my side. I call the company and tell them to send a car our way, while Cara and I walk down the street taking in the beautiful day. We have to wait for the car to arrive so I steer her to the giant guitar by the front. "Want a picture?" I ask her, pointing to it.

"You're not annoyed at my excessive amount of pictures yet?" she asks, grabbing her phone from her small brown purse with the giant glittery heart and handing it to me.

"I could never be annoyed by anything you do. Plus, you look absolutely adorable standing in front of the camera. Do you like pictures? Take your pictures."

"Are you sure you're a man? Because you sure as hell don't act like one sometimes," Cara quips and I flinch. "I didn't mean it like that. I just mean you're so patient and, like, encourage all my shenanigans and you don't complain when I ramble. It's just odd," she adds.

"It's not that hard, Carita. Is that where your bar is set? With men who won't listen to you or take your picture? All the way on the damn ground it seems."

"The swoony man only exists in books and in front of people; behind closed doors, they turn into monsters." That sentence hit me right in the chest. She doesn't know how much I feel that about my own dad and how he portrays himself as a family man when truly none of us are ever enough in his eyes. He is kind to our mom and that's the main reason we tolerate him but the man is a piece of shit sometimes. It also makes me want to kill every man she's ever been around with that gave her that same feeling.

I walk to her, closing the gap between us, forgetting the picture I was trying to get. "Cara," I whisper, bringing my hand up to cup her face, "Can't you see? You deserve the world. You deserve patience, and swoony moments. You deserve to have your picture taken, and your chicken tenders for dinner. You deserve slow dancing and someone to hold your purse when you just want to spin around. You deserve to be driven around and be taken to places *you* want to go. I've heard you tell all your friends they deserve better, why don't you think the same for you? Why is it so hard for you to believe that you deserve better too?

A silent tear rolls down her face as she leans into my hand and says, "I don't want to cry in front of all these people, Manny."

"Then let's disappear, bebé. Just you and me, okay?" I ask and with her nod, we walk toward the vehicle already waiting for us.

We drive around, away from the city and the crowd, quietly watching out the window as we get further and further from the chaos. We are dropped off in a wooded area secluded enough to have privacy in the park, but still on the private property where I want to take her—if she's up to it after we talk.

Opening the door of the vehicle for her, I give Cara my hand and help her out, walking side by side with her until we reach a large swing under a tree in the park. When I was researching things to do in Nashville, I found this spot. It's quiet and beautiful and I knew we could find some privacy here.

She takes a spot on the swing next to me, tilting her head back onto the backrest and kicking her feet as if trying to rock herself but not reaching the ground—so I help her. We rock softly, keeping each other company and sharing the silence. Somehow, this quiet moment has spoken to me more than years of words. I sit in silence next to Cara for five, ten, fifteen minutes now, just aimlessly swinging, watching the sun disappear behind high mountain peaks, letting the change in the air pass us by with every minute—and just be.

I don't remember the last time *just being* was enough and I like it. I love it. I think I love *her*. Maybe I always have, deep down, secretly, behind closed doors. Maybe I never put it into words or thoughts because why would I when it wouldn't be reciprocated? But now, how could I help it? How could I not see that she brings out the best in people—in me? That she sets people free. With her carefree spirit and her silliness. With her funny highway games and her childish drinks. She lets her inner child free and it's beautiful to see. So yeah, I think I do love her.

I want to give her time and space. I want to let her tell me what she's thinking if she wants to, but I also want her to know I'm here to listen or to just keep her company if that's what she wants.

"Carita," I say, my voice comes out groggy as if I've been sleeping for a while but it's the emotion building up inside of my heart that won't let me clear my throat. Like those three words are threatening to come out and it won't clear until they do.

"Mm hm," she mumbles, her eyes closed, and her perfect lips relaxed.

"You know you can talk to me, right? I know you shared some of what was bothering you the other day, but I'm here. For as long as you'll have me, share with me. I may not be able to give you good advice but I'm a good listener."

Her mossy green eyes snap open, tilting her head to face me and looking at me she says, "You are a good listener and it's not that I don't want to talk to you it's that I don't know why I'm still dwelling on shit that happened a long time ago."

"It doesn't matter how long ago, if it's still bothering you should talk about it. Even if not with me. When you let things cook inside of you, they might eat you alive. Sometimes you just need to let them out."

She kicks her feet under her softly, barely touching the ground. "Just like you share so much about yourself?" she asks, and when I flinch she sits up straight and apologizes. "That was unfair and mean, I'm so sorry. I'm just so tired. So tired of feeling too much of *being* too much." She brings her hands to her face as she shakes it softly and lets out a small grunt. She's frustrated and I hate that I can't ease her mind. I hate that I haven't been able to show her how much of me I've already shared with her and how much more I wish I could share for longer.

"You are not too much. If there's anything I say you hear, let it be that. You're perfect." I bring my hand up to caress her cheek tenderly but instead of leaning into my touch, she pulls away.

"It's just because you and I, whatever this is, is new and exciting, and hot. So freaking hot," she adds, with a smile on her face before looking somber again. "But eventually you'll find out all I'm good for is a short and fun time, not a long time."

I lift her chin to look at me. "Why on earth do you think you're only good for a short time? I don't know where you'd get that from but have you seen your friendships? You've had the same group of best friends your whole life. You're so loyal, Cara, fun and funny too which are two completely different things, and fuck, bebé anyone would be so lucky for you to give them any time, even if for a little while. I'm so lucky about this time you've given *me*. Your time is a gift, not the other way around."

"Then why couldn't he love me, Manny?" she asks, immediately covering her face and dropping it back to her lap.

"Cara, come here," I say, trying to pull her by her hands onto my lap. Trying to soothe her the only way I know how. She fights it at first but then she lets me pick her up and I manage to sit her on my lap. Her head rests on my chest as I rake my fingers through her soft hair.

"No, it's okay. I'm a damn mess over a man. A man I don't even love anymore but, like, if he couldn't love me after giving him twelve years of my life, then who could ever?"

I can. I do, I think but I don't say out loud. "He's an idiot. Anyone who doesn't see how incredible you are or how lucky they were that you even gave them the time of day is an idiot. He doesn't deserve you. He didn't deserve you then and surely doesn't deserve you now. Not your laughter, not your thoughts, not your time, not your tears." I kiss the top of her head but leave my lips on it before she sits up and looks at me kindly.

"It's just so hard to look past it, you know? I still don't understand why I thought begging him to love me was what I needed. And you know, after talking to my therapist I definitely see he wasn't good for me, but how do you shut up the little voice in your head? The one that says that maybe if I drank champagne instead of sprite with grenadine or maybe if I didn't drive the stupid Barbie van, maybe he would've taken me seriously?" *I'm going to kill him.* The more I hear about this douche, the more I want to smack him in the face.

"If someone can't see all those little things as what makes you unique and freaking adorable, they truly don't deserve you, Cara. Your friends, your sister, your parents, they all love you so loud. Hell, you tell my sister all the time to never settle for less, and to fuck all the people who think otherwise, right?" I ask, waiting for her reply, and when she nods I continue, "Then why do you think you don't deserve the same? You don't think you deserve better than a jerk who couldn't appreciate everything you are? Barbie van, Dirty Shirleys, jumping deer, and all?"

Her breath catches in her throat before she wipes her eyes. She takes a long, slow breath, and I can feel her shoulders sag, like a weight just lifted off. Then, without saying a word, she leans her head against my shoulder. Her fingers twist into the fabric of my shirt, seeking something solid.

"He's an idiot, isn't he?" she whispers.

"The biggest idiot." My arm instinctively pulls her closer to my chest in a tight squeeze. "You deserve to be loved, Cara. All of you. I'm sorry he couldn't see that."

She doesn't say anything at first. Just breathes, her hand still gripping my shirt as though she's afraid to let go. A small, almost imperceptible laugh escapes her. "Thanks, Manny." Her voice softens, the sadness still there but wrapped in a hint of something lighter. "Maybe I shouldn't be paying my therapist. I should just pay you instead?"

I grin, the corners of my mouth pulling up. "Nah, that's her job. I'm just here for the important stuff. Moral support and... kisses, you know. Top tier package deal."

Her laugh breaks through, quiet but real, and for a moment, the weight of it all seems a little lighter.

She laughs loudly, coming from her belly this time, deep within her emotions and it's the most beautiful sound. "You like kissing me, huh?"

"I do, and I would very much like to kiss you right now so let me know when you're ready," I add, squeezing her leg.

"You can kiss me anytime, Manuel Zabana," she replies.

"Don't say things you don't mean, Cara." I hold her gaze, letting her see the full meaning of my words. I let her see that I want her to mean it. I want her to let me kiss her, touch her, and worship her anytime. She deserves to be front and center all the time.

"I mean it." She smiles softly and I know she does mean it. Even if she means it like *now*, on this trip, there's a part of me that truly wishes she meant any time forever.

I hold the back of her neck, threading my fingers through her hair and pulling her to me to kiss her tenderly on her lips. Not the hungry way I've kissed before—ready for more. I want to take my time with this kiss. I want to savor it and love this moment forever. I want to imagine this is a never-ending kiss and that all our worries will disappear. I want to think that with every kiss I give her, I take a little longer in the hopes that it never ends. In the hopes that this, this between us never does.

We break our kiss and rest our foreheads together. I whisper against her lips, "Can I show you what we came here for?"

"What is it?" Cara asks and I pull her up by her hands, walking toward the platform where a little bird is waiting for us to let her fly.

30

THE BEST SEAT IN THE HOUSE
WILDEST DREAMS (TAYLOR'S VERSION), TAYLOR SWIFT

Cara

A HELICOPTER. A damn helicopter ride. I know money doesn't buy happiness or whatever but this little ride is making me extremely happy. I can't believe how this man takes things he's known about me for years and just makes them happen. I used to be obsessed with helicopters and little planes, the total contrast to Allie. She hates flying, I wish all I could do was fly. I used to dream about going on helicopter rides all my childhood and when I was eighteen, that was part of my parents' graduation gift. I've been wanting to do it again and now, Manny just made it happen.

"Look!" I shout, pointing at the people dancing on top of a party bus in the middle of Broadway Street. The lights from the buildings form a beautiful picture and from up here, we're getting the best view. I grip the edge of the seat and laugh as we make a quick turn and get a tilted view of the city. I lean closer to the window, straining to get a better look.

"Look at this view!" I shout again. When I turn around to see if Manny is watching, I find him looking at me. "Stop looking at me, you weirdo, and look at the city."

"I have the best seat and view in the house, Carita," he says, and I hear the pilot chuckle. I forgot he can hear us too but Manny clearly doesn't care. I roll my eyes and look back out.

We're approaching our descent after viewing the city for the past twenty minutes, there's nothing to clear your mind more than feeling small. Seeing the city buzzing below you, full of people, buildings, and cars will do that to you. What an instant serotonin boost. We finally make it to the ground, Manny reaches over and unbuckles me. After stepping out he proceeds to hold the door open for me and helps me to step out.

The night air is different, or maybe I'm different. A crying session, a reassuring moment, and then a helicopter ride? Who am I? Actually, who is this man and where has he been hiding? We walk hand in hand out of the driveway, until we reach the vehicle that dropped us off.

"Manny, I hope you're paying this man well."

"Which man?"

"The driver." I mention it because he has been at our beck and call for the past two days and I don't know if that's normal.

"I do, sunshine, don't you worry." He opens the door for me and grabs my hand as he slides into the seat beside me. He holds my hand in his and never lets go the entire ride. We get to the house and after walking up to the entrance, I see a giant bag that looks like takeout by the door. Manny grabs it and we walk inside.

"You hungry?" he asks, taunting me with the bag .

"What do you have in there, Manuel?" I ask and he gives me a mischievous smile before pulling out a wrapper the size of a burger.

I fucking love burgers and fries. They're my top-tier choice every time, and the only thing to make it better would be—I don't finish my thought when I gasp, loudly shouting, "Gimme!" because this man not only has a burger in his hand, he has a mayo packet and this is exactly what dreams are made of.

I squeal and grab the food from him, walking to the couch and plopping down. He follows me, cackling and sitting on the opposite end. I try to take my shoes off but he stops me and says, "Let me." He takes my shoes and socks off, putting them down and keeping my feet on his lap. He pulls one of my toes and I gasp in surprise. He smiles, doing the same with the rest of them.

He must know. "How do you know?"

"How do I know what? That you like your toes popped? One time in the Dominican, our parents paid for that group of masseuses to come give us massages by the water, do you remember that?"

Barely. Forever ago all of us took a family vacation to the Zabana's beach house in the Dominican Republic. That family knows how to splurge. And one of the things we got there were massages by the beach. "Yeah," I reply.

"You kept asking how to say 'toes' and getting all tangled up about why 'toes' and 'fingers' are the same in Spanish. It cracked me up. But long story short, all you really wanted was for that girl to pull your toes. I remember how much you liked that, so I thought it might still be a thing."

"You remember that?" My voice catches, warmth washing over me.

"I remember it all, Cara." Manny meets my gaze, and for a moment, the world around us fades. I can see the memories flicker in his eyes—the laughter, the little moments that made up our shared history. It's like he's holding onto every silly, tender detail, and it makes my heart so damn happy.

He grabs my other foot and does the same as I unwrap my

burger and my fries, adding a dollop of mayo on the wrapper so I can dip my fries. I'm a happy camper, eating all the greasy food and enjoying the company. I start thinking about how our arrangement is coming to an end and how I don't want it to end. It also hits me that Manny hasn't worked, or at least I haven't seen him work in the past few days.

"How's work?" I ask, chewing the last of my burger before scrunching the wrapper and tossing it in the bag.

"I wouldn't know," he replies, taking a bite of his wrap. I fucking knew he wouldn't eat a burger because even though I have the habits of a toddler, he doesn't. "Last time I talked to Gus, they were doing fine and I asked to be kept in the dark since the whole Virgil debacle."

"That's a first," I say.

"Yes, for the first time in my life, I'm actually taking a break, and it feels amazing, Cara. I don't know if I would've done it without you, so thank you."

"I didn't do anything. If anything, I'm the one who should be thanking you." I glance at him, the warmth of gratitude blooming in my chest. "You've driven me around, kept me fed and entertained, and even played therapist. You're a good friend, Manny. I'm lucky to have you."

He swallows hard and if I didn't know better I would think that the word *friend* affected him just as much as it felt odd coming from my mouth. *He's more than a friend* flashes through my mind in bold neon signs but instead of Manny saying something about it, he gives me a playful smile. I guess that glimpse and short moment was a lapse in judgment. Maybe I wanted to see that.

"My goal is to keep you relaxed too," he says playfully as he winks at me. My cheeks heat up, a rush of warmth spreading through me as I glance away, trying to hide my smile. Why do I keep hiding from him when I know damn well that all I want right now are his hands on me.

"Oh yeah? Do you have something in mind? I'm pretty tense all of a sudden," I say as I lay the rest of my food on the table and sit on my knees next to him.

He does the same with his food but instead of setting everything aside, he grabs the styrofoam cup from the bag and removes the lid.

"I have a few things in mind," he replies as he keeps his eyes on me and my whole body becomes alive with awareness. Awareness about everything.

I'm painfully aware of the way his Adam's apple bobs as he dips his fingers into the cup, rattling the ice. I am completely aware of his eyes on my neck and then my legs as I clench my thighs. "We've done so much in the past couple of days, Carita. I think your body could use a treatment, you know, to help your muscles. Are your muscles sore, bebé?"

His raspy voice sends a shiver down my spine—my body even more aware of him than it was before. "Yes," I manage to breathe out.

He scoops out an ice cube at the same time that his eyes darken and I lick my lips. He's watching my every move too because when I bring my hands over my knees and rest them on my thighs he practically growls.

Manny gets closer to me, bringing his mouth to my ear and whispering in a raspy voice, "You know what's really good for your muscles? Ice." I feel a cold sensation down the side of my neck. He traces my neck and collarbone with the ice cube and when I hiss, he lifts it and traces the same path with his hot tongue. The cold and hot contrast has my body set in overdrive and I'm immediately as turned on as if I was naked and his tongue was everywhere on my body. I place a hand on his neck but he immediately lifts his mouth from my skin. I feel the loss of his touch immediately and arch my back trying to close the gap between us. "Patience, Carita mia, patience."

Manny moves the ice cube to my ear lobe, touching it and moving it side to side before removing it and chasing the cold with his mouth, sucking on my earlobe and biting gently. The temperature contrast has my brain in overdrive and I can feel every bit of my body tense under his touch in the best way possible.

"Fuck," I say, spreading my knees to try to get some friction from the seam of my shorts. He brings the ice back up, but this time runs it right behind my ear and all the way down to his favorite spot on my neck. I love when he kisses me there and so does he. He applies pressure with the ice until the skin feels almost numb—the ice melting, sending drops of water running down my shoulder. Before I realize it, he removes the ice from my neck, his mouth covering my now frigid skin, erasing the numbness and licking my skin back to life.

I spread my knees wider on the couch, lowering next to him and positioning the inner seam of my shorts to rub against my clit through my dainty panties. I wore a lace thong today, hoping I would have the chance to show it off, but luckily for me the fabric is creating the friction I'm seeking. I hook my fingers under the band of my shorts and pull the strings above the shorts to give me the right pressure against my sex and my ass. Manny's eyes snap to mine once he notices what I'm doing and there's pure fire in them.

He grabs me by my waist, pulling me up and sitting me on top of his leg. He reaches back to the cup on the table for another piece of ice. This time instead of teasing my ear and neck, he lowers the strap of my top over my shoulder, pulling it down while tracing my arm with his fingers and freeing my breast in the process. Another day that going without a bra works in my favor. Because the moment Manny takes a look at my pebbled nipple, he bites his lip and slides the ice around the sensitive skin.

I hiss at the contact but it feels so damn good. I roll my hips and pull the string of my thong higher.

"Is that enough pressure for you? Is this the right temperature?" Manny asks as he stops moving the ice and leaves it on top of my nipple, making me see stars at the cold sensation. When I roll my hips again, he lifts the ice and lowers his mouth to my nipple, licking it and biting it while his hand grips my back, keeping me in place and not allowing me to move away from his tongue. His mouth feels so warm against my cold skin and the mixture of temperatures, plus almost crossing the line between pain and pleasure, have me extremely turned on. I feel my shorts getting wet.

"Yes," I moan and he pulls my nipple between his teeth before removing his mouth and replacing it with the ice. "Fuck, Manny, more," I plead while rolling my hips over and over trying to chase a high I didn't know I could accomplish without anything touching myself.

He uses both of his hands to spread my legs as wide as they'll go over his leg and then drops his mouth to my breast again. His hand on one of my thighs is wet and cold, as if he still has the piece of ice, just melting away as I burn. But then he brings his cold fingers to my other breast, cupping it and letting me feel the nearly melted piece of ice. His mouth biting, licking, and pulling on one nipple while rubbing the ice until it melts in the other, has me right on the edge of my orgasm. Manny slides his hand up my back and into my hair, gathering the length and wrapping it around his fist and pulling gently backward making me scream, "Oh, yes."

"Ride my leg baby, let me see you come undone with your pretty tit in my mouth and your clit ready for me to touch. Ride it, baby, ride it," he groans before going back to biting my breast. He pulls on my hair, arching my back and pressing my breast harder against his mouth and his other hand pinches my nipple to the edge of pain. I roll my hips again but then, he bites my nipple and that does it. That sends me right over the edge and I come, hard. I rock wildly continuing to chase the sensations—his mouth and hands on my body and my ass grinding on him.

"Manny," I whisper. Falling onto him, limp, after coming down from the hottest high of my life, and I had my fucking pants on.

He smiles against my skin, picking me up, and walking us back to the room. We kiss as we strip our clothes. Shirts off, shoes left behind, and pants being unbuckled all without dropping our mouths from each other. He puts me down and sets the cup of ice he managed to bring on top of the dresser. I push him onto the bed, and seeing him there, laying half naked, his dick hard and straining in his pants, and his eyes on me, taking in all of me, is making me feel like a damn goddess.

I pull his pants down, his dick springing free and I notice he's ready for me—a bead of moisture making his head glisten. I take a card from his own deck and grab an ice cube. I pop the ice in my mouth as I walk back toward him. I bring my hand to his balls, cupping them and squeezing gently.

"Fuck, Cara. Are you trying to kill me?" Manny asks, folding his hands behind his head and using them as leverage so he can see. I kneel next to him on the bed, bringing my mouth over his dick, and taking as much as I can into my mouth. I pull back, my tongue flat, licking all the way back up. "It's so cold."

"It's so good," I smirk before taking him in my mouth. I lick and suck, up and down, until I feel him harden more against my lips. His legs tense under my touch and his breathing becomes shallower. I keep sucking and licking, tasting every inch of him.

"If you don't want me to come all over your pretty mouth,

you need to stop," Manny says and that just gets me more excited to keep going. I work him harder, digging my nails into his thighs and moaning against his dick when I feel him tense up. I swirl my tongue around the tip as he brings his hands to my hair, pulling it up into a made up ponytail. I snap my eyes up at him and I find them locked on me. I feel like I can do it all in this moment. On a high of desire as I have him under my mercy. I smirk and hum around him and he tilts his head back with a groan.

I lick again, this time swirling my tongue around his thick and hard dick until I feel his hand tightening on my hair. "I'm going to—" he groans but he cuts off as I hollow my cheeks and increase the pressure. I immediately feel the salty taste on the back of my throat at the same time that he lets out a groan. I continue to suck, until I feel him still and then swallow it all. "You are so damn perfect. Perfect," Manny says, tilting his head back and raising his hand to my head.

He pulls me up to him, I nestle my legs around his hips as he finds my lips. Kissing me softly at first and then changing pace to hard and needy. His lips and mine dance around each other in perfect rhythm. The world around us fades away as his tongue touches mine intensely, claiming me.

He hooks his hands into my shorts, and pulls them down my hips, as I lift myself up so he can slide them down my legs. As soon as I kick them off, I lower myself over him again. We touch and we kiss some more. He teases my clit with his thumb, pulling a moan out of me.

"Manny." His name a breathy whisper on my lips.

"I love it when you say my name like that," he murmurs, keeping his eyes on me as his hands roam my naked body.

"How?" I ask, entirely aware of his hands touching my back gently, making it down to my ass and squeezing hard.

"Like you want me to take you to the highest high and chase

you all the way down as you fall." I'm so fucked is all I think about. His eyes intensify the stare on me, looking at me like he never wants to see another woman in his life.

I push up from his chest, bringing my hands to my breast as I grind on his pelvis and feel his dick harden under me. He lifts me up with his hands and lowers me over his dick.

I moan, loudly, bringing my hands to his hair, brushing it backward and then giving it a slight pull. "I want you to make me come all over you, Manny."

He groans before saying, "That's what I like to see. You—full of my cock and ready for me." He brings his thumb over my clit and rubs on it until I'm completely adjusted over him. It takes me a minute to stretch around him, as it does every time he's inside of me, but it feels so good I don't care.

He guides me up and down with his hands on my hips, picking up the tempo as we both moan and gasp against each other. I bring my hands to my breast, squeezing them tight and then dropping my hands to his chest, using him to steady myself and keep his tempo. I'm so wet, I can feel it dripping between us and with the sound of his dick sliding in and out of me, I'm close. "I'm almost there, Manny," I whisper.

"I know. Go ahead and come, bebé. Come all over my cock." Right on command I do, my pussy throbbing around him and my chest collapsing onto his, letting him move my hips until I feel him tense up, and then he's coming again. There's something fucking hot about knowing that I just made this God of a man come twice and that he still wants to kiss me and touch me. If I never felt like a goddess before, Manny definitely makes me feel like one.

"Fuck," he groans against my mouth, once we both stop moving and it's just the sound of our breaths around us. He squeezes my ass and says, "Your whole body is perfect, but this ass, this ass is worthy of sculpture."

"Oh my God, stop. My ass may be big but it's full of cellulite," I grumble, burying my head into the crease of his neck.

"You literally need to have a fatty ass to have a big ass, Carita. It's perfect, so damn perfect. Come on, let's go shower," he replies, getting us both up and into the bathroom.

PRETENDING

PRETENDING, GLEE CAST

Cara

FIVE DAYS OF HIKING, exploring, swimming, and dancing. Reading books every night, whispering sweet nothings into each other's ears as we spend time together with our bodies and our souls. I know I was supposed to find myself on this road trip but what I think I found was him

instead. Opening my eyes to the amazing human that is Manuel Zabana has been an utter delight.

I don't know how I didn't notice him before. He's so funny and sweet and kind and freaking listens. He's giving me so many good memories, so many moments to keep as mine and I wish I could keep him too. I have no idea how anything long term would work with him. There's no way that I can keep a man like that forever but God what wouldn't I give to try to.

I love spending time with him. I love how we can go from laughing until we're crying at breakfast, to him reading books to dogs at the shelter, to hiking up to a waterfall in the afternoon, to skinny dipping and fucking under the water while being afraid of being caught. I like spending time with him and sharing small and big moments. He never gets tired of my silly games and now he's even pointing when we see a turtle-ish road or a jumping deer sign, he said that the highway patrol should rename them because my cute names are better.

We went to a soap-making class and he enjoyed smelling all the combinations for me because my sense of smell isn't great so I don't trust my nose. He then purchased all the soaps I loved because he said he needed to smell like my favorite scents at all times.

We saw a field of sunflowers and he pulled over to let me walk through them. I loved it. And he knew I wouldn't want to pick any, just wanted to see them and snap some pictures. He even posted one of me on his social media from the back, you can't tell it's me which is why I didn't say anything but he titled it "catching sunflowers" and I don't know what else could've been more fitting since he kept running behind me trying to catch me as I bee bopped around through the flower field.

We went wedding outfit shopping and I made him do the runway strut for me which he did happily. Have you ever met a human puppy? Because that's exactly what Manny is. Loyal, funny, and playful. Adventurous too. We have gone hiking countless times, we tent-camped one night, even though he hates bugs. Jumping from bridges into the river and eating food we couldn't pronounce were some of the things he decided he wanted to try. We also had sex in the most adventurous and public places and I don't think I would've done that with anyone else. I've never been as comfortable as I am with him. I feel protected, cherished, and happy, and the fact our trip is coming to an end is hurting my soul.

Another thing Manny does? He communicates. We had a whole conversation about safe sex after our condomless shenanigans that could've been awkward with anyone else but not with him. We talked about how important it was for me especially since I didn't use protection before and then I was spiraling thinking the worst when I found out he cheated on me. He got a full STD panel after that. It came back clear, which I had a suspicion it would, but it felt good having that conversation and doing the responsible thing.

I've talked to my parents and they're ready for me to be back home but I haven't been able to reach Nellie. Mom says she's traveling a lot which doesn't surprise me since she's about to start working full time. Nellie is such a wild child, wild grown-up now, I guess. All I can do is hope she stays safe. There's no taming her, so might as well just show her how to not die while she's trying to live her life.

We spent the day at the Georgia Aquarium yesterday, knowing that today will be the wedding of hell and that we wouldn't get as much time together. We took our time and explored downtown Atlanta on electric scooters. And we ate so much food that I was seriously worried my dress wouldn't fit today—but you only live once so I ate it all.

I'm lying in bed in this beautiful hotel, that's also the wedding venue, waiting for Manny to come back up with break-fast, and texting Allie to check if I'll see her before the wedding.

> The Bestie: Do you want me to come to your room and we can get dressed together? We need to talk about all the things.

Fuck. I forgot I had told her to do that with me but now that

I'm in this room with her brother, I really don't think that's a good idea.

> Me: I don't feel great so maybe I'll see you right before the wedding? Do you want to get drinks before? Pregame so we can deal with the shit show that today's gonna be?

I hate lying to her but what am I supposed to say? Oh yeah, you can't come over because I'm sharing a room and a bed with your brother? I don't think it would be a really big deal if I told her we were hooking up, but I also don't want to deal with this when we only have two more days on this trip. Tomorrow, we're heading home and then I can start my new life on Monday. And on top of the Manny stuff, there's the whole thing with Tasha and Cole and I don't want to add more stress to an already stressful night.

> The Bestie: Sure. Is Manny still coming? Let's all go get drinks at the hotel lobby. 3:00?

> Me: YASSSS! Can't wait to squeeze you future Mrs. Clarke.

> The Bestie: 😍 😍 😍 😍 😍 😍 😍 😍 😍

"Croissants, eggs, grapes, and coffee for my queen," Manny shouts from the door. When I look up, I see him carrying a tray and a giant smile. He's in such a good mood today and has been since he woke up at the crack of dawn and said he was going to the gym.

"How was your workout session and thank you! That sounds delicious." He puts the tray on the bed and kisses me on the forehead, before sitting across from me and grabbing a water bottle. He stretches a leg over his lap and takes a sip.

"It was good. I'm ready for a shower, you want to join?"

"Do you ever get enough, hotshot?" I ask, pulling the covers over my chest and grabbing the food, ready to snack on something before figuring out when to start getting dressed. The wedding is at four but if we're meeting Allie and Jake at the bar, I need to start getting ready soon. Especially blow-drying my hair—which takes forever.

"Of you, sunshine? Who could ever get enough?" Manny gets up, removing his shirt with one hand, like Adonis himself, and walking toward the bathroom. His workout pants hang low on his hips and when he makes it to the bathroom door, he turns around to look at me before saying, "I promise a good time and you know I can deliver."

Fucking hell, I know he's right. I shove a piece of croissant into my mouth and follow him into the bathroom to hopefully get in my Manny fix before the day ends.

"BITCH, YOU LOOK STUNNING!" I shout when I see Allie in her smoke-show navy blue gown. Her skin glows under her dress and her hair pulled up in a bun with her curls falling over her face makes her look even more stunning than usual.

"Me? Look at you!" she says, holding my hand and spinning me so my gown twirls around me. I'm wearing this off-the-shoulder black gown with a slit almost to my hip. I thought I was going to die when I put it on and swore I wouldn't wear it, but Manny had other things to say and he offered to buy it in every color they had. So I did.

"Enough about our fabulous selves, let's go find our seats." I pull her by the hand and outside to the patio where the ceremony is taking place. We ended up canceling drinks because according to her she was having hair issues, which I can't tell by looking at her. However, I'm sure dealing with her curls can't be easy all the time so she gets a pass.

It worked out in my favor in the end because my stomach has been in knots thinking about the possibility of seeing Tasha and Cole tonight. Manny can tell I'm tense because he spent all day exploring my body and helping me relax in so many ways. Or at least he tried. It's not only the wedding that's been looming over my head. The fact that our time together is coming to an end is bothering me too. I'm not happy about it and it's stopping me from living in the moment and more like in my head. He, on the other hand, seems to be enjoying every minute we do have together. Taking my bracelet advice and making it his own.

We sit side by side, Jake and Manny next to us as we wait for the ceremony to start. Alex found the love of his life in Livie, something we never saw coming because that man is as grumpy as they come to everyone but us. We never thought he would ever let himself love anything more than football and his mom. When his career ended his whole life stopped, too. His attitude became worse and he was almost unbearable to be around. He healed through a shit ton of therapy and yoga but he still was a little dull. Then Livie happened, literally almost crashing into his arms and the rest is history. They dated for, like, four months before he put a ring on it and they decided not to waste time and get married right away. I usually don't believe in insta-love but those two are proof that when you know, you know. My radar must be off though because I also thought I knew, and I was clearly mistaken. I'm hoping theirs is a lot better than mine.

I'm so lost in my thoughts that I almost missed everyone standing up to look back at Livie walking down the aisle. She's radiant in her princess style gown as she glides all the way to the arch at the front made with beautiful white and beige flowers.

My gaze wanders to the second row in front where I see Tasha's pretty blonde hair draped over Cole's shoulder. I tense at the sight but quickly avert my gaze back to the soon to be husband and wife. When Livie reaches Alex, he steals a kiss from her before anyone can say a word.

"Sorry, I had to," he says and the crowd laughs.

We take a seat and watch this beautiful ceremony take place while I'm constantly wondering if that will ever be me. Not necessarily the girl holding the flowers and wearing the pretty white dress but the girl walking to someone who is looking at her like *that*.

"You're beautiful tonight," Manny whispers in my ear. "I meant to tell you earlier but I was starstruck and couldn't form coherent thoughts."

"You don't look so bad yourself," I whisper back, squeezing his thigh quickly before settling my hand back on my knee. I force my attention back to the couple but my mind is completely torn thinking about Manny and about how good he feels next to me, and how much I like talking to him, and I almost choke on a laugh at the most inappropriate moment thinking about how fucked up this whole situation is.

Even if I were to tell him that I think I like him, what would he do with someone like me? There's only so much I can give him. We seem to fit together on this summer road trip where responsibilities don't exist and he doesn't have to go to work functions and fancy events. When he doesn't have to parade me around in front of cameras or investors. I'm his silly summer fling—a good time. All I'm good for.

Looking at the back of Cole's head as the ceremony continues I remind myself of everything he used to say, not with his words directed at me but with his actions and little innuendos. Never taking the time to do anything I wanted to do made me feel like I wasn't important. Never having a wedding talk with me and letting me think he wasn't ready until he broke up with me and put a ring on someone else's hand. I pump my leg up and down rapidly with all the thoughts swirling in my head. Manny brings his hand to my thigh, settling it down with his touch and grounding me back to the present moment.

"You may kiss your bride," the officiant announces and we quickly stand up to clap for the newlyweds. I have a few minutes to get my shit together before I'm sitting at a table with Manny, Allie, and half our friends, pretending that I'm not falling in love with this man.

32

I'M GOING TO KILL HIM

LATCH (ACOUSTIC), SAM SMITH & PEACE, TAYLOR SWIFT

Manny

THE WEDDING HAS BEEN GOING on for hours now. Wine, champagne, food, music, and dancing have been good for not only my soul but everyone else's. Except I might be breaking from the inside out thinking about this trip coming to an end. How do I tell this girl that I'm in love with her when I know she doesn't reciprocate the feeling? How do I ask Cara to take a chance on me when she deserves so much more?

I've been trying to keep her from running into the idiotic ex all night. I couldn't avoid her staring at him during the ceremony, taking into consideration that they were sitting just a few rows ahead of us, but I sure as hell can avoid her running into them every other time. I could see how she tensed up or how her gaze kept going over her shoulder looking back most of the night. Always wondering if they were going to run into her, but I kept my mouth shut and just tried to guide her somewhere where they were not at.

She's in the middle of the dance floor, dancing and twirling, having the time of her life and my eyes are nowhere else but on her and her pretty smile. I stopped trying to fight the fact that my eyes seem to keep roaming toward her no matter where we are or what she's doing.

"You love her, don't you?" Allie's voice sneaks up on me and when I look next to me, she's sitting there watching the dance floor where my eyes were just locked on the most beautiful girl with the pretty smile.

I close my eyes, take a deep breath, and think about how I'm going to answer this question. I think about what I want to say and how I want to say it but at the end of the day, there's only one right answer to that. "Yes, I think I do. Actually, I know I do." I turn to look at her and find her smiling at me with her caramel eyes shining bright, full of emotion.

"When are you going to tell her, baby bro? Because I can guarantee she can't tell, even though everyone with two eyes can see it."

"What can they see? That I'm completely fucked because the girl I've had a crush on for my entire life, might be the love of my life and she's clueless? Or can they see that she's so out of my league it won't even matter if I tell her?"

"Oh Manny, why do you think that? From what I can see— the way she's around you and how at ease she seems to be with you— she might love you too, baby bro. I had my suspicions before but after seeing the two of you around each other in Nashville, there was not a doubt in my mind. I didn't even say anything to her because it was as clear as day to me. She's also not out of your league. I think you're perfect for her. You're sweet, funny, kind, handsome, and annoying, just like she is. You both get along fine and honestly, she could use a man who puts her first and that's what you would do, right? You don't do shit half-assed which is why you never dated anyone. Because you couldn't give them the time they deserved?"

Allie is asking the right questions. And if I'm honest with myself, that might be a big reason why. But I worry, who am I without my job? And if I'm giving my all to my job, there's no heart to give to anyone else. But now, I know that the job can wait. I know I can be successful, or at least my business can, without me spending my life rotting in my office. I stopped answering emails and let them handle things. Yes, I lost Virgil's account according to the email I read this morning, but at the cost of being able to breathe for the first time in years? Worth it. I may not have been able to think about this before this trip but fuck it feels so good. When I texted Gus to tell him, his only reply was "Thank God." I guess he hated him as much as I did.

"I don't even know who I am without being at work all day, Allie. Cara, on the other hand... I mean look at her," I say, pointing at Cara currently dancing in a circle with all the kids at the wedding. Twirling the girls around, while her laugh fills the room. The music may be loud but her laughter reverberates through my body like every cell in me is in tune with her melody. *I'm so fucked.*

"Pure sunshine on legs," Allie replies.

"Sunshine and rain. Beautiful and necessary. Her whole life is full of the things she loves. How do I fit into that?"

"Manny... you have to tell her. She deserves to be loved like that. She deserves someone who knows her to that extreme. Someone who knows her so well. A man that can see all that she is, not only what she shows others." She looks away to the farthest table from us where Cole and Tasha are sitting next to each other and rolls her eyes.

"That—" she points at them "—was never what she deserved. You, on the other hand, are. I won't say anything. Manny, but you have to." Allie stands up and pats me on the arm.

"To be honest, you deserve a love like that too. Love each

other, lean on each other, grow together, you both deserve it. Her life may be full of people and things she loves, but she doesn't have a partner to share it with and that's what she has wanted since we were kids. Maybe you can give her that." She kisses my forehead and walks toward the bar where Jake is sitting talking to the groom.

I turn around just in time to see Cara walking my way—with a pretty smile and a sexy walk. Her dress has an open slit up her thigh and with every step her hips are perfectly accentuated. She looks like a goddess. I was stopped dead in my tracks when I saw her come out of the bathroom earlier—long hair bouncing when she walked, a shimmery black dress fitted perfectly to her body. Even though we went together to buy it, and she let me see when she tried it on, nothing could've prepared me for seeing her tonight. Mix that with her perfume and with how carefree she's been, even knowing that the asshole of her ex is here, it's a lethal combination.

"You wanna dance, hotshot? You've barely gotten up all night and I'm starting to think there's something wrong with you," Cara teases, extending her hand, palm up, waiting for me to take her up on her offer.

"I always want to dance with you, Carita," I reply, guiding her back to the dance floor. Sam Smith plays in the stereo, an acoustic version of Latch, and how fitting is it in this moment, this weekend, this trip. It's been more than serendipitous. It feels like the universe is trying to say something. Couples are slow dancing around us on the checkered dance floor lit by beautiful chandeliers. I want to be able to talk to her, not just dance, so I tuck us away toward the end of the space.

I walk us around until we make it to the perfect spot and with one quick swoop of my hand, I pull her into my arms and she immediately relaxes. This is where she belongs, and even if she doesn't say it, I think her body is showing me that she knows.

I turn her around and her body dramatically shifts from one way to another. I bet she can see them and that's what has her on edge now.

"Hey," I whisper as we slowly follow the music, both feeling the words as they float around us and me turning her so she's facing a different direction than them. Cara loves to sing and dance, and I love to feel the music. Together, right now, we're doing both.

"Hi," she replies, peering at me through her lashes and following my steps.

"Are you having fun?"

"I am, thanks for asking. Are you?" she asks, her eyebrows frowned with concern.

"Always having fun with you," I say, trying to keep my tone light.

"That's what I'm known for, bringing the fun," she replies, but her voice is flat, devoid of the spark I crave. It's like a punch to the gut, leaving a bitter taste that lingers longer than it should.

I reach for her, my fingers brushing her cheek as I tilt her chin up. "You're fun, bebé, but you're so much more. Can't you see that?"

Her eyes flicker, but the warmth usually there is absent now. "You're a good friend Manny. Of course, you would say that."

The words hit like a knife, buried deep, twisting painfully as they sink in. "Do not say that." My voice cracks, a mixture of anger and something deeper, something I can't quite articulate. *Hurt.* That feeling is hurt.

"Sorry, you know what I mean. Like you have to like me, it's like Allie and my friends. There's no getting rid of me so might as well accept it."

"Cara, where is this coming from, huh? You know how incredible you are. You're always telling everyone how much of a gift you are, which is true, so where's this self-doubt coming from?" I ask and she drops her face immediately, keeping me from seeing her eyes.

"No hiding, remember? Don't hide, show me. Show me what you're feeling, let me see all of you."

She lowers her gaze, looking a little lost and maybe a little sad. I'm worried she won't tell me what's going on but suddenly her eyes snap back to mine.

"I got a text from Cole," she admits. *The fucking jerk. I'm going to kill him.*

"When?" I bite. I'm ready to stop being civilized when it comes to him. My hands tighten around her body because I feel her tense under my touch and I don't want her to leave without telling me.

"I don't know... last week, the week before and at some point tonight," Cara replies, biting her lip and blinking rapidly. I can bet she's trying to keep herself from crying and the thought of that motherfucker ruining her night. I fucking knew that something happened on those days she seemed to be harder on herself. I knew that something else was going on. I should've pressed more. I should've asked more questions.

"What did he say?" I ask, continuing to dance with her. Pretending I don't wanna kill him, pretending we're just two friends having a conversation. She tenses and shakes her head instead of telling me. "I know we're in a death to the patriarchy era or whatever you want to call it, Cara, but I need you to tell me what he said."

She scans the room and drops her hands from my body. "I'll show you," she says, walking toward the table and I follow her. The room is filled with people dancing, kissing, and talking, completely unaware of the hearts that are breaking. We make it to the table and she gets her phone out of her black leather purse.

"Here."

I grab it and sit down and scroll up looking at the texts he has sent. The first one is dated the first week of June so either she erased all the messages before this month or it's been months since they messaged, so why message her now?

MAY 31

He who-shall-not-be named: I heard you're moving back. You don't have to worry about us being here, we're moving out of Baker. Happy at last.

The day she sang that song at karaoke. The day she looked so sad and her voice sounded so broken as if her light was being dimmed by something. I attributed it to finishing the school year but now, reading this, maybe I had it wrong all along. Or maybe it was a combination of both.

JUNE 7

He who-shall-not-be named: I don't know if anyone told you but I'm going to the wedding with Tasha. I figured you knew but didn't want you to show up alone and then be miserable when everyone else has a partner. Maybe you should avoid the heartache and not go.

Jesus. This was the day we kissed and then she spiraled and told me to forget about it. *Damn it, Manny. You stupid idiot.* Of course she was feeling all types of ways. She probably spent the day thinking about this. No wonder she was drinking so much and overall flighty. She was overcompensating and I made it somehow worse.

TODAY

> He who-shall-not-be named: Manuel Zabana, Cara? Are you a cougar now? Actually he might be perfect for you, the two of you will have fun and then he'll trade you for his next flavor of the week while you try to find your next man to trap. Congrats, you finally picked right

I'm going to kill him. "Where the fuck is he?" I snarl, standing up ready to find him and kill him.

"Stop." Cara grabs my arm, stopping me from doing what I was trying to do. "Sit down," she says, this time with firmness in her tone, so I listen and do as she asks. "It's not worth it, Manny, and I don't want to ruin Alex's wedding. I want to keep dancing until the wedding is over and then you can help me forget he's an ass later. We've avoided them all night, let's not change that now."

"I have no problem erasing every single memory of him out of your mind, bebé, but someone needs to put him in his place. He's acting like a bitch ass boy, not a man. And why the hell has been texting you all this time and why, Cara, why didn't you say something?"

"Because I'm a damn masochist, Manny. Clearly. But you know what? I blocked his number now and Allie said that they moved from Baker this past week, so this will hopefully be the last time I see both of them. His parents don't live in Baker anymore, and Tasha—well I really don't care about her. You asked me to show you and now I did, so please drop it."

"Cara." I wait and give her a few moments, not dropping her gaze so she can see I'm not backing down. I know she needs me to listen to her and to be calm but I can't. Not when I can see how much he's still trying to mess with her head.

"Please drop it. You said you love my voice and hearing me

talk; now I want you to listen to what I'm saying too. I know you hear me, but can you listen?"

If there's something I learned at a young age it's how to do exactly that: listen. And I do, loud and clear. I know her choices were never respected before and I want to do that. I want to respect everything. Every boundary and every limit.

So I say, "Okay." Maybe she doesn't need saving from him, just listening ears and a hand to hold, and I can be both even if I can see her physically getting ill over this whole situation.

"I'm going to run to the potty real quick and then I'll be back and we can finish dancing, okay?" she asks, standing up and squeezing my shoulder. When I nod, she smiles at me and walks away disappearing behind the narrow hallway that leads to the bathroom. I hit my fist on the table and shake my head. I know she's not okay, I know it. How does one balance in the line between respecting her wishes and protecting her? How do I show her that I would kill for her if I have to but that I also respect her wishes, no matter how bad I want to do the opposite.

33

GOLD & GLITTER

FLOWERS, LAUREN SPENCER SMITH & LOSE YOU TO LOVE ME, SELENA GOMEZ

Cara

YOU'RE NOT ENOUGH. I hear him deep down as I rush to the bathroom to try to drown out the noise. The last thing I need is to cry in public so I had to walk away from Manny before he could see beyond the strong front I'm putting on.

You're just a teacher. I make more than you in a day. You're only good for a good time.

I run my hands under the cold water until my fingers go numb and then move the handle to as hot as it'll go. The bathroom is empty so at least I don't have to share this moment with anyone else.

Why would anyone like to do that, Cara? Are you fifteen, Cara? Why don't you drink wine like an adult?

The water goes hot and as I see my fingertips get red, I can hear him again, shaking me to my core.

Eat a vegetable Cara. Can you be quiet for a minute? You're going to make us crash with your stupid nonsense, Cara. I don't have time for that. Nobody likes to go down on women, get out of your romance books. Life is not a romance book. When will you grow up?

Stop.

Stop.

Stop!

Stop!

I splash water on my face and flinch at the temperature and the memories that invade me suddenly. How stupid was I that I didn't see him for who he was? A misogynistic asshole messing with my head. Completely tearing me down instead of growing with me, instead of trying to build me back up. I was so blind. How come I didn't see it?

I turn off the faucet and pull some paper towels out of the rack to dry my hands and pat dry my face, wiping the paper towel under my eye and erasing any proof of the tears shed. *No more, Cara. He doesn't deserve any more of your tears.*

I leave the bathroom, ready to go find Manny and get the hell out of here. But as I find him in the crowd, I notice Tasha and Cole walking my way. *Kill me now, please.*

"Natasha. Cole," I say politely, nodding and trying to get away from them as quickly as possible.

"What? You're not even going to wish us well? Tell us congratulations?" Cole snaps, holding Tasha's hand up and flashing her ring at me. She's beautiful, I'll give her that, but only on the outside. Long glossy blonde hair, pretty eyes and legs for days. Wearing a tight dress that leaves nothing to the imagination, she looks like a mermaid but she's more like a siren than anything. Wrecking lives.

"Oh yeah, congratulations are in order. I hope you two live a very long happy life together. Now if you excuse me," I persist. But before I can turn around, Tasha speaks up.

"You're all the same, aren't you? Only happy when it's you. Only worrying about each other's happiness—damn everyone else. You couldn't make him happy but you can't be happy for him? I thought you loved him," she spits out. And now? Now I'm not upset, I'm angry. How dare she?! After everything she has done, she's still blaming others.

"Don't worry about her, baby, let her go. We won in the end," Cole snaps behind me and now I'm not only mad, I'm furious.

"Tasha, you know what? I've tried taking the high road. I've tried being civilized, but you... You have to push, and push, and push until someone snaps." I turn my body around to face them head on before channeling my inner badass and saying, "And you—you fucking misogynist asshole. Just full stop. Just stop. The best thing that could've ever happened to me was you dumping me because I deserve better. And you know what? So do you, Tasha. It's not normal what you two are doing and if you can't see it, I feel sorry for you. But I do wish you the very best." The commotion from our heated argument must be causing a bigger scene than I thought because suddenly there's people crowding near where we are. Exactly what I was avoiding.

"You stupid bitch, don't talk to her like that," Cole shouts and I gasp at the same time that Tasha holds his arm back. It's not only my gasp I hear and when I look to the side, I find some people doing the same. I'm so damn thankful Livi and Alex are probably outside at this moment because this is enough of a shit show as it is.

"If I were you, I would consider very carefully what I say next," I hear an unmistakably deep voice say. I look to my left and I see Manny walking toward us with his eyebrows furrowed and his eyes dark locked on Cole. *Oh shit.*

"Now you need a man to fight your battles for you?" Why is he being even more of a jerk right now? He was always short fused but now he's being evil for no reason. He dumped me. He got the other girl. He can live happily ever after and leave me the fuck alone. But no, he has to nudge and nudge the bear.

"I don't need a man to do anything, especially not put you in your place." *The bear got nudged enough.*

"You needed me for years," he says, completely ignoring Tasha and standing up straight.

"Well you're not a man, Cole. Because a man wouldn't talk to a woman like that. A man wouldn't want to make a girl feel bad about being happy and being herself. A man—" I say stepping forward closer to him to point at his chest "—wouldn't cheat on his long term girlfriend with her fucking friend. I may have been blind before, Cole, but I can finally see. You two," I say pointing between them, "you two deserve each other. Have a nice life." I walk away from them, standing near Manny but before I can chicken out, I turn around and say, "And Cole, lose my fucking number. You're not a middle schooler, grow the fuck up." Tasha looks at him after that statement like this is news to her too. Ha, good luck, sweetie. He won't change.

"Don't you walk away from—" Before he can finish that statement, Manny turns around and punches him dead in the face.

"Manny!" The group of people watching has gotten bigger and so many of them gasp at that movement. I see Alex rushing through the murmuring crowd of people, finally making it to where we are standing and enjoying the show.

"I told you to watch it and I heard enough. Someone should have punched you a long time ago." Manny shakes his hand and walks to me, his features softening but still looking concerned.

"You need to go, now!" Alex shouts at Cole, who is now by the wall holding his face. "Get out!" Alex shouts.

"Are you okay?" he asks me as Cole and Tasha walk away from us and some of the people go back to the dance floor. I don't want any of them here though.

I nod my head, looking at them and then saying, "I'm so sorry for ruining your perfect night."

"There's nothing for you to be sorry about. I'm going to get people to walk away and give you some privacy. I'm sorry," he repeats before standing up and walking the people back to the dance floor.

As he leaves, Manny stops right in front of me, his hands coming up to hold my face, he asks, "Are you okay?"

I nod because if I open my mouth to talk my voice will be shaky or I'll end up crying, and I'm done shedding tears over this shit. I'm closing this door and never opening it again. Done with him, his bullshit, and getting hurt by a man who is not even worth it. Not worth my time, my tears, not even worth my thoughts. Manny searches my eyes and I'm sure he can see the turmoil behind them because his features were just hard a minute ago but now soften as he traces my cheek tenderly.

"Do you want to get out of here?" he asks, not dropping my face from his hold or his eyes from mine. I blink once and that's all the answer he needs. He grabs my hand and pulls me toward the exit. We stop at the table for my purse, my head still down avoiding eye contact, and then I let him lead me through the hotel. I'm not sure where he's taking me but I'm not questioning him because if there's one thing I do know it's that I trust him.

We walk through some doors that look like an employee-only area and after a small dark hall, he pushes through white double doors that lead to a lively kitchen. It's full of cooks and people dancing around the stoves, moving ingredients, and creating magic in the form of food.

"You can't be in here!" someone shouts and Manny ignores them, walking until we reach the refrigerator. He opens the top door and pulls out a bag of frozen peas, before picking up the pace and walking us both out of here.

"Manny, slow down," I protest, trying to keep up with him.

The heels are not cooperating and honestly, we probably shouldn't be running either way.

He holds my hand tighter and continues to guide me through the hotel and into the beautiful back garden. It's dark with just a few garden lights illuminating a small path to a bench near a fountain. He doesn't slow until we're by the fountain and then he finally turns around and hugs me tight.

"Are you okay?" he whispers against my hair.

"I'll be when you let me breathe again." My words get lost against his warm and solid chest. He eases me back, but not before drawing us both down onto the bench. I settle onto his lap, a tangle of limbs, and as I shift to get up, his grip holds me still.

"Hold on, Carita, just stay with me for a minute," Manny adds with his head buried on my chest. The adrenaline of what just happened must have gotten to him and he needs time to settle it down.

"I'm not going anywhere, Manny. It's okay." I thread my fingers through his hair, feeling the silky curls slip between my fingertips. It's softer than I remembered. "I love your hair."

"Good, because I love yours." He lifts his head and grins when he sees my face. He pulls out the bag of peas and places it over his hand.

"I can't believe you punched him," I say, as I pull his hand forward so it rests on my lap while I hold the frozen bag still.

"Someone had to; I'm surprised it took me this long to do it. I've never punched anyone before though so I don't know if my hand will be okay." He pouts at me with his big puppy eyes.

"Oh my God, you're so dramatic. You'll be fine," I say and we both laugh softly. We stay silent for a moment or two. Feeling the warm breeze on our faces while listening to the crickets singing and the distant horns of the cars keeping the city alive.

"I'm proud of you," he finally says.

"Proud of me? For what?" I bring my hand up and tuck one of his soft locks behind his ear.

"Are you kidding me, Cara? You telling that jackass to fuck off was incredible. Needed, but overall I bet it was shocking for him to hear how you don't care anymore. How you wish him a long and happy life and to leave you alone. You know what's worse than being upset at someone?"

I shake my head and wait for him to finish his thought.

"Indifference. You showed him today that he doesn't have a hold on you anymore and that probably hurt worse than anything else you could've done." I think about what he says and I truly think I meant it. I was so anxious to see them today I didn't stop to think about how I truly felt. Sometime in the past year and these last three weeks, I must have put him behind me. I'm sure his words will have an effect on me for longer but I truly felt nothing when I saw them. Other than anger because he keeps trying to fuck with my brain.

"I don't want to hurt anyone though, at least not on purpose," I reply and that's honestly the truth. I really just wish them well. I hope he changes and grows and that she kicks him out if he doesn't. Overall, I just want them out of my life so I can move on. So we can all move on.

"Because you're made of gold and glitter and not hate like most of us."

"Gold and glitter, huh?" I ask, lifting my eyebrows and with tears in my eyes.

He gets closer to me and whispers against my lips, "And flowers galore."

Manny kisses my lips softly. His lips are a tender caress against mine, reminding me that there's still good in this world, even if it's for a little while. We kiss slowly, like we're frozen in time and nothing else matters but his lips on mine. He doesn't speed the pace and neither do I. Life is always rushing toward something but with Manny, that's not the case. He makes me feel like nothing else matters but the right here and right now. He reminds me of the *me* I love. The *me* I've lost through the years of trying to comply. Oh, how I wish I could bottle this feeling because this is how I want to feel for the rest of my life.

I've missed so many moments that I could've enjoyed being wrapped in hurt and feeling lost when I could have been treasuring them all. Taking my own bracelets into consideration instead of letting a crappy man dictate my feelings. One thing's for sure, I will remember every single day of this trip, even when it ends.

The kiss slows to a stop and he rests his forehead against mine. His eyes still closed when I ask, "How's your hand?" I bring my hand over it, feeling the bracelet he hasn't removed since I gave it to him.

"It's been better but I'd do it again." He smiles against my lips.

"You'd punch Cole again for me?"

"Him and everyone else who would ever speak to you like that again." He kisses my lips again and then lets go, pulling my head to his chest. I keep my fingers over the bracelet, tracing it with my fingertips.

I bring my face up, kissing his cheeks and then his soft lips. "Thank you," I whisper against his lips.

"My absolute pleasure, Carita" We settle into a quiet moment, the soft rustle of leaves whispering above us, the gentle breeze teasing the edges of my hair. I close my eyes, leaning into him, feeling the steady beat of his heart beneath my ear, each thump a reassuring anchor. Grounding me. It's incredible how his earthy scent, and his strong arms have done to my brain. They have rewired me to find the most comfort in him and I'm about to lose that. I do get comfort in the fact that I'll have all these memories to look back on.

His hands move slowly, tracing the curves of my neck as his fingertips brush against my scalp in a way that sends a pleasant shiver down my spine. I can't help but smile against him, the warmth of his body wrapping around me and keeping me at peace.

For a moment, everything outside fades—just us, the breeze, and the soft thud of his heart against my ear, a quiet reminder that we're here, together, suspended in this fragile peace.

Until we hear everything shutting down and we walk back to our hotel room, where he makes love to me all night long. It's not just sex and I can feel it in every moment that his lips are on mine. I can feel it in every touch of his fingertips on my skin or the way that he whispers onto my body what his words are not saying. He isn't just having sex with me, he's saying goodbye.

34

YOU PROMISED

LOVE ME TIL' YOU LEAVE ME, GAVN!

Manny

This trip is coming to an end and I can feel the ominous decisions looming over us. Do I let her go? Do I keep my end of the deal and take Cara home, or do I tell her how I feel and hope she feels the same? I know she likes spending time with me but would that ever be enough for someone like her? Do I help her shine brighter like she deserves or will I dim her light when everything is said and done?

We were only five hours away from her house this morning but I took us down the back roads and up through a little town a couple of hours away from Baker where they have a fair. We've been here all afternoon, eating too much greasy food and riding all these carnival rides while the ticking time bomb follows us around, threatening to detonate at any point.

The fairgrounds' atmosphere buzzes around us—music, children's laughter and machines announcing winners everywhere. Even though the bright lights twinkle above, and the air is thick with the scent of cotton candy and fried dough, I can't seem to find the joy in this moment. It's hard to feel anything but dread, with a knot in my stomach thinking about Cara and leaving her at her house tomorrow, never looking back. Like I didn't just learn what love was and now I'm supposed to move on like it didn't happen. Like I didn't learn what is like to truly live and not just go through life.

I glance at Cara, her face is illuminated by the neon glow of the carnival rides and she turns to face me, opening her eyes wide and pointing in front of her. "Oh. My. God. Look at the puppies!" She laughs and pulls me by my hand, her hair catching the light and flowing in the air, both pulling at my heartstrings with excitement and making my heart ache. I want to capture this moment and etch it into my memory forever, make it into a bracelet moment. Deep down, I know time is slipping away. Every second, every moment feels like a damn countdown. One laugh and I'm taken back to the day she set the rules. One look into her eyes reminds me of the inevitable. She wants this to end tonight and I don't know how to fix it.

We weave through the crowd until we make it to the pen full of puppies with a sign that says, 'Ready for a furever home.' She asks the worker if we can play with them and when she nods, Cara opens the pen and lets us in.

"Hi puppies," I say, holding out my hands to all the golden, brown, and black puppies. When they start swarming around me, I drop to the cold dusty ground. They crawl on my lap, reminding me how much I love dogs and how I've always wanted one.

"I knew you liked dogs after seeing you pet one everywhere we go, but I didn't know that it was a sit-on-the-ground, let-them-lick-your-face kind of love," Cara explains, picking a puppy of her own and snuggling it close to her face, never dropping her eyes from mine.

"I've always wanted a dog but moving all my life didn't let it happen."

"What about now?"

"Now? I don't have the lifestyle I need to have a happy dog. I don't want a dog that won't see me ever or that will only get me for two hours at night." I see there's a line of kids waiting to enter the pen so I get up and offer my hand to Cara to help her up.

"Thank you," I say to the girl waiting by the gate as we walk out and past the kids. We fall into an easy pattern, walking slowly toward the Ferris wheel. She tucks her hand into mine, intertwining her fingers and laying her head on my shoulder.

"Maybe now that you've taken a break from work... you could consider scaling back?" she asks.

If you'll have me, I'll take all the time, I want to reply, but I don't. I just nod and walk us through the line waiting at the bottom of the Ferris wheel.

"Are you going back to work tomorrow?" she asks, stepping through the gate and waiting for me to hand our tickets to the worker. We get into one of the baskets, sitting next to each other, and I pull her under my arm.

"No, not tomorrow, but after that I will. I don't think I'll keep working the crazy hours I was, though. I don't think that would fulfill me anymore, Cara." I bring my hand to her face and pull her hands on my other one.

Her eyes sparkle when she looks at me as we ascend slowly, allowing time for other people to sit in the baskets below us. "What would fulfill you, Manny?" I don't know if she asked that question knowingly. Can she see the turmoil in my eyes? The love? Can she see that I would live these three weeks ten times over if it meant I get to spend more time with her? Just with her.

"We spent so much time talking on this trip about me and so little about you, other than seeing how happy you seemed. What would make *you* happy?" She grabs my baseball cap, flipping it backward and gives me a quick kiss.

It's now or never. I've asked her over and over not to hide from me and now it's my turn to do the same and tell her how I feel. "You," I whisper against her lips.

"I—what?" she asks with confusion in her eyes. The light of the sunset reflects off her beautiful green eyes and I don't know if it's the yellow dress she's wearing today, reminding me of the pure sunshine she is, or the fact she's so close to home she can taste it but her eyes are so light today. Instead of deep green pools of emotions, today they feel like soft feathers flying in the air. Light. Airy. Safe.

"You would make me happy, Cara. You do, actually. Not only you being with me, but who I am when I'm with you. You've shown me so much in these three weeks. So much more than I've learned in my entire life. I'm a better person because of you and honestly I want that for more than just these three weeks."

"Manny," she whispers, closing her eyes.

"No, no, let me finish. You showed me how to enjoy and appreciate every moment, every hour, every minute, of every day and I want that for longer. I also want all your moments. I want to spend so many moments with you and turn them into memories together. I want to wake up next to you and cuddle under the stars. I want to hear how many names for street signs you have and how long you can dance before falling asleep in my arms. I want to spend more time getting to know you like nobody has ever known you before. I want to spend time showing you how easy it is to make you my priority. I just need you to let me."

Two silent tears drop over her cheeks and her eyes find

mine. "I know I don't deserve you. I know I don't deserve the moments you collect like these bracelets on your arm but let me show you I can earn them. I will spend the rest of my life trying to make more memories with you, Cara. If you let me." I mean that with everything I have. Turning moments into memories with her might be the only purpose I have left in life. I want them all and I want them all with her.

The minutes pass and she stays quiet; speechless in a way I've never seen her before. Silent tears keep rolling and her skin turns blotchy as the sounds of the fair fade into the background. We start the descent and she still hasn't said a word. If there's anything that I've learned about Cara through the years is that she rather stay silent than say something that would be hurtful. She's making the silence the answer I need. *She doesn't feel the same.*

"Please say something, Carita."

She tenses in front of me as my words hang soundlessly between us. I wanted to wait until the perfect moment to tell her how I feel, but there was never going to be a good moment if she didn't feel the same.

"I'm flattered, Manny, I am. You know how much I care about you and this trip was more than I could ever imagine." Cara brings her hands to her eyes and wipes the tears off her face.

"I care about you too," I reply.

"I had no expectations on these three weeks, Manny, but if I did, you would've surpassed them all. I forgot how happy I could be just doing the things that fill my cup and you gave me that back."

"But..." I add because I can feel it coming and I want her to know that whatever it is she can trust me. Even if it breaks me in the process.

"I don't know that I actually make you happy, Manny.

Three weeks is not enough time to turn your life upside down to follow a girl just because you think she brings you joy," she says, completely serious and turning her knees away from me. She's putting a barrier up with her words and her body, hitting me with a harder blow.

"But you do, Cara. I've always been happier around you, my whole life actually. All my damn life and now that I had you in my arms, now that I know exactly what my life feels with you in it, I don't know that I could ever go back."

"I hear you, Manny, and I agree to an extent. I just think a lot played into the happiness we both felt these three weeks. Outdoor time, time away from work and the rest of the people who may bring us problems. You haven't taken a vacation in years and your brain is probably high on dopamine from not being stressed out all the time. And yeah, I'm sure hormones played a big part and the whole forced proximity thing. But tomorrow... tomorrow when we go back to reality, you'll go back to your corporate life and I'll be trying to rebuild my life."

I lean against the cool metal railing, the air warm against our skin. "And I don't fit in that plan," I answer flatly, rubbing my chin, trying to ground myself amidst the storm brewing in my chest.

"What are you saying, Manny? Are you saying you'll quit your job and move to Baker Oaks and go on hikes with me after I get home from school?" Her voice is sharp, piercing through me and leaving me hollower with each word.

"No, Cara, that's not what I'm saying." My words hang in the air, heavy and unwieldy. Below us, the carnival lights flicker like fireflies trapped in glass jars. We're suspended at the top, caught in the cycle of this conversation—one that spins around and around with no end.

"Exactly, Manny. I finally want to do something for myself."

She gazes out at the horizon, where the silhouette of the town is just a shadow against the darkening sky.

"I want to move to Baker and learn my new job and be around my friends. I want to be in the town I've loved all my life from afar, and for once I want to be happy." Her voice cracks, the truth of her words echoing between us. *You don't make her happy, Manny.* Once, maybe, but now that she remembers who she is, she doesn't need me anymore.

I swallow hard as she says, "We said this was over when the trip was done, and now it is. You did promise me, though."

"I promised you what, Cara?" The lump in my throat grows thicker, making it hard to breathe as I search her eyes for the answers I'm terrified to see.

"You promised you'd still be my friend at the end of this and you're a man of your word, right? I don't want to lose you, Manny."

She doesn't want to lose the happy-go-lucky, go-with-the-flow Manny. Her friend Manny. But that's it. When I tell her that I want *her* in my life, then that's not what she wants. I did promise her that and I am a man of my word. So even if I hate it, that's what I'll be. I'd rather be her friend and be in her life than be nothing at all. She wipes her tears under her eyes as she gives me a tentative half smile. She's afraid I will say no. She's afraid she'll lose me and I rather lose myself than lose her.

"You're right, Cara. I did promise to be your friend at the end of this, so that's where we're leaving it now." I pull her to me, kissing her on the forehead and swallowing those three words I've been dying to say all day.

"I'm sorry," she whispers as the basket makes it back down, completing the ride and marking the end of our conversation. I was exactly what she needed, but now it's over and I'm not in her plans anymore. Her perfectly curated bullet points don't include me beyond tomorrow. Point taken. It's funny, really.

How something so simple, so innocent, can turn into something this heavy. Something I've carried with me every day without even realizing it—this longing, this wish that maybe, just maybe, before just wasn't our time. That the years and the distance between us was just shaping us into who we are today and that I wasn't too late in telling Cara how I feel. But the truth is, I've always been too late. I've watched her from the sidelines for so long that I've forgotten how much my heart desires her. And now that I finally crossed that line she doesn't feel the same and there's no point in stretching out longer. We had fun. She healed. And now we get to go our separate ways.

I will show Cara respect even if it means going against what I think is best for both of us. She spent twelve years in a relationship with someone who didn't respect her or her wishes and I won't be the one doing that to her. Even if it kills me. So I squeeze her shoulder as I step out of the basket, giving her my hand to help her come out. Guiding her out softly. I fall into a silent step next to her. There's nothing else to say or do, so we might as well head home. I might as well drive her home.

35

WELCOME BACK
BEFORE YOU GO, LEWIS CAPALDI

Cara

> The Bestie: Ronnie's tomorrow?

> The Badass: Lord yes. I have to train first but then I can. 8:00am? Is that too early for you Cara?

> Me: 8:00 works

ADDS THE SWEETIE TO THE CONVERSATION

> Me: Hey Nats, want to have breakfast tomorrow? I'M BACK!

> The Sweetie: I can! I'll leave Bella with her grandparents. Ronnie's?

> Me: Yup, 8:00am

> The Sweetie: you're waking up early on purpose?

I DOUBT *I'll even sleep,* I think as the message comes through. We're already in my neighborhood. We left the fairgrounds after the conversation and we've been in silence ever since. I opted to grab my phone and pretend I'm busy doing something because I don't have it in me to continue talking to Manny. There were only so many words I could offer without telling him that I'm terrified of trying something more permanent with him just to not be enough or be able to compete against his job.

The music is playing softly in the background as Manny drives up my parents' long entry road. If there's something I love about living in Baker, it's how every home has so much land before you even get to the actual house. My parents' cars are in the driveway but no sight of Nellie's. I was hoping she would be back home by now, but it looks like it's just them and me tonight.

It's already almost 11:00pm so I doubt they're awake, and if I'm being honest with myself, I don't want to talk to them tonight. I don't want to talk to anyone. I just want to lay my head on my pillow. Laying my body on the bed that has held me through so much, that has supported me as I cry myself to sleep more nights that I can count. The bed that has been there since I was in high school because my parents refuse to turn my room into anything else. *You'll always have a place to call home* they say, so they keep both of our rooms intact for us to crash into whenever we want.

"This is me," I murmur like a damn idiot. Manny has the address on GPS so of course he knows that. We agreed he'll take the van with him tonight and we'll figure out tomorrow how I can pick it up. He's staying the night at his Jacksonville condo so at least it's not too far away.

He parks, walking to my side of the door and opening it for me. Helping me to get out, he then leans in to grab my bags from the backseat. We walk in silence to the door, the week and the whole Ferris wheel conversation hanging between us. My heart is on my throat and the words "stay with me" are right on the tip of my tongue but I don't think it's fair to either of us.

He places the bag next to the wooden door. "Thank you for everything, Manny," I offer quietly. "This trip was truly the highlight of my year." *Of my life,* I want to say but I don't. I bring my hand to his arm and squeeze it gently, his muscles tightening under my touch.

"No need to thank me, I was happy to do it, Cara." *Cara.* Manny stopped calling me Carita the minute I told him I thought he was wrong and I truly didn't make him happy. *What if you do, Cara? What if you are exactly what he needs and he is what you need?*

"Talk to you tomorrow?" I won't ask any more questions; I won't admit to him I think I want more. I won't tell him because I know for a fact there's no good way out of this. He would want me until he's busy with work again and then he won't need me anymore and I can't do that again. I can't go through this again.

"Yup, sounds about right. Good night, Cara." Manny brings his face down, kisses me on the cheek and walks away from me. I open the door, step through it and slide myself down to the floor. Letting all the tears I've been holding for what feels like a year all at once.

IT'S funny how Manny called me sunshine for three weeks straight, because right now I feel like the complete opposite of that. I feel like I'm standing at the edge of the cliff watching the storm form on the horizon. But instead of the storm being far away, the storm is reflecting my heart. My sorrows. It's brewing deep within me.

All night I couldn't sleep. My chest tightening around my heart and my lungs making me feel like I couldn't breathe. The pit of my stomach in knots telling me that I'm wrong. Telling me that I made the wrong call. How could I have made the wrong choice when my heart was already breaking at his words—and that's without giving it the chance to wither even more? Without giving it the chance to grow more attached and to connect with him even more. Eventually he would get tired of this small town life. I don't belong in his perfectly curated world; at least this way, I can mourn what I wish I would have and not what once was. There's no surviving losing Manny so at least this way I get to keep him as a friend, without fucking it all up by trying to make a relationship work. I know I'm enough, I know that. I know that Cole wasn't really it for me or for anyone for that matter. I know that the years he made me feel like I was a shit show and not good enough for him were just a reflection on him; I know that my relationship with him doesn't dictate the way the rest of my relationships will go in life. But I need to take time to do the things I want to do without worrying whether my partner wants to do the same too.

Even though this feeling of despair is not dissipating by any means, I'm sure it'll go away once I shower, eat something, and see my girls. Maybe it's just the crash after spending three weeks filled with adrenaline or the exhaustion of it all. But either way, something's gotta give.

I'm fully expecting my van keys not to be on top of the granite countertop in the kitchen, where the rest of the keys lay, so I take a step back when I see them there. My bright pink cowgirl hat keychain attached to my keys lies on top of a note. I grab the keys and read the note, immediately letting out a sigh because I think I broke Manny's heart. If I actually did, I will never forgive myself. The thing is, how do I let him down gently when I'm trying to protect my heart too? How do I prioritize his when I know how much it hurts being replaced by someone more accessible? I refuse to go back to the spot I was, thinking I was worthless and useless because I wasn't enough for a piece of shit of a man. *But Manny is nothing like him,* the little voice of reason echoes in my head. Deep down I know it's right but I just can't risk it. Not right now.

Cara,

I know I was supposed to come back tomorrow to return the keys and the bus but I decided to just call a car instead. I got my things out of there so it's ready for you to take on new adventures. I hope I didn't leave any trace of me being there but if I did, just toss it away. I have a lot of work to catch up on this week so if you don't hear from me, that's why.

Welcome back home, Cara. I hope you get everything your heart desires and I hope Baker brings as much light as you brought into my life these past three weeks.

Don't let other's shadows cast over your light but don't let yourself dim your own flame either. You are the sun, Cara. Never forget.

Love,

M.

I wipe away the tears that were threatening once I saw the note but that quickly were unable to be held back at his tender words. How did I manage to spend three weeks with Manny and somehow it feels like it was both longer but also not enough? He opened his heart to me. He let me in. He let me see *him* and I did the same; but is that enough for us to mess everything up and try to make this work? He needs more and I'm not in the position to do it. I'm not in the position of dropping everything and becoming the type of girlfriend he needs. Fancy and put together and a good representation of his brand everywhere. One thing's for sure; whoever he decides to share his life with will be the luckiest girl in the world. I just need to be brave enough to be able to offer him the one thing I asked from him: friendship.

THREE WEEKS **Later**

BEING BACK HOME HAS BEEN every bit of the dream I thought it would be. Breakfast at Ronnie's, coffee with my mom, daily walks with Allie, drinking with Roe, hanging out at Natalie's shop's couch while I blabber nonstop about random shit, and so much more. It feels so good to be back, except something's missing.

I feel like part of me is not really here but rather stuck on the road trip. Stuck in those three weeks of bliss. I haven't talked to Manny much, just quick text messages here or there. I'm sure he's busy with work but I miss him. I don't know how many times I've written and deleted those words in text to him, because what am I supposed to say—"Hey does that offer to see where this thing goes stands? Do you still think you could be happy with me?"

Allie had sent out some frantic SOS text, so I just got to her house to see what the hell is going on. If she tells me she's pregnant, I'm going to be very happy but also, give a girl a call and stop with the SOS texts. I walk in, not bothering ringing the doorbell. I look around and although I don't see Allie, Roe and Natalie are both here.

"I'm sorry, Cara, but you look like absolute shit," Roe confesses.

"What are you sorry about? That you're telling me I look like shit, or because I actually do?" I snap, my voice sharper than I mean it to be. Without waiting for an answer, I collapse onto Allie's couch, the cushions sinking beneath me like they're trying to swallow me whole.

"Both? Either? What's going on?"

"Nothing is going on other than me being tired. What if I told you that you looked like shit, huh?" Roe huffs and I roll my eyes, taking a deep breath. It's the same question I've been hearing over and over, and it's wearing me down, piece by piece. I'm happy, I truly am. I love my life here. Is something missing? Yes. Is that something Manny? Maybe.

"I'm fine," I reiterate, but it feels like a lie in my mouth. "Just... tired. The move here's been more than I thought."

It's the same line I've been repeating to everyone, including myself when I catch a quick glimpse of my smile not reaching my eyes or my eyes roaming, wondering if Manny is thinking about me or if he's lost in work again.

I know it's not just the move. It's everything—the house I've been obsessing over, the one that should feel like a fresh start? It feels right but when I keep looking at it, it just seems emptier than it is. It feels quiet and eerie. I can't even pinpoint why. So I just keep avoiding it, keep putting off making an offer even though that is literally the house of my dreams.

Natalie's gaze is soft but heavy with concern. "Cara, we're

just worried. You haven't been yourself. You've been... pulling away." Her words hang in the air between us, a sharp ache.

I hold up my hands, palms out, like I can ward them off. "Nothing's wrong. Really. I'm just... tired. Can we please stop talking about it?" The words tumble out sour in my mouth at the lie I keep repeating.

Natalie's eyes are soft but relentless. "We're not gonna stop asking, Cara. Not until you talk to us. We're your friends. We know you're struggling. We know you, we see it. Do *you* even know? Do you even know you're not happy?"

I bite down on my lip to keep from saying something I'll regret. I don't want to be seen. I want to keep pretending everything is fine and nothing is missing until that becomes a reality.

Before I can say anything, Allie walks out of her bedroom, looking both annoyed and determined. She sits next to me with a sigh, her eyes locking onto mine with that look—the one she always gives when she's about to say something she knows I won't want to hear.

"You're not fine. We all know it and we're done beating around the bush. Today, we're talking about you and Manny because you two idiots can't get it together on your own."

The room falls into a heavy silence. The air feels thick with unspoken things, and for the first time, I'm not sure I can hide behind my tired excuses anymore.

"What?" I ask.

"Don't even try to hide it, Cara," Allie demands, her voice cutting through the tension in the room like a knife. She doesn't wait for me to reply, her eyes already narrowed, like she's been holding this in for far too long.

"When you came back into town, I was hoping you'd tell me the truth—any version of it, since you already talked about it in Nashville leaving me out of it completely. I'm not an idiot, and I'm not blind. I saw it, okay? And then at the wedding, I told my stupid brother to finally tell you how he felt. So imagine my surprise when you came back, and we went to breakfast, and you looked even more heartbroken than when I left you in Chicago almost a year ago. You didn't say a word, not a single thing. And that's when I knew something was off. The minute we left the restaurant, I called Manny. He didn't answer, so I put two and two together."

My stomach lurches. I stare at her, wide-eyed, as if the words are still circling around my brain, trying to find their place. I knew Roe and Natalie had figured out what happened with the fling, but this? This is something else entirely. Allie knew *everything*? How had I not seen that coming?

"What the hell, Allie?" I manage to choke out, the shock in my voice louder than I want it to be.

She doesn't flinch. Doesn't back down. She leans forward, her eyes hazel eyes hard but still kind. "No, Cara. *You* don't get to 'what the hell' me. Listen up." Her words are slow, deliberate, like she's making sure they land where they need to. "For the past three weeks, I've watched you—this version of you. You pretend you're fine, you wake up and you go places with your fake smile on your face that I think even you believe, when in reality you're heartbroken. You've been sad—and I mean really sad. A kind of sadness that's deeper than I've ever seen in you. And if it was for a good reason—if you were hurting because of something real, something we could work with, we could deal. But you didn't say anything. You just kept it to yourself. Have you even admitted to yourself you miss him?"

I feel the weight of her gaze like a physical pressure on my chest. She's right—I have been sinking into something darker, something I don't know how to explain. Something I can't seem to shake.

"You didn't say anything. I gave you three weeks, Cara. We're supposed to be best friends and you didn't say anything about being in love with my brother and missing him. So I went to see Manny," she continues, her voice lowering just slightly, as if the next part of this story might be a little too much for even her to say. "And guess what I found? He's just as bad off as you. Equally sad, maybe worse."

I blink, stunned. Manny? My Manny, the guy who always made me laugh, who had his flaws but somehow made me feel seen in a way no one else ever did. He has his job and his back into his life. Why would he be sad and why hasn't he told me?

"What? Why?" My voice cracks on the question, and I hate how vulnerable I sound. But I can't help it. I'm actually worried about him now. I'm worried about both of us, if I'm being honest. My stomach churns as I imagine him, sitting in some dark corner, just as lost as I feel. I need to know. I have to know.

But Allie just shakes her head, her jaw tight. "I don't know yet, Cara. But something's broken between the two of you, and I can't keep watching you both fall apart like this." She rubs her temples, like the weight of it all is finally hitting her too. "You two need to figure it out. You need to talk."

The silence that falls between us is thick, suffocating almost. There's no easy way to undo what's been broken, no neat bow to tie around this mess. And now, knowing that Manny's just as wrecked as I am? It feels like I'm standing at the edge of something, too scared to jump, but not sure I want to climb back up, either.

"Talk about what, Allie? We're friends. We got closer on this trip, yes but he said he was going to message me when he was done with work. I'm sure he had a lot of catching up today now that he's back but overall, he doesn't owe me anything. And honestly, he's back at work doing what he loves. And yeah, we haven't talked as much as we did on the trip but that's no reason for him to be desolate like you are implying. Why would he look miserable?"

"Because he loves you, you clueless, clueless girl! I'm pretty sure he has loved you all his life. Didn't he tell you?"

I'm a better person because of you and honestly I want that for more than just these three weeks. The words that have been echoing in my mind for the past three weeks come out loud now, even clearer than before. *You'd make me happy, Cara. You do.* Was he trying to tell me that he loved me? Was he trying to tell me more than what I let him say? I know I interrupted him and I've been playing that interaction in my mind every night all this time. But I've considered that sharing while with words may be hard for him, he did spend weeks showing me I was priority for him, and I just didn't listen.

"He told me he cared about me, not that he loved me."

"I'm pretty sure what he said was that he wanted more than three weeks with you and that he was ready to wake up next to you every day, or am I wrong?" Allie asks.

"Allie," I whisper.

"Am. I. Wrong?" she asks again. Allie found her backbone for sure.

"Well shit, remind me to never pissed Allie off," Roe chimes from her spot on the chair and Natalie just laughs at that.

I shake my head and Allie continues. "I know I'm not wrong because I have asked him to repeat to me what happened over and over again. I have begged him to call you and tell you—to show up, to beg, to do something—but all he says is that your choices were not respected once and he refuses to be that person. He said that he'd rather be your friend than nothing at all and Cara, you don't think that's love?"

"Fuck, I don't know," I add, bringing my hands to my face. "I clearly don't know the first thing about love. I don't know the first thing about lust versus love. Caring versus friendship. He told me I made him happy but he's always happy you know?

How am I supposed to believe all of those feelings were love? How do I know?"

"You do know, babe," Roe adds. "You know love is not supposed to hurt. You know love is friendship. Love is companionship. Love is finding yourself while you're learning to love someone else, while you're learning to share your ups and downs with someone else. You know that love is not selfish and that love is patient right?"

Her words settle over me, warm but heavy, and I feel a pang deep in my chest. It *should* be that way, shouldn't it? Love should feel like something solid, like a foundation you can build on. But right now, it feels like everything is crumbling beneath me.

"You can't fall in love with someone in three weeks." I wipe my tears with the palm of my hands as the three of them look at me with softness behind their eyes.

"Oh but you can and you did, didn't you?" Allie asks. I look around and shake my head. Refusing to believe this. This is crazy. This can't be true. I know that I miss him but is this loneliness, this longing, this yearning for more, because I'm in love with him?

Natalie leans forward, her expression soft and understanding, like she's trying to catch every fragment of my heart that's falling apart. "You know love is acceptance," she adds, her voice gentle but firm. "Love is respect. It's about joy, and laughter, and finding someone who sees you for exactly who you are—no filters, no pretending." She smiles, that kind of smile that makes everything feel a little brighter, even though I know she's talking about something I can't seem to reach.

I swallow hard, trying to hold myself together as her words hit me one after the other. It feels like they're sinking deeper than I want them to, like they're chiseling away at the walls I've built around my heart. But maybe that's the point. Maybe I need to let them break through.

Allie's voice is the next to wrap around me, her tone both fierce and warm, like she's trying to light a fire inside me, something I can hold onto. "Cara," she says, leaning closer, her eyes searching mine like she's trying to remind me of something I've forgotten. "You know exactly how to love without saying those three words. That's how you love all of us. Fiercely. Without hesitation. You're there for us no matter what, no questions asked. Don't you see it? All he wants is to be that person for you, bestie girl."

Her words hit me hard. I've been so wrapped up in my own hurt, in all the ways I've convinced myself that love is supposed to be *hard*, that I've forgotten what it really is. I've forgotten how to *let* it in and to let myself be loved.

But Allie, Roe, and Natalie—they're right. Love is supposed to feel like home. It's supposed to build you up, not tear you down. And maybe, just maybe, I've been pushing away the one person who's trying to be that for me. The one person who has always seen me. I just kept seeing it all as a game that even when he tried to tell me he wanted more, I brushed him off.

They're not wrong. Manny may not have said that he loved me but he sure as hell tried. He also showed me every day for weeks how much he did with his actions and his listening ears. With his patience and his demeanor. And then he tried to tell me he wanted more, and I shoved it all down for fear of not being enough. For fear of not being able to compete with his job.

"What about his job?" I ask between a sob I'm not able to hold. Did I mess it all up? Am I too late?

"What about it? That's something for the two of you to discuss but you need to stop being a dummy and go tell that man that you love him, too," Allie insists and those words shock me to my core.

"You love him, don't you? It's written all over your face. I've never seen you so connected with someone like you were in Nashville, and then at the wedding," Natalie adds, a teasing grin on her lips.

"Stop lying to yourself, Cara. What are you really afraid of?" Allie presses, her gaze sharp.

A knot tightens in my stomach, and I can feel it pulling, twisting, like a weight sinking deeper and deeper. If I can't admit this to them, how the hell am I supposed to face it myself? How am I ever going to tell Manny? I swallow hard, the words fighting to escape, the truth I've been avoiding for too long.

"What if what I have to give is less than what he wants? I don't want to uproot my life for a man. I want to live it fully the way I've always wanted without feeling like I'm failing a partner for not putting their wants first," I finally blurt out, my voice cracking on the edge of the question. It's been lingering in my mind for weeks, maybe longer; a nagging, relentless whisper that refuses to let me go.

The room falls into silence for a second, but then Natalie leans in, her expression soft yet firm, like she's pushing the doubt away with nothing but the sheer force of her belief in me. "You are enough," she urges, her voice warm and steady like a lifeline. "Just because that jerk couldn't see it doesn't mean no one else will. *We* see you, Cara. And you're worthy just the way you are. Nothing about you needs to change. What you have to give is plenty and I'm sure you and Manny can come to an agreement on things but Cara, I don't think you understand... his job is not as a priority as you think anymore. I'm pretty sure *you* are his only priority."

I raise an eyebrow, the smallest flicker of curiosity sparking through me despite the heavy weight of my thoughts. "I'm whose priority?"

"Manny's!" she says with a grin, and her eyes sparkle like

she's sharing a secret only we're in on. "I'm sure he'll give it all up to make *you* happy but you have to let him."

The laughter that follows bursts from them, deep and free, and it catches me off guard. I can't help it. I laugh, too. It's a sound that bubbles up from somewhere inside, loosening the tightness in my chest, even if just for a moment. I look at them—at these women who have held me up more times than I can count—and the tension starts to slip away, piece by piece. Maybe I am seen. Maybe I'm not as invisible as I feel sometimes.

"Agh, this is so hard," I groan, flopping dramatically back onto the couch. I let my body go limp, surrendering to the weight of everything I've been holding in. The room spins for a second, and I let the comfort of these familiar people settle around me like a warm hug. Keeping me safe and warm and sound.

"It really isn't," Allie says, her voice carrying that no-nonsense tone she always uses when she's ready to shake things up. She crosses her arms, sitting up straighter, that determined gleam in her eyes. "It's just a matter of you believing it. Manny believes it. We all believe it. Now it's time for you to believe it, too."

The words hit me, not like a blow, but like a wakeup call, a reminder that I've been holding myself back for too long. I close my eyes for a moment, letting their laughter echo in my mind. Maybe, just maybe, I don't need to fight this alone.

"And you're okay with all of it? You're acting entirely nonchalant about this. This is your brother, Allie."

"Who better to become my sister than you, my sister by choice? It's not a big deal to me, Cara, because I can see how much he cares about you. And if how shitty you've been feeling for the past few weeks is any indicator, I think you feel the same. Actually, I know you feel the same," she replies, smiling softly at me as she brings her soft fingers to touch my hand.

"So what? I'm just going to call him and be like 'Forgive me, Manny. I love you,'" I mock, looking at them with worry in my eyes but seeing nothing like that in theirs. They all seem to feel strongly about this in a different way than I thought they would take it. Even if I realized it before that *he* is the piece I'm missing, by the time I realized that it was too late. It's been too many days.

"Welp, that's when we come in for help. We have an idea," Natalie announces with a big smile that mirrors both Roe and Allie on their faces.

36

THE CONTRACT

MILLIONAIRE, CHRIS STAPLETON & I GUESS I'M IN LOVE, CLINTON KANE

Manny

"LUCIA, why do I have a meeting at 4:00pm? I haven't worked past 4:00 in weeks," I tell Lucia who just came to bring me the folder. I know old habits die hard but after I came back from the road trip, I held a meeting with everyone in the office and outlined new rules. No more staying past 4:00pm, last meetings at 3:00pm, everyone needs to take a fourteen-day vacation a year, and no more checking emails from home. It's been a challenge for some, but not for me. I came back from that trip with a different mindset and there's no going back.

It didn't stop with work. I go for walks or runs every afternoon outside and when I don't, I'm in a bad mood. It's crazy how much I needed nature and never realized it before. They said that people spend one thousand hours a year on technology and that number multiplies by three when you work on a job like mine. Cara had mentioned she was doing that outdoor challenge, so I researched it and I've been tracking my hours. My mental health has been better since. I also started therapy. That was weird but needed. I've been to four sessions and I think Mark and I will have a long road ahead together. Apparently, I have some issues that need to be worked on.

"She said it was urgent, and she named you and Mr. Augusto by full names when she used the family and friends card. She said your sister sent her. I called Mr. Augusto to confirm and he said she was right. I'm sorry, sir, it seemed important," Lucia rambles.

I pinch the bridge of my nose; at the same time, I comb my loose curls back and shake my head. "It's okay, Lucia. Thank you. Just bring her in whenever she gets here. I'll look at the file in a minute," I add.

Another thing that I learned from Cara? Patience. You never know what someone is going through; sometimes you just need to be a little patient and have some empathy for that person. Then, anything everyone does starts to feel less and less annoying.

I walk to the desk to look at the folder, thinking about how crazy it is that I went on that trip supposedly to take Cara from one place to another—but what actually happened was that I ended up finding myself instead. Even if we didn't end up together, I will always be thankful for every moment we spent together.

I drag my hand over the cold glass of my desk and open the folder when there's a knock on the door. I look up to see the last person I was expecting.

"Your four o' clock, sir," Lucia announces as she lets Cara in. She walks toward me, stealing my breath and catching me by surprise. She's wearing a tight little gray skirt with a soft pink button-down shirt tucked in, showing every single curve. She's wearing high heels and dark tights making her legs look a mile long and she has a giant bag over her shoulder.

"Thank you, Lucia. Close the door please and you're good to go. Have a good night," I stammer, trying to keep my voice calm. Lucia nods as she walks through the door, shutting it behind her and leaving me to face Cara.

"Cara," I say sharply trying to hide how my heart almost leapt from my chest when I saw her.

"Manuel." She walks closer to me, crossing her legs one in front of the other, accentuating every step as if she has a sole purpose in life and that purpose is to kill me. Her hair is styled in loose waves that bounce with every step she takes and her smile—her damn smile—could light up the whole building.

"How can I help you?" I ask her, trying to stay professional. I tuck my hands to my pockets, the only place I can keep them so I don't run around this desk and pull her to me. Actually, so I don't bend her over this desk and fuck some sense back into her. How do I make her see that I just need her to let me love her the way I know I can and the way I know she should? I just need the chance to show her, nothing else.

"I need help with something and I think you're the only person who can do it. Did you look at the folder?" she asks, pointing to the folder on top of my desk. I opened it right when she walked in but I didn't even see what's in it. The minute my eyes landed on Cara, I couldn't think about anything else but her.

I see a picture of a beautiful farmhouse with a classic gable roof and what seems like weather-resistant siding. The front porch wraps around the side, complete with rocking chairs framing a soft yellow door with a label that says 'like sunshine and lemons'. Now that I'm paying attention, there are labels in different parts of the photograph. The porch has one that says, 'for stargazing' and the front yard says 'for dancing under the stars'.

I turn the page and find more pictures. One of an open-concept living space that feels warm and inviting with a label that reads 'for family dinners.' I can almost see myself sitting by the cozy fireplace, surrounded by exactly that—friends and family. Surrounded by her 'bestie girls' as she calls them, or a double date dinner with Allie and Jake. The kitchen catches my eyes, with sleek stainless steel appliances, a farmhouse sink, and a spacious island with a label that says, 'for all chicken nugget dinners and whatever salad you want to eat.'

My heart is pounding hard against my chest as I continue through the pages, looking at different parts of the house with labels that are too close to what I would like my house to be. What I would like my house with *her* to be. The last page has the master bedroom, a spacious room with a California king bed in the middle and a label that reads 'too much room just for me.' That's the last page in this packet so when I turn it over and upside down to make sure I didn't miss something I look up to find Cara with tears in her eyes and a soft smile.

"You see, Manny, I found the perfect home but it has two big issues. One, every place in that house is perfect to do something that I want but it's also perfect to do something I enjoyed doing with you. Every inch of that house is exactly as what I pictured I wanted for myself and a family one day."

"Okay and how is that a problem? I can look at your finances and advise," I reply, trying desperately to appear unphased.

"Well, the problem is that it's too big and, although every space in it is exactly what I want, it feels entirely wrong without you in the picture."

I look into her eyes, searching for something. I don't want to assume anything. I want her to tell me with her words exactly what she means.

"I—"

"Let me finish. I heard you, now I want you to hear me. I *need* you to hear me. I've been house hunting for weeks now and every house I find has an and, if, or a but. But then I realized why. It's because it's a house I'm not sharing with you. And yes, I know how crazy this looks and how this sounds but, Manny, I think I want more than those three weeks with you, and I sure as hell don't want any of these three weeks, I've spent without you. I want to make more memories with you. I want to share more moments. I want them all. If you'll have me that is."

The moment her words hit me, everything inside me stops. It's like the world freezes—no ticking clocks, no buzzing phones, no noise at all. Just her voice, soft and tentative, weaving through the thick air between us. I can't even process what she's said at first. I just... *feel* it.

I want more than those three weeks with you.

God, she wants more. The fear that had gnawed at me for weeks—the fear that it all was too much, too soon—dissolves in the heat of her words. And yet, I can't breathe.

A second. A full minute of silence stretches between us. My pulse is louder than anything else. I feel the heat of her gaze on me, steady and uncertain, like she's waiting for me to say something—anything—but my tongue feels thick, my thoughts tangled in the mess of this moment. I just... I want to say *something*—anything to keep her from second-guessing herself. From walking away thinking she misread me. But I don't trust my voice. I said how I felt once and then it all fell apart.

Instead, I step forward. I don't think, I just move. One step, then another, until I'm standing right in front of her, so close I can feel the heat of her breath. I look at her—really look at her—willing myself to take this in, to memorize the way her eyes flicker nervously, how her lips part just slightly like she's about to say something but doesn't. It's like my heart is pumping faster in my chest, but my body can't keep up with the speed of my emotions.

"If it's too late, I understand," Cara mutters before continuing, "but I'm not leaving here without a fight, Manny. I want more than just your time now. I want all of you. All of it. I want to know the quiet parts of you, the ones you keep tucked away. I want to share days and nights where we don't have to rush, where we don't have to hide behind *just* the moments that pass by too quickly. I want to show you how much I love you, Manny. How much I fell for you in those three weeks, even if that sounds crazy. I want to prove that I can be enough for you."

Then, she pulls out another folder from her bag and hands it to me.

The gesture feels so... *her*—like it's the most vulnerable thing in the world. I stare at it, confused. She's always so put together, always the one who has everything in line, and here she is, handing me something that looks like it belongs in a school supply closet. I look at the letterhead—apples, hearts, Ms. Thompson.

"What is this?" I ask, opening it, not sure if I'm supposed to laugh or take it seriously.

"A contract." She says it casually, like it's no big deal. Like she's offering me a cup of coffee instead of... this.

I blink. "A *contract?*" My mouth feels dry.

"I wasn't sure if you'd believe my words," she replies, almost shy now. "So I figured if I showed you in your *business* language, it would make more sense."

I can't hold back a smile; a genuine, full-blown smile that stretches across my face. This—this is insane. It's ridiculous and adorable and makes me want to pick her up and kiss her until neither of us can breathe. The way she's looking at me now, the hope and fear tangled up in her eyes, it's everything I've wanted. *Everything.*

I can't stop myself from laughing softly. It's a mix of disbelief and pure joy. "What would make sense, Carita?" I ask, my voice teasing but soft. My heart is still pounding. I'm still overwhelmed.

And then she looks at me—really looks at me—and says the simplest thing, the one thing that pushes every last wall I've built around myself crashing down.

"That I love you, you goof."

The words land like a bomb, and I feel them in my chest, like the world just made sense. I'm shaking. My hands want to reach for her, to pull her into me. But I hold back, not because I'm unsure, but because I want to take this moment in. I want to soak in every piece of her—every word, every small gesture, the way she's standing there, so vulnerable, so perfectly *herself*.

She loves me.

I never thought I'd hear those words. Hell, I never thought I'd get to *feel* this. And now, here it is—her love, like a gift, like something so pure that it makes everything else fade into the background.

I don't know what to say. I don't know how to respond to this. But I do know one thing: I'm not letting go. Not now, not ever.

And as I reach for her, pulling her close, I whisper into her ear, "You don't know how much I needed to hear that. But you know I'm not a lawyer though, right?"

She giggles, bringing her hands to her mouth and then responding, "Then maybe you can take the time and teach me what it is that you do in this fancy office of yours."

"Cara, I don't need any of that. I just need you. I was willing to take whatever you would give me and this, this is more that I could've imagined. In case it's not obvious, I love you, too."

"You do?" she asks, putting some space between us as she

looks me in the eyes, tears finally falling from her eyes as she looks at me with a soft smile.

"I do, Cara Thompson. I've loved you all my life. It's about time for you to let me show you." I bring her closer, kissing her softly, bringing my hands to her neck and not letting her go. Her lips taste salty from the tears and like lemon scones, just as she always tastes. Sweet and citrusy, the perfect blend. I'm lost in this kiss when I hear a soft yelp and let go to look around.

"What the hell? Did you hear that?" I whisper looking around and she laughs loudly.

"Mm, yeah, about that. I came here ready to fight dirty if I had to."

"Is that why you're wearing that sexy-ass Legally Blonde inspired outfit?" I don't know how many times I watched that movie growing up but it was enough to know that Elle Woods would approve of this moment.

"Yuuuup aaaaaand..... why I brought this," she adds, lowering her giant bag to the ground and pulling out the tiniest and fluffiest puppy I've ever seen.

"Cara, what is that?" I ask, taking the puppy from her hands.

"This is Foster. Our double doodle."

"Our double doodle?" A dog? She brought a dog?

"Yeah, I adopted him today. I was planning on fostering, hence the name, but then he needed a forever home. Didn't you, pup?" she coos, rubbing his head. "He's coming home with me but maybe you can stop by and we can figure all of this out? I'm ready to give this a try, Manny. We don't have to move in together or anything like that, but I'm ready for us to give this a real chance. I'm ready to let you love me if you let me love you back. I want us to be on the road for longer, Manny."

"We've wandered down the road sometimes taken, but now

it's not a path you'll ever leave—it's ours forever. Is that what you want, Cara?"

"I want to at least try," she says.

"Fuck trying. You were made for me, Carita mia. For me." I kiss her again, with the puppy in my hands and with the promise of what's to come. I don't need anything in the world but this girl in my arms now and until the end of times.

EPILOGUE
I LOVE YOU, ALEX & SIERRA

One and a half years later

CARA

"YOU LOOK STUNNING," I say to Allie who is currently standing in front of me wearing her royalty-worthy wedding gown. We have dreamed about our weddings since we were little and for the past year, we've been planning this like our life depended on it. She gets to marry her best friend today and I don't know two more deserving people.

"Thank you, babe. I feel like a princess," she beams, smiling at me as she touches the top part of her dress.

"You are a fucking queen. Feel it!" I tell her, giving her a hug and being careful not to smear her makeup everywhere. Allie is an emotional babe and today won't be the day she stops crying about everything. Neither will I.

"Alright, I'll see you out there," I add, kissing her cheek and holding her hands in mine.

"I'll be the one walking down the aisle," she sniffles, her eyes glossy with emotion.

"I'll be the one sitting next to the hottest man I've ever seen, waiting for her best friends to finally seal the deal."

"Please stop calling my brother hot, Cara."

"You'd think you'd be used to it by now."

"I don't think I'll ever be used to it," Allie adds. "Maybe next year when you officially become my sister."

Manny and I got engaged last week after he surprised me at school with a flash mob. A freaking flash mob. This adorable puppy-in-human-form pulled it off, and it was the most precious thing I've ever seen in my life.

The past year and a half has been... well it has been something. I wish I could say that it was easy but it was really hard work. Not Manny, Manny is so easy to love. What was hard was trying to work through all of our insecurities while trying to build a life together. We moved in together soon after the whole love declaration. Sharing a puppy in two different households was hard, plus Foster really liked my house better, so Manny just moved in. We attended couples therapy soon after because we kept living in fear that at any point we were going to come home and find the other one gone. I had the fear he would leave me for someone else and he had the fear I wasn't going to take him seriously once he decided to cut his hours at work. As if having less work made him less desirable.

We worked through it and here we are ready, to start the next chapter of our lives together. Well, after we get his sister married, that's for sure. Allie was really the most supportive person through it all and she said she always knew we would end up together. What she never saw coming—I mean none of us did—was Gus and Nellie ending up together, too. Those two are something else for sure but I'm happy for both of them. They have been through so much and they deserve each other.

Even if I wanted to kill Gus half the time for pursuing my little sister.

The wedding venue is beautiful, right by the water with a mix of earthy colors. I sit in one of the outdoor chairs we brought, per Allie's request, and wait for Manny to take his seat next to me. He's probably been walking Foster around since we brought him with us this weekend and he will be alone in the hotel room for hours while we celebrate with our friends.

All of our friends are here. Well not all of them, considering Natalie is sitting with baby Vero and Bella and an empty chair with a portrait of Nick next to her. Jake wanted to still pay tribute to his best friend so there's an empty chair, a beer, and a picture of him on top of it. They went back and forth about it but finally Natalie said that Nick would've wanted that way too. I've never met anyone stronger than that girl and I just need to keep checking on her through the night. It can't be easy sitting at a wedding after losing the love of your life less than two years ago but she's still here supporting her friends.

"What's going on in that pretty head of yours?" Manny asks as he kisses the top of my head and sits next to me. He holds my hand and traces my pretty ring with his fingertips. Manny picked the perfect ring for me and I also can't stop looking at it. The band is crafted in white gold and at the center it has a stunning round diamond that mimics the heart of a flower. It's surrounded by smaller petals formed from clusters of smaller diamonds. It's delicate and enchanting and perfect.

"Just thinking about how unfair life is sometimes." When he follows my gaze to Nat, he nods.

"I'm sorry, Carita. I know it hasn't been easy. Just let me know if I can help in any way."

"Always," I reply.

The music plays, signaling the ceremony is starting, and we all stand up to see Jake walking down the aisle.

MANNY

"TONIGHT WAS SERIOUSLY SO MUCH FUN," Cara exclaims as we walk through the hotel room door. I have her shoes in one hand and her purse in the other because she said she was a tired girl and couldn't deal with life. I'm surprised I didn't have to carry her here judging by how much she danced, cried, and drank all night.

She plops herself onto the bed, pulling herself back with her arms until she reaches the top of the bed. She's laying down in her beautiful terracotta gown, with that damn slit that drives me crazy over her legs. Barefooted and wild on top of the bed.

I stand there looking at this beautiful girl I still can't believe is mine. Rosy cheeks, disheveled hair, sweaty body, and tired legs. *And mine.* I still pinch myself every morning waking up next to her.

The past year and a half has been movie worthy. Living in Baker, as much as I hate to admit, is what I needed—and stepping away from working every day of my life was too. I have two full-time assistants right now and my life has never been better. I let the company run itself and I just oversee the operations. The empire we built is finally working on its own and now we get to enjoy our lives.

"You need help taking that off?" I ask Cara. She brings her hands to her chest seductively, pulling her hair up and away from her face and twisting it into a loose bun. I still don't know how she manages that without a hair tie, but she's magic so I don't question it.

"You first," she adds with fire in her eyes. There's not a day that passes where I don't feel like the most desired man in the world by the way she looks at me. I unbutton my shirt slowly, taking it off and then tossing it to the ground. I climb onto the mattress and crawl to Cara.

She bites her lips as I reach her, pulling the lip from her teeth and kissing her softly. I will never get tired of kissing her either. That's for sure. I break the kiss, bringing my lips to her ear as I growl, "Turn around."

She turns around, placing her head sideways on the pillow as I kiss her cheek, her ear, and her neck. I pepper kisses all the way to the middle of her back where her zipper rests. I pull the zipper down slowly, enjoying seeing every inch of her skin revealed to me. The zipper stops right above her ass and when I pull the dress off her body, I see the tiny lace panties she has on. *Such a tease.* She knows how much I love these and she only wears them when she's hoping I'll see them, which is practically every night if she'll let me.

I climb her body again, peppering kisses over her back. She's eerily still which is unlike her considering she's a ticklish wiggle worm. I kiss her neck again and when I go to kiss her cheek, I see her lips slightly parted and notice her breathing is heavier now. *She fell asleep.* My sweet, sweet girl. The day must have gotten her bad because she's sound asleep right now. Her body is relaxed across the bed, her hand tucked under her face and her eyes closed peacefully. I love seeing her like this. So at peace with everything that she can just close her eyes and sleep soundly. She danced for so long tonight that I'm not surprised at all.

I get up, finish taking my clothes off and after a cold ass shower, I dry myself up and walk to her. I pick her up gently, moving the blankets and placing her back on the bed. I cover her up and give her a kiss goodnight at the same time that she whispers, "I love you, Manuel Zabana."

"I love you too, Cara. I love you too." I hop in the bed next to her, bringing my arm around her and pulling her flush to me. Right where she belongs, next to my heart.

THANK YOU FOR READING! I hope you loved The Road Sometimes Taken. If you'd like a peek into teacher Cara living in peace knowing Manny has her heart subscribe to my mailing list and click the link (or scan the code) to receive this Bonus Chapter.

100% swoon guarantee

Coming mid-2025—Preorder Now

Nellie

My dad always said tragedy comes in threes. I never understood what he meant by that—never understood until now. Not until I was drowning, that first taste of salt creep into my mouth, my lungs filling with the cold, sharp sting of the ocean's depths. It felt like the world was lifting me up—then, in an instant, it crashed down around me, pulling me under, twisting me into its unforgiving grasp.

He used to talk about the "harmful trifecta," and I always thought he meant the simple, painful things children fear—hunger, loss, death. I never knew that you could starve even when you have food, that the pain could be so deep, it's like a wound that would never close, and that the death he spoke of didn't always come with a body, but with a soul slowly slipping away. You can be alive but not living—not truly, not in the way you were meant to.

I didn't know tragedy wasn't just something that struck you

from the outside—it's something that's already buried deep inside you, waiting, just beneath the surface, its weight pressing down on you until you can no longer breathe. I didn't know that when it hit, it would feel like a rush, a storm of adrenaline, confusing my heart's beats with excitement instead of the panic I should've felt.

And even after the first blow, I was so swept up in the force of it all that I didn't notice the warning signs, didn't see the danger until it was already too late. The wave came too fast. It was too cold. Too powerful. And I was caught in it, being dragged down. Deeper. I was drowning in the overwhelming weight of it all, with no way back.

Then came the silence—the eerie calm that followed the chaos. But it wasn't peaceful. It wasn't a reprieve. It was hollow, suffocating. The quiet didn't heal me; it wounded me even more, drawing out the pain I hadn't even known was still there. The weight of it pressed harder, dragging me straight to the undertow, until I could barely breathe, until it crushed me under its weight.

And that's when the third wave came. But this one didn't come from the outside. It came from within me—from somewhere deeper than I even knew I could feel. And as I was sucked under again, I lost everything. Everything I thought I had. Everything I thought I was. Everything I thought I deserved.

I didn't know tragedy was this close, this intimate, and that none of us could escape it.

I didn't know one day it would hit *me*.

Until it did.

Preorder TLAT: A secret relationship, age gap, angsty romance.

JOIN THE BABE TRIBE!

Be the first to know when I have a new preorder or book ready to be released: Follow my Amazon Page Here!

Biweekly updates (and giveaways) on what's going on in my life and book recs? Join my newsletter Here!

Do you want weekly updates (and giveaways)? Join Ambar's Babes Here!

ACKNOWLEDGMENTS

Hi!!

Thank you so much for reading The Road Sometimes Taken. Manny and Cara's story took me on a wild ride of unexpected roads and long nights. I loved writing them and I hope you loved reading them too.

I have so many people to say thank you to but I want to start with YOU because without your love for my stories and your support, I wouldn't be here. This story would probably not exist if it wasn't for you so thank you. Thank you for reading, for recommending my books to others, for telling me how much my words mean to you, and for being there. I may not know who you are but I want you to know how important you are to me and my dream. You are literally a dream maker!

Per usual, I'm thanking my husband, Joey because without his support, I wouldn't be able to spend countless hours being lost in these fictional words. Thank you for showing me how love is patient, kind, and fair. Thank you for being my adventure partner and for renaming road signs with me. I never want to take a road trip with anyone else but you for the rest of my life.

To my alphas and betas, Mandy, Adriana, Sophie, Erica, Raquel, Kristina, Kai, Karen, Michelle, Rachel, Brittney, and Jayné, thank you for the invaluable feedback that made this story better. PS, Michelle, I hope this release date is double special for you and your husband <3

To my author friends, Sarah, Rachel, Hailey, Hollie, Jenn, Allie, and Alexis, thank you for being my sanity during this drafting process. Thank you for the sprints and for the unconditional support. Thank you from the bottom of my heart for being there for me for more than just writing. Thank you Veronica, Nicole, Emily and Bella for continuing to be my moms in this journey. I would be so lost without you all.

To my kids because there's nobody who wants to see me succeed more than you. Thank you for your patience as mami navigates writing, working, and parenting.

To Kendra from Spice Me Up Editing, these stories are a lot more polished and readable because of you.

To Kim from KBG Designs and Mayhara from Mayharate for the most beautiful cover in the entire world. I'm forever obsessed with the two of you. You will never get rid of me, that's for sure.

To Aliyah with Ever After Cover Design, the discreet covers are always so perfect. The hidden tears and rain drops?! Gold!

To the behind the scenes crew: Lemmy from Luna Literary Management, thank you for all that you do! Courtney from Marketing with Courtney, I could breathe more this time around with all your templates. Thank you.

To Cassie, I don't even know what to call you. My right hand? My sanity? My ultimate hype girl? I don't know what I would do without you and Cassie's Creative. Thank you. Thank you. Thank you. (I've said it before and I'll say it again. Everyone needs you in their life.)

To my street team. I love you all. Our discord is my favorite place to be. Thank you for being the best hype girls and for going to bat for my books.

To my ARC team, thank you for reading and reviewing my work. Thank you for reading my stories and for sharing the love.

To the 1,000 Hours Outside Group. Starting this challenge a few years ago changed my life and my family's too so when I decided to write this book and all of you helped me craft the perfect road trip, I knew I had something special in my hands. Thank you.

To some of the locations in this story that exist in real life, Camp Aramoni, The Wilds, and Arrington Vineyards, thank you for letting me share your true magic with my fictional characters.

And last but not least, thank you to Joey again. Thank you for being the road I want to travel forever.

Now, off to cry in author tears and on to the next book.

143,

Ambar

ABOUT THE AUTHOR

Ambar is the author of small-town and multicultural romance that brings emotional twists to her readers. Her debut novel The Truth Never Spoken, is book 1 in the Baker Oaks series: A small-town series based in Florida. Ambar is a wife and mom who has been living in Florida since 2015, and who loves the small town where she currently lives in. Born and raised in the Dominican Republic, she embraces cultural differences and brings that to her books,

When she is not writing, she is enjoying time with her family, traveling, and reading.

To learn more, scan or click here

Grab a book, fall in love, stay a while ♥